9 to 5

Falling for the boss…

They're working side by side, nine to five…
But no matter how hard these couples try to
keep their relationships strictly professional,
romance is undeniably on the agenda!

But will a date in the office diary lead
to an appointment at the altar?

Find out in this exciting series!

The Tycoon's Reluctant Cinderella
by Therese Beharrie

Available now!

A BRIDE FOR THE
BROODING BOSS

BY
BELLA BUCANNON

First Published in Great Britain 2017
By Mills & Boon, an imprint of HarperCollins*Publishers*
1 London Bridge Street, London, SE1 9GF

© 2017 Harriet Nichola Jarvis

ISBN: 978-0-263-92282-0

23-0317

Our policy is to use papers that are natural, renewable and recyclable products and made from wood grown in sustainable forests. The logging and manufacturing processes conform to the legal environmental regulations of the country of origin.

Printed and bound in Spain
by CPI, Barcelona

Bella Bucannon lives in a quiet northern suburb of Adelaide with her soul-mate husband, who loves and supports her in any endeavour. She enjoys walking, dining out and traveling. Bus tours or cruising with days at sea to relax, plot and write are top of her list. Apart from category romance, she also writes very short stories and poems for a local writing group. Bella believes joining RWA and SARA early in her writing journey was a major factor in her achievements.

To my special husband, whose extra help enabled
me to conquer the challenge of a deadline.
To Brett for expert advice, once he and other friends
had stopped laughing at the idea of technically inept
Bella's heroine being a computer problem investigator.
To the Paddocks Writing Group for support
and encouragement, and to Flo for her advice
and belief in me. My grateful thanks to you all.

CHAPTER ONE

LAUREN TAYLOR ALIGHTED from the taxi, smiling in surprise. A multi-storey glass and cement edifice had replaced the six-storey building with a bank at ground level she remembered from years ago.

Anticipation simmered through her veins. A rush job. Urgent—which usually meant challenging.

Her initial reaction to her employer's Monday morning call had been to refuse. She had managed to squeeze in a much-needed week off and had planned on some 'me' time—seeing movies, reading in the park, aimless walking… The promise of an additional week on completion of the assignment, plus a bonus, had won her over. A few days of Adelaide in March wouldn't be too hard to take.

The flight delay at Sydney airport the next afternoon meant it was three o'clock by the time she'd booked into her hotel and caught a taxi to the address. A quick phone call to a brusque Matthew Dalton raised some apprehension but he *was* the one with the critical dilemma.

Dalton Corporation's reception area on the eighteenth floor suited the building. A patterned, tiled floor drew the eyes to a curved redwood desk and up to the company name, elaborately carved in black on a gold background. Sadly the lack of human presence, along with the almost complete silence, detracted from the impact. The three doors in her sight were all shut.

Scrolling for the contact number she'd used earlier, she stopped at the sound of a crash from behind the second door along. Followed by a loud expletive in a woman's voice.

Lauren knocked and opened the door.

A blonde woman stood leaning across a desk, her hands shifting through a pile of papers, a harassed face turned to-

wards Lauren. A document tray and its previous contents
lay scattered on the floor.

'You want Mr Dalton.' Uttered as a hopeful statement.
'Sorry about this. I'm usually more organised. Last door
on the left. Knock and wait. Good luck.'

Her words heightened Lauren's unease as she obeyed,
instinctively smoothing down her hair before tapping on
the door. The light flutter in her pulse at the raspy 'Come
in' startled her. As did the unexpected allure in the deep
guttural tone.

Without looking up, the man with a mobile held to his left
ear gestured for her to enter and take the seat in front of
his desk. Matthew Dalton was definitely under pressure.
No jacket or tie, shirt unbuttoned at the top, and obviously
raked through, thick chestnut-brown hair. He continued to
write on a printed page in front of him, occasionally speaking in one- or two-word comments.

Lauren sat, frowning at the oblique angle of his huge
desk to the wall-to-wall, floor-to-ceiling windows with an
incredible view of the Adelaide Hills. Made of dark wood,
it held only a desktop computer, keyboard, printer, land
phone and stacked document trays. The only personal item
was a plain blue coffee mug.

The man who'd requested her urgent presence swung to
his right, flicking through pages spread on the desk extension. His easy fit in the high-back leather chair with wide
arms suggested made to measure. And he needed a haircut.

She continued her scan, fascinated by the opulent differences from the usual offices where she was welcomed
by lesser employees. From the soft leather lounge chairs by
the windows to the built-in bar and extravagant coffee machine, this one had been designed to emphasise the power
and success of the occupier.

The down light directly above his head picked up the red

tints in his hair, and the embossed gold on his elegant black pen. She shrugged—exclusive taste didn't always equate with business acumen. If it did she might not be here.

Reception had been bare and unmanned, the blonde woman agitated. How bad *was* the company's situation?

Normally tuning out sounds was an ingrained accomplishment. Today, nothing she tried quite prevented the gravelly timbre skittling across her skin, causing an unaccustomed warmth low in her abdomen. She steadied her breathing, mentally counting the seconds as they passed.

Then the man she believed to be a complete stranger flicked a glance her way. Instantly, with a chilling sensation gripping her heart, she was thrown back ten years to *that* night.

The dinner dance after a charity Australian Rules football game organised by interstate universities and held here in Adelaide. Limited professional players were allowed and her parents insisted the whole family come over in support when her elder brother agreed to represent Victoria.

The noisy function seemed full of dressed-to-kill young women draped over garrulous muscular males, many of whom twitched and pulled at the collars of their suits. Though only two or three years separated her from most of them, at sixteen it was a chasm of maturity and poise. Unfamiliar with the football scene and jargon, she blushed and stammered when any of them spoke to her.

Escaping from the hot, crowed room, she found a secluded spot outside, at the end of the long balcony. Hidden by tall potted plants, she gazed over the river wishing she were in her hotel room, or home in Melbourne. Or anywhere bar here.

'Hiding, huh? Don't like dancing?'

The owner of the throaty voice—too much enthusiastic

cheering?—was tall. Close. Much too close. The city lights behind him put his face in shadow.

She stepped back. The self-absorbed young men whose interests were limited to exercise, diet, sport, and the women these pursuits attracted held no appeal for her. Men like her brothers' friends who teasingly came on to her then laughed off her protests. Never serious or threatening, merely feeding their already inflated egos. Shy and uncomfortable in crowds, with a tendency to blush, she was fair game.

'I saw you slip out.' She detected a faint trace of beer on his breath as he spoke. When he took a step nearer, causing her to stiffen, a fresh ocean aroma overrode the alcohol. Not drunk, perhaps a little tipsy.

'We won, you should be celebrating. You do barrack for South Australia?' Doubt crept into the last few words, the resonance telling her he'd be more mature, maybe by two or three years, than she was. So why seek her out when there were so many girls his age inside?

'Y… Yes.' How could one word be so hard to say? How come her throat dried up, and her pulse raced? And why did she lie when she didn't care about the game at all?

He leant forward. 'I did kick two goals even if I missed out on a medal. Surely I deserve a small prize.'

He *was* like all the others. Her disappointment sharpened her reply.

'I'm sure you won't be disappointed inside.'

'But an elusive prize is much more rewarding, don't you think?'

Before she could take in air to answer, he gently covered her lips with his.

And she hadn't been able to take that breath. Hadn't been able to move. Hadn't been able to think of anything except the smooth movement of his mouth on hers.

The urge to return the kiss—have *him* deepen the kiss—

had shaken her. Terrified her. The quick kisses from the boys she knew were just being friendly had been gentle, nice. Never emotionally shattering.

Why did she sigh? Why were her lips complying, pressing against his, striving to be in sync? Until the tip of his tongue flicked out seeking entry and she panicked.

Frantically pulling away, she fled past him to the safety of the packed ballroom and a seat behind her parents and other adults in a remote corner. As she drank ice-cold water to wet her dry throat, she realised all she could recall was a glimpse of stunning midnight-blue eyes as his head had jerked back into the light.

The same midnight-blue eyes that had fleetingly met hers a moment ago.

Why was she so certain? She just knew.

Would he recognise *her*? He'd had a drink or two and it had been dark. She finally had a reason to be thankful for her mother's instructions to the hairdresser. Darker colouring with extensions woven into a fancy hairdo on top, plus salon make-up, had altered her appearance dramatically.

She'd been a naive teenager who'd panicked and run from an innocent kiss. He'd been an experienced young man who'd have known scores of willing women since.

Gratitude that she hadn't seen his face flowed through her veins as she studied the man to whom she'd attributed so many different features over the years in her daydreams. If, along with those memorable eyes, she'd imagined high cheekbones, a square firm jaw and full lips, she doubted she'd have slept at all. Even his lashes were thicker and darker than she'd pictured.

She dipped her head whenever he looked at her, wasn't ready for eye-to-eye contact. Forced steady breathing quelled her inner trembling.

Matt Dalton's mind ought to be totally focused on the

information he was receiving. Instead his eyes kept straying to the brunette sitting rigid on her seat, politely ignoring him. The one who'd caused a tightening in his gut when he'd glanced up at her.

In an instant he'd noted the sweet curve of her cheek framed by shoulder-length light brown hair. If she hadn't dropped her gaze, he'd also know the colour of her eyes.

Shoot! He asked the caller to repeat the last two figures. Blocking her out, he carefully wrote them down. After ending the call, he clipped all the pages together, and dropped them into a tray.

He could now concentrate on this woman, and her technical rather than physical attributes. Her employer's high fees would be worth it if she found out what the heck had happened in the company's computer system.

'Ms Lauren Taylor?' He pulled a new document forward.

She turned, and guarded brown eyes met his.

He immediately wished they hadn't as a sharp pang of desire snapped through him and was instantly controlled. Women, regardless of shape, colouring or looks, were off his agenda for the foreseeable future. Probably longer. Betrayal made a man wary.

'Yes.' Hesitant with an undertone he didn't understand.

He'd requested her services on a recommendation, without any consideration of appearance or demeanour, which for him were unimportant. The female colleagues he'd associated with overseas were well groomed, very smart, and always willing to offer their opinions. His equal on every corporate level.

Lauren Taylor was neatly dressed in a crisp white blouse under a light grey trouser suit, and wore little make-up. With her reputation, she ought to project confidence, yet he sensed apprehension. Was it a natural consequence of her temporary assignments or the confidentiality clause creating a desire to keep a distance from company employees?

No, this ran deeper, was more personal. He cleared his thoughts, telling himself his sole interest was in her technical skills, conveniently discounting his two reactions towards her.

'I'm Matt Dalton. I contacted your employer because I'm told you're one of the best computer problem investigators. My friend's description. Was he exaggerating?'

A soft blush coloured her cheeks, and her eyes softened at the compliment. They were actually more hazel than brown with a hint of gold flecks, and framed by thick brown lashes. He growled internally at himself for again straying from his pressing predicament.

'I don't… I rarely fail.' She made a slight twitch of her shoulders as if fortifying her self-assurance.

He gave a short huff. 'Please don't let this be one of the times you do. How much information were you sent?'

'The email mentioned unexplained anomalies a regular audit failed to clarify.'

'Two, one internal, one external. The detectable errors were fixed but no one could explain the glitches or whatever they are, and I need answers fast.' Before his father's condition became public and the roof caved in.

'May I see the reports?' Again timidity, which didn't fit the profile he'd received, though to give her credit she didn't look away.

'In the top drawer of the desk you'll be using along with a summary of our expectations, file titles et cetera. I assume you can remember passwords.'

She frowned, making him realise how condescending he sounded. Was he coming over as too harsh, overbearing? Her impression of him wouldn't be good either.

'Staff turnover has been high in the last two years, sometimes sudden with no changeover training. Recently I found out passwords had been written down and kept in unlocked drawers.'

She waited, and he had the feeling he was being blamed for some personal misdemeanour. He decided he'd divulged as much as she needed to know to start. Anything else necessary, she'd learn as the assessment progressed.

'Most of the errors were from incorrectly entered data, exacerbated on occasion by amateur attempts to fix them. Apparently not too hard to find and correct if you know what you're doing.'

'But surely the accountant…?' Her hands fluttered then her fingers linked and fell back into her lap. 'Why weren't they picked up at the time?'

Damn, she was smart. And nervous.

'The long-term accountant left, and was replaced by a bookkeeper then another. Neither were very competent.'

Her eyes widened in surprise. For a second there was a faint elusive niggling deep in the recesses of his mind. As her lips parted he forestalled her words.

'I'd like you to analyse from July 2014 up to the present date. Everything your employer requested is in the adjacent office. How soon can you start?'

Too abrupt again but it was imperative he find out what had been going on. The sooner the better. Four weeks ago, at his original inspection of his father's company accounts, would have been best.

'If I can see the set-up now then I can begin early tomorrow morning. Being a short week because of Easter doesn't allow much time.

'Are two days enough?'

'Doubtful if I'm a last resort. I have a family commitment in Melbourne for the weekend then I'll come back.' She made it sound like an obligation rather than a pleasant reunion.

'That's acceptable.' He flicked his hands then put them on the edge of the desk to push to his feet.

'Human error and deliberate action are different. Is it the latter I'm searching for?'

He sank back into his chair. She was *too* smart.

Lauren had been in critical corporate situations before and recognised desperation, even when well hidden. This man was heading for breakdown. His taut muscles, firm set lips and weary dark eyes all pointed to extreme stress.

And her question had irritated him so he definitely suspected fraud, probably by someone he'd trusted. She certainly wasn't going to push it now. Not when she'd behaved like the skittish child she'd thought she'd conquered years ago.

'I won't make guarantees I might not be able to keep. I can only promise to do my best. Having the straightforward errors already adjusted helps.'

He relaxed a little, and his lips curved at the corners, almost but not quite forming a smile.

'Thank you.'

He rose to an impressive height, letting his chair roll away, indicating a door to her left.

'Through here.'

Lauren picked up her shoulder bag and followed, wishing she were one of those women who were comfortable in killer heels all day. And an inch or two taller. Having to tilt her head gave him the advantage. When he suddenly stopped and turned, her throat tightened at the vague familiarity of his cologne. Not the same one, surely? Yet she recognised it, had never forgotten it. And this close, the lines around his mouth and eyes were much more discernible.

'I apologise. I should have offered you a coffee. Do you—?'

'No. No, thank you.' The sooner she was out of his presence, the better. Then she could breathe and regroup. 'You're obviously busy.'

His relief at such a minor point enforced her opinion of the strain he was under.

'Like you wouldn't believe. Any answers you find will be extremely welcome.'

He opened the door and ushered her in, the light touch of his fingers on her back shooting tingles up and down her spine, spreading heat as they went. Unwarranted yet strangely exciting.

The décor in the much smaller room matched his office, and included two identical armchairs by the window. But the position of the desk was wrong, standing out from the wall facing the door they'd entered. She walked round to check the two desktops and a keyboard, all wired up ready to go. He followed, stopping within touching distance.

'Your employer asked for the duplication. Easier for comparisons, huh?'

'Much. What's the password?'

He told her. While she activated the computer, he removed a blue folder from the drawer, and placed it on the desk.

'Anything else you require?'

'I'll need a copy of the report for highlighting and a writing pad for notes.'

'Help yourself to anything in the cupboard. The copier is in Joanne's office off reception.'

'The blonde lady?'

'Yes, currently we don't have a receptionist. If you have any questions regarding your task ask me. If it's office related Joanne or any one of the other five employees can help.'

He walked out, not giving her a chance to say thank you, leaving his heady sea-spray aroma behind. Did he treat everyone in the same offhand manner?

Lauren felt like pounding the desk. She'd handled ruder employers who'd been under less pressure with poise and conviction. I'm-the-boss males with autocratic, archaic, even on occasion sexist, views were certainly not an endangered species. It didn't wash with her. They were in a predicament and she was the solution so she made it clear: no respect and she walked.

The personal aspect here had shaken her composure, giving the impression she doubted her abilities. She'd show him. Tomorrow she'd be the perfect detached computer specialist.

She selected stationery from the cupboard, skim-read the printed files, then spent ten minutes perusing the computer data prior to closing down. The few pertinent notes she'd written would save time in the morning.

Carrying the audit reports, she tried the door leading to the corridor. Finding it locked, she went into Matt Dalton's office. He was standing, sorting papers on his desk. His gaze was less than friendly to someone he'd hired to solve his problems.

'I'll copy these then I'll be leaving. What time is the office open in the morning?' Polite and stilted, following his lead. The fizz in her stomach could and *would* be controlled.

'I'm here from seven. Do you need transport?'

'I'll sort that out.'

'Good.' He returned to his papers.

She swung away, heat flooding her from head to feet at his dismissive action. All her fantasies came crashing down. Spoilt, rich, I-can-take-what-I-want teenager had become arrogant, treat-hired-staff-with-disdain boss. Was that why people had left without notice? She'd never wished bad karma on anyone, but she was coming close today!

Long deep breaths as she went out helped to settle her stomach and stop the trembling of her hands.

Before re-entering Mr Dalton's office, printouts in hand, she reinforced her prime rule of contract work. Never,

never, ever get involved. Someone always ended up heart-broken.

Swearing the oath was easy. Sticking to it when con-fronted with those hypnotic blue eyes that invited her to confess her innermost secrets was tougher than she'd ex-pected. Especially when his lips curled into a half-smile as he said goodbye.

She stabbed at the ground-floor button, angry that she'd smiled back, dismayed that even his small polite gesture had weakened her resolve. The thrill of the chase ought to be in his computer files, not in dreaming of— She wouldn't dream of anything. Especially not midnight-blue eyes, firm jaws or light touches that sent emotions into a frenzy.

CHAPTER TWO

MATT STARED AT the open doorway, perplexed by his reactions to a woman so unlike the outgoing, assured females he usually favoured. He raked his fingers through his hair. They were strangers, so why the censure in her alluring eyes when they'd met? It irked. It shouldn't have affected his attitude but he knew he'd been less than welcoming.

His finding her delicate perfume enchanting was also disconcerting. And she'd stiffened when he'd touched her. Had she felt the zing too? Please not. He had enough complications to deal with already.

Would it make her job easier if she knew the whole story? Loath to reveal family secrets to outsiders, he'd tell her only if it became relevant to her succeeding. Despite his friend's glowing report, he'd been less than impressed.

Dalton Corporation was in trouble. His only choice was to trust her on the corporate level. He had little reason to trust her, or any other woman, personally. Especially as her manner said she'd judged him for some transgression made by someone else.

Had she suffered the same indignity as he had? The soul-crushing realisation that you'd been used and played for a fool. The embarrassment of how close you'd come to committing to someone unworthy, incapable of fidelity or honesty.

The dark-haired image that flared took him by surprise. Any affection he'd felt for Christine had died when she'd proved faithless. He hadn't seen her since he'd walked out of her apartment for the last time after telling her the relationship was over, and why. He'd rarely thought of her either.

They'd both spent nights in each other's homes but he'd held back from inviting her to live with him. Looking back that should have been a red flag that he had misgivings. Thankfully he'd told no one of his plans to propose to her.

Admitting he'd been stupid for assuming mutual friends and lifestyle expectations would be a good basis for a modern marriage hadn't been easy. He wasn't sure he'd ever consider that life-changing step again.

God, he hated being here handling this mess. He'd hated even more being in London where people gave him sympathetic looks and wondered what had happened.

Letting out a heartfelt oath, he banished both women from his mind. There were emails to read and respond to, and he'd promised his mother he'd be there for dinner. He grabbed his coffee mug, feeling the urgent necessity for another caffeine boost.

Nearly two hours later he pulled into the kerb outside his parents' house, switching off the engine to give himself time to prepare for the evening ahead. He regretted the loss of unwavering respect for his parents, wished he'd never found out his father had been having affairs. He'd lost a small part of himself when he'd come home that evening nine years ago, and had never been able to obliterate what he overheard from his mind.

'I suppose this one's as gullible as the rest and believes she has a future with you. How many more, Marcus?'

'Man wasn't meant to be monogamous. If you want a divorce, be prepared to lower your standard of living.'

'Why should I suffer for your indiscretions? I'm giving up nothing.'

Somehow his mother's acceptance of his father's infidelities made her complicit. In disbelief he'd fled to his room, changed into a tracksuit and taken off, pounding the footpath trying to drive what he'd heard from his mind. His hero had fallen. He'd returned to a silent, dark house where, for him, nothing would ever be the same.

He scowled, thumping the wheel with an open hand. He'd always been confident, sure of himself and his judgement of cheating and affairs. Now he felt remorse as his father had turned into a stranger who'd made drastic mistakes in the last eighteen months, sending Dalton Corporation on a downhill path.

Pride dictated he fix those glitches and return the company to profit status, along with preserving its good name. Only then could he consider his own future, and for that he'd need a clear head. The only people he'd give consideration to would be family and his partners in London.

He started the engine, and drove through the elaborate gates, grimacing as he entered the luxurious house. This was his father's dream, a symbol of wealth and prestige, bought during Matt's absence abroad. He hadn't told his mother their financial status was in jeopardy. If Lauren Taylor was as good as her reputation, and he'd inherited any of his father's entrepreneurial skills, he might never have to.

Adelaide had a different vibe from the city Lauren remembered. Not that she'd seen much of the metropolitan area when she'd lived here, or much of anywhere besides ovals and training grounds. Beaches in summer, of course— swimming and running on the sand were part of the family's fitness regimen.

As she'd strolled past modern or renovated buildings a window display advertising Barossa Valley wine triggered a light-bulb moment. The Valley, the Fleurieu Peninsula and the Adelaide Hills, plus many other tourist areas, were all within easy driving distance, and she'd been promised a two-week vacation as soon as the assignment ended. All she'd need were a map, a plan and a hire car.

She picked up Chinese takeaway, and spent the evening poring over brochures and making notes. In full view from her window a group of young athletes were training in the parklands over the road. On the side-lines some adults watched and encouraged. Others sat on the grass with younger children, playing games or reading with them.

Her eyes were drawn to a man sitting with a boy on his lap, their heads bent as small fingers traced words or pictures in a book. Her chest tightened and she crossed her arms in a self-hug. Why didn't she have any memories of those occasions? Why had she never asked either parent to read to her or share a favourite television show with her? She'd always been too afraid of rejection.

Why had *they* never noticed her quietly waiting for some of the attention claimed by her boisterous brothers? If it had been intentional maybe it wouldn't hurt so much. Being overlooked cut deeper than deliberately being ignored. And she'd never been able to summon up the courage to intentionally draw attention to herself.

The boy looked up, talking with animation to his father. Eyes locked, they were in a world of their own.

It conjured up the image of Matt Dalton holding her gaze captive as they'd talked. Even thinking of those weary blue eyes spiked her pulse, and memories of that long-ago kiss resurfaced. Her balcony secret she'd never revealed to anyone. Never intended to.

Lauren chose a different route to work in the morning. She felt more herself, determined to show her new boss she was the professional his friend had recommended.

Last night no matter how many positions she'd tried or how often she'd thumped the pillows, sleep had eluded her. Reruns of her two encounters with Matt Dalton had kept her awake until she'd given in, got up, and researched the company. Something she normally avoided to keep distance and objectivity.

There'd been no reference to him, only a Marcus Dalton who'd become successful by investing in small businesses, and persuading others to participate too. The website hadn't been updated since November last year, indicating there'd been difficulties around that time.

No, wait. She'd been asked to assess twenty-one months. So the anomalies had been discovered only recently but long-term deception was suspected.

The sleep she'd eventually managed had been deep and dreamless, surprising since her last thoughts and first on awakening had been of full grim lips and jaded midnight-blue eyes.

The door adjacent to Mr Dalton's was still locked. From the piles of folders on his desk and extension, he'd arrived very early. He appeared even wearier, the shadows under his eyes even darker.

Lauren tried to ignore the quick tug low in her abdomen, and the quickening of her pulse.

'Good morning, Mr Dalton. Would it be possible to have the outer door unlocked so I won't disturb you going in and out?'

Or be disturbed by my immature reaction to you.

Intense blue eyes scanned her face, reigniting the warm glow from yesterday.

'Good morning, Ms Taylor. I'm not easily disturbed.'

Of course you're not. You're a cause not a recipient. Ignite a girl's senses with a soul-shattering kiss then forget her. Though to be fair she'd been the one to run.

'My watch alarm is set for an hourly reminder to relieve my eyes, stretch and drink water. To ease my back, I sometimes walk around or up and down a few flights of stairs.'

'Not a problem.' He glanced at the bottle in her hand. 'Keep anything you like in the fridge under the coffee machine or there's a larger one in the staffroom.'

Without looking, he flicked a hand towards a door in

the wall behind him. 'There's an ensuite bathroom here or, if you prefer, washrooms on the far side of Reception.'

Why the flash of anguish in his eyes? Why was she super alert, her skin tingling during this mundane conversation?

'Thank you.' She turned towards the bench, away from his probing gaze, popped her drink bottle and morning snack into the fridge, then went to her desk. Keeping her eyes averted didn't prevent his masculine aroma teasing her nostrils as she passed him.

She settled at her new station and, while the system booted up, filled in the personnel document he'd left for her. Once everything was laid in her preferred setting, she stood by the window to stare at the distant hills for a slow count of fifteen.

Now she was ready to start.

For two hours, apart from a short break for her eyes, she focused on the screens in front of her. But like a radio subliminally intruding into your dreams, some part of her was acutely aware of each time the man next door spoke on the phone or accessed the filing cabinets in this room.

The feeling in the pit of her stomach now was different, familiar, one she found comfortable, the exhilaration of the chase. The minor errors matched those in the audits. The one anomaly she found was puzzling enough for her to recheck from the beginning, puzzling enough to tease her brain. A challenge worthy of the fee her boss charged Dalton Corporation.

She headed for the ensuite to freshen up ready for coffee, cheese crackers and relief time. There was one door on her left, another along the corridor to her right.

She regretted choosing the latter the moment she saw the iron-smooth black and silver patterned quilt covering a king-sized bed. For a nanosecond she pictured rumpled sheets half covering a bare-chested Matt, his features composed in tranquil sleep. She blinked and pivoted round. Not an image she wanted in her head when she locked eyes with this cheerless, work-driven man.

On her return to the office, his posture enforced her last description. His chin rested on his hands, his elbows on the desk, his attention fully absorbed by the text on his screen.

Stealing the opportunity to observe him unnoticed, she stopped. A perception of unleashed power bunched in his shoulders, a dogged single-mindedness showed in his concentration. The untrimmed ends of his thick hair brushed the collar of his shirt, out of character to her perception of a smart, city businessman.

His mug had been pushed to the edge of his desk, presumably empty. She picked it up, startling him.

'Would you like a refill?'

He nodded. 'Thanks. Flat white from the machine, one sugar. How's it going?'

'Progressing. Do you want details?'

His eyes narrowed.

She pre-empted his next remark. 'People who hire me have varying knowledge of technology and require different levels of explanation.' *Many don't like to betray their ignorance in the field.* 'My daily report will be comprehensive.'

'Do whatever's necessary to get results. I'll read the report.' Again an undertone of irritation further roughened his voice, a darkening glint of angst flashed in his eyes.

Matt made a note in red at the top of the paper in front of him, and regretted being repeatedly terse with her. He closed his eyes, clasped his neck, and arched his back. He felt bone tired from sitting, reading, and trying to make sense of his father's recent actions.

He wished he could shake the guilt for not being around, for not noticing the subtle changes on his trips home for family occasions. Maybe if he'd spent more one-on-one time with Marcus he would have. Instead he'd apportioned blame without considering it was their lives, their marriage.

For nine years he'd kept physical and emotional distance from two of the most important people in his life.

He heard the soft clunk of a mug on wood. By the time he straightened and looked, a steaming coffee sat within reach, and Lauren was disappearing into her room. She'd discarded the light jacket she'd worn on arrival. Tired as he was, the male in him appreciated her slender figure, her trim waist. The pertness of her bottom in the grey trousers.

Inappropriate. Unprofessional.

As he drank the strong brew the sound of a quirky ring-tone spun his head. The friendliness of Lauren's greeting to someone called Pete rankled for no reason. Her musical laughter ignited a heat wave along his bloodstream.

He strode to the ensuite to splash water on his face and cool down.

'Hey, it's nearly twelve o'clock.'

Lauren started, jerking round to see her temporary boss standing in the doorway, the remoteness in his eyes raising goosebumps on her skin. She blinked and checked her watch.

'Two minutes to go. Are you keeping tabs on my schedule?' Some clients did.

'Not specifically.' He moved further into the room, closer to her desk. To her.

Her pulse had no right to rev up. Her lungs had no right to expand, seeking his masculine aroma.

'Your work's high intensity.' His neutral tone brought her to earth.

'I've learnt how to manage it. Results take patience and time.'

He gave a masculine grunt followed by a wry grin. 'The latter's not something we have plenty of. Take a lunch break. I need you fully alert.'

Eight floors by foot before taking the elevator to the

ground helped keep her fit. She smiled and walked out into the light drizzle. Adelaide was like a new city waiting to be explored. Chomping on a fresh salad roll, she strolled along, musing on that dour man, wondering what, or who, had caused the current situation. And why Marcus Dalton was no longer in charge.

Matt was clearly related. He bore a strong resemblance to the photograph on the website she'd accessed. Even with the ravages of the trauma he was under, he was incredibly handsome with an innate irresistible charisma. Was he married? In a relationship?

She chastised herself, chanting silently, *Never let anyone get to you on assignments.* Stupid and unprofessional, it could only lead to complications and tears. However, she had never been in this situation before…she'd never been kissed by one of her clients.

'There's definitely a recurrent anomaly. Finding when it started may tell me how and what,' Lauren informed Matt as she gave him her report prior to going home.

She was leaning towards it being deliberate because of the number of identical anomalies. No reason to mention she had no idea how it had been achieved.

He nodded and dropped the report in a tray. 'How's the hotel? I asked Joanne to book somewhere not too far out.'

'Oh.' Was he trying to be sociable? Make amends for his abruptness? 'Very nice, and my room overlooks the parklands.'

'Not too noisy on that corner?'

She couldn't suppress her grin. 'I live in Sydney, remember. You tune it out or drown it with music.'

His gaze held hers for an eon, or longer. The darkening in the midnight-blue coincided with heat tendrils coiling through her from a fiery core low in her abdomen. Her eyes refused to break contact, her mouth refused to say goodbye. Her muscles refused to obey the command to turn her away.

It was Matt who broke the spell, flinching away and shaking his head. His chest heaved as his lungs fought for air. He clenched his fists to curb the impulse to—no, he wouldn't even think it.

'Did you bus or taxi?' He didn't particularly care but was desperate to keep the conversation normal. To ignore those golden specks making her eyes shine like the gemstones in his mother's extensive jewellery collection. His voice sounded as if he'd sprinted the last metres of a marathon.

'I walked. It's not that far.'

His eyebrows shot up. 'Walked?' To and from a bus stop or taxi rank was the furthest most women he knew went on foot, apart from in shopping centres.

She shrugged. 'Beats paying gym fees and clears my head.'

'I guess. Just take care, okay.' He had no reason to worry, yet he did.

'Always. Good afternoon, Mr Dalton.'

'I'll see you tomorrow, Ms Taylor.'

As soon as she'd gone he slumped in his chair, stunned by his reaction to her smile, quick and genuine, lighting up her face. His pulse had hiked up, his chest tightened. And his body had responded quicker and stronger than ever before.

His fingers gripped the armrests as he fought for control. This shouldn't, couldn't be happening. Women, *all* women were out of bounds at the moment. Even for no-strings, no-repercussions sex. She was here on a temporary basis. She was an employee, albeit once removed.

He groaned. She was temptation.

He forced his mind to conjure up visions of the life he'd left behind in London, crowded buses and packed Tubes, nightclubs, cafés and old pubs. Teeming, exciting. Energising. Attractive, fashionably dressed women in abundance. Great job, great friends. And one woman he'd thought he'd truly known.

It had been a near perfect world prior to his trust going down the gurgler and his existence being uprooted into chaos. Now he had little social life, even less free time, and collapsed wearily into a deep dreamless sleep every night. And woke early each morning to the same hectic scenario.

CHAPTER THREE

MATT WAS PACING the floor, talking on the phone when Lauren arrived Thursday morning, hoping for a repeat of yesterday when she'd been left pretty much alone all day. He'd been absent when she'd finished so she'd left her report on his desk.

On the way to her room she returned the preoccupied nod he gave her, grinning to herself at the double take he gave her suitcase and overnight bag. She'd booked out of the hotel, confirmed she'd be returning on Monday and been promised the same room.

She did her routine and began work, fully expecting an apologetic call some time from her eldest brother, who'd been delegated to pick her up on arrival in Melbourne. She'd long ago accepted she was way down on her family's priority list.

Her priority was to complete her designated task. Her expertise told her a human hand was involved. If—*when, Lauren, think positive*—she solved what and how, fronting Matt Dalton was going to be daunting. The few occasions she'd had to implicate someone in a position of trust had always left her feeling queasy, as if she were somehow to blame.

In two days she'd become used to the sound of him in the background like a soft radio music channel where the modulations and nuances were subtle, never intrusive. Every so often the complete silence told her he'd left the office. Occasionally someone came in. Few stayed more than a couple of minutes.

There was no sign of him when she went to the fridge, though an unrolled diagram lay spread out on his desk. She resisted the impulse to take a peek, and consumed her snack while enjoying the view from her window.

Matt's return was preceded by his voice as he walked along the corridor not long after she resumed work. She glimpsed him as he strode past her doorway to the window, ramrod-straight, hand clenched. Not a happy man.

His temper wouldn't improve when her report showed all she'd written down so far today was a slowly growing number of random dates.

'Dad!'

His startled tone broke Lauren's concentration.

'Sorry, mate, I'll call you back. *Dad*, what are you doing here?'

He came into her view and stopped. By craning her neck, she could see him clasping a greying man to his chest.

'You came alone?' There was genuine concern in his tone.

'Haven't been in for weeks so I thought I'd come and find out what's happening.' Apart from the slower pace of the words, the voice's similarity to Matt's was defining.

'Everything's going smoothly. Come and sit down. We'll talk over coffee.'

Blocking his father's view of her, he guided him towards the seating, then continued talking as he passed her door on the way to make the drinks. Without breaking step he made a quick gesture across his throat when their eyes met.

'There's a new espresso flavour you've never tried, rich and aromatic.'

He wanted her to shut down and not let his father know what she was doing. What if Marcus came in here? Asked who she was? As far as she knew, it was still his company. And it was his son's fault she couldn't escape through the locked door.

The papers and folder were slipped into the drawer, a fresh page on the pad partially covered by random notes for show. Acutely conscious of the mingled sounds of the coffee machine and Matt's muted voice making a call, she reached for the mouse.

Matt slid his mobile into his pocket, and picked up the two small cups. What the hell had prompted his father's arrival? If his mother was aware he'd come into the city, she'd be worried sick. Had Ms Taylor understood his silent message? Could things get any worse?

'Here, Dad, try this. Tell me if you like it.' He sank into the other armchair, torn between the desire to hug his ailing father, and the recurring craving to demand why he'd cheated on his wife. So many times.

He'd never understood why so many people he knew treated cheating casually, as part of modern life. To him it was abhorrent. Why claim to love someone and then seek another partner? Why stay with someone who had no respect for your affection?

He had never declared the emotion, deeming that would be hypocritical, but had always insisted on fidelity. He'd found out the hard way that for some people promises meant nothing.

It churned Matt's stomach that his father considered affairs a normal part of life, his due entitlement as a charismatic male. The man he'd revered in his youth and aspired to become had seen no reason why they should affect his marriage.

He was torn between the deep love of a son for his father and distaste for his casual attitude to being faithful. And behind him, hidden by the wall in Matt's eye line, was the room where he brought the women. His coffee turned sour in his mouth.

Marcus sipped his drink cautiously, savouring the taste.

'Mmm…good, real coffee. I'll take a pod home and ask Rosalind to buy some.'

'Take a box.' Matt cleared his throat, hesitant to ask the

vital question. *Please don't let the answer be he drove.* 'How did you get here, Dad?'

'Caught a cab at the shopping centre near home.' He glared at the desk, set not too far away. 'You've twisted my desk.' It was an accusation.

'Don't worry, it suits *me* that way. We can always put it back.' He'd never place it in the former position that had given the user a direct eye line to the person working at the desk next door.

'Hmph. Now I need the bathroom.'

Marcus put his cup on the table, and went to the ensuite. Matt let out a long huff of breath, and took another drink of the hot, stimulating liquid. A glance at his watch told him his cousin should be here in a few minutes.

Swearing softly when his desk phone rang, he strode over to answer. He missed his father's return as he searched his in-tray for the letter the caller had sent.

Lauren stopped typing as Marcus came into her office. The eyes were a similar colour, the facial features bore a strong resemblance, but he lacked the firm line of his son's jaw, his innate sense of character.

'You're new. What happened to Miss…?' He tapped his palm on his forehead. 'Um, long dark hair, big blue eyes.'

'I believe she left. Can I help you?'

His gaze intensified, then he came round to stand beside her, and stared at the screen.

'She was a good typist. Fast and accurate.'

'Dad.'

Matt stood in the doorway, the same forbidding expression he'd worn at her interview directed at her. She lifted her chin, determined not to be part of whatever games this family was playing.

The older man spoke first. 'There's too many changes, Matthew. My girl was good. She left. People kept leaving.' Slow with pauses at inappropriate times. 'Who hired this one?'

He tapped her on the shoulder as he spoke, and she involuntarily flinched, knew from the frown on Matt's face he'd seen. He came over, and wrapped his arm across his father's shoulders.

'Let's leave Ms Taylor to her work, Dad. Come and finish your coffee?'

Although Matt barely glanced at her screen, he gave her a reassuring nod as he led his father out. He'd seen the bogus letter she'd started typing up.

'It'll be cold.'

She heard the outer door open, and saw Matt's body sag in relief.

'Here's Alan, Dad. He and I will drive you home and Mum will brew you another when we arrive.'

They moved out of her sight and she heard muffled exchanges then Matt's clearer words.

'Give me a minute. Grab that box of pods from the bench.'

He came into her room, his grateful expression telling her she'd pleased him, creating fissions of pleasure skittling from cell to cell.

'Quick thinking, Ms Taylor, thank you. I'll be gone for an hour or so. Joanne has a key to lock my office if you go out.'

He paused, swallowed as if there was more he wanted to say but couldn't find the words, then disappeared leaving her with a bundle of questions she'd never be game to ask.

The man she'd just met hadn't looked all that old but his behaviour and actions were certainly not those of a fast-thinking entrepreneur who'd built a thriving business.

She deleted the text as soon as she heard the door close, and brought up the files she'd been scanning. The events replayed in her mind as she sat, hands lightly resting on the keyboard.

Matt had been protective yet somehow detached from his father, desperate to get him out of here. He'd called this Alan to come and help, not wanting to escort him alone.

From Marcus' remark she deduced Matt had taken over his office. A woman had worked in here so he'd been elsewhere, probably the empty room by reception. Had Marcus kept such tight control Matt had no idea what was happening in the accounts and records?

That would explain his underlying antipathy and hostile manner but why towards her? She was his solution, his last resort. She was used to being warmly welcomed and treated with respect.

Matt was an enigma, his words and tone not always matching his body language and often conflicting with the message in those stunning blue eyes. He resented whatever it was that sparked between them, and must have a reason she couldn't fathom.

At all costs she had to find and fix his problems and get away without him finding out they had a past.

Matt quietly placed his keys into his desk drawer, wondering what he was going to say to Lauren.

My father has Alzheimer's. He's losing his memory. He's lost most of his good staff in the last year, and he's possibly screwed up the company.

His condition had escalated in the last month and Matt's mother was finding it harder to cope. Some very tough decisions would have to be made in the near future.

Matt would never blame Marcus for anything that could be attributed to that hellish affliction. But it was his father's screwing around that had sent him to the other side of the world. If he'd been here, possibly working with him, he'd have noticed the deterioration in time to prevent this debacle.

He would have. His fingers bunched. He squeezed his eyes shut and gritted his teeth. *He would have.*

Only the family, their doctor and a few select friends knew. Matt believed his chances of success hinged on keeping it a secret, and Lauren's employer had emphasised her discretion and trustworthiness. He was about to test it to the max.

She stopped working as he came to her doorway, her face inscrutable, her eyes wary. His stomach clenched.

'We'd better talk. Please come in here.'

Once they were seated by the window he paused to think, weighing up how much to tell her.

'There aren't the words to thank you enough for your understanding today. The man you saw isn't the same person who started this company. He has Alzheimer's.'

She leant forward. 'I suspected something like that. I'm sorry. It must be so hard on your family.' Empathy rang true in her voice and showed in her expression.

'Unfortunately, he kept his illness a secret from everyone, including my mother. We have no idea how long he faked his way until the progression sped up and his errors in the business became obvious. I'd have come home sooner if I'd known.'

'You weren't here?' She recoiled, eyes big and bright, fingers splayed.

She didn't know? There'd been no reason to tell her but he'd assumed she'd guessed. He nodded. 'I've been living in England for seven years.'

'Oh. Did you ever work here with your father?'

'In my late teens. My interests are in different fields of business.'

A pink blush spread up her neck and cheeks.

'Is something wrong?' He tensed, flexed his shoulders, and his hand lifted in concern.

Lauren cursed her lifelong affliction. What *could* possibly be wrong?

Only that the instant he mentioned his teens she remembered the balcony. Only that the sight of his mouth forming the words had her lips recalling the gentle touch of his.

'No, and I promise never to divulge any personal or company information to anyone.' Her hands clasped in her lap, she could barely take in that he'd shared this most personal secret with her. Now she understood.

His unplanned return from abroad to take control of a company in financial trouble explained the tension, the curtness. The urgency. She couldn't begin to imagine the daunting task he'd had thrust upon him.

'I'd appreciate it.'

'You're welcome. That's why you wanted my scanning hidden from him and called a friend for help.'

'He has good and bad days. Normally he becomes agitated whenever anything to do with the company is mentioned yet today he gave the taxi driver the correct address for the office. There was no hesitation in finding his way here or to the ensuite.'

'And he remembered the girl who worked here, though not her name.'

'He would.' The bitterness in his voice shook her and she jerked back, receiving a half-smile in apology as he continued.

'I was told her departure a few months ago was acrimonious to say the least. There were others who left because of his behaviour too, but replacements have to wait until you succeed and we sort everything out.'

She'd go and new staff would come. There'd be another woman at her desk, chosen by him...what was she thinking? This was not a valid reason to be depressed. Did he prefer blondes or brunettes?

Must. Stop. Thinking like this.

She snapped herself out of it and went to stand. 'On that note, I'd better get back to my task.'

He stood, and held out his hand to help her. The warmth from his touch spread up her arm, radiating to every part of her. She doubted even ice-cold water would cool her down. She prayed he couldn't detect her tremor and didn't demur as he kept hold.

'I am truly grateful, Lauren. I owe you big time and I never forget a debt.'

The message in his smouldering dark blue eyes painted a graphic picture of the form his gratitude might take, scrambling every coherent thought in her brain. Her throat dried, butterflies stirred in her stomach and it felt as if fluttering wings were brushing against every cell on her skin.

His grip tightened. Her lips parted. He leant closer.

The phone on his desk shattered the moment, and he glowered at it as he moved back, and reluctantly released her. She caught the arm of the chair to avoid collapsing into it.

His rasping, 'We'll talk again later,' proved she wasn't the only one affected.

As he picked up the handset he added, 'Alan's my cousin, family.'

The instant he answered the call he was in corporate mode. That irked because she needed time to compose herself, cool her skin, but he clearly didn't. When she returned from the ensuite, he was leaning on his desk, phone to his ear, watching for her. His engaging smile and quick but thorough appraisal from her face to her feet and back threatened to undo her freshen up. Not so calm and composed after all, just better at covering it up.

* * *

Lauren closed down early, allowing time for the ride to the airport, loath to suspend her search for four days. She had an inkling of an idea she'd heard somewhere but couldn't remember where or when. There'd be plenty of time to dwell on it in Melbourne.

Collecting her luggage, she took her report to Matt, whose stunned face and glance at his watch proved he'd forgotten her early departure.

'That late already? Have you ordered a taxi?'

'I'll be fine. I've noticed they always seem to be driving past.'

He grinned. 'Unless you need one. I'll finish this page and drive you.'

'There's no—'

'Humour me.'

Lauren's knowledge of cars was limited—there wasn't a necessity to own one in Sydney—but she recognised the Holden emblem on the grill. Matt's quiet assurance as he eased into the traffic didn't surprise her.

'Did you drive in Europe?'

'Yes, rarely in London, a lot through the country. Nowhere is too far if you can put up with dense traffic and miles of freeways. So different from Australia. Driving in Paris was a unique experience. Have you travelled?'

'A week in Bali with friends two years ago. We're planning a trip for this year if we can decide on a destination.'

She was aware of him glancing at her, but she kept her focus on the road where his should be.

'You mentioned family in Melbourne. Do you visit often?'

'Three or four times a year. This is my niece's first Easter.'

Matt willed her to look his way. She didn't. The ten-to-fifteen-minute drive in heavy traffic was hardly conducive to a meaningful discussion. That would have to wait until she returned.

'Why did you move to Sydney?' Why did he want to know? Why the long silent pause as she considered his question?

'Why did you go to London?'

Because I couldn't stand the sight of my parents feigning a happy marriage when it was a complete sham.

Because even moving into a rented house with friends in another suburb hadn't given him sufficient distance.

'Rite of passage to fly the nest and try to climb the corporate ladder without favour from associates of my father.'

'And you succeeded. It'll all be waiting for you when you've got Dalton Corporation back on track. Your family must be glad to have you home even under sad circumstances. I'm sure they've missed you.'

Matt picked up on the nuance in her voice, but didn't respond as he flicked on his indicator and turned into the airport road. So she had an issue with family as well. She'd rather not go.

He pulled into a clear space at the drop-off zone and switched off the engine. Before he had a chance to walk round and assist her, Lauren had unlatched her seat belt and jumped out.

He wiped his hand across his jaw, fighting the urge to reassure her, feeling he'd left so much unsaid today. He'd make time when she came back. She *was* coming back, and that pleased him.

She let him lift her luggage from the boot, and seemed reluctant to say goodbye.

'Thank you for the lift, Mr Dalton. I'll see you on Tuesday.'

'My pleasure. Enjoy your long weekend.'

I don't understand why, but I'll miss you.

CHAPTER FOUR

DRIVING BACK, MATT felt like laughing out loud at the incongruity of the situation. They could have spent time together during the four-day break, working alone, sharing lunches, maybe even dinner. Learning more about each other. Instead they'd be in different states paying lip service to family traditions.

With a complete turnaround, he wondered what the hell he was thinking. This was insane. Lauren Taylor was a temporary employee. Not his type at all. Yet he'd been so close to kissing her today in the office. The action and location were both bad ideas. So why did he wish that call hadn't come at that moment?

And how the hell had she managed to avoid answering his question?

Lauren closed her novel, and stared at the landscape rushing by then disappearing as the plane gained height. How could she concentrate on spine-thrilling action when her mind was in turmoil because of a man? She had male friends, a few of them treasured and platonic with whom she felt completely comfortable and totally at ease.

There were none who made her forget to breathe, who created fire in her core and sent her pulse into an erratic drumbeat. The thought of the magic those now skilful lips might evoke had her quivering with anticipation, earning her an anxious mutter from the older woman in the adjacent seat.

She gave her a reassuring smile, and turned back to the window. The fantasies she'd concocted for the last ten years had been childish daydreams based on teenage romance. The two relationships she'd drifted into had been more from affable proximity than passion. That they'd remained friends to this day proved how little anyone's heart had been involved.

No way would any woman accept friendship after an affair with Matt Dalton. His touch created electrical fissions on her skin, turned her veins into a racecourse and curled her toes. If they ever made it to the bedroom… She gulped in air, imagining the tanned, hot muscles he hid under expensive executive shirts.

'Are you sure you're okay?'

Her head swung round to meet a concerned gaze.

'Yes, thank you. I'm fine.'

Opening her book, she pretended to read, flipped pages and didn't take in a solitary word.

Late on Saturday night Lauren curled into the pillows in the guest bedroom, wondering what Matt was doing. She almost wished she'd gone with her parents and the grandchildren to visit friends. Her brothers were having the inevitable barbecue in the back garden.

She'd spent a great day with friends from university, who had insisted on driving her home, dropping her off at the corner because of all the cars parked in the street. Deciding to try to be more sociable, she'd attempted to join in with her brothers' party.

She'd lasted ten minutes among the raucous crowd, with whom she had little in common, then she'd finished her sausage sandwich, drained the soft drink can and said goodnight. A chorus of, 'Night, little sister!' had followed her into the house, most of it slurred.

She'd gone slowly up the stairs, reappraising her attitude to her upbringing. Had she been the one to pull away, uneasy with the openness of the rest of her family? Had she taken their leave-her-in-peace approach for indifference?

Not understanding why she'd begun to analyse her relationships, she'd shaken it away. She had a good life, a great job and supportive friends. Maybe she'd talk it through with them when she went home.

Putting on headphones and turning her music up loud, she'd logged into her computer and accessed her favourite game, which necessitated super concentration, blocking everything else out.

Now it was quiet except for an occasional passing vehicle. Was Matt asleep? Did he live alone or with his parents? Did he have siblings? There were so many questions that might never be answered.

Matt laughed out loud as he stood chest-high in his parents' pool on Sunday afternoon, pretending to fight off his nephews. He picked up Drew, the youngest, and tossed him, squirming and shrieking, about a metre away. Alex immediately latched onto his upper arm.

'Me next, Uncle Matt. Me next.'

He obliged, knowing this game could last until they were exhausted. He was surprised they had so much energy after the active Easter egg hunt around the garden this morning. One after the other, they kept coming at him and he revelled in their joy of the simple pleasure. They rejuvenated him whenever he was with them.

These were the times he regretted never marrying, and having children of his own. He took a splash of water in the face, shook his head, and laughed again. Hell, he wasn't even thirty, he had plenty of time.

He grabbed them both, one in each arm. Knowing what was coming, they giggled and clung to his neck. 'Deep breath.' Taking one himself, he dropped to the bottom of the pool, bending his legs to give him leverage. Pushing up, he surged from the water in a great spray, their happy squeals deafening him.

'Again. Again.

'Time out.'

His sister, Lena, was walking across the lawn carrying a tray of drinks and snacks. He let the boys go and they immediately swam for the ladder. Hoisting himself up onto the side, he took the beer she offered. She sat beside him, letting her feet dangle into the water, and studied him as he drank.

'What?' He looked at her and grinned. 'Am I in trouble?'

She shook her head as her eyes roamed over his face, and rested a caring hand on his arm. 'There's something different about you, Matt. I can't quite work out what.'

'I'm bone-tired, grabbing fast food most days and need a haircut.'

And I am inexplicably missing a woman I have only known for three days.

'Nothing's changed there since I last saw you. Bigger problems at work? No, that you'd handle in your usual indomitable manner.'

She tilted her head and arched her eyebrows, a ploy that usually produced a confession. They were as close as siblings could get but Lauren was new and he hadn't quite worked out how and why she affected him. And what he was going to do about it.

'Every trip you made home I hoped you'd have found peace from whatever drove you to go so far away. It never happened though you hid it well, and I know you only came now because Dad needed you.'

He didn't reply because he couldn't explain. He shrugged, put his arm around her and drew her close.

'I missed you, Mark and the boys more than I can say, Lena. You're the biggest plus on the side of me staying for good.'

Her face lit up at his remark he was considering relocating back to Adelaide. He meant it, wanted to be here for all his nephews' milestones. Skype was no substitute for personal hugs.

She kissed his cheek. 'You'll tell me when you're ready. In the meantime, add an extra plus sign.'

He frowned then grinned even wider and bear-hugged her. 'That's great. When?'

'November. You're the first to know.'

'Whatever happens I'll be here.' It was a promise he intended to keep.

When the boys went inside with their mother, he slid back into the water, working off restless energy with strong freestyle laps. His strokes and turns were automatic, leaving his mind to wonder what Lauren was doing and who she was with. And why the hell it was beginning to matter to him.

'Hang on, Lauren. The door's locked.'

Lauren turned her head towards the sound. It was ten past seven on Tuesday morning. Where was Matt? He'd said nothing about being absent today.

Joanne appeared, carrying a small bunch of keys, and they walked along the corridor.

'Mr Dalton's at a site meeting in the northern suburbs, called me last night. If he's not back by morning break, I'll join you for coffee.' She pushed the door open and left.

Being alone in the office didn't daunt Lauren, who'd always preferred having no surrounding noise or motion. Today her body was all keyed up as if waiting for some fundamental essential that was missing.

She had no interruptions until ten-thirty when Joanne walked in carrying a plate of home-baked jam slices.

'Family favourite. Let's sit by the window. Tea or coffee?'

'Tea, thanks.'

Lauren never indulged in gossip at work. She couldn't define why she felt tempted now, unless it was because Matt Dalton had invaded her peace of mind, and aroused her curiosity. The more she learnt about him, the easier it might be to resist him. If she couldn't she knew who'd end up heartbroken.

'How long have you worked for the Daltons?'

'Over six years. Since my youngest started secondary school. Of course, that was in a smaller office near the parklands. I like having familiar faces around. How do you cope, travelling and working with new people all the time?'

'I prefer it. I'm not much of a people person, never quite got the hang of casual socialising.'

'Mr Dalton senior was a natural and had no problems persuading people to invest with him. He was good with computers, installing quite a few new programs himself, and very easy to work for until a few years ago. We lost good long-term staff because he became secretive and less approachable.'

'And now Matt's in charge.'

Of everything. Thankfully he was unaware that included her emotions, unaware of how intriguing she found him.

'He came back from Europe when his father's heart trouble was diagnosed. Put a great career on hold, I understand, and not very happy to be here. I'm not sure whether it's the business, the problems or having to leave London, maybe all of them. He'll be heading back once his father's in full health again.'

Lauren let her babble on, regretting she'd instigated the topic. Matt had led her to believe he trusted Joanne yet he'd given the staff a fabricated story and let them believe his father would be coming back.

Did he really think any of them were involved in the computer anomalies? If not, it was cruel of him to give them false hope. Why did he keep giving out mixed messages? Or was she misinterpreting them?

Oh, why wasn't he older, content with a doting wife, and heading for a paunch from all her home cooking?

***

Lauren's mobile rang as she wrote notes on the last hour's work. Convincing Matt of her beliefs wasn't going to be an easy task.

'Ms Taylor, I need a favour.'

No preamble. No 'how are things going?' And the rasping tone was rougher. Why did she sympathise with his stress when he obviously intended to unload some of it onto her?

'Yes, Mr Dalton.'

'This is taking longer than I anticipated. If a Duncan Ford arrives at the office while I'm out, can you entertain him until I arrive?'

'Me?'

Meet and socialise with an unknown corporate executive?

Dealing with them when they needed her skills and the conversation centred on their technical problems was a world away from casual chit-chat. Knowing she was capable gave her confidence.

'You. Will it be a problem? Joanne's compiling figures for our meeting later.' He sounded irritated at her reluctance.

'That's not what I do. The few businessmen I've met have only been interested in how quickly I can fix their problems. A comment about the weather is as personal as we'd get.'

'It won't be for long. I'll be there in an hour or so, depending on traffic.'

She heard another voice in the background, followed by his muttered reply.

'Please, Ms Taylor. He's just a man.'

Yeah, like you're *just a man.*

His coaxing tone teased goose bumps to rise on her skin, and the butterflies in her stomach to take flight. She'd do it for him, and he knew it. She could hardly tell him fear of messing it up for him contributed to her reticence.

'Give him coffee. Ask him about the weekend football or his grandkids. Pretend he's an android.'

She pictured him grinning as he said that, and sighed.

'Okay, I'll try.'

After an abrupt 'thanks' he hung up, leaving her with a sinking stomach and a strong craving for chocolate, *her* standby for stress. Grabbing her bag, she raced for the lift and the café in the next building, mentally plotting dire consequences for all the too-good-looking, excessively privileged, overly confident males who'd ever tried to manipulate her. Including her three brothers.

'Mr Ford has arrived, Lauren. I'll bring him along.' Joanne phoned to give her warning.

Shoot. Only ten minutes since Matt called to say he was finally on his way. She swallowed a mouthful of water, pulled her shoulders back and prayed she didn't look as apprehensive as she felt. On her way through his office she added an extra plea he had a clear traffic run.

Mr Ford was average height, slightly overweight, and wore an apologetic smile. So much for Matt's word picture. He also held a small boy by the hand.

'Ms Taylor? Thank you for offering to look after us until Matt gets here.'

Offering? Us? Someone tall and desperate had bent the truth a tad.

'You're welcome. Come on in.' She indicated towards the armchairs. 'Please take a seat. Would—?'

Squealing with excitement, the child had broken free and was running to the window.

'Look, Granddad. Look how high we are. Look at the tiny cars way down there.'

Granddad smiled at Lauren and shrugged. 'The world's a wondrous place at that age.'

He walked over and hunkered down, his arm around the boy's shoulders, and let the child point out the amazing things he could see.

Pain clamped round Lauren's heart and she couldn't bear to watch them. She clasped her hands together over her stomach and stared at the floor. She'd never shared a special moment like this with either of her parents. They'd been happy to supply her with books, computers and assorted accessories, hoping they would keep her occupied. Never seemed to have time to spend exclusively with her.

There'd never been other relatives either. Her father's family lived in Canada, her mother had left home in her teens, and contact was limited on both sides. No wonder she felt inept in any new social situation.

'I believe you were about to offer coffee, Ms Taylor.'

She looked up to meet a quizzical gaze. Knew she was being appraised and managed a shaky smile. Matt had requested her to hostess and he was paying her wage, so a hostess she'd try to be.

'Of course. We have water or soft drinks if the child is thirsty.'

And then what do I talk to you about?

Take out the economy, sport, politics and local events, none of which she was up with, and she was left with the weather.

Matt Dalton, I hate you for putting me in this position.

He'd hired her to sit and scan his computer files, not make small talk, which she'd never ever been able to comprehend.

'Flat white for me and lemonade for Ken, thank you. I came in to take care of him while my wife and daughter saw a specialist, took a punt that Matt might be free. Ken

has a game pad, and I have a magazine to read so we won't
be a bother.'

He reached for the satchel he'd placed on the floor and
opened it.

It's no trouble,' she lied.

His expression said he didn't believe her, and knew exactly how she was feeling. He'd be a formidable opponent
in a boardroom. She turned away, heart hurting, stomach
churning. Still the same tongue-tied girl she'd always been.
Always would be.

Mr Ford was settled into a chair and Ken sitting cross-
legged on the floor when she brought the drinks over. The
boy was frowning as she put his on the low table.

'Thank you. Granddad, the frog won't jump.'

Without hesitation she dropped down alongside him.

'Show me.'

He studied her with narrowed eyes, assessing if she
could be trusted with his new favourite toy. He gingerly
handed it over, shuffled closer and didn't take his eyes off
the screen as she read the game rules and started tapping.

Matt couldn't remember breaking a mirror or running over
a black cat but he sure as hell was raking in bad luck. At
least there'd been some positives in his inspection of a new
recommended site today.

Duncan Ford was a man reputed to be fair and honest
in business, a trustworthy partner and an admirable opponent. A man he'd met on a number of occasions over the
years, usually with his father. Lately through a business
acquaintance and his own initiative.

If Lauren had managed to keep him happy, he'd have
a chance to pitch his proposition in the near future. If he
secured a deal with Duncan Ford on the development of a
vacant factory, it would go a long way to solving the com-

pany's present dilemma. Unfortunately ifs weren't solid happenings.

He strode towards his office, his heart sinking. No sound, no voices. Until, as he reached the open door, he heard a triumphant 'yes' in a child's tone.

The man he'd hoped to impress was sitting in one of the armchairs reading a magazine. Lauren and a young boy were kneeling by the coffee table, heads bent over a bright yellow pad.

'Matt.' Duncan stood, and came forward to shake hands. After putting the cardboard tube containing site plans on his desk and his satchel on the floor, Matt willingly complied.

'I apologise for not being here, Duncan.'

'Hey, it was an off chance. Lauren's been the perfect hostess.'

Matt flashed a grateful smile in her direction. He'd thank her properly later. The daggers she sent back warned him he'd have to grovel, big time. To his surprise he found the prospect stimulating rather than daunting.

'I got a call late yesterday to say this particular site goes on the market next month. I couldn't refuse the chance to inspect it.'

'We'll schedule a meeting when you've finalised your proposal. My coming into town was unexpected and I should be hearing from my daughter any minute. Once she and young Ken are on their way home, I'd like you and Lauren to join my wife and me for lunch.'

'Me?'

Matt's head swung at the panic in Lauren's voice. Exactly the same as earlier, yet, whatever her fears, she'd obviously impressed Duncan, which didn't surprise him. She certainly fascinated him.

'My treat for keeping Ken amused.'

'Thank you but no. I have work to do and I've brought my lunch.'

Her agitation was clear in her voice, and, though she managed to keep her features calm, Matt saw the plea in her wide-open eyes. And that intangible niggle flicked in his memory, and was gone just as fast.

The gentleman in him leaned towards letting her off the hook. The desperate male striving to secure a solid future for the company and its employees won.

'It'll keep 'til tomorrow, Ms Taylor. Never refuse a chance to eat out in Adelaide.'

If she was about to protest, Ken forestalled her, patting her arm and holding up his pad.

'Your turn, Lauren.'

She knelt to attend to the child. The chagrined look she gave Matt ought to have annoyed him, as she'd be wined and dined in style. Instead he was already planning ways to help her relax with the Fords.

CHAPTER FIVE

CLAIR FORD AND her daughter were Lauren's idea of true corporate wives, dressed in the latest fashion and groomed to perfection. If their greetings and appreciation hadn't been so sincere and friendly, she might have cut and run.

With young mother and son safely on their way home, the remaining four walked to the Fords' chosen restaurant. They led the way, allowing for private discussion.

'I owe you big time for today.' Matt's voice was low and subdued, proving the tension he was under.

'I'll keep tally, Mr Dalton. This counts too. What do I have in common with Mr Ford and his wife? The nearest I come to their world is walking past executive offices.'

'Under the current circumstances, Lauren, I think you should call me Matt.'

Lauren. Matt.

This made it personal, more familiar.

She'd liked the way he'd remembered the pronunciation of her name from her first phone call. She wasn't so sure about the butterfly flutter in her belly as he said it or the pleasurable shivers over her skin every time he guided her past oncoming pedestrians.

'I don't understand. You meet and deal with new people all the time. Why the reluctance?'

How could he understand how she felt? He oozed confidence and charm, would have no qualms on walking into a room full of notable people he'd never met. He'd been brought up to meet and greet strangers with ease.

'I can't do small talk. My family are all outgoing, garrulous, and at ease with anyone. I was shy. I'd freeze up and hide in my room. I...'

Duncan turned to check where they were as he and Clair turned off towards a waterside restaurant. The warm glow to her belly from Matt's gentle squeeze at her waist eased her misgivings. The tingles from his hot breath as he bent to her ear generated entirely different reservations.

'She's a down-to-earth mother and grandmother who enjoys serving on charity committees. He's into football and car racing. Trust me, Lauren, I'll be right beside you.'

They were escorted to a round table by the window. Matt held her chair, leaning over to whisper, 'Just be yourself, Lauren. I like you as you are.'

His fingers gently brushed a strand of hair from her shoulder, making her quiver, making her heart expand 'til her chest felt full and tight. So much for her internal lectures on the return flight to Adelaide, reinforcing how vital it was to keep distance between them.

Clair insisted on sitting next to her rather than opposite. 'The men will talk shop,' she said without rancour, smiling as she accepted a menu. 'Always say they won't. Always do. Nature of the beast.'

At the moment the two of them were discussing wine with one waiter while another poured iced water into their glasses. Lauren drank some, and felt cooler, more in control.

'What do you fancy, Lauren? The veal scaloppini is always delicious, and the perfect size to leave room for dessert.' Clair put down her menu, her decision made.

After ordering the same, Lauren almost refused wine until she caught Matt watching her, and decided why not? It was a light refreshing Sauvignon Blanc and one glass might give her courage. It would also fortify her for later if she told him the most likely outcome.

'Duncan's a stickler for supporting local wineries and we're rarely disappointed,' Clair said, leaning closer. 'Ken really enjoyed himself today, told me you taught him how to win games faster.'

'He's very bright, picked up what I showed him easily.'

'Maybe I ought to get him to teach me. I'm hopeless. My

worst fault is somehow sending files into folders they're not supposed to be in. Then I can't find them. I've also seized everything up a few times.'

'Have you taken any courses?' Chatting came naturally when someone took a genuine interest in you. Knowing they were all grateful to her, albeit for different reasons, helped too.

'A couple. I read the notes, and try to remember. Drives Duncan crazy. He says I rush too much. How do you do it all day?'

'Different people, different skills. Put me in a kitchen with any more than four or five ingredients, and I'm in trouble. Or rather, whoever wants to eat is.'

Their meals arrived, and the conversation became general until Clair suddenly announced, 'I'm thinking of asking Lauren to give me a lesson or two on my computer.'

Lauren saw a delighted smile replace the initial surprise on Matt's face. Duncan's exaggerated groan and loving expression towards his wife filled her with a longing she couldn't explain.

'I'm sure she's dealt with more incompetent people than me, Duncan Ford.' Clair's put-on piqued expression caused laughter round the table. Three pairs of eyes turned to Lauren for a reply.

'I'm sure I have. The trickiest ones are usually when they've tried to rectify the error but can't remember what they did. Or when they deny knowing.'

She shared a story of an ongoing promotion feud where two women had been sabotaging the other's computer, costing both of them their jobs. With encouragement she continued.

'A friend was asked to retrieve permanently deleted emails from the client's wife's laptop. He'd found romantic messages between her and another man, lost his temper and deleted them. Became angrier when he realised he now had nothing to confront her with.'

'Teach him to be destructive even *with* provocation. Did he get them back?' Clair asked.

'My friend refused to get involved so I have no idea.'

'Duncan, remember when…'

Clair's voice faded and Duncan's took over but Lauren barely heard his words. As she'd told the story, she'd become aware of Matt tensing beside her, hadn't dared look that way. She forced herself to focus on their host.

They were all laughing at the anecdote of his son-in-law wrongly directing an email about a surprise party when she glanced sideways. Matt was looking at her, a speculative expression on his face.

The world around them blurred until she could see only him. Her heart blipped then began to race. Warmth spread up her throat and cheeks. He arched his neck and his eyes darkened to almost black. She didn't dare guess at the thoughts behind them as he reached for his glass.

In fact Matt was wondering what the heck had happened. The quiet woman, who was so guarded with him, was captivating their hosts. There was only a hint of the hesitancy he'd perceived in the office. She listened to Clair with a genuine smile on her lips, and gave the same consideration to Duncan as he spoke.

So why the barrier with him? Instinct told him Lauren had a history with someone, painful enough to make her wary of men, or a particular breed of men. He was torn between letting it alone or finding out more and proving to her he couldn't be categorised.

It would be treading dangerous ground trying to discover the woman behind the technical façade. But, oh, it would feel good to see her smile focused on him, feel those sweet lips yield under his, trail a path of kisses down her slender neck as he held her in his arms.

'Have you finished, sir?'

He flinched as the waiter's arm appeared at his side.

Finished? Unless he lost his mind, he had no intention of starting.

'Oh. Um… Yes, thank you. The steak was perfect.'

He met Clair's knowing look across the table, and knew by the heat his cheeks were flushed. She was as astute as her husband; he'd bet she wasn't easily fooled. He had to try.

'Great restaurant. I'll keep it in mind for entertaining.'

Thankfully the wine waiter distracted her as he topped up her glass. Matt noted Lauren declined.

As they left the restaurant Clair caught his arm.

'I like her, Matt. She's very natural, down to earth. Pity she'll be returning to Sydney.'

'It's her home.'

'Adelaide used to be.'

He didn't answer. He hadn't known.

Duncan hailed a cab, telling Matt they'd drop him and Lauren at the office on their way. As they said goodbye Clair tapped Matt's arm through the window.

'We'll see you Saturday night. I do so love dressing up for corporate dos.'

'I'll be wearing my best tuxedo.'

He took Lauren's arm to guide her into the building, and sensed her guard was back up. Which made his burgeoning idea even more incongruous.

Lauren strove to keep her emotions under control in the lift, fought to keep her fingers from fisting. She didn't have proof yet, only assumptions. Saying anything would detract from the positives of the day.

Matt unlocked his office door, moved aside to let her enter then suddenly stiffened and caught her arm.

'You're trembling. Why?'

She looked into concerned blue eyes, and was swamped by the desire to caress the shadows away from underneath, to ease his burden. To say it was all okay.

'It's been an eventful day. I'd better get back to work.'

'Hmm, and I have to check in with Joanne and the others.' He let go, shrugged off his jacket, and hung it on his chair. Halfway back to the door, he swivelled round and gave her an ironic smile.

'I know I haven't been the easiest of people to work with or approach since taking charge. You're a courageous lady, Lauren Taylor, and I will find a way to repay you for stepping in for me.'

His unexpected compliment threw her. Her first opinion of him eroded a little more as new aspects of his enforced position emerged.

Opening up to her on Thursday wouldn't have been easy. He'd been forced by circumstances to take her into a confidence he'd rather have kept private. Something he only shared with those close to the family.

She went to her desk, determined to crack this puzzler and alleviate the pressure he was under. Her life in Sydney was on hold, her friends were there. When she returned everything would revert to normal. Except her vague fantasy was now a handsome, magnificently built real live male whose aroma, and every look, every touch weakened her knees and sent her pulse skyrocketing.

Her professionalism partially blocked him out at the office, and she managed to focus when dealing with hotel staff and other people. During those hours he was like an undercurrent in her head, surging to full force as soon as she was alone. With his muscled torso—clearly defined under his shirt—his trim waist and flat stomach, his image flicked through her mind like pages of a fireman calendar.

She'd succeed and then she'd have to leave him behind.

Matt returned to his office an hour later. Talking plans and strategies hadn't kept his thoughts from straying to Lauren. The way her chin lifted when she became defensive. The way her hair swung across her shoulders when she turned her head. Her soft hazel eyes betraying every emotion.

They'd crossed a threshold today, and he wasn't sure where it might lead. Surely they could become friends and stay platonic? Yeah, tell that to whatever part of his body was revving up his pulse and stimulating his libido. Initiating a closer relationship while she worked for him was fraught with danger.

She leant forward over her desk as if being closer would make something happen, her eyes riveted to the screen. Delightfully intense. She hadn't noticed his arrival, and started when she did, falling back with her hand covering her heart.

'Sorry, I didn't mean to disturb you.'

She'd gone a delicate pink again, a shade fast becoming a favourite of his. Leaning on the door jamb, he wondered how far it spread, immediately banishing the enticing image.

'I've got a call to make then we'll talk.'

Why? Lauren blinked, stretched, and changed her mind about going for a cold drink. She did a few leg raises, wriggled her fingers, and resumed work.

She tried to ignore the steady drone of his husky voice, interspersed with laughter and long pauses. The gentle tone she'd never heard him use before implied it had to be a woman he cared for. Her stomach knotted and her fingers curled. If she'd dared, she'd have closed the communicating door so she wouldn't have to hear.

His call ended, and she sighed with relief, entered a date for checking, and scrolled down peering at the screen. Neck tingles alerted her as he walked in and sat on the edge of her desk.

Letting her hands fall into her lap, she looked up. Her throat dried, and she wished she'd gone for that drink. Her chest tightened under the intensity of his gaze. It was as if he were searching for her innermost secrets.

'Do you have plans for Saturday night?'

'What?' She jolted upright, gripping the armrests for support. Stared, mouth open, too shocked to think.

His sudden wide smile confused her more, sending her body temperature soaring. Heart-stoppingly handsome before, even with the ravages of fatigue, he was elevated to drop-dead gorgeous.

'It's a simple question. Are you free on Saturday night?'

'I may not be here by then.' Breathless and throaty, not sounding like herself at all.

'No.' Sharp. Irascible. 'No.' Gentler, more controlled. 'Even if you find the cause of the anomalies, there'll be tidying up to do.'

'Why are you asking?'

What could he possibly want from her?

His light chuckle skimmed across her skin.

'I'd like you to be my partner at a corporate dinner.'

'Dinner? Why me?' Her common sense brain patterns seemed to have deserted her.

He leaned forward, and what little breath she managed to inhale was pure ocean breeze.

'A thank you for having my back today. Duncan and Clair like you, and we'll be at their table.'

'Surely there's someone else you could take.'

'After seven years away and working up to eighty hours a week? Anyone I knew is long spoken for. My sister only consented to accompany me out of pity.'

His sister. She flopped. She'd been jealous of his sister. *No! Not jealous.*

'Well?' His eyes were like laser beams searching for the answer he wanted.

'Won't she be disappointed?'

'Ah, that's where my negotiating skills came in. I've offered to babysit my two nephews, and shout her and her husband dinner at the restaurant of her choice. She'll have a romantic evening for two instead of set menu, speeches and dancing with her brother.'

Dancing. In his arms.

Too close. Too dangerous. You're already in too deep. Say no, thank you.

The phone on his desk rang. He muttered a low hoarse sound, and appeared reluctant to move.

'Will you come with me, Lauren?'

'Yes.'

Wrong. Idiot. Wrong.

He stroked a feather-touch path down her cheek, immobilising her senses, then smiled again, sending them all haywire.

'Thank you. I promise you won't regret accepting. Do you want to take an early leave? You've had an eventful day.'

'I'm fine. I'll keep going, and you need to reply to that call.'

Fine didn't come near to describing how she felt. Adrenaline coursed through her veins, her lungs were having trouble pumping air and her heart was pounding. And she couldn't tell if it was joy or fear driving them.

Matt had avidly watched the ever-changing emotions in her eyes. Confusion, surprise, shock when he mentioned his sister, and then pleasure as she blurted out her answer. It was as if she were afraid her brain would rebel and refuse his request if she dithered any longer.

He'd gripped the desk to prevent his arms reaching for her, the urge to hold her stronger than he'd ever felt. And then what? He had no idea; with her he was in uncharted waters.

He was, however, determined that before he let her go he'd persuade her to reveal her inner torments, and help her overcome them. He knew with an innate certainty the inner woman was as beautiful as her outward appearance.

* * *

Lauren arrived early the next morning even though she'd taken extra time on her hair and make-up. She'd fallen asleep thinking of ball gowns—she'd have to buy one, plus matching accessories—romantic music and dancing with a stunning male in tailor-made formal wear.

It had been dark when she'd woken, her mind buzzing with an idea generated by her discussion over the phone with Pete in Sydney. Eagerness to try it had warred with the desire to look extra good for Matt, so she'd skipped breakfast and bought a sandwich on the way.

The disappointment at his absence was countered with optimism that she'd be able to give him the answers he'd requested. Her fingers hesitated over the keyboard. If she was correct, today might be her last day in this room, so close to him. Even when he was elsewhere in the building, she felt his presence, and his unique aroma lingered in the air.

She'd spend the rest of her working life breathing in expectantly and being disenchanted. Not even the same brand would suit because it wouldn't have his essence.

She booted up. She'd promised to do her best for him, and would, even if it meant she lost out.

Matt arrived mid-morning, eager to see her. He was perplexed by her reticence on the phone when he'd called to say he'd been delayed. If she was having second thoughts about Saturday, he'd have to talk her round.

In his hurry to see her he left his jacket in the car. Not caring, he barrelled through his office to her door where her grave expression pulled him up short. Even as the truth hit home his subliminal mind noted she wore extra make-up. Subtle and captivating.

'You've solved it.' It was what he wanted, had hired her for. So why the heaviness in his chest, and the sudden nausea attack?

She nodded and he swung away to fetch his chair, wheeling it over to her desk. His gut told him it wasn't good and he braced for the worst. Her delicate fragrance taunted him with every intake of air.

Her blue screen was blank except for a familiar symbol.

'And this is…?' He already knew—wanted confirmation yet dreaded receiving it.

Lauren hesitated, hating that what she was about to reveal would hurt him, She had no choice, pressed enter, and a box with a request for a password appeared.

'It's deliberate and there are limited people who had access. Joanne said—'

'You've discussed this with her?' His body surged forward. Anger flashed in his eyes, giving them more animation than she'd seen since they met.

'No! We shared a coffee break yesterday, and she said they'd lost good employees. You referred to the staff turnover last Thursday.'

'I did. I apologise.' It was terser than he'd been lately, with no relenting of his indignant stance.

'It wasn't gossip. Joanne admires your father very much. I got the impression his health had worried her for ages. She said how well he and the staff got on, what a great boss he was, and that he'd installed a number of the programs himself.'

'I didn't know. I wasn't here.' He ground one fist into the other palm.

'It has to be my father.'

CHAPTER SIX

HIS WORLD HAD imploded at the sight of the icon. This was confirmation of the suspicion that had grown as he'd checked the records, hoping his father's worsening dementia had been responsible for the unaccountable swings. Saying the words out loud enforced the actuality.

He moved closer and typed in the heading on the plaque in his father's home study, his fingers surprisingly steady in contrast to the agitation in his gut. Two screen changes and he had the answers he needed. And a whole new bunch of complications.

Elbow on the desk, hand clenching his jaw and mouth, he gaped at the folder titles, anger building at the subterfuge of the man he'd admired. What the hell had he been planning?

'Would you like me to leave while you examine the files?'

He didn't turn, couldn't face her. Needing air and time to come to terms with the harsh reality in front of him, he pushed away from the desk, shot to his feet and swung away from her.

'No. Close it down.'

He strode out of both offices, his mind churning with distasteful words: fraud, embezzlement, jail. Ignoring the lift, he went to the stairwell and headed down. There was no more doubt, no more hope of technical glitches, or outside scamming.

If he reported what they'd found his father would be investigated. If he didn't...not an option. He'd fight like hell to save the company and his new enterprise with Duncan but the appropriate authorities had to be informed. Whatever the cost to his own personal reputation, everything had to be open and above board.

He wasn't sure how many floors he pounded down and

up again. As his head and his options became clearer, he realised he'd left Lauren in the lurch. She'd succeeded in the task he'd given her, and he'd growled and walked out. Had she left? Would she equate him with his father?

His angst eased a little when he found her sitting by the window in her office writing in a small notebook. She raised her head and he gazed into sweet hazel eyes, full of compassion and offered with complete sincerity. A haven from the tempest.

Lauren sat stunned after he'd barked out the order to shut down and stormed out. He hadn't even glanced at her, just bolted.

After closing down and writing out instructions to access the files, she went for a drink of water, pondering her future, which might be closer than she'd expected. She'd done the job, found what the anomalies hid. Not knowing what the folders contained, she assumed they'd need to be audited, and that wasn't her expertise.

Did this change his invitation for Saturday night? Would she be starting her exploration of rural South Australia earlier than anticipated? She was no longer required so why didn't she feel the usual elation of success? The bubble of enthusiasm for the next assignment?

She took a notebook from her bag and tried to makes notes and failed. Her mind was on the distraught man who was trying to come to terms with his father's deceit. This was a major blow for him. He deserved privacy to come to terms with tangible proof of his father's duplicity and the fallout effects to his family.

His entrance was as abrupt as his departure. He paused for a second in the doorway then walked slowly towards her, midnight-blue eyes dark and unsure of his reception. Her skin tingled, and her heart somersaulted. She trembled as she met his gaze, stood and dropped the book and pen onto the chair.

He took her hands and squeezed them, his Adam's apple convulsing, and his mouth opening and shutting without sound. Slowly, gently he caressed up her arms to hold her shoulders, and inched closer. He stroked her cheek, caught a strand of her hair and twined it round his finger. When she placed a hand on his chest, he shuddered.

If Lauren's heart swelled an atom larger, it would burst from her body. Heat spiralled from deep in her belly, drying her throat, searing her from within. He evoked feelings she'd never have believed herself capable of, made her aware of a physical wanting she'd only read of in books. He coloured her dreams in brilliant shades and sunshine.

His eyes were searching for her soul and she couldn't look away. Mesmerised by their power, she leant forward in a mirror image to his movement. Stilled when he straightened up, a guttural sound coming from deep in his throat. His hands dropped to his sides, leaving her cold where his fingers had been.

'I… This… *Hell*.' Forceful. Passionate. 'I'd planned for a special lunch with you so we could talk.'

He rubbed the back of his neck and his face contorted as he stared at the computer.

'I have to deal with this now and find out what he's done.'

She understood the battle he was fighting—his family's good name was in jeopardy—but it hurt. She felt as if she'd been dismissed. Gathering up her pen and book, she moved to the desk for her bag and took a sheet of paper from the top drawer.

'These are the access instructions.' She put it on the desk top, Had to get out before she broke down and cried.

'Lauren?' The anguish in his voice tore at her heart.

She turned and saw a different battle in his eyes, one that clogged her throat and tripped her heartbeat.

'Thank you. I may not seem grateful at the moment but I do appreciate all you've done.' He gestured at the computer. 'If possible we'll have lunch tomorrow or Friday.'

'I'd like that.' Much, much more than like.

'There can't be much you don't know or haven't guessed so you must know the ramifications could send us under.'

The potency had gone from his voice, giving him an endearing vulnerability, making her care for him even more. With his strong will, it would only be a temporary effect of the devastating blow.

'If there's anything I can do.' She moved forward until she inhaled his cologne. She was so going to miss the fragrance. The walks she always enjoyed along windswept beaches, especially prior to an impending storm, were going to be a mixture of pleasure and pain for ever.

His rueful smile made her long to wrap her arms around him for comfort.

'I'm sure there will be at some stage. There's nothing now so take a few hours off.'

When she left he was talking on his mobile, an open file on her screen in front of him.

The size of the hidden program astounded Matt. There were accumulated folders and files dating back six years, money transferred in, none out. He studied names and figures, made calls to his accountant, lawyer and Alan. No amount of trying could curb the resentment at his father's deception beginning long before the onset of his dementia.

Cheating was unjustified, in any form. Marcus, acquaintances, even friends deemed nothing wrong with bending rules or breaking promises. A few months ago he'd let himself be fooled by a scheming woman, and had been on the verge of pledging his life and honour to her. She'd claimed to love him, a blatant lie.

Now he was more cynical, and had no faith in romantic declarations. He'd make that clear before entering into any relationship. No emotions, no lies, and nobody got hurt.

Which meant no involvement with Lauren. She was a for-ever kind of girl who'd weave romantic dreams around kisses and…hell, again he'd come so close to kissing her today.

It might be for the best that she'd be leaving soon. It wouldn't be until he was sure there was nothing else hidden, and not until he'd treated her to a night she'd always remember.

He clicked the mouse, and rechecked the folder list. He'd need hard-drive copies of everything plus paper copies of the folder list, maybe others. Lauren's help would be invaluable as he dealt with any authorities who'd have an interest in any aspect of the clandestine accounts.

Bracing himself, he accessed another file, and resumed his onerous task.

Lauren rarely shopped for social events. Her new 'uniforms' of trouser suits and blouses were purchased in the January and June sales. Outside work she wore casual clothes, unless on special occasions. What she did have was in Sydney but nothing in her wardrobe came close to being suitable for a corporate dinner.

She fluctuated between longing to go and fearing she'd embarrass him as she wandered from shop to shop, sifting through racks of dresses and tops. Standing in the change rooms of an international brand store, she almost gave up.

Why this alien urge to buy something bold and extravagant? *So* not her, sleek and clinging, showing off every curve and a seemingly long expanse of leg? Like the low-cut sapphire-blue on the wide-eyed image staring at her from the mirror.

'Do you require any assistance?' the salesgirl called through the door.

No. Though, if she were ever to wear anything like this out in public, a huge hike in self-confidence would definitely help.

'I'm fine, thanks.'

She found what she was searching for in a small off-the-mall boutique. A dress that fitted perfectly and boosted her self-esteem, one she hoped would make Matt proud to escort her. Shoes and a matching clutch bag were bought in a nearby shop, and by mentioning Joanne's name she managed to book an appointment for Saturday at her recommended hairdresser.

Stepping towards the kerb to hail a taxi, she remembered he'd spoken of lunch, a special lunch for two. She dropped her arm and headed back into the mall.

The driver who took her and her parcels to the hotel waited and drove her to the office. She'd rather be there helping him than on her own in her impersonal rented room.

Lauren watched the file names speed through as they were copied to the second hard drive, so many more than she'd expected. Surely this would have a huge effect on the company. Had any of it been declared to the tax office?

She'd be long gone before anything official happened. Matt might remember her as part of his father's downfall, not much more.

He'd been making and taking calls since she'd returned to the office, a pleasant background to her thoughts. She was going to miss his gravel tone when she left. Rougher under stress; she doubted it would ever be smooth. Not even in moments of passion. Which she so should not be thinking about. Ever.

He was absent when she'd finished so she made herself a cup of tea. The man who walked in as she deposited the used tea bag in the bin was tall, handsome and had to be related. His resemblance to Matt was striking, and his instant smile in a familiar face reminded her of Matt's when he'd invited her to the corporate dinner.

Hi, is Matt here?'

'Right behind you, mate.'

She watched enviously as the two men hugged and slapped shoulders, indicating a very strong bond.

'I've made a couple of calls, thought I'd come round to talk. It's quieter here than my office. Then I'll shout dinner. Shall we make it for three?'

Whoever he was, he spoke to Matt but looked at her, with unashamed interest in eyes that were a much lighter blue than Matt's.

Matt noticed the direction of his gaze, his brow furrowed and his eyes narrowed. For the first time since they'd been in high school, he was loath to introduce his charming cousin to a girl. They walked over to her.

'Lauren Taylor, our computer expert from Sydney. Lauren, my cousin Alan Dalton.'

Her quick glance at him told him she'd heard the edge to his voice that surprised him as well.

'Hello, Lauren.' Alan held out his hand, and she accepted it.

'He said he'd hired an expert from Sydney, didn't say *she* was young and beautiful.'

Matt tensed, his breath lodged in his throat. She'd never acknowledged the few times he'd touched her, though he'd sensed her reactions. He'd barely been able to hide heat rushes from contact with her.

She certainly didn't seem to mind Alan holding on longer than protocol required while he continued his smooth talk. Bile surged in his stomach. He knew how persuasive his cousin could be and felt an indefinable impulse to move between them, break them apart.

Thankfully Lauren appeared to be impervious to his charms, deftly stepping away as she freed her hand. In fact she wore a similar guarded expression to the one he'd first encountered on the day she'd walked into his office. So perhaps it was all eligible men she had a problem with... not just him.

'Thank you. I have plans for tonight.'

Matt knew she didn't and her words inexplicably pleased him.

'Maybe the three of us could have lunch another day.' Not if Matt could prevent it. Alan was a persistent devil.

'I'll be leaving soon so probably not. Matt, the hard drives are in your top drawer. Excuse me.' She took her drink and went to her office.

'Wait here, Alan.' Matt followed her to the chairs by the window, and dropped onto the vacant one. Her sombre hazel eyes caught at his heart.

'You've finished the copying?'

'Yes, is there anything else you want me to do?'

A hundred things flashed through his mind, none of which he could voice out loud. All of which he'd be happy to participate in with her, however inappropriate. A complete reversal of his earlier decision.

'I have no idea until I've seen the accountant and solicitor. I do know I don't want you to leave yet.'

She smiled, her eyes lit up and he fervently wished his cousin were back in his own office two city blocks away.

'It's heading for five. Go home, and if you want time off tomorrow to shop for the dinner that's fine.'

'About that...'

His finger covered her mouth, preventing her from changing her promise and creating a zing along his arm.

'Alan's waiting. We'll discuss details tomorrow. The

function's black tie so it's long dresses, or pants and glittery tops. The women usually scrub up good too.'

'Idiot.' Her stuttered laughter raised the hairs on his nape, made his fingers itch to reach out and pull her from her chair onto his lap. He liked that his teasing had rekindled the sparkle in her eyes.

Feeling happier, he stood up, inhaled her enchanting perfume and fought the impulse to stroke her hair.

'I'd better get back to Alan and pick his brains.'

She looked puzzled.

'He studied both law and commerce at university. They make a useful combination and I need all the good advice I can get.'

Alan was perched on his desk checking his mobile when Matt walked in.

'Too busy to make the coffee, huh?' He set the machine for two cappuccinos as his cousin came over to join him.

'I've never been able to work that machine. Too elaborate for me.' Alan leant on the bench, picked up a teaspoon, and twirled it through his fingers.

'How long will Lauren be in town?'

'As long as I need her, and I'd rather she wasn't distracted.'

'You've got to admit she's cute.'

'She's also quiet and dedicated to her job. Not your type at all, cuz.'

The spoon stilled in Matt's peripheral vision. He looked up to find a wide grin and knowing eyes.

'Getting territorial, are we, Matt?' The smile faded as Alan's gaze intensified. 'You *are*!'

'She's here to work—an employee. I have no idea if she's free. I'm strictly solo for a long time. Take your pick of reasons.'

He heard the curtness in his tone, regretted being terse with the one person he trusted unconditionally. The only person he'd confided in when he broke off his relationship. The one secret between them was his father's infidelity and he hadn't been able to admit to his father failings, or his mother's acceptance of them, to anyone.

'Alan, I'm sorry. You've been my rock throughout this mess. Put it down to fatigue and frustration.' And, he admitted to himself, maybe jealousy.

'No problem. I'd have buckled weeks ago.'

They were seated by the window when Lauren came through and said goodbye. Alan replied in kind.

Matt held her gaze for an instant, wishing they were alone. 'Enjoy the rest of the afternoon. I'll see you tomorrow.'

'Definitely territorial,' Alan stated after she'd gone. 'Don't give me the guff you spouted earlier. I know you, Matt Dalton. What's the problem?'

'Trust.'

'Hers or yours? I thought you were over the woman in London.'

'There was really nothing to get over. I was angry as hell that she'd cheated on me but my pride took more damage than my heart. So how do you tell if it won't happen again?'

'I reckon Lauren's worth taking a chance on.'

Matt silently agreed.

Thursday morning was muggy with depressing grey clouds and intermittent showers. It was a perfect day for Lauren's mood as she kept close to the city buildings, avoiding raindrops and dodging umbrellas. Which she'd always hated, even the one she'd received on her last birthday. Transparent and shaped like a dome, it made her feel like one of those stuffed birds you saw in old houses and museums.

She'd been rehearsing how to approach Matt since she'd woken, hadn't found an easy way or the appropriate words. Every hasty decision she'd ever made had brought remorse.

Though doubtful, proximity might lead to him remembering their meeting on the balcony. Their lives were different. They were different.

She shook out her light raincoat in the building's entrance and folded it over her arm. Sensible, coherent excuses ran through her head as she entered his office, and scrambled in her brain with one look at his striking features, his toned chest muscles moulded to his light blue shirt, and one long leg crossed over at the ankle as he leant against the bench.

'I've changed my mind.' She blurted it out without a greeting, not allowing him to charm her with his gravelly voice or expressive eyes. Not giving him the chance to captivate her with his smile.

CHAPTER SEVEN

HE TURNED HIS head towards her and his body stiffened. His jaw tightened, eyebrows arched and eyes widened, darkened. His lips curled as he did a slow, oh-so-slow scan from her flustered face to her feet. When he finally looked her in the eyes he wore a wide grin and his raspy voice dropped an octave.

'Is this for my benefit?'

'What? Oh.' So focused on her speech, which she'd stuffed up anyway, she'd forgotten she was wearing the new green dress. At the time of purchase she'd hoped the scooped neckline, fitted waist then flared skirt to just above her knees would impress him. Seemed as if she'd succeeded big time.

'You look too exquisite to be spoiling for a fight, Lauren Taylor. I like the dress. Colour suits you.'

'I thought it…you're trying to confuse me.'

He didn't need to try. A look, a smile, a touch and her brain addled.

'I truly don't think I should be your partner at the dinner.'

The mug in his hand clanked as it hit the bench. In two strides he stood in front of her, a determined gleam in his eye. Close. As close as he'd been on the balcony. If he leant forward…

Blushing at her thoughts, she stepped back, out of range. Maybe not. He had long arms. The long, muscular arms she'd last night dreamt of encircling her as they danced to a Viennese waltz.

His lips firmed as her cheeks warmed.

'Okay. We are going to talk this out now and then forget it.'

With surprising tenderness he took her arm and guided her to the chairs, settling her into one then placing her bag and raincoat on the floor. He sat opposite and didn't say a word until she looked up at him.

'I confirmed you'll be my date when I called in to see my sister last night.'

There was an implacable edge in his tone. His eyes, now alert and locked with hers, were corporate mode. She tamped down her longing to surrender and mustered logical arguments.

'You can phone her. I should never have agreed. I'll get tongue-tied and embarrass you.'

'No, I won't. You're beautiful, intelligent, and the Fords want you there. In fact it was Clair who subtly put the idea into my head.'

He thought she was beautiful? Clair had really liked her? Her heartbeat kicked up.

'It's a woman's privilege to renege, of course, but then you'll be the one who has to break the news to my sister and nephews.'

She lifted her chin and glared at him. He was teasing. The gleam in his eyes was back, more compelling than before, and his lips seemed tantalisingly fuller. It was a complete change from her interview meeting. Did he really believe she'd relent on that flimsy statement?

'Why? You can stay with them another night so their parents can go out.'

'No problem there. The camping trip they decided to have seeing they now had no commitments for the weekend might be. The boys were writing a packing list when I left and I'm not going to be the one to disappoint them.'

'Oh.' Her bubble burst. She broke eye contact, fighting not to hug her stomach to quell its churning as she squeezed her legs together to hide their trembling. She gulped when he leaned towards her, fingers linked between his knees.

'You meet and deal with new people every day, Lauren.

Your boss receives glowing reports about your interaction with others. How is this different?'

Because it's not work, not technical. Not transient. She realised she'd linked *her* fingers and was grinding her palms against each other. Stopping the action, she drew in a deep breath.

'Those are usually people who want my help. I fix the glitches and leave. And, yes, there are a few regular clients, and our rapport has built up over a number of visits. Not the same and mostly workers on my level.'

Matt held back the chuckle that threatened to erupt. She sounded so earnest, so desperate to have him believe she'd be a hindrance. So scared of putting herself in an unfamiliar environment.

'Lauren, it's just a roomful of couples wanting to have a good night out and raise money for charity. There'll be set tables for dinner, then people tend to mix once the dancing starts.'

'That's another thing, the dancing. I'm not sure I can in company like that.'

'Ah. Which worries you, traditional or modern? In the first I promise you won't be pressured to join in. And my experience with modern is there are no rules, and the men with the least coordination seem to have the most fun. Especially after a few good wines.'

Her brow cleared, her stiff posture loosened. He was making headway. She knew about his father's condition and financial deception. If either leaked out saving the company could become almost impossible. And he needed her to understand the evening wouldn't be a prelude to a personal relationship.

'You're smart. You must know Dalton Corporation is in trouble. As things stand, your findings could tip us either way. I've been upfront with Duncan Ford and promised he'll be kept informed of all proceedings. Thankfully he has faith in me.'

He reached out and unclasped her hands, covering them with his.

'Please, Lauren. If it will make it easier to accept, treat the evening as an extension of your assignment.'

The gold specks in her darkening eyes were becoming more pronounced. They brightened and softened with her unconcealed changing emotions. He willed her to agree, his own responses heightened by the softness of her skin under his fingers, and the gentle blush on her cheeks. His pulse quickened, and every muscle felt taut as he willed her to agree.

She raised her chin, and her lips curled into a sweet smile.

'You'll come.' If she still wavered, he'd go down on his knees. And pray no one came in while he was there.

'Only so your sister can have her romantic evening.'

If punching the air wouldn't have seemed patronising he'd have done it. He didn't care about her motive, which he suspected she'd grasped at rather than admit she wanted to come.

'Thank you, Lauren. I promise to give you a night you'll never forget.'

She pulled her hands free and leaned away from him as if needing space and distance.

'So what would you like me to do today?'

'I know it's not your field but Joanne says the day-to-day data is behind. I've got meetings this morning and later this afternoon, which should give me some idea of what repercussions I might be facing. Midday's free so I've booked our table for one o'clock'

Shame flooded Lauren. He was fighting for the future of the company and its employees and she'd dumped her insecurities on him. He'd even allowed time to take her for lunch.

'I'm sorry, Matt. I've been selfish, worrying about myself when you've got much bigger problems.'

He stood and held out his hand, his eyes sending a message that weakened every resolve she'd made, and every muscle in her body. Her legs threatened to buckle as she accepted his assistance to stand.

'I'll forgive you almost anything as long as you keep saying my name, Lauren.'

That would be breaking down another barrier between them, and she wasn't sure how many were left. She smiled and stepped away.

'I'd better go and find Joanne.' Her head had demanded poise and self-control. Her voice had proved breathless and aroused.

Wind had blown the dark rain clouds away, bringing in their place white fluffy banks that drifted slowly across the now bright blue sky. The sun had dispelled the morning chill and raincoats could be left behind. The taxi dropped them off at the gates to the botanical gardens and they walked to the restaurant inside.

There were so many shades of green, so many different plants and flowers, all fresh and glistening from the showers. Ducks waddled over the lawns and birds swooped from tree to tree, their different calls mingling in the air. For Lauren it had become a magical spring day. Made doubly so by the sight of the shimmering white pavilion at the edge of a pond.

'This is where we are eating?' She drew them to a stop to drink in the image, and fumbled in her bag for her mobile to take a photo, though she knew she'd never forget.

'Here, let me.' Matt took it from her. 'Turn around.'

She faced him, the building behind her, the breeze teasing her hair and her heart twisting while she smiled on his command. Twice for her camera then, to her surprise, twice more for his.

The interior was as pristine. White linen covered the

tables and chairs, even extended to the serviettes. Silver cutlery, crystal glasses and a delicate floral centrepiece completed an impressive décor.

They were seated by one of the open arches overlooking the waterfall and pond featuring a reed-covered island and a family of colourful ducks. Matt declined wine, opting to share the water she'd asked for. As the waiter left with their orders she gazed round full circle in awe.

'It's so incredible. I can't believe I never came here in all the years I lived in Adelaide. I have a vague recollection of the zoo so that must have been when I was young.'

'You never came to the city on weekends or in the holidays with friends?' As if that made her unique but not in a good way. 'How old were you when you moved?'

'No and thirteen. My family life revolved around my brothers' sporting events. And before you judge, it wasn't so bad.'

Why was she defending what she'd always decried? Unless she was beginning to understand her own personality's part in it all? She sipped water from the delicate glass and smiled. If she had visited the gardens, it would have been in a plastic bottle on the benches outside.

Matt stretched across the table, stroking her hand with his long fingers.

'Believe me, Lauren, I never make judgements on anyone's family. The reason you're here is proof you can never tell what happens behind closed doors.'

Nausea gripped his stomach as he recalled the moment she'd shown him evidence of his father's duplicity. The secret deals and bank accounts, even the location of a large amount of cash. Preparation for what, a new life with another woman? A suspicion he'd keep to himself as long as he lived.

He gazed into hazel eyes, and found warmth and understanding. Something tight around his heart shifted and softened unexpectedly.

'How do you explain nearly five years of lies and deceit, Lauren? What the hell was he planning?'

'Will he even remember?'

'I have no idea how much is real or how much he's been faking, and I'm praying I can keep the truth from my mother. She's defended his behaviour all my life, and I can't bear to disillusion her.'

He found the simple act of caressing her small, delicate hand comforting. The kitchen could take all the time they wanted; he was in no hurry.

'Does she have to know anything?'

'If there are legal proceedings against him or I fail to revive the business, yes. In either case I won't be able to protect her from the consequences. I've accepted my father is guilty and I'll handle whatever happens as it occurs.'

He noticed the waiter approaching with their meals, grudgingly removing his hand.

'No more work talk. This was intended as a get-to-know-you meal before the dinner.'

Get to know you? Lauren already responded to him in ways she hadn't believed were real, much less that she'd be capable of. He could turn her inside out without any visible effort. He was going to haunt her for ever.

She picked up her knife and fork, and made the mistake of looking into his contemplative midnight-blue eyes. It was as if he were seeking a path out of the quandary he'd been coerced into handling, and she might be his beacon.

He ran his finger over his mouth—oh, heck, the mouth that had covered hers so gently, so masterfully. So long ago.

'So, do you follow the footy at all?'

About to begin eating, she almost bit her tongue. Had he remembered?

'Only as a talking point with clients. Sport's never interested me.'

'What does?' He bit into his bread roll, showing neat white teeth.

'Why the sudden interest?' She heard the words, hadn't meant to say them out loud.

'Indulge me. Saturday night I'll be your escort. It would help if we knew something about each other.'

But we are strangers and I have to keep it that way so I can relegate you to 'memories never to be intentionally accessed'. Ever.

He started on his meal, chewing slowly, and studying her as if committing her to *his memory*. Agreeing to go to this dinner was so one of her worst decisions ever. Though it could turn out to be one of the best.

'Does it work both ways?' Again she voiced her thoughts. She didn't wanted to know, hoped he'd refuse.

'I'm an avid Adelaide Crows supporter, and watched every match on the Internet while I was overseas. I played competitive squash—now I fit in games or workouts with Alan whenever I can, and run. My movie taste is for high adventure, fast action. And there's not much I won't eat.'

Wow, more detail to flesh out her fantasies and spice up her dreams of an unsuitable, never ever for her, completely unattainable man. She instinctively squirmed in her seat and pushed into the back.

'Your turn.' He wasn't going to let her off.

'I rarely watch sport, enjoy any well-made science fiction, and Australian historical movies or series and walk whenever possible. I use a gym on a casual basis. I enjoy spicy food, not too hot, and eat limited takeaway when I'm home.

'And you like your job?'

'I love the challenge of a mystery and the adrenaline rush when I succeed. Unfortunately most jobs are mundane, the result of human error and complications when they try to undo without really knowing what they did.'

She heard her own dissatisfaction. Maybe it was time for a change.

'Is there anything else you'd like to do?'

'I'm not sure. It's a new concept.' She frowned at him then smiled. 'Talking to you might not be good for my career. Where did you live in London? I heard houses and units are super expensive.'

'Correct. I got lucky. I own a one-bedroom suburban flat within walking distance of the Tube. Actually, the bank has a major share, but my name is on the deed. And I could buy a new three-bedroom house in Adelaide for less. It's rented out to a colleague while I'm away, which looks like it's going to be much longer than I anticipated.'

He pushed his empty plate aside.

'New topic: favourite ways to relax.'

Matt didn't mention Saturday night arrangements during their meal or on the way back, and kept the taxi waiting while he came in to pick up the folder he needed for his meeting with the solicitor.

He turned to go, made a move towards her and the air stilled between them. The flash in his eyes triggered a surge in her pulse. She waited, holding her breath. His eyes narrowed, his lips parted then his Adam's apple bounced as he struggled for words. The sound he made was guttural, masculine. She felt its effect skittle down her spine.

'Don't go until I get back, okay?'

She could only nod as his finger brushed her lips and he walked out through the door.

Joanne hadn't been kidding about the backlog but by normal finishing time Lauren had made good progress. She tidied up, then went to the nearby shop and bought a magazine and a packet of chocolate biscuits.

She was curled in a chair by his window, filling in a cross-word when he appeared and dropped the folder on his desk.

'Stay right there. Another drink?' He indicated the mug by her side.

'No, thank you.' She closed the book and watched him. She'd expected dejection with the prospect of prosecution for Dalton Corporation, his father or both hanging over him. Couldn't see it in his face or movement.

He sat and stretched out his long legs, taking a deep swallow before putting his mug down.

'That tastes good. Thanks for waiting for me.'

His attitude puzzled her. Blasé as opposed to taut as a wound spring as he'd been most of the time she'd been here. As if he read her mind, he arched his back, linked his hands behind his head and smiled.

Where had the dour, weary-eyed man from ten days ago gone? Only the dark shadows under his eyes and the deep lines around his mouth and eyes proved the strain he'd endured.

'Not the same guy you first met, huh? Your finding that screen has taken away the uncertainty, the unknown factor hanging over every decision I made. Now I have true facts and figures to deal with. We'll be audited and investigated but if we're honest we'll survive.'

'So your meetings went well.'

'I've told the truth, and produced all the records and Dad's medical assessment. Now I can concentrate on the new project while the experts work it all out. My priorities are to keep the company going, even if I change its direction, and to protect my mother from any fallout from Dad's actions.'

He drained his coffee, and stood, pulling her to her feet. Close but not quite into his arms.

'You've already exceeded expectations and completed

your original assignment. Now I'm asking you to stay here a little longer in case I need you. Please, Lauren?'

How could she refuse when his fingers clasped hers, his voice dropped low with emotion and the pleading in his eyes wrenched at her heart.

The urge to step closer, reach out and trace his strong jaw line, to feel the slight rasp of his almost undetectable stubble, consumed her. Her pulse fluttered, her legs trembled, and swallowing had no effect on her dry throat.

'As long as you think I can be useful.'

'Thank you.'

A buzzer sounded from the reception area, newly installed for visitors. 'Anyone here?'

'That's for me.' He led her to the door and called out, 'Be right with you,' before giving her a quirky smile.

'No peace, as they say. You go home and I'll see you in the morning.'

He didn't. He called as she walked to work telling her he probably wouldn't be in the office at all. How could such a short sentence turn her day cloudy?

'I wanted to talk to you about tomorrow night. Pre-dinner drinks start at six-thirty so I'll pick you up at your hotel around then. It's only a short drive.'

That meant thirty-four hours until she saw him again. She hid her disappointment with a cheerful voice.

'I'll be ready. Call me when you're nearly there and I'll come down to the lobby.'

'I'm looking forward to it.'

In a crazy way with mixed feelings, so was she.

'I'll see you then, Mr Dalton.'

'The name's Matt, remember?'

Matt. Imprinted on her brain, hero of her dreams. Of course, she'd never forget.

CHAPTER EIGHT

MATT WASN'T A teenager on his first date so why did his heart race, his chest feel tight? Why were his palms sweating? Escorting a colleague to a corporate dinner hardly qualified as a date anyway.

Quit fooling yourself, Matt Dalton. She's not a colleague. She's a beautiful woman you are attracted to. And it bugs you that she's so wary of men like you.

He'd called her as the taxi was pulling into the hotel driveway, wanting to be there when she walked out of the lift. The look on her face as she'd agreed to stay on Thursday was imprinted in his brain.

It had been a mixture of fear and hopeful expectancy. If it wasn't complete delight when he brought her home tonight, he'd deem himself a failure. His aims were to see her smile, hear her laugh. And to develop his bond with the Fords.

Cold and objective maybe, but he'd learned that love and happy-ever-afters were more advertising hype than reality. Tonight he'd forget business, relax and enjoy himself. Lauren would go home with happy memories rather than those of nights spent alone in a hotel room.

The lift came down twice while he paced the foyer. She'd said five minutes, four had passed so...

His jaw dropped, his heart pounded. He looked into big anxious hazel eyes and the resolution to keep the relationship casual and platonic shot into Netherland.

She was exquisite, captivating. Every red-blooded man's dream. From her gleaming newly styled, honey-brown hair framing her lovely face, to her red-painted toes peeping out of strappy gold shoes. Her sunshine-yellow dress, which fell loosely to her ankles from under her enticing breasts, shimmered as she walked towards him. A double gold chain around her neck enhanced her smooth peach skin. And she had to be wearing higher heels because she barely had to tilt her head to meet his gobsmacked gaze.

He took both hands in his and held them out, felt *her* speeding pulse under his thumb, and had to clear his choked throat before he could speak.

'Stunning. Lauren Taylor, you are enchanting.'

Her eyes misted. Her glossed lips—oh, he so wanted to kiss them right now—parted.

'I am?' She was genuinely surprised by his compliment. Didn't her room have mirrors?

The lift beside them pinged and opened. As soon as the occupants left, he ushered her in, facing her towards the mirrored wall, and standing behind her.

'Look at yourself, Lauren. You are gorgeous. I'll be the envy of every male in the room.'

His first aim was achieved as she smiled at their reflections. A soft glow appeared in her eyes and grew until they sparkled, and all apprehension disappeared. His arms ached to wrap around her, and if they didn't leave this instant he most definitely would claim a kiss.

After they'd buckled in their driver handed him the corsage he'd left on the front seat.

'I chose this one without knowing what colours you'd be wearing. It seemed…well, you.'

'It's beautiful, perfect.'

He echoed her words in his head, not referring to the flower.

When she reached out to touch the delicately shaded orchid with its deep purple centre, he caught her hand and slipped it onto her wrist. Resisting the whim to press his lips to her pulse, he compensated by linking their fingers and keeping hold. He gave her the same advice he'd given himself.

'Relax and enjoy the evening. It's one of the biggest events of the year, all profits benefitting children's charities.'

He felt her fingers twitch against his, saw the colour in her cheeks fade. But her eyes were clear and steady when they met his.

'Big crowds are less daunting than smaller ones. They're easier to hide in.'

A puzzling remark that intrigued him. Why wouldn't she want to be seen?

'No hiding tonight. Not that you could looking the way you do. Duncan arranged our tickets, and the other two couples at our table are friends of theirs so you'll be in good company. I'll stay as close as I can and make sure you're never alone.

Which was going to be a pleasant task, not difficult at all.

Matt being close might well be her biggest problem, Lauren thought, floating on air from his compliments. He wore formal wear with an innate ease. Had he been so elegant when he'd kissed her years ago? She could only remember those devastating startled blue eyes.

As the taxi joined the line-up waiting to discharge their passengers, she craned her neck to watch them heading for the entrance. These were the elite, the rich and influential, and the corporate climbers—a mingling horde of people eager to see and be seen by their peers. Unlike her, they'd be at ease with each other or skilled at hiding any nerves.

'Lauren?' She turned her head to find Matt regarding her with a pained expression.

'I'll need that hand to eat dinner.'

With a gasp she realised how tightly she was gripping his fingers, and let go.

'I'm so sorry. Does it hurt?' Mortification stung her cheeks.

He gave a low chuckle and wriggled his fingers. 'My friends will say any damage can only improve my guitar playing.'

The car inched forward, stopped and a uniformed man opened Matt's door. She sidled across as he alighted and offered her the hand she'd squeezed. She felt his strength as she allowed him to help her, felt hot tingles race along her veins as he drew her closer for protection in the throng.

The foyer was a kaleidoscope of colours, bold and lurid, pastel and muted, interspersed with the stark black of tuxedos. The overhead lights glistened off the dazzling displays of precious gems adorning necks, wrists, and fingers, hanging from ears and even woven into elaborate hairdos.

Being part of the excitement was worth the initial sick feeling in her stomach, the harsh dryness of her throat. Matt pressed her to his side in his efforts to manoeuvre them to the designated meeting point with the Fords, and the adrenaline rush was intoxicating.

Even he seemed surprised by the number of people who greeted him and held them up. So many inquired if his parents were attending. Others asked when he'd arrived in Adelaide, how long he was staying, and when they could catch up.

They declined drinks until they'd joined their hosts, Matt selecting a white wine and Lauren a soft drink. Duncan introduced them to a middle-aged couple then, when the men began to discuss today's games, Clair drew the two women aside and grinned at Lauren.

'And at these occasions they talk sport.' She turned to the other woman. 'Lauren's a computer expert and I'm—'

'A danger to any active program,' the woman cut in playfully.

They laughed and Lauren noticed Matt's short nod of approval in her direction. She'd also felt the reluctance with which he'd released her hand. Or was she reading too much into his protective mode?

The doors to the dining area opened and they were asked to locate their seats. As she began to follow Clair, Matt appeared beside her, drawing her close.

'This is incredible,' she whispered, admiring the ornate decorations on the uncountable number of tables.

The dimmed lights gave everything a magical feel, coloured spotlights played across the room, randomly picking out guests for a second or two then moving on. Classical music was supplied by a string quartet on stage, and along the backdrop hung brightly coloured banners bearing the names of sponsors and the charities that would benefit.

Matt guided her to her seat at a table near the front and sat alongside. Duncan and Clair were on her left. She swung her head, determined to memorise every detail, and shared a menu with Matt as bread rolls and wine were being served.

'Main course is served alternately, chicken or steak. If you'd prefer what I'm given, we can swap. The other courses are set.'

'Thank you. I'm not keen on steak unless it's well done.'

'Good evening everyone.' A deep voice boomed through the sound system urging latecomers to take their seats so the caterers could begin serving entrees. The welcoming thank-you speech was short and amusing, and the quiet music during the meal allowed over-the-table conversation.

Matt and Duncan made sure Lauren was included and she felt at ease enough to join in. Not often and not unless she was sure of the subject but it felt good. Except when Duncan asked if she had siblings. Giving a quick glance to check Matt wasn't listening, she admitted to three brothers, found herself telling him they were all professionals, two footballers and one cricketer. He seemed impressed, wanted more detail. To her their jobs were no different from hers, his, or any other person's.

As the waiters cleared the dinner plates, people began to move around the room, stopping in small groups to talk or wander out into the foyer. Band gear was set up on the stage and the group began to play a slow ballad.

There was a trickle of couples at first then more and more until the floor was crowded. No room for any more, she thought with relief.

'Dance with me, Lauren.' Matt's eyes gleamed, his breath tickled her ear, and his hand on her bare shoulder evoked a quivering in her stomach that had nothing to do with nerves.

'You promised no pressure.'

'True. If you refuse I won't push. But I'll be disappointed, and regret not having even one dance with you.'

Oh, so smooth. No wonder he'd won the Fords over and, according to Joanne, been very successful in England. She'd regret it too; the difference was she'd always remember.

She stood, and accepted the hand he offered. 'Do you always win?'

'The important battles, yes.' The victorious sparkle in midnight-blue eyes proved he believed this counted with those.

He led her onto the dance floor, and slipped his arm around her waist, enclosing her hand in his over his heart. Her legs trembled and her head clamoured for her to cut and run. Her heart leant into him, taking her body along.

Matt had planned his move. The packed floor gave him the excuse to hold her nearer, move slower. Her body aligned with his perfectly, she followed his steps with ease, and her perfume—or her—stirred feelings he'd been denying all week.

Somehow in the last two days the anger he'd carried for

weeks had begun to dissipate. Tonight the pain of betrayal had been replaced by an unfamiliar emotion. It took him a few minutes to recognise the alien feeling as contentment, and a little longer to realise that his thumb was caressing her fingers.

The music stopped, and as other couples split to applaud the band they stayed together, his eyes on her face as she looked towards the stage. She was happier and more relaxed than he'd ever seen her. Suddenly however long she'd be here was too short.

'Lauren.'

Bright hazel eyes met his, her lips parted, and only the first few notes of a classic seventies heartbreaker stopped him from kissing her there and then. The couple behind nudged her and he automatically pressed her closer for protection. Her head nestled on his shoulder, his cheek brushed her hair. And he wanted the music to last for ever.

It didn't of course. The singer announced desserts and coffee were being served, and the band was taking a break. He escorted her back to the table, pleased she seemed as reluctant as he was.

'Duncan's gone walkabout,' Clair said, moving along next to Lauren, beckoning her female companion to join them. 'Are you planning to network too, Matt?'

He ought to, it was the sensible thing to do, the best action for the company. Their desserts arrived, and he grinned and took his seat.

'And miss double chocolate gateau with strawberries and cream. Maybe after.'

'Have Duncan's too, if you like. I'm watching his weight,' Clair offered.

'You want double delight, Lauren?' he teased and was rewarded with a rosy blush.

'I'm not sure I can handle what's in front of me,' she countered without breaking eye contact and his heart leapt into his mouth. Heat flared in the pit of his stomach, and his fingers itched to reach for her and…

'Coffee for anyone?' A waiter held up cups and saucers on the other side of the table.

Yeah, black and strong for me to drown in. And is that a tiny smirk on her face?

If they were alone he'd be kissing it off in an instant.

'I'll take one, thanks.' Duncan loomed up behind Matt and sat down. 'After that, and the dessert I'm going to be scalded for eating all weekend, I want you to meet a trusted friend of mine, Matt. If we decide to proceed with the bigger project an extra investor might be welcome.'

Matt glanced at Lauren.

'You go. I'll be fine.'

She was. Too much so. Catching up with business acquaintances and meeting new contacts should have been a pleasure but his mind was on Lauren, and how long he'd been away. He'd left her talking to Clair and her friend. When he returned she was in deep conversation with a blond-headed man who, in his opinion, was leaning too close.

His gut hardened, his jaw clenched and he strode over to where the two of them sat alone.

'Sorry I've been so long, Lauren.' Not much regret in his tone.

They turned, and the man rose to his feet, extending his hand.

'Matt Dalton, isn't it? I'm sure I played high-school footy against you a few times. I'm John Collins, a friend of Lauren's brother. Haven't seen her for five or six years so this was a pleasant surprise.'

Matt's irritation abated and he accepted the greeting.

'Your face is familiar though I can't remember the name. Too many over the years.'

'Yeah, I know.' John glanced at his watch. 'I'd better go

find my wife and say our goodbyes. My mother-in-law's babysitting. Great catching up with you both.'

'Where is everyone?' Matt asked as soon as he'd gone, shaking off his discomfort. An old friend of the brother's. Married and bending close, as *he* was now, because of the constant hum of voices combined with the now louder and upbeat music.

'Out there having fun.' Lauren laughed and pointed at the dance floor.

It was hard to tell who was partnering who as arms were waving, bodies writhing and legs kicking, stomping and twisting. Clair was easily spotted in her bright red dress, grinning and waving as she recognised friends. Duncan, now coatless, followed no rhythm but his enjoyment was clear.

'Let's join them.'

She demurred.

'Look at them, Lauren. No rules. No cares.' He seized her wrists, lifting her to her feet. 'Come on.'

She'd shrunk. He looked down at her stockinged feet. Felt the grin spread across his face.

She grinned back. 'My new shoes started to pinch. Besides, I can hardly dance like that in those heels.'

'Not without spiking someone, probably me. Hang on while I ditch my coat.'

This was the best and the worst idea he'd had all night. The way Lauren's body synchronised with the rhythm created havoc in his. Her dress outlined shimmering hips as she swayed. Her lustrous hair brushed her shoulders as she swung her head and her skin glowed under the spotlights. Even watching her delicate energetic feet with their red tips gave him a warm glow.

Completely in the moment she'd let go of whatever cares she had, given herself to the magic of the music, and was in a world of her own. A world he wanted to be part of for as long as possible. He tasted bile in his mouth at the thought of her leaving, swallowed it down. Emotion-inspired happy-ever-afters were a myth.

'Last dance, ladies and gentlemen. Slow or fast?'

Couples were already coming together, calling out 'slow' and drowning the requests for fast. A few left the floor. Lauren's eyes shone as he stepped closer. She didn't resist at his pressing her head to his shoulder. She was smaller without her heels, making him feel more macho, more protective. He caressed her back, drawing her tightly against him, and swore he heard a contented sigh.

Lauren sighed again as the taxi eased into traffic. This was an enchanted evening. A night to cherish always, for so many reasons. The man responsible for those unforgettable memories shifted across the seat, put his arm around her, and nestled her into his side.

'Glad you came, Lauren?'

His voice was low, gruff, his breath tickled her ear. She turned, put her hand on his chest, and wished she could snuggle into him and fall asleep. Any dreams she had tonight would surely be pleasurable.

'Mmm, it was wonderful. I didn't want it to end.'

'It hasn't yet.'

Her fingers curled, her heart chilled and she stopped breathing. He didn't think, wouldn't expect… No. That wasn't the man she…could she possibly learn the true man within less than two weeks, four days of which were spent apart?

'We have the drive home and I'll ask the cab to wait while I escort you to your room.'

'There's no need.' Her words came out in a rush of air.

'My pleasure. Would you like to hear the compliments Duncan paid you?'

'He and Clair are nice, so easy to talk to though she

made a few enigmatic remarks during the evening, and asked twice how long I'd be here. Said she'd like to meet for lunch before I go. Oh.'

She gasped as he suddenly squeezed her as if annoyed at her remark.

'Don't think about leaving yet. Don't think about anything but tonight. Did I mention you were the most beautiful woman in the room?'

She smiled up at him. He was smooth and charming, handsome as hell and his midnight-blue eyes glowed with an intensity she'd never seen. Ever. From anyone.

'Once or a dozen times. Thank you for everything.'

He tapped the folder under her clutch bag on the seat. 'And you have the photos.'

'They're mine?'

'All yours.'

So he didn't want any reminders. She'd behaved as he'd asked, been a helpful social partner, and he was simply grateful. But in the end she was just the skilled technician hired to fix his system. A chill settled over her. The gloss faded. The evening was tainted.

A few moments ago she'd been elated, not wanting the evening to end. With two simple words, he'd burst her blissful bubble. She felt tired, numb… She wished she were alone, yet contrarily didn't want to leave the warm haven of his arms.

CHAPTER NINE

HE PUT DISTANCE between them in the lift as if sensing her withdrawal. She kept her eyes downcast, and hung onto the photos like a lifeline. They and the exotic orchid on her wrist were mementoes she'd treasure for ever.

She should be grateful. She would be, when common sense rid her of the dull ache. Not now. Maybe once they'd shared polite platitudes, and she was alone.

Her key card. She'd better have it out ready and limit any awkward time. The doors opened and he guided her towards her room, turned her to face him, gripping her elbows, his features composed, his eyes dark as ebony.

They held her captive, mesmerised her. Seconds. Minutes. She was drifting, vaguely aware of him freeing her arms.

'Sleep peacefully, Lauren.' Rough as if forced over jagged stones.

Then, like déjà vu, his lips were on hers, moving smoothly yet more masterful, more mature. Like ten years ago their only physical contact. And like ten years ago she instinctively responded, wanting his kiss to last for ever.

Breaking away, eyes now narrowed and puzzled, he stepped back, and gave a slow short shake of his head.

'Goodnight, Lauren.' He sounded bewildered before walking away.

Had he remembered? Realised who she was? Her hand shook as she blindly tried to swipe her card without taking her eyes off his rigid departing back. She froze as he turned, strode back and yanked her into his arms, taking her mouth with a fierce male grunt. Causing her to drop everything and cling to him.

This wasn't the exploratory tenderness of the teenage boy, or the polite goodnight of a moment ago. This was raw, masculine need, a hunger that swept her up and demolished any inhibitions. He caressed her back in wide strokes, urging her closer, searing her skin wherever they touched.

A yearning to arch into his warmth overwhelmed her. She couldn't breathe, didn't care. Her legs shook, her body quivered, fire flared in her core. And her lips parted willingly as he deepened the kiss.

She tasted wine and rich coffee, a hint of chocolate and—

His head flung back, his chest heaved. His stunned eyes raked her face, and his lips parted without sound. He backed away, arms wide. He hit the wall opposite and swallowed, dark eyes roaming her face as if he'd never seen it before.

With his gaze locked with hers, he came slowly forward and lightly traced shaking fingers down her cheek, settling under her chin.

'Wow.' Incredulous. Deep and husky. He seemed to struggle for breath. 'I... I'll see you Monday.'

By the time she'd blinked he'd gone, heading for the stairs.

Lauren fought for composure, unable to move. What had she done to provoke such a reaction? Where had *her* response come from?

The lift's ping brought her back to the present. She scooped up her belongings and a moment later was secure behind her closed door. Dumping the stuff on the desk, she flung herself onto the bed, reliving every second since they'd exited the lift.

She studied the photo of the two of them, searching for something to explain his behaviour and sudden flight. There was no clue in his open expression or his smile. Nothing to indicate he had anything but enjoying the function on his mind.

So it had to be her. What deficiency did she have in her personality that discouraged more familiar contact? Did she give out negative vibes? She had close friends, some from back at school and uni in Melbourne.

Their common interests had been the original base but their friendships now went much deeper. She knew she could always depend on their support in any situation. It was her family who seemed to find excuses not to be with her. Or was it she who put up barriers, subliminally deterring closer intimacy for fear of being rejected?

She set the photo against the lamp on the bedside table, placed her corsage in front of it, and prepared for bed. They were clearly visible in the light from the street lamps. She fell asleep with her fingers on her lips.

Matt fisted one hand into the palm of the other as the taxi drove him home. He could smell her perfume on his shoulder, see her shocked expression when he'd pulled away and left. He still savoured the taste of her on his lips.

He'd meant that first kiss to be gentle, an affectionate ending to a memorable night. Her initial response hadn't surprised him. Its effect on him had been astonishing. His libido had gone into overdrive and that damn niggle had drummed in his head. Breaking free had been instinctive.

But he hadn't been able to walk away. The invitation he'd seen in her hazel eyes had driven him back and he'd let his pent-up desire run free. He'd moulded her body to his, caressing her back, and exploring the curves he'd delighted in all evening. He'd invaded her mouth, savouring her sweetness, craving more.

Her soft moan had slammed him back to reality. To the shame of his actions. He'd never lost control before. Getting the hell out of there had seemed the only option; now it branded him a coward.

Going back to apologise while he still ached for more intimate contact would exacerbate the pain he'd caused.

Phoning would be even more cowardly. He hadn't felt so much like a louse since…

Since the night he kissed a girl hiding in the dark on a balcony. The niggling cleared like a light-bulb moment in his head. An irresistible allure. A barely heard sigh. Soft lips under his.

The kiss he'd never forgotten, had relived so often in his dreams, and that had been so entrenched in his memory that his body had known her the instant their lips had met tonight. He'd never had a face to picture, only a curled mass of dark hair, and a recollection of a slender body in a blue dress. And throughout the ten years since, no lips had ever felt as soft or tasted as sweet.

He'd searched the ballroom for her, and spent the rest of the evening repeatedly scanning the crowd without success. Deep inside he'd never given up hope of finding her.

Now he understood the guarded look and apprehension the day he'd interviewed her. She'd recognised him, must have remembered their meeting as well.

Tomorrow he'd begin to make amends for tonight's ending. Monday morning was going to be very interesting.

Matt's jacket hanging on the back of his chair was the only indication he was in the building. Lauren wasn't sure if she was upset or relieved.

Tucked into her purse was the florist's card that had accompanied the arrangement of orchids delivered to her hotel room yesterday morning. Another memento, personally inscribed, *Forgive me, Matt.*

For the kiss or for running?

She'd imagined a number of scenarios for when they met again, none of which eased her apprehension. She couldn't shake the re-emerged doubts. Their lives, their interests, their personalities, all were polarised. If it weren't for the undeniable attraction, they'd have nothing in common. She sighed and gazed out of her window lost in a daydream of music, lights and feeling cherished as they'd danced.

'Why were you hiding?'

She jumped, spun round to find him standing halfway across the room. Her heart stuttered. She covered it with her hand, and fought to steady her erratic breathing. How come he looked so cool and calm? So unruffled?

'I wasn't.' She cursed her wobbly voice. 'I'm just doing my normal preparation.'

Three rapid paces brought him an arm's length from her side, leaning on the glass nonchalantly. The firm set of his jaw belied his calm demeanour, giving her composure a tiny boost. He gestured in the general direction of the river.

'On the balcony, a good cricketer's throw away from where we had lunch with the Fords.'

He knew—had to see the blush heating her neck and face, the embarrassment in her eyes. Her teeth as they bit on her lip, something she hadn't done since she was a child.

As she struggled for breath and an answer, his lips—lips that had filled her waking hours since he'd strode away—curled into an apologetic smile.

'I have no idea why I followed you. I saw a mass of dark curls and a hint of blue dress going through the door alone and wondered why. Couldn't find you at first.'

He inched a little closer.

'You running away shook me. I swear I looked for you to apologise, and I've always regretted frightening you but never the kiss, never the sweet taste of your lips.'

'I hated being there,' she blurted out without thinking. 'Hated the way I was forced to be part of a world I had no interest in. Places like the balcony were sanctuaries. I didn't belong inside with those people.'

Fleetingly stunned by her outburst, he recovered to run his fingers in a light path down her cheek and under her jaw, sending fissions of delight skimming across her skin.

If he let go, her legs would give way and she'd end up a trembling mess on the floor.

'And I invaded your peace. Did you know who I was before the interview or recognise me then?'

She felt her skin heat again and dropped her gaze, only to have him tilt her head until she looked him in the eyes. His eyebrows quirked.

'Lauren?'

'There were lights behind you that night. I didn't see your face but as I pushed away your eyes became visible. They're very distinctive.'

His low chuckle zinged through her. Laughter shone in his eyes and they crinkled at the corners.

'My eyes, huh. We'll have to talk more but not *here*.'

He grated the last word and then his tone softened.

'The next few days are going to be gruelling. I'll be juggling appointments regarding Dad's actions with meetings, on and off site, about new projects. They'll all take time away from where I want to be.'

His affectionate expression said he meant her. The gap between them diminished. His movement or hers?

'Come to dinner with me tomorrow night.'

There was an edge to his voice that she didn't understand. Her first inclination was to refuse but then she'd always wonder.

He claimed he'd tried to find her. If she agreed—and her heart and logic warred about the sensibility of that— she'd have personal time to learn more about him, be able to return to Sydney with no what-ifs. His persuasive voice, his hypnotic gaze, and his touch on her skin were an irresistible combination.

She meant to nod, swayed forward instead. As if in answer to her silent plea, he bent his head. Suddenly jerked away.

'Not here.'

Growled in anger. Why?

His fingertips tracked lightly across her neck, triggering a goose-bumps rush from cell to cell, from her scalp to the soles of her feet. Awareness flared in his eyes, his chest heaved, and suddenly there was a wide space between them.

'I have to make a couple of calls, and talk to Joanne before I leave.'

'What am I supposed to do after I've finished the data entries?'

He spread his arms, fingers splayed.

'Whatever Joanna needs help with. I know it may be below your expertise but…'

He struggled for words. 'I don't want a stranger coming in when we transfer those accounts into the mainstream. I want you.'

The inflection in the last three words was personal, nothing to do with accounts or computers. Leaving wasn't an option.

'I'll stay.' Data entry. Filing. Basic office work. Tasks that would allow her mind to wander to midnight-blue eyes and smiles that lit up her day.

'You're an angel. I'll be here for half an hour then out for the morning. My mobile will be off most of the time so leave a message if you want me.'

His hand lifted towards her. Dropped. He walked out, picking up his jacket on the way.

If she wanted him?

Her body hummed with a need more disturbing than anything she'd ever felt. So much stronger than the mild desire she'd felt during her two previous relationships. She now recognised them as more mind melding and merely physical rather than zealous ardour.

There'd be no 'let's be friends' when the passion died for Matt. He'd walk away and she…she'd survive. Somehow.

* * *

Matt strode to the boardroom, praying it would be empty. He was pleased he'd been able to persuade Lauren to stay. Having her at his home for dinner was risky, considering the way they both responded to the proximity of the other. But how else were they going to talk without interruptions? How else could he find out why she hadn't trusted him before she knew him?

He'd almost kissed her again this morning. Never, ever going to happen here. He would never follow in his father's footsteps. Would never use that bedroom, no matter how late he worked or how tired he became.

Footsteps sounded in the corridor. He refocused on the project he and the team were working on, the one he was determined would revitalise the company.

Everything hung on a precipice. His father could be facing fraud charges. He and, in his doing, Dalton Corporation had probably committed tax evasion. Duncan Ford might decide to suspend their talks of investing until Matt could prove he and the company were clean.

He should be broken, anxious of the future. Instead, now he knew the truth he found the challenges stimulating. If it all collapsed around him, he'd start again. Staying down wasn't an option.

Lauren collected information needed from Joanne's office and settled at her desk. She tingled from his touch, her stomach had barely settled, and her brain was in the clouds.

Logging in took two attempts at the password. When she went to write the date on her notepad, she'd left her pen in the drawer. Unless she pulled herself together, today would be a shambles.

Get it together, Lauren.

A fingertip tap on each of her work tools, a muscle-loosening back-stretch, followed by her slow-count-to-fifteen habit, and she moved the cursor.

Engaged in more simplistic tasks, she found her mind had a tendency to wander, always to Matt and his effect on her. After an hour, she took a break, ran up and down eight flights of stairs and refocused. Apart from taking messages from occasional phone calls, she was undisturbed.

At midday she joined Joanne and three of the male staff for lunch for the first time, making an effort to contribute to the weekend football match discussion. She didn't comment when one of the men raved about her youngest brother, who'd kicked four goals including one as the siren sounded.

'Mr Dalton seems happy with the progress we've made on this new venture, Joanne. It's completely different from anything we did for his father, quite stimulating. Do you think the changes will be permanent?'

Lauren lowered the mug she'd been raising to her lips. She noticed Joanne's hesitation at the man's question. How much did she know of the true situation?

'I know he's doing all he can to sort everything out and he'll be tied up with meetings most of the week, nothing else.' She rose and went to stack her utensils into the dishwasher. 'Break's over. Do you have enough to do, Lauren?'

'Yes, I'll find you if I need more.'

Every employee she'd met addressed him as Mr Dalton. Although he used their first names, he kept distance between himself and his staff except for her. Because he intended to return to London?

Was there someone special there? Someone prepared to wait for him? Someone he'd taken to Paris?

A no-strings arrangement by two mature people. How did they do that? She couldn't imagine becoming involved with anyone who also dated other women.

Reinforcing that in her head didn't stop her stomach from fluttering at his call sign on her mobile.

'How's it going, Lauren?'

'Fine. Joanne says she can keep me occupied today and part tomorrow, after that I may be on cleaning duty.'

He laughed as she'd hoped he would, deep and raspy, making her ear tingle.

'Anything to keep you here. I won't get to the office until late today, or tomorrow morning. I'll call you when I can.'

'Is it bad?'

'I'm dealing with reticent legal and financial professionals. They hardly commit to black or white coffee but at least it's not all doom and gloom. Hang on.'

She heard his name and him replying, 'Thank you.'

'I'm being summoned back to the world of ifs, maybes, and it all depends. I'll see you tomorrow, Lauren.'

'Tomorrow.'

She sat as still as stone, staring at her mobile. He'd called her Lauren twice; she hadn't said his name at all. He used hers every time he spoke to her. At the function she'd made a deliberate attempt to say 'Matt' in the presence of others. In front of work colleagues it was 'Mr Dalton', to conform with them. Alone with him she omitted to call him anything.

He was smart, quick to notice nuances and actions. He'd have to know she deliberately avoided the intimacy of first names.

CHAPTER TEN

MATT DIDN'T WANT to be sitting in his parents' dining room that night pretending nothing had changed. His head ached from all the legal jargon, the implications of what might or might not happen, and from reading some of the complex forms and documents he'd been given. And the processes had only just started.

It had taken supreme effort to keep focused and not picture Lauren alone in her office or Joanne's. Or ponder on dinner tomorrow. No disruptions, no phone calls with both mobiles on silent. Quiet time for conversation.

It's more than talk you want.

'Matthew?'

'Sorry, Mum. Miles away. It's been a long day.'

'This is all taking a toll on you. I wish I'd acted sooner, but Marcus kept assuring me he was just tired and overworking.'

'It's okay, Mum. I've got good help and everything's coming together.'

Though there's a fair chance it might implode in my face.

'His mood swings are more frequent, and persuasion doesn't work as well as it did. Today he became angry when I suggested he shouldn't go for a walk alone.'

His jaw tightened, and he glared at his father, nonchalantly eating his meal. He softened his features as he asked, 'When's his next appointment with the doctor? I'll make sure I'm available and then we'll have a family meeting.'

'I want to keep him at home as long as possible. Please, Matthew.'

He reached across to cover her hand with his.

'For as long as possible, Mum. We can arrange for day help and, if necessary, I'll move in.'

His gut churned at the thought of living here again, in

the house where his naive adulation of his father had been shattered, and his admiration for his mother diminished in a single stroke. Where he'd discovered human weakness could overrule honour, and betrayal could be overlooked if it meant the continuation of a preferred lifestyle.

His honour dictated he had no choice. His heart demanded he call into his sister's on the way home to spend time with a truly happy couple. And to kiss his nephews as they slept.

Crouched behind the desk in Reception, Lauren almost missed Matt's arrival at five past two the following day. Checking the stationery, she sprang upright at the faint hint of sea-spray aroma.

'Matt.' Instinctive. Spontaneous.

As natural as the smile he gave her. He looked frazzled and energised at the same time, jacket slung over his shoulder and sleeves rolled up to reveal muscular arms covered with fine dark hair. One glance at finger-ruffled hair and blue crinkled eyes, and her senses sprang to attention.

'Hi, how's it going? Come and tell me over coffee. With normal everyday words.'

'Joanne's run out of work to give me.' She straightened the desk phone as she glanced up, and met narrowed eyes and a scowl.

By the time she come round to his side, they'd gone. He patted his satchel as they walked to his office. 'And I'll be occupied for days. How's your legalese?'

'My what?'

'Legal mumbo jumbo. Guaranteed to cause headaches or a craving for alcohol.'

She laughed. 'Sorry, all I know is the few foreign phrases I learnt from friends at uni. Unless it's cyber-speak.'

'Might just as well be for me. So what time are you finishing?'

'Ten minutes and I'm all done.' She swallowed, glad he wasn't looking at her. Thankful he couldn't see her disappointment.

His brow creased again as he held the door open for her, not moving aside, ensuring she brushed against him as she passed. He dumped his satchel on his chair, draped his coat over the back, and scraped his fingers into his hair. When he spoke she swore there was a catch in his voice, growing more pronounced towards the end.

'You're not going home?'

She shook her head. 'I promised I'd stay.'

'You're one of the few people aware of the full situation and I trust you. We'll find something for you to do.'

He trusted her. Her heart soared and dipped, raced for a moment then blipped. She couldn't deny she had continuing issues with where he'd come from, the class he associated with.

'You don't have to. I decided last week to spend my promised fortnight vacation being a tourist in South Australia.'

His face cleared and he caught her hands in his, skittled her breathing with his beaming smile.

'Two weeks, huh? That's good. Can you fit any work I need done between trips?'

'If I'm needed.'

'You are—very much.' His intense appraisal was unnerving, as if commanding she hide nothing from him. His undisguised admiration made her insides glow, yet roused a prickling unease on her nape.

'Is there a special dress code for tonight?'

'Neat casual. Whatever you feel comfortable in.'

Your arms.

Thankfully thought and for once not voiced. She cursed her seesawing responses.

'I'll call when I leave here and pick you up.'

'I'll be ready.'

* * *

She was sitting on a bench near the revolving doors two minutes after he phoned. It gave her a clear view of the curved driveway and the road beyond the garden bed. Her fingers tapped on her right thigh and she clasped them with her left hand.

It was just another dinner in a public place, nothing to make her nervous. Unless you counted the confident, charismatic male striding, head high, on the opposite side of the road. At twenty-six, she really ought to be able to control these sudden spikes in her pulse and these inexcusable urges to run to meet him.

She went to the kerb, keeping track of him between passing vehicles. He stopped when he noticed her, his smile easily visible at this distance, and beckoned her to come across. Took her arm as she reached his side.

'Hi, has anyone ever told you that you are remarkably punctual?'

'For a woman?' She tilted her head, and raised her eyebrows. Relished the pleasurable quiver in her stomach as he laughed.

'For a human. The car's not far.'

He didn't speak during the short walk, obviously preoccupied. Lauren was all too aware of his guiding touch on her arm. Warm and protective.

The lights flashed to unlock his car but he didn't open the door. He leant on it instead, placing his hands on her waist. He looked at the grass under their feet and exhaled.

'When I said dinner, I meant takeaway or home delivery to the unit I'm renting. You and me. No phones, no demands from anyone. No distractions. I should have been explicit. If you'd prefer, there's a local hotel with good food and friendly atmosphere.'

His preference matched hers. No noisy chatter or waiters hovering to serve, clear dishes or top up glasses.

'Do I get to choose what we pick up?'

She hadn't realised how tense he was until his shoulders dropped.

'Food, wine and anything else you want.' He moved aside, allowing her to get into the car. 'You amaze me almost every day, Lauren Taylor.'

Lauren was the one surprised as she entered the modern single-storey town house not far from the city. He'd driven into the garage, led her through the door into a laundry and then along a hallway into one of the most sparsely furnished rooms she'd ever seen.

There was a long soft leather lounge, a coffee table and a television on a wooden cupboard. No rugs, no cushions. No books, ornaments or pictures.

She appreciated he was renting, and had been working long hours under extreme pressure, but…

Matt's eyes followed her astonished gaze, and for the first time he saw his home as it was. He'd bought the barest necessities, hadn't been planning on long term or entertaining.

He shrugged and gave a rueful grin.

'Not exactly home beautiful, but I don't spend a lot of time here.'

'Are the other rooms the same?'

Leaving the Thai food and bottle of white wine on the table, he held out his hand.

'Guided tour included with the meal. Any constructive opinions welcome.'

She didn't say a word as he pushed open doors to reveal a desk and office chair in one room, suitcases and boxes in another, the bathroom, and finally the main bedroom.

It contained bedside drawers and a rumpled king-sized bed, which dominated the space but he never slept well in anything smaller. Since moving in he'd crashed every night into deep, unbroken sleep, including a few times in the lounge. Except for the last two nights, and his restlessness was evident from the unmade bed.

His senses were on super alert, tuned for her slightest reaction. He heard the faint intake of breath, saw her shoulders twitch and the convulsive movement in her throat.

Berating himself for his insensitivity, he drew her away, and pulled the door shut behind them, praying she didn't think he had an ulterior motive bringing her here. He couldn't ignore the picture that had flashed into his head as he'd looked from his bed to Lauren, or its effect on his body.

'I signed the lease in the morning, made the saleswoman's day in the afternoon, and moved in two days later,' he said, hoping to distract her as he took her to the kitchen area.

'No dining setting?'

'Not yet. The only person who visits is Alan, and we eat while we watch TV, usually the footy.'

She winced and he remembered her outburst yesterday morning. She hadn't exaggerated her dislike of sport. Tonight he was determined to find out why.

'We'd better eat before the food goes cold. Plates are in the corner cupboard. I'll bring the glasses and cutlery.'

Clicking on the TV, he scrolled to the relaxing music channel, keeping the volume low. He sat, giving her space, and opened the Riesling, poured a glass and slid it in front of her.

'Thank you. I'm guessing you like leftovers, from the amount of food you bought.'

'It'll taste as good tomorrow.' He lifted his glass in salute. 'To you, Lauren. You have my eternal gratitude for everything you achieved.'

She tapped her glass to his. 'Even with all the angst it's going to cause you?'

'Hard facts can be dealt with. The uncertainty is what

fuels suspicion and creates tension. I'll be guided by the professionals and handle any repercussions.'

Lauren savoured the tang of the sweet and sour pork, and the mellow taste of the wine, but found the depth of the settee uncomfortable. It was built for taller people or for curling up on. A few thick cushions would solve the problem.

She put her plate on the table, slid onto the floor, and folded her legs.

'Can we pull this closer so I can lean against the sofa? I don't have your long limbs.'

He complied immediately. 'I'm not rating too well, am I? I'm all set up for myself, didn't expect to have visitors very often if at all.'

Then why that huge bed, looking as if there'd been plenty of action there last night? Did he have similar expectations tonight?

She choked on a piece of pineapple, took a soothing drink of wine, letting it glide down her throat. He'd said only Alan visited and she had no reason to dispute his word.

'Are you all right?'

No, but admitting it might start a conversation she wasn't ready for, probably never would be.

'I'm fine. This is delicious.'

'Hmm.' He relaxed, elbow on the leather arm, his legs stretched out with one ankle over the other. Looking as hassle-free as a newborn baby.

Unlike her. Sitting down here might be easier on her spine but now he was only in her peripheral vision and other senses heightened. She became aware of muted sounds as he shifted or flexed muscle against the leather, and his ocean aroma teased her nostrils, overriding the piquant sauces of their meal. Occasionally his foot twitched.

The companionable silence stretched, the music soothed. She picked up her glass and sipped, letting her mind drift to a gentle touch, a guiding hand. A bewitching dance she'd never forget.

She turned her head, and caught him watching her, his lips curled, his dark eyes gleaming with unconcealed desire. He blinked and it vanished. Or had it been a reflection of her own?

'Full?'

She could only nod, her throat too clogged to form words. He wanted to talk; she'd prefer to delay it any way possible. If he wanted her history, dared she ask for his? Wouldn't it be better to have only memories of *their* time together untainted by his past?

The dishwasher was stacked, the food containers stored in the refrigerator. Lauren curled up in the corner of the settee cradling the remnants of her drink.

'Top up?' Matt waved the bottle in front of her.

Why not? She'd make it last 'til the end of the evening.

He half-filled hers, gave himself more then took the remainder to the fridge. Settling at the far end, he twisted towards her, one ankle balanced on the other knee. His arm lay along the back of the lounge, forming a perfect angle with his body for someone to snuggle into.

She stifled the sigh that threatened as she remembered the firm warmth of him, and the way her head rested cosily on his shoulder during the slow dances. A quick self-rebuke, a sip of wine and she met his gaze with a bravado her internal fortitude didn't match.

'So you didn't inherit the sporting gene like your brothers?' A coaxing tone, probably developed with his nephews, with an edge that said he wouldn't give up until he'd learned all he wanted to know.

'I was uncoordinated, couldn't catch, throw or jump and had no interest in being coached to improve. Lately I've been wondering if I was the one who withdrew from my family rather than it being them who ignored my interests.'

'Maybe lack of compromise on both sides.'

'I believed I didn't count so I stopped attending anything sporty and made a life on my own.'

He scooted along the cushions, stopping inches from her knees. His fingers caressed her neck and tangled into her hair.

'You count, Lauren, in every way that matters.'

'I know that now, just not sure how much with them.'

She suddenly hit him, flat-handed over his heart, making him jerk away.

'Admit it, Matt Dalton, you were one of those guys like my brothers, who assumed being athletic made you better than those who weren't. And more deserving of attention from girls.'

Matt's fingers stilled, his stomach clenched. She'd nailed him. Major benefits of being in the school's A-grade had been the accolades, the admiration of lesser-gifted pupils. The chicks he could take his pick from.

Hell, that sounded egotistical.

'And I'll bet you barely noticed anyone who wasn't beautiful, confident and out there.' Her jaw lifted and one finger tapped on his chest. Her hazel eyes flashed with challenge.

'Ah, but I did.' He grinned at her defiance. 'I was nineteen, surrounded by adoring girls yet I followed a shy, unknown escapee into the dark and kissed her. She ran and I ended up going home alone because I couldn't find her again.'

'You didn't?'

She doubted his word. Understandable maybe but it irked. He prided himself on his honesty. Taking her drink, he plonked it on the table heedless of the splashing droplets. He bent forward, splaying his hand on the lounge arm, enclosing her and forcing her to lean away.

'You don't believe me? How can I persuade you it's true?'

'You can't.' Proud and playfully stated.

She had no idea how provocative she looked arched over the armrest, enticing full lips parted and bold eyes sparking.

Or did she? The tapping stopped. Pity, he'd liked it from her. She sucked in a deep breath, her head tilted and wariness drove defiance from bright hazel.

Ashamed of his brash behaviour, he shifted but kept within reach. Picking up the glasses and holding hers out, he noticed the motion of the wine. *From his trembling.* He drained the remainder of his, shaken by his reaction.

'Forgive me. I said tonight was for talking. I won't make that promise for the future though. There's something between us, Lauren, something too strong to ignore.'

'It'll pass. There'll be other women in your life.'

'You're the only one now. It's you I want.'

Her head swung from side to side in slow motion as if that would change his statement. He halted the movement by cupping her chin.

'I don't lie, Lauren. And I can wait until you're ready to admit it too. In the meantime, we could call Alan, who'll confirm my story. I shared a cab with him and his date.'

She flicked him a half-smile. 'No phones tonight, remember.'

Almost an admission she believed him. He feigned an affronted air.

'You questioned my word. I deem that an emergency.'

Her instant laughter hit a spot deep inside, denting the armour he'd placed around his heart. Scaring the hell out of him. He'd sworn never to be vulnerable again.

'So why Sydney?' Out of the blue to give him recovery time.

'I was offered a challenging position interstate from Melbourne.'

'A long way from your family.'

'I didn't disown them. I keep in touch, visit reasonably regularly, and always see them when they come to Sydney for a sporting fixture.' She spoke defensively as if she'd heard censure in his voice.

'Which you don't attend.'

'No. They seem to have accepted I'm different. I'm hoping they give this new consideration to their grandchildren.'

'My eldest nephew loves anything involving kicking or hitting a ball, the younger one can take or leave it. We're trying to keep it all fun for as long as possible.'

'There's only the two?'

'Alex and Drew.' He recalled Lena's expression when she'd told him she was pregnant, felt the same rush of affection he'd had then. 'Lena and Mark would love a little girl as well.'

'I wish them success. What did you do in London?'

CHAPTER ELEVEN

STUPIDLY BECAME INVOLVED with a scheming adulteress. Confused physical idolisation with love and almost got sucked into a nightmare.

'I'm a partner in a consultancy firm. We tailor business strategies, give advice and bring investors and companies together. Unlike my father, we don't invest in them though I do have my own portfolio. And I'm very good at what I do.'

She looked away, tightened the hold on her glass, and seemed to shrink in front of his eyes. He thought through his statement, trying to pinpoint what might have upset her.

It hit him like a hammer to his gut, almost overridden by the elation that flooded him. The present tense, still committed. Planning to return.

His heart flipped and his pulse raced. Had she already thought about making love with him and now believed she'd end up hurt if they became involved? It didn't have to be that way if they were completely open and honest. If they didn't let emotion rule their heads, they'd have no regrets when it was over.

He fought the urge to reach for her, draw her into his arms, and tell her that was how it would be. She wasn't ready for such a declaration yet.

'I haven't changed my status as a partner because of the uncertainty. The best scenario would be to get everything legal at Dalton Corporation, and any due taxes paid. I'll get the new project running then I can decide on my future.'

Her sceptical gaze met his. Somehow he had to convince her he was telling the truth, that his main objective was to make the company strong and viable. He hadn't allowed himself to think beyond that.

'Legal proceedings allowing, I'll try to use the same procedure we have in London with Dad's clients, making them independent. The project with Duncan is different, a change of direction for me, but it will stabilise Dalton Corporation.'

Her body had inched forward as if drawn by a magnet. Now the only movement was the slow rise and fall of her chest. Her eyes didn't waver from his.

'It sounds long term.' Husky with a hint of hope. Dared he wish too?

'Anyone's guess. There are too many factors involved.'

Lauren's anticipation deflated. She stared at the glass in her hand, wondering when she'd drunk the remaining wine. From the moment they'd met tonight her emotions had taken her on a loop-the-loop ride, twisting her in knots, ending with a crash landing.

The agenda he'd described would take time and effort. He'd shrugged it off as no big deal, easily done. Then Europe and his partnership would beckon and he'd go with no looking back. And while he might caress and cajole, he'd never pressure her against her will.

She just wished she could decide what she wanted most.

'Your glass is empty.'

His fingers brushed hers as he took it and she trembled. Something fiery flared in his eyes.

'Would you like a hot drink?'

'No, thank you.' She snuck a glance at her watch as he turned away, torn between wanting to stay and having space to fortify her defences against his charm.

'Hinting it's time to go home?' The laughter in his husky voice teased, and she dipped her head to hide the inevitable blush.

He shuffled closer, avoiding contact, the glasses clinking in his hand, and waited silently for her to raise her head. And the funfair ride took off again at his tender expression. Her stomach flipped, her heartbeat pounded and, she wasn't exactly sure but…had her toes curled? Without even a touch.

'Your choice, Lauren. I'll call a taxi if you want to.'

'Taxi?' Sending her home alone. Shortest funfair ride ever.

'I haven't long finished the second wine. We'll take a taxi now or have coffee and wait a little longer. I don't take chances when I drive.'

A cosy trip in the back seat or more disclosures here?

'Make mine weak white. Do you need help?'

He only had big mugs so hers wasn't full. It was rich and sweet, complementing the meal. She sipped and enjoyed, noticed he took fewer, bigger swallows.

'Sydney's an expensive city to live in too. Do you live alone or share?'

His polite words were belied by the set of his shoulders, the slight tilt of his head and the heat in his midnight-blue eyes. There'd been no necessity to say he wanted her. Every look, every touch proved he did.

Did she give out the same signals? Her curiosity about him was all consuming yet he'd managed to avoid revealing much personal information.

'Three friends and I put in a bid for one floor of an un-built apartment block. One of them is in banking and arranged the mortgages. We got a special price and an input into the layouts and décor.'

'And?'

And what? The other half of his question. He was fishing about her private life.

'I live alone. The other three have partners so it's rare there's not someone around. What about you?'

He ran his hand up her arm creating electrical zings on her skin. All over her skin. He faced her full on, his shoulder pressing into the leather back of the lounge, his arm flat along the top. His fingertips played with her hair.

'Occasionally I have guests.' His face darkened for a second as if remembering an unpleasant experience. 'Not for a while.'

Matt brushed away the past, trying to concentrate on the now. She lived alone, she was single. There was no one who'd have cause to feel offended if he kissed her again.

A companionable silence settled. He gazed into his empty mug, multiple questions racing through his mind, each one too personal to ask unless he intended to make a move tonight. Common sense said it was too soon, they knew little about each other, needed time to build trust. However, would he ever fully trust a woman again?

His libido said he knew all he needed. He wanted her and he'd bet whatever part of the London flat he owned that she wanted him too.

A movement in the corner of his vision broke his reverie in time to see Lauren try to smother a yawn behind her hand. Guess it wasn't going to be tonight.

'You're tired. What do you have planned for tomorrow?

'I'm picking up a hire car and heading to the Barossa Valley for a couple of days. No schedule, just drive and stop whenever something takes my fancy. I'll book into a local hotel each night.'

Two nights.

Plus almost three days without seeing her.

He straightened, tried to swallow past the lump in his throat, tried to ignore the tight band constricting his lungs.

'You'll be back in Adelaide on Friday?' He had to know. Didn't understand why.

'Will you need me then?'

He choked back his instinctive reply.

'I'll keep in touch. Now I'd better get you home.'

He took her hand, led her to the laundry and reached for the door knob to the garage. His brain urged caution.

Every muscle tensed with craving. Every cell in his body clamoured, 'Ask her to stay.'

Lauren wasn't his ex, she was as wary as he was. He saw his knuckles whiten and he let go, slamming his hand onto the wall beside her head.

Her eyes widened, her lips parted and her breasts lifted as she sucked in air. He drew her into his arms, his forehead resting on hers. He heard her bag hit the floor and felt one arm encircle his waist. The other hit his chest between them.

It felt good, so good. But not enough. He ached for something unattainable, something that didn't exist. He'd have to settle for whatever she was prepared to give. For being close and building up memories that wouldn't turn sour in acrimony.

She leant into him, and had to be aware of his harsh breathing, how hard his heart was thumping. How aroused he was.

He bent his head. She lifted hers to meet him. He kissed her gently, using every ounce of restraint he could muster, shuddered as her fingertips pushed up his chest to trace a fiery path over his already heated skin. Her unique aroma stirred him with every breath.

He teased her lips into opening, and tasted sweet coffee, mellow wine and Lauren. Encouraged by her muted sighs, he strengthened his hold, stroking and caressing, binding her to him. Only when his lungs screamed for air did he break the kiss, trailing his lips across her neck.

Her eyes moved under closed lids. Her trembling vibrated through him, or were his tremors affecting her? He willed her to look at him and his heart slammed into his ribcage when she did. Gold specks glittering, her hazel eyes smouldered with desire. She wanted him. Primal macho pride surged through him.

But before he allowed himself to accept what her eyes

were offering, that same pride decreed he be totally honest, even if it meant she didn't stay. He pressed her head to his shoulder, not wanting to see her expression change, fighting for a softer way to tell her.

There wasn't one. He watched his breath stir her hair as he forced out the words.

'One thing life's taught me is there's no rose-covered cottage with two dogs and a cat and a happy-ever-after waiting for you to find it. Flowers don't last and having a one true love is as rare as a priceless diamond.'

She made a strangled gasp into his shirt. He cupped her chin, raising her head until their eyes met, and felt a strong urge to take it all back just to see the pain vanish. He couldn't. He wouldn't deceive her.

'I want you, Lauren. I want to make love to you so badly it's driving me crazy. But I won't lie. I don't believe in soulmates and endless romance, I've seen too much anguish caused when others have. However, I do believe in and expect complete fidelity.'

Lauren's heart twisted. Someone *had* hurt him, broken him, making him doubt every other woman he met. She fought for composure. If she gave in to desire, she'd be the one counting the cost.

Her heart didn't care, deeming every moment spent with him worth any pain. There was no yesterday, no tomorrow, only now. There was only Matt Dalton, his skin hot under her hand, his body trembling in sync with hers and his heartbeat pounding against her breast.

She inhaled, drew in ocean spray and aroused male. Wanted, ached for more. All-consuming heat coils spiralled from her core. Her fingers itched to unbutton his shirt and caress the muscles it defined.

'Matt?' A dry whisper, pathetically weak for the powerful emotions controlling her.

Passionate blue eyes darkened, his nostrils flared, his

lips parted. Something akin to euphoria swept through her. He was no longer the aloof, self-contained executive of fourteen days ago. This was primal man. And tonight she would be his.

'Lauren. I…' Rough. Grating. Emotional.

She touched one finger to his mouth. 'No promises. No tomorrow. Only us tonight.'

With a triumphant growl, he scooped her up, claiming a conqueror's kiss as he strode towards his room. To that massive bed with its rumpled sheets and pillows sure to smell of ocean waves.

The sudden shudder from head to feet took Matt by surprise. His body resonated with the aftermath of the most intense, satisfying sex of his life. As if they'd been transported to a new dimension where only they existed. Lauren had been his, totally, utterly his from the moment he'd lain beside her, kissing and caressing her, moulding her body to his form.

Tightening his arms around her, he held on, riding out the incredible feeling, wishing he could see her beautiful face and her lovely expressive eyes. There was only the faintest light seeping round the edges of the window blinds, only enough to see shadowy outlines.

She was stroking his chest, threatening to reignite the fire that had consumed them both. His willingness to be engulfed by the flame warred with the suspicion that she didn't realise the fervent effect her gentle action evoked.

He placed his hand over hers, sought and found her lips. Keeping the kiss soft and light, he tried to let her know how he felt, elated yet humble, primal yet emotionally moved.

Her soft sigh motivated action.

'Don't go away.' He went to the ensuite, turned on the light, then left the door ajar, allowing subdued light to spill into the room. Bunching up the pillows, he slid into bed and nestled her tight against his side, her head on his shoulder. Her breath blew across his chest, tickling his skin in the nicest sensation imaginable. Her hand lay over his rapid-beating heart.

He'd never initiated after-sex talks, curtailed them as quickly as possible if his partner did. This new desire to learn all he could about Lauren was unnerving and compulsive, so not him. Confidences led to familiarity, which equated with vulnerability. And that he'd determined never to risk.

He stroked her hair for a moment, pressed a kiss on her forehead.

'Why are you so wary of guys like me? Maybe not me so much any more, but it's there. With Alan too.'

Lauren didn't answer. Her body stiffened, she stared at his chest, and her fingers curled. Idiot, he'd pushed too soon. If he could see her face...hell, he knew what he'd see. Fear. Reluctance.

He'd had no choice but to tell her about his father, had given her no reason to believe she could confide in him.

'There was a woman in London I'd known and dated for quite a while. I liked her a lot, though after I wondered if she'd shown her true self to me at all. We shared mutual interests and friends, got on well and I believed we could have a mutually advantageous marriage. It's surprising how many people settle for that. Love wasn't a factor at all.'

He had no idea why he'd confessed his humiliating experience unless it was to show her she could trust him, that she was different from other women he'd known. His calm, rational approach to the relationship with Christine was worlds away from the mind-blowing emotions Lauren aroused simply by being in the same room.

She stirred as if preparing to pull away. He held on, needing contact, and rushed the end of his embarrassing story.

'Luckily for me I discovered she was also involved with a married man before I proposed. I ended the relationship immediately.'

She raised her head and he was stunned by the honest sympathy in her eyes, not a hint of disapproval for his cold approach to a lifetime commitment. He kissed her, holding back the passion that flared. Having her confide in him was paramount even if he wasn't sure why at the moment.

'We've all done things we regret or had them done to us. I have no right to judge anyone, Lauren. Will you tell me? Whose actions did you brand me, Alan and umpteen other guys with?'

Her eyes clouded a second before she dropped her gaze to his throat. She quivered, and sucked in a long breath. Feeling like a louse, he was about to tell her it didn't matter.

Lauren blurted the first words out in a breathy rush then steadied as Matt soothed her back with rhythmic caresses.

'Just after Christmas, the same year you and I…you know… There were often weekend barbecues in our place, crowded, noisy, lots of drinking. My brothers' friends got a kick out of teasing me, and calling me little sister to make me blush and get tongue-tied. To them it was harmless fun. I hated it.'

The almost forgotten feeling of helplessness crashed back, clogging her throat, rendering her speechless. Followed just as suddenly by an empowering sensation. She was no longer a victim. She'd grown and moved on. Hadn't she talked to them at Easter without any childish awkwardness?

'I can see now it was thoughtless but never ill intentioned. If I'd been closer to any of my family I'd have been able to tell them how I felt. Instead I used to spend most of my free time with friends. That night the house was quiet inside when I was dropped off. I didn't see my brother's best friend leaning on the dining room door jamb until he lurched out and grabbed me in a bear hug.'

Matt pushed up against the bedhead, taking her with him. 'Lauren, if you—'

'He mumbled, "You're pretty, *li'l sister*," and kissed me. He stank of beer and sweat and to me it was gross. I remember kicking his shins, breaking free and looking over the top of the stair rail with revulsion. He was slumped against the wall, finishing off his can of beer.'

'And you lumped our kiss on the balcony with that?' His incredibility was tinged with anger.

'No! You were…' In her eagerness to appease him she almost divulged how special his kiss had been, how she'd created fantasies of him over the years.

'Matt, I'm sorry, truly sorry. I let one drunken incident influence my judgement of certain types of good-looking men. From his attitude on the few occasions we've met since, I'm convinced he doesn't remember it at all.'

'Lauren Taylor.'

She recognised the corporate tone from their earliest meetings and squeezed her eyes shut as if that would prevent the coming declaration. He tilted her chin up, coaxing her to look into determined midnight-blue eyes.

'You are very special and I intend to banish every skerrick of that image from your memory. In the best, most personal way possible. And I promise you won't want to run from me.'

His kiss was sweet and tender, and, for her, much too short. Humour glistened in his eyes as he raised his head.

'So you think I'm good-looking? Tell me more.'

CHAPTER TWELVE

THERE WERE FEW vehicles on the roads as Matt drove home after leaving Lauren at her hotel room in the early hours of the morning. Gently nudging her through her door and not following tested his resolve. Pulling it shut to enable him to walk away from her sweet smile, flushed cheeks and slumberous hazel eyes was the hardest action he'd ever taken.

He could still feel her soft lips responding to his in the longest, sweetest goodnight kiss he'd ever had. No holding back. No expectations.

He'd asked her to stay all night but understood her need for distance after their shared confessions and lengthy conversation after. It had been soul-searing for them both. They'd have distance all right, three days, two nights and who knew how many kilometres.

He parked in his garage, switched off the engine and clicked the remote to wind down the roller door. Didn't move. Didn't want to go into that empty unit where her tantalising perfume lingered and her presence was now indelibly implanted into the atmosphere.

Reclining the seat and pushing it back, he lay staring at the roof. New, clean, unmarked, like everything else he owned in Australia. Limbo land. Between the old and the unknown.

He closed his eyes—body weary, mind wide awake. His impulsive kiss so long ago had caused repercussions he'd never have believed, and distress for Lauren. He'd allowed his perception of his parents' relationship to affect his attitude. Love might not be blind but maybe it blurred faults in those you cared for.

Lena and Mark, Duncan and Clair. There were other happy couples he knew too. Did his mother's love override the pain of his father's affairs?

He yawned, ought to go in, get a few hours' sleep to cope with the long day ahead. He'd miss her in his bed— probably lie awake remembering the passion they'd shared. Had those harsh, ecstatic groans of release mingling with her joyful cries come from him? His lips curled, his body shifted as he remembered her kittenish mews. He slept.

Lauren woke early, a faint ray of daylight competing with the street lamps to dispel the night. She quivered as memories teased her from sleep, and grew stronger, more vibrant. More intimate.

She blushed as she recalled how forward she'd been, so unlike the compliant participant in her other relationships. Matt had gently encouraged her, kissed her until she was molten lava in his arms then taken her to the stars and beyond.

It was because of those new and tumultuous sensations, followed by the sharing of their innermost secrets, that she'd asked him to take her back to the hotel. Part of her had longed to stay, to sleep cradled to his body and make love in the morning as the sun rose. The other half had felt vulnerable, shocked by her ardent responses, and needing solitude to decipher why now? Why him?

A similar duel had her torn between knowing how much she'd miss him and feeling an inexplicable inclination to re-erect the defence shield round her heart. She had three days to…who was she kidding? Her surrender had been complete.

Thirteen hours later she pushed her dinner plate to the far corner of the table and opened the green patterned spiral notebook she'd bought in the quirky gift shop a few hours ago. Along with presents for friends' future birthdays.

She'd never been one for writing copious holiday descriptions, relying on photos, brief notes and her memory.

She'd kept Matt's image at bay as she drove, forcing her mind into work mode where nothing was allowed to intrude on the task at hand. New vehicle, new roads, though there were fewer freeways than in New South Wales.

As she wrote and sipped delicious rose tea she noticed the small ceramic vases on the dining-room tables, each one unique and holding two fresh flowers and a sprig of greenery. *Her* vase with orchids was swathed in bubble wrap and secured behind the passenger seat of the car.

Laying her new special green pen down, she cradled her cup, recalling his tenderness and sensitivity, and the way his passion, matching hers, had overridden both. No one had ever made her feel so feminine, so aroused. She relived the evening from the initial eye contact across the road to his reluctant expression as he'd closed her hotel-room door.

Lost in reminiscence, she jumped when her mobile rang, rummaged for her phone with unsteady fingers.

'Matt.'

'Hi, having a good day?'

His now oh-so-familiar raspy voice triggered a rush of heat through her veins. She leant her elbow on the table, and pressed her mobile tighter to her ear as if the action would bring them together.

'Yes, I turned off at any interesting sign, and stopped at almost every town I went through. The autumn colours are incredible. I took lots of photos and bought a few presents.' She was babbling, couldn't seem to slow down.

'Did you miss me?' Deeper, hopeful tone.

'If I say yes, you'll claim an advantage. How did your meetings go?

'Chicken. I missed *you*. Only had one. Where are you now?'

She clutched her stomach to quell the fluttering his confession created, steadied her breathing, and fought for her normal placid tone when she replied.

'Nuriootpa for the night. Tomorrow, who knows?'

'You will be back on Friday?' The teasing note disappeared. He sounded serious, surprisingly uncertain.

'That's the plan. Is there a problem?'

'Not from my end. You'll be getting a call from Clair in the next hour or so. We've been invited to their home in the Hills for the weekend.'

'We?'

'As in you and me, Lauren. Duncan wants to discuss the company's current position, and the business proposal I pitched to him a couple of weeks ago in a relaxed atmosphere. They want you to come with me.'

'Why? I'm not part of your deal at all.'

'They like you.'

Not exactly the answer she wanted to hear.

'Lauren, *I* want you to come. You know them, said you liked them. If it's our relationship worrying you, I promise nothing will happen between us unless you want it to.'

Of course she wanted it to; the location was irrelevant. Last night had been the most wonderful experience of her life. The dilemma was the when and where.

'A whole weekend in someone's home is a giant leap from having dinner with them.' With added pressure if they believed she and Matt were involved.

He made an exasperated noise in his throat.

'I wish I could see you, reassure you. Will you please consider it? Talk it out with Clair?'

She shared the same desire to be with him but she was also aware of how much he was counting on making a deal with Duncan Ford. Would it make a difference if she could see his expression? Moot point so far apart.

'Okay. I'll decide when I talk to Clair.'

'Let me know. Now tell me where you went and what you did.'

* * *

Matt almost rolled off the lounge as he lunged for his mobile an hour or so later, failing to stifle a harsh groan as his elbow hit the side of the coffee table, and his mug fell off.

'Lauren.'

'What was that?'

Simultaneous voices, then silence.

'Matt, are you there?' He liked, more than liked, the concern in her tone.

'I knocked my elbow on the table. You can kiss it better on Friday.' He sat on the sofa's edge, ramrod straight, stomach taut.

'Try pawpaw ointment, it works quicker.'

'Not as much fun. Clair phoned?' He held his breath.

'The two of you are very persuasive. She reminded me I offered to have a look at her computer some time, so I could hardly refuse. And she promised it'll be a weekend to remember.'

His commitment as well. He rose to his feet, adrenaline surging, his free hand fisting and pumping the air. Couldn't, didn't want to stop the grin from forming but managed to keep his voice steady.

'It will be. Are you tired?'

'A little. I'm in the motel room ready for bed.'

A vivid image from his bedroom filled his head, he barely managed to stifle the zealous groan.

'Too sleepy to talk? You're a long way away, and I don't want to say goodnight.'

'What about?'

'You and your family. Why you took the job in Sydney.'

He waited as she pondered his question, a habit he'd learnt to expect, professionally and personally.

'What I went through might have been because I was so different, too shy and inhibited to join in boisterous games. My parents and brothers were all extroverts, loved any kind of physical sport and had no problems interacting with strangers.'

A decidedly male growl resonated in Lauren's ear.

'They didn't allow for you being quiet and gentle, didn't make time to understand who you were?'

She sensed Matt's anger, found his defending their lack of sensitivity towards her exhilarating.

'I'm beginning to see how I contributed to the problems. I wasn't interested so I didn't make any effort. I never complained or told them how I felt except to refuse to attend any more sporting events once I turned thirteen. To them I seemed happy to bury myself in books and homework. At least I always got good grades at school.'

Another growl so she quickly added, 'If I hadn't I might not be working with computers. Might not be here.'

'Eighty odd kilometres away. Much too far.'

She snuggled into the pillow, striving to keep grounded. He made her feel warm and light-headed even along a phone line. With each word, her pulse had quickened, electric tingles danced over her skin, and the overwhelming desire to touch him, feel his strength surrounding her was almost frightening. He could make her feel strong, empowered. He could also hurt her more than anyone else in the world.

Lauren returned the hire car early Friday afternoon, and was given a sealed package Matt had left for her containing a key to his unit. Finding a round dining setting in the appropriate place and three large bright blue cushions on the settee left her speechless.

She texted him to say she'd arrived, found a tea towel in a kitchen drawer, and set it on the new table. It was the perfect place for the orchid arrangement he'd sent her. They were as fresh as when she'd received them, having suffered no ill effects from their journey to the Barossa.

A cup of tea, an open packet of chocolate biscuits, and

she was ready to sort out her belongings in the lounge room. The items she chose for the Hills visit were packed into the new suitcase she'd purchased, everything else was wrapped and stored in her original one ready for the trip home.

Home. Her own apartment. Her sanctuary. It was never going to feel quite the same. The memories she'd be taking with her would change the way she viewed her life, her work. Her future. She chomped into another biscuit and vowed, no matter what, there'd be no regrets. Her friends would be there for her though she'd never be able to tell them the full truth. Matt would be her special *good* secret, hers alone.

She heard his car pull into the garage, his footsteps in the passage, his delighted raspy tone. 'You're here.' She saw his captivating smile, was swept into his embrace, and held as if she was fragile and precious. She slid her arms around his waist, revelling in his strength and the satisfying sense of security.

His lips feather-brushed her forehead. She cuddled up, wanting this serenity to last, and he seemed in no hurry to end it either. Quiet harmony. An idyllic memory to cherish.

'You kept the orchids?'

She arched her neck to meet questioning eyebrows and curved lips. 'Of course. They're beautiful, Matt.'

His eyes shone as he gathered her in. 'So are you, Lauren. Beautiful and intoxicating.'

His kiss was light, gentle, spreading a warm glow from head to toes. Her lips instinctively moved with his. Her heart soared, and she wanted to freeze-frame this precious moment for ever.

With evident reluctance he eased away.

'If I don't let you go now, we'll arrive in the dark. I know which I'd prefer…'

'But the Fords are expecting us for dinner. I'm packed and ready.'

'Give me ten minutes to shower and change.' He dipped his head for a brief hard kiss and walked out of the room.

When they left Lauren kept silent at first allowing Matt to concentrate on the driving through peak traffic. She stared out of the window, trying to identify the suburbs and buildings, surprised by the number of new houses and renovations on main roads.

Once they hit the freeway to the hills, he turned on the radio, keeping it muted in the background.

'Any listening preference, Lauren?'

'Whatever you usually have on is fine.'

'Which would mainly be news and sport. Not for you. How are you on county and western?'

He had to be teasing. One look at his profile said he wasn't.

'As long as it's ballads and not yippee-ki-yay stuff.'

'Whatever pleases you.' He glanced over and her mouth dried up at the fire in his eyes. She quivered inside at the thought of the two nights and two days ahead.

'I've been meaning to ask you for days, kept forgetting because you have a habit of distracting my mind and scrambling my brain. What's the name of your perfume?'

She couldn't answer, her own brain turning to mush at his compliment. He was claiming to be as affected as she was when they were together. Did he have the same heat rushes, the tingles? The heart flips?

She'd been wearing the same brand for years, had one of the fragrances in her suitcase. So why couldn't she remember either name?

'It's from a small rural company who produce different aromas from Australian native flowers. I keep three and wear whichever suits my mood at the time.'

'It's been the same one every day since you arrived. Are the others as enticing?'

'I've no idea. Why do you always wear the same sea-spray cologne?'

'The truth?'

'Yes.' *Please don't let it be because it was a gift from a girlfriend.*

'I forgot to pack mine for when I changed after a game and borrowed Alan's. Apart from when I've been given others, it's the one I use.'

'You wore it that night.'

'For the first time.' He flicked her an incredulous look. 'You remembered how I smelt?'

'You did get pretty close, Matt.'

'Yeah, and then I lost you.'

They drove in silence for a while, both lost in thoughts of their meeting on the balcony, Matt's focus on the road and Lauren's out of the window.

Because of the long hot summer, the vegetation wasn't as green as she'd hoped. Sneak views of houses between the trees, horses and sheep grazing, and colourful native plants drew her avid attention. Seeing a herd of alpacas in a small fenced area of a paddock thrilled her.

After exiting the freeway, they followed the signs through the small typical hills town and onto a winding, tree-lined road. High overhanging branches covered with autumn leaves of brilliant orange and brown shaded them from the setting sun. The verges were covered with more, tempting walkers to romp through them.

'This is so peaceful. So Australiana. When we lived in the suburbs I used to dream of moving to a hills town. Any one of them.' She shrugged. 'Didn't happen of course.'

Matt pulled over, switched off the engine and unbuckled his seat belt. He stretched his arm and unclipped hers, unfazed by the sudden apprehension in her eyes. Twisting to face her and taking her hands in his, he yearned for the glowing satisfaction he'd seen after they'd made love.

'You had a few unfulfilled childhood wishes, didn't you?'

She shrugged. 'Doesn't everyone?'

'No.' He ignored his ambition to work as a partner with his father. 'Most of mine came true. I played Aussie Rules for the school, graduated from uni and travelled overseas. Considering my lack of vocal ability, becoming an international singing sensation was never going to happen.'

His heart swelled at the sight of her hesitant smile. Give him time and he'd make her radiant and happy.

'I dreamt of being a dancer for a year or so.' She gave a self-conscious laugh. 'Of course, in my imagination I had no fear of appearing on stage in front of hundreds of people. The one time I was selected to read a poem I'd written at parents' night, I took one look at all those faces, froze and bolted.'

'So you wrote?'

'I have a stack of notebooks full of poems and short stories, only ever shown to my best friend. Childish and not very good but fun. I haven't written anything for years except reports or emails.'

Her fingers gripped his. His pulse accelerated. The temperature in the car rose rapidly.

'I've been reflecting on my life lately and I'm beginning to realise my family and I just didn't gel. Maybe they weren't as much insensitive as bemused by the alien in their midst. And there were no other relatives around who might have made a difference.'

'Will you discuss it with them when you see them?'

'No.' Short and sharp. 'There's no way it wouldn't sound accusing and the past can't be changed.'

He silently agreed with fervour.

'I'm an adult with a good career and great friends. It'll achieve nothing, and only cause pain.'

A car drove past, the driver beeping in customary rural

friendship. Matt checked the time, then cradled her face in his hands.

'Most assuredly an adult, Lauren Taylor. Beautiful and desirable.'

He intended the kiss to be gentle, reassuring, but almost lost control when she returned it with enthusiasm. Her hands slid up his chest to tease his neck, heating his blood to near boiling. Her body pressed to his fuelled the urge to have her alone somewhere quiet and private.

He broke away, expelling the air from his lungs, gasping in more as he feasted on her blushed cheeks and brilliant eyes. His hand shook as he redid his seat belt and started the engine.

As he struggled to find his voice again he mulled over her confessions of the last few days. He needed to know everything if he was to help her completely overcome her insecurities before she left.

Before she left. The very idea depressed him. Having her near lifted his spirits.

'In five hundred metres turn right.'

The GPS interrupted his thinking and he slowed down.

CHAPTER THIRTEEN

LAUREN'S LIPS TINGLED from his kiss, and her heartbeat loped along in an erratic rhythm. She wanted to be alone with Matt, wasn't ready for a whole weekend with comparative strangers who'd probably invited her for his sake. Her first sight of the property increased her reservations.

Well-maintained tall hedges formed the property's boundaries with ornate stone columns and high elaborate gates protecting the entrance. She could see neatly trimmed red- and green-leafed plants skirtinged the winding gravel driveway, and a variety of trees and shrubs hid the house from view.

Matt pressed a button on a matching bollard, answered a disembodied voice and the gates swung open. They passed through, and for Lauren it was like entering another world, where money was no object and the traditions of generations would be strictly upheld. She had no logical reason for the feeling yet it was strong and overwhelming, negating all the assurances Matt and Clair had given her.

She gripped her hands in her lap, drops of sweat slid down her back and her stomach churned. Having lunch in public, with eating and waiter service taking up time, hadn't been as bad as she'd expected. The dinner function had been so noisy, so crowded and bustling, interaction had been kept to a minimum.

She'd been coerced into a weekend with Matt and the Fords, dining with them three times a day, sitting with them in the evening. She'd be alone with Clair while the men discussed business. What did she have in common with a rich, influential woman whose life revolved around her husband, family and society friends?

She... Oh, they'd stopped as the car rounded a curve. Wide expanses of lawn had been laid as a fire break on the sides she could see. Ahead stood the house, a beautiful sprawling example of a colonial family homestead with a shady wide veranda on all four sides. It was painted in muted shades of green and brown, including the shutters, to blend with the surroundings. A peaceful harmonious haven. A millionaire's paradise.

She was vaguely aware of the lack of engine noise, then Matt's hand covering hers, raising the hairs on her skin, triggering warmth deep inside. Somehow it intensified the trembling she tried to hide.

She looked into sympathetic blue eyes and wished she'd been more honest and refused the invitation. So much hung on the impression he made this weekend, and she'd be a liability he'd regret.

'I'm sorry, Matt. I made a mistake. This is a mistake. The dinner was one thing—this is way bigger. You and Duncan talk business, sport, topical news. You were brought up in the same social environment, probably went to the same private school. I'll never fit in with your elite circles.'

A guttural rumble came from his throat and he placed two fingers on her lips. She swatted them away.

'Clair is a caring, generous person with all the social skills. I'm a computer geek with hardly any. We'll run out of conversation in minutes.'

His features hardened, sending an icy chill shooting across her skin as if she'd entered a supermarket freezer. She pressed into the seat, wishing she could disappear into it.

'Those statements are beneath the person I believe you are, Lauren. They met you and thought you were a charming, intelligent, and gracious young woman. Duncan's exact words when he asked me to thank you for your kindness to Ken. And, believe me, Clair would never have invited you just to make equal numbers.'

He stroked her hair, clasped her nape and gently drew

her upright. His gaze intensified as he studied her face. What was he searching for? And why? His smile obliterated her logic and created chaotic fantasies.

'They'd like you to have a relaxing weekend in one of the most beautiful places in South Australia, the same as I do. I'm sure Clair knows we're attracted to each other but there's no way she'll say or do anything to make you feel uncomfortable.'

Shame made her blush and she bit her lip. She gave him a remorseful smile, and flattened out her hands with linked fingers in supplication.

'I guess deep inside I know that's true. Sometimes the insecure child overrides the logical technician. Being with you plays havoc with my rationality.'

Too late she heard what she'd admitted, knew from his smug grin he'd understood, and wouldn't hesitate to use it to coerce and cajole her.

'You've just paid me one of the nicest compliments I've ever had. If I wasn't parked in view from the house, and constrained by my seat belt, I'd put it to the test.'

He covered her lips, teasing and coaxing yet with an underlying restraint. She returned the kiss, safe in the knowledge it could go no further. For now. She wound her arm around his neck to hold him closer then let it slide slowly away when he lifted his head. Embraced the surge of power at the emotion in his voice when he whispered in her ear.

'And don't think for a second I won't remember every word and every touch next time we're alone.'

Bringing her breathing under control as they drove up to the house, she silently echoed his words. Except *she'd* remember them as long as she lived.

Clair was waiting on the front steps and came out to meet them, leaning into Lauren's window.

'Glad you made it. We've opened one of the garage doors

for you round the back. I'll meet you there.' She didn't comment on the five-minute time gap from gate to front door.

They parked and Matt was unloading the boot when she joined them, giving Lauren a warm hug and a kiss on the cheek. So different from the casual greetings from her family. Did her reticence cause the awkwardness between them?

'Do you need a hand with the luggage?'

'She's brought less than any woman I've ever travelled with,' Matt chipped in as he received the same greeting. 'And that includes the carton of wine from the Barossa.'

'Oh, how thoughtful. Let me take your suitcase.'

She led the way to the steps, wheeling Matt's case, accompanied by Lauren with hers and an overnight bag. Matt locked the car and followed carrying the wine, his satchel and parka.

'I've put you in the guest wing, three bedrooms all with an ensuite, a sitting room and small kitchen. Completely self-contained if needed.'

As they stepped onto the veranda two black and white dogs raised themselves from their snug positions in the corner and came over to sniff and be introduced. The larger one, a mixture of collie and a few unknowns, nuzzled at Lauren's hands and she dropped her bags and stroked him. The other sat by Clair and studied the two newcomers.

'Cyber's an addict for attention. He'll stalk you the whole time you're here if we let him. Cyan is pure collie, and quieter. Both are very protective and great guard dogs. Go settle, you two.'

Turning to the right, she walked a few steps and opened a door to reveal a wide corridor with a high ceiling. Entering first, she placed the suitcase by the wall.

Lauren's eyes widened at the incredible décor, presumably historically accurate with the appearance of being freshly painted in shades of blue. She'd always enjoyed colonial movies, now she felt she was on the set of one. The carved wooden mirror on the wall with a narrow matching table fascinated her. She moved closer. Clair came to stand behind her.

'We inherited these and a lot more furniture with the house. Tomorrow I'll take you on a tour if you like.'

'I'll look forward to it.'

'You'll find we've mixed and matched different time periods. If we like it, we fit it in. Use any rooms you want and join us in the main lounge when you're ready. Shall I take the wine?'

'It's heavy so I'll bring it. We won't keep you waiting.' Matt had already put it on the floor.

'I just need a quick freshen up,' Lauren said.

'Take all the time you want, then come through here.' Clair left through a door midway along the hall.

'Well, Lauren, would you like to choose where you sleep?'

At odds with its rough timbre, his voice glided as smooth as silk over her skin and the only answer in her head was, *With you.*

The first room was a cosy corner lounge with windows on two sides. Matt opened the next door to reveal a king-sized bed with a padded green headboard and quilt. The light green wall complemented white woodwork and built-in wardrobes.

Shuttered windows overlooked the veranda, and the Queen Anne dressing table and stool between two closed doors matched the bedside drawers. One door led into a very modern ensuite, the other to an almost identical bedroom with a floral theme.

Lauren gazed from one to the other then to Matt's inscrutable expression. His taut jaw and the slight curl of his fingers showed the depth of his tension.

She bent her head to hide a smile. If she said separate

rooms, he'd accept her decision without censure though she'd bet he'd use his charm and every seduction technique he could think of to change her mind.

Her stomach quivered and she trembled as she imagined a few of them. In an instant, he was holding her arms, sombre eyes scanning her face.

'Whatever feels right for you, Lauren. This is for happy memories, no regrets.'

She reached up to caress his cheek, and felt his tremor through her fingers. Felt a surge of elation at the power her touch had on him. She tilted her head, and curled her lips in what she hoped was a beguiling smile.

'I've never been a flowery décor girl, and I can't imagine *you* sleeping under a floral quilt.'

His smile lit up her world, his bear hug squeezed her ribcage, and his deep, passionate kiss had her craving to be in the bed behind them right now.

Lauren expected dinner to be in a formal room. Instead the round dining setting overlooked a native garden scattered with inconspicuous bollard lights, illuminating colourful flowers and leafage of all shades of green. Picture perfect scenery.

Duncan opened a red wine she'd purchased in the Barossa Valley and one of his own chilled whites.

'Lauren, which would you like? We are firm advocates for indulging in your own preference.'

She chose white, the others elected to try the red. They toasted good friends and she was complimented on her choice, making her relax and laugh.

'I can hardly claim responsibility. Matt recommended two of the wineries and I merely asked the people in those, and a third near Angaston, for a selection of their bestsellers. It's a gift from both of us.'

'Very much appreciated. Shall we take our seats?'

Clair went to fetch the starters, declining Lauren's offer to assist.

'They're all ready to be served. You can help clear and bring in the other courses.'

Any apprehension Matt had felt regarding this visit faded away as conversation flowed. Lauren was curious about the plant varieties in the garden, admitting she'd had a successful vegetable plot in Melbourne and missed the straight-from-the-ground taste. When laughingly challenged by Clair to name the home-grown on the table, she amazed them all by being correct.

'I thought I'd get you on the peas from the market. We'll pick some fruit for you to take home on Sunday.'

The conversation ranged from orchards to the history of the house and the restorations the Fords had undertaken over a number of years. Matt admired the gentle banter between them, the friendly teasing solidly based on an enduring love and evident companionship.

He'd been convinced he'd never feel such a bonding, yet lately that belief had become blurred. Was it possible he might be wrong?

His eyes met Lauren's as she stood to help with the dinner plates, and her smile tripped his heart. His mind flashed to the night ahead with the enchanting woman who'd agreed to share it with him.

Pavlova, coffee and liqueurs rounded off a delightful meal, his senses heightened by the promise of a perfect ending to the day.

All Lauren's senses were acute, tuned like a maestro's violin, as they approached the door that would shut them off from the rest of the house. Matt's fingers were laced with hers. She could hear the long breaths he took. His aroma surrounded her, tempting her lungs to breathe deeper.

Tonight there'd be no drive back to her hotel. She'd nestle into his warmth and fall asleep. And wake in his arms to be kissed and loved some more as the sun's rays lit up the room.

No expectations. No recriminations. She'd accept what he freely gave and not regret what he was not able to give. Every moment spent with Matt inched her further along the path of surrendering her heart. There was no going back and in front she could see no happy ending.

As soon as the door closed behind them, he twisted her round, and stepped closer, trapping her against the wall. He stroked her cheek with his knuckles, and she could feel his heart pounding under her palm. His free hand slid around her neck and he bent his head to claim her lips.

The fire that had smouldered since he'd arrived home roared into flame, and she returned his kiss with an ardour that shook her to her core. He quivered then his arms enfolded her, tightening until there was no space between them.

Time stood still, stretched endlessly to infinity. Too short an eon later, he raised his head to take a shuddering breath. Her own came in gasps, and she let her forehead rest on his chest.

'Wow.' Placing one hand on the wall above her head, he blew air out and inhaled new in. Stared at her for a long time as if trying to see inside her head, trying to puzzle something out.

'I've missed you, Lauren. Ached for you for three long days and two endless nights and I can't wait any longer.'

He lifted her into his arms, carried her into the bedroom, and laid her on the bed. Without relinquishing hold, he settled beside her, rolling onto his side to lean over her. His fingertips skimmed across her shoulders and arms then over her hips, making her squirm with anticipation. His lips kissed a path from the pulse by her ear to the corner of her mouth, driving her crazy with need.

'Matt?' She hardly recognised the breathless, needy plea as coming from her. Her hand pressed on the back of his neck, dragging his head down to hers, and her fingernails scraped his skin.

'You're mine.' His voice was harsh, deep with passion. Macho. Triumphant.

'Yours.' Hers was breathless. Elated. Proud.

For as long as he needed and wanted her.

Lauren leant on the veranda rail waiting while Matt showered so they could join their hosts for breakfast. The universe was different, sharper, brighter. *She* was different.

She huffed and watched her breath evaporate in the cool air. She'd been changing since Matt had glanced up at her with his mesmerising midnight-blue eyes. A little every time they were together, stronger from the kisses outside her hotel room and a giant leap when they first made love.

Last night the metamorphosis had become complete. There'd been no sign of the shy, vulnerable caterpillar. She'd given herself to him completely, no hesitation, no restraint. And been shown a realm of soaring passions and sensations far beyond her imagination.

She'd fallen into contented sleep wrapped in his arms, his lips on her forehead, her hand on his thundering heart.

She felt a nudge at her side, and hunkered down to pat Cyan, almost fell over as Cyber also claimed attention.

'Save some for me.' Matt stood in the doorway, hair damp, eyes gleaming.

He could have all of her for as long as he wanted.

Breakfast was served on the balcony facing the large vegetable patch. Lauren loved the crispness in the air, and the light breeze stirring the foliage, making the garden appear to be alive. She could imagine sitting here all day and into the evening enjoying the changes of light and sound.

'This is all so idealistic. I can't imagine a more soothing place. Working in the city must be so much more tolerable if you know you have a haven to go home to.'

'And work's better now I can do a lot electronically,' Duncan chipped in. 'You can keep your high-rise views. Nothing beats what we have here.'

'Do you get out of the city much, Lauren?' Clair asked as she buttered her toast.

'Occasionally. We drive up to the Blue Mountains or along the coast to go hiking. Beach walking is fun any season and easily accessible in Sydney.'

'And who's we?'

Lauren noted she gave no apologies for being inquisitive, didn't need to. It was part of her caring nature.

'A group of friends I've met since moving there. We now live in the same apartment block so we're like family.'

As she spoke she looked across the table at Matt's thoughtful expression, remembered earlier conversations and wondered if he'd come to the same sudden realisation. She had a second family, of her own ilk, and who she gelled with comfortably.

He quirked an eyebrow and his lips curled, causing fluttering in her belly and heat waves in her veins. She lifted her glass, drank the remainder of her freshly squeezed orange juice, and tried for a nonchalant demeanour.

CHAPTER FOURTEEN

MATT STRUGGLED FOR the same effect. His body still buzzed from the exhilaration of waking from deep satisfying sleep with Lauren curled into him, warm and irresistible. He had no idea what he'd eaten, drunk or said since they'd joined Duncan and Clair for the meal.

She was radiant. Her skin glowed and her expressive hazel eyes shone as brightly as any stars in a country sky. He'd heard and understood what she'd said. She had friends and support. She'd be all right when she went home.

Home. His half-empty barren unit. She'd taken three days of her leave. Allowing for the day or two he'd need her at work, she'd only be here for two more weeks. Forget the hotel. He'd ask her to stay with him.

The prospect of spending long evenings with her was intoxicating. The image of her sharing breakfast and dinner across the new table he'd bought because of her upped his pulse to uncountable. And as for the nights...

'Matt?'

He crashed to earth with a thud. Clair's eyes twinkled as she held up the coffee jug.

'More coffee?'

'Um... Please.' He pushed his cup and saucer over to her, hoping his face wasn't as red as it felt. She'd caught him out again.

'As you two will be in Duncan's study for most of the morning, Lauren and I will walk the dogs then I'll show her over the house,' Clair said, topping up her husband's drink.

'Just don't let her get you in the small room off the lounge, Lauren,' Duncan quipped. 'That's where her troublesome computer lurks and you'll be trapped in there until dinner.'

'Brute.' Clair gave him a playful flick of her hand and they smiled blissfully at each other.

The painful gut wrench took Matt by surprise. Their affection was obvious after nearly thirty-five years of marriage. Duncan had mentioned their anniversary was in June and he intended to make it an extra special occasion.

He'd assumed it would be for show like his parents' celebrations. Not any more. Like Lena and Mark, the interaction between them proved their feelings ran deep and true.

The dogs bounded down the back steps as soon as Lauren and Clair came out of the door, raced halfway across the lawn then stopped to ensure they were following.

'They're better than any exercise programme I've ever tried,' Clair remarked. As the two women caught up with them, they shot off again.

'Walking anywhere around here would never seem like training to me. This trip has got me rethinking my priorities and future,' Lauren replied.

'The trip or the man?'

Lauren wasn't sure how to answer as they went through a gate and onto a bushland path.

'It's complicated.'

'It needn't be, Lauren. The way you look at one another, whenever you touch, the attraction's obvious but there's also constraint. My children tell me not to interfere…'

'Advice is always welcome.' Lauren would gladly accept guidance. 'It's whether it can be acted upon that counts.'

'Don't give up on him, Lauren. Matt's mother and I belong to the same organisations, and she's hinted at Marcus's medical problems. Apart from that and the company situation, I sense Matt has personal demons to conquer.'

'You may be right.'

He's certainly determined to have me exorcise mine.

'He also has a reputation for tough, ethical dealing. If he

didn't Duncan wouldn't be considering a partnership. Let him find his own way and be there when he does.'

As things stood she'd be on the east coast fixing glitches, living on memories and dreaming of midnight-blue eyes.

'Cyber. Cyan.' The dogs had darted to the left at a fork, and obediently returned to Clair's side.

'There's a magnificent view this way. Luckily the koalas don't seem at all perturbed by our noisy pets so keep an eye out for them in the gum trees.'

'I envy you all this beauty and peace. Matt told me the property was quite run-down when you moved in.'

'I inherited the estate from two wonderful stubborn-as-mules grandparents who refused help and died within weeks of each other. Life wasn't easy, especially in those early years, but it's always worth fighting for what you love.'

But what if the one you are fighting for doesn't want to be won?

The talks with Duncan couldn't have gone better; now all Matt wanted to do was find Lauren, and see her smile. Had she had a good morning? Was she happy she'd come?

He found her in the kitchen helping Clair prepare a salad lunch, and restrained the desire to kiss her in company. Until her face brightened at the sight of him and the invitation in her bright eyes was too hard to resist. He slipped his arm around her waist and softly covered her enticing lips with his.

She laid her hand on his arm, and welcomed the kiss, recreating the heat sensations from last night. His pulse tripled and his heart pounded. All overridden by an unfamiliar longing to hold on for ever and cherish.

Shaken by this new emotion, he broke the kiss, fighting for control. He wanted to find solitude to assess what was happening, and perversely ached to scoop her up and carry her to a quiet place and be with her.

'How'd the walk go?' Reality slammed home at Duncan's remark from the doorway.

Matt set Lauren free, nearly pulled her back in at the sight of her sweetly bemused expression.

'The air was fresh and crisp at the south lookout and the hills were shrouded in mist—very bracing,' Clair replied. 'You two can carry the salad bowls and meat plates. Lauren and I will bring the rest.'

The dogs padded round the veranda to join them, squatting close in anticipation of being fed as well.

'We also had a session on my computer,' Clair announced with pride as they helped themselves to food.

'And?'

Duncan wasn't merely playing lip service to his wife. Matt heard the genuine interest in his tone, saw it in his eyes. She was his number one priority as he was hers. So different from his parents. A cold fist crushed his heart, and his chest tightened.

'I'm not so bad after all. Lauren gave me a beautifully covered notebook and bright green pen and I wrote down everything step by step as she told or showed me.'

Lauren's knee bumped against his and stayed. A simple nod of her head plus a look that said 'you were right' sent heat surging throughout his body. He echoed her action then concentrated on Clair.

'No one's ever explained the things I have trouble with in simple English I can understand. Lauren did, and I have her email address and phone number so I can contact her any time I need help.'

Matt couldn't prevent the swell of pride even though all he'd done was persuade Lauren to come. With a start, he realised it was pride in her, something he had no justification for. She was her own person. An enchanting, self-sufficient woman.

'So I'm going to take her into Hahndorf this afternoon. What do you have planned?'

The men exchanged glances.

'Another couple of hours and we'll break for the day. You'll find us on the side veranda with a bottle of wine and a selection of cheese and crackers.' Duncan grinned at Matt. 'They'll have to come get us to carry all the shopping from the car.'

Clearing the table was accomplished in a few minutes with everyone helping then Matt went with Lauren to fetch her coat and shoulder bag. And to kiss her, longer and deeper than he'd be able to do in front of their hosts.

It left them both hot and gasping for air. And bedtime was a lifetime away.

'Glad you decided to come, Lauren?' He watched her face for any sign of regret.

'Got coerced you mean. Yes, I'm very glad.' Her eyes darkened, highlighting the gold flecks. His body responded to the thought she might be remembering last night.

'Clair says she'll take me round the house tomorrow.'

He'd been in umpteen old renovated homes. A few days ago he'd have politely declined joining them. Today the chance of seeing what the Fords had achieved through Lauren's eyes was appealing.

'Tell her I'd like to be included.'

His wanting to join them delighted Lauren. When the offer of two weeks' leave had been made it had sounded like ample time for a break. Now, with three days taken, it was a pitiful amount to store memories to last a lifetime.

Lauren flicked at the insect biting her earlobe, sighed and snuggled into her pillow. It returned, pulling her a little further from sleep.

'Wanna go for a walk and watch the sun rise?'

Whispered throaty seduction.

In an instant she was wide awake, catching at the hand whose fingernails were tickling her lobe. Matt lay beside her, fully dressed in jeans and warm jumper, eyes gleaming with mischief. The only light came from the open en-suite door.

How come he wanted to go hiking and her main desire was to drag him close for a repeat of last night? And later. And some time in the early hours of today. It would take only his touch to turn her languid muscles molten and re-kindle the passion he'd ignited again and again.

'What time is it?' She stretched, and shivered as the cold morning air hit her arms, glared at him when he pulled the quilt off her. He sucked air between his teeth as she tried to drag them back.

'Early. I've got snacks, drinks and directions to the best lookout.' He was excited, eager like a puppy ready for his daily walk. 'You've got five minutes.'

'You asked for ten on Friday,' she muttered, pretending to be annoyed. Secretly she was thrilled he wanted to share this outing with her. His laughter followed her to the shower.

He took her hand as they left, guiding her down the back steps and over the lawn, his torch lighting their way. They followed the path through the trees, accompanied by only the sound of the breeze rustling the vegetation, the scuffling of animals in the undergrowth, and dried leaves crunching under their sneakers.

Lauren relished the chill on her face, the night hiding the factual mundane world and the warmth of his fingers linked with hers. This was more than special, this was super memorable. A never-to-be-forgotten occasion to be taken out and savoured in the future whenever she felt sad.

Matt stopped suddenly in the centre of a small clearing,

and bent to place his backpack on the ground. She heard a click and the beam disappeared, leaving them in complete darkness, surrounded by black velvet. Magical. Ethereal.

He drew her into his arms, and she wrapped hers around his neck. His lips were soft, his kiss firm yet holding a tenderness that touched her heart. No bells or fireworks. This was a moment of profound contentment. The moment she acknowledged the truth. She was in love with Matt Dalton.

With their lips a whisper apart Matt breathed out Lauren's name, too stunned to form any other words. He'd switched off the torch for effect, to heighten the ambiance when he'd kissed her in the dark. Hadn't expected to be so unsettled by his own emotions.

Only she could access his soul and revitalise the beliefs he'd long discarded, make him yearn for a better time when he'd had faith in for ever. She fitted him perfectly, her soft form to his hard muscle. He didn't want to—couldn't—let her leave until he...he wasn't sure what.

Keeping one arm around her as much for his comfort as hers, he bent to retrieve the torch, waved it round and led her to the gap in the trees. In the light's limited sphere there was a valley below and hills beyond, vague mysterious shapes. The wind was stronger here in the open, blowing up and over the edge, causing him to strengthen his stance.

His intention had been to give Lauren a weekend of pleasurable memories. Now he was storing them up for himself.

Taking the picnic rug from the rucksack, he laid it out between the trees near the edge of the cliff. Lying down on one elbow, he held out his hand. His already racing heartbeat hit rocket speed as, without hesitation, she joined him, eyes sparkling, lips parted. She stroked his cheek, and ran her fingers across his jaw, triggering reactions that blew his control.

Shy, exquisite Lauren was teasing him, playing havoc

with his libido. She tempted him with her inviting smile, her tongue-tip tracing her lips, and her feather-light finger touch. He bent over her, lowered his head and clicked off the torch.

The first small pink and orange rays shimmered on the horizon. Matt leant against a tree trunk, nestled Lauren's back onto his chest, and rested his chin on her shoulder as they stared across the valley. He breathed in her delicate scent, tinged with his cologne and their personal aromas.

This was an extraordinary moment, life changing. For those few incredible minutes, they'd been one entity, bound by a force he didn't understand. Knew he wanted to relive it again and again.

For ever? She wriggled, reigniting the desire. His body would willingly comply for as long as he lived. His resolute mind clung to the hard lessons he'd learnt. He refused to make false declarations to gain any advantage or to give false hope of any kind.

No deception. No lies. What they had was good, much better than good. There was no reason they couldn't continue to be together until she flew home. His arms tightened, reinforcing his hold, and she gave a cute gasp. He nuzzled her neck and she sighed. He nibbled her earlobe.

'Oh-h-h…' Her breath whooshed out as vibrant colours tinted the edges of emerging clouds and gradually spread across the sky. Dark shadowy shapes began to appear on the landscape, slowly taking recognisable form. Unforgettable. Unbelievably spectacular.

His own breath caught in his throat. His body stilled, his pulse raced. This was supposed to be a unique experience for Lauren to treasure, along with the other special occasions they'd shared. He hadn't expected to feel anything more than he did at fireworks displays or the like.

Instead nature at her finest tugged at his heartstrings,

and raised the hairs on the back of his neck. The adrenaline rush was greater than when he'd skied the Swiss Alps and white-water rafted in Wales, heightened by sharing it with Lauren.

The sun's softer morning rays revealed the delicacy of her skin, rapture in her wide-open eyes, and ecstasy on her beautiful face. He burned it into his memory, to be recalled at will.

'Matt.' Husky with emotion. Crumbling what little composure he had left.

'Darling Lauren.' Rough, dragged over the constricting lump in his throat.

'It's wonderful. Unbelievable. Thank you.'

He cradled her cheek, leant forward and kissed her, wishing the earth would stop spinning and the magic would never end. He laid his head next to hers and pretended it hadn't.

Lauren wished she could reverse time, have the sun set then rise again. In slow motion. With her senses already heightened by his gentle loving only minutes before, she'd been enthralled by the fluid change of colours. The panorama in front of her, the solid wall of his chest behind her, and his muscular arms enfolding her intensified the sensation of being snugly cosseted in a vast open universe.

She loved the mystical atmosphere of night becoming day, of small pockets of mist among the trees. Of feeling they were alone in the cosmos. Even the nocturnal creatures were silent in mutual reverence.

His kiss was magical, soft with an underlying hint of yearning. A longing echoed in her heart. A craving for this never to end.

Lights flickered in the distance, and the wind picked up, bringing with it faint sounds of traffic. They ate the chocolate bars and drank the hot coffee he'd brought. Cuddled close in their padded winter jackets, neither ready to leave and return to the real world.

Only when they heard the dogs barking did they stand and pack up.

'I think I need a bigger car,' Matt joked as he juggled the luggage into the boot for the late-afternoon return to the city.

'Don't whinge. I'm the one who'll be paying for excess weight on the plane.' Lauren's light retort masked the pain of knowing every moment brought her departure closer.

They'd have a few evenings, maybe part of the weekends together, and distant phone calls while she was driving around being a tourist. All too soon she'd have used up her ten days and they'd say goodbye.

There hadn't been, nor would there be, any promises or declarations of keeping in touch. And she'd never ask for them.

'It might be cheaper for me to drive you home.'

CHAPTER FIFTEEN

HER HEARTBEAT SPIKED. His tone was light but his eyes were grave, his lips firm and unsmiling. She couldn't have replied to save her life, and ached to have him add he meant it.

'Got room for more?' Clair came down the steps carrying a huge bunch of flowers. 'Duncan's bringing the fruit we promised.'

Lauren pressed her hands together, her index fingertips on her lips. How had she ever been daunted by this considerate, generous couple?

'They're beautiful, Clair. Thank you for a wonderful weekend. It's been unforgettable.'

She recognised roses and tiger lilies, others were unknown. When she reached up to kiss Clair's cheek as she accepted the stunning gift, she was drawn into an unexpected motherly hug.

'You'll always be welcome, Lauren,' Clair said, and gave her an extra squeeze.

'Even when she hasn't stuffed up on her computer.' Duncan laughed as he appeared behind her with a big cardboard box. 'Should last you a few days,' he added, handing it to Matt.

Lauren buried her face into the blooms and inhaled their perfume before placing them on the back seat alongside her overnight bag. Gently touched the petals, blinking back tears at the Fords' kindness.

She noticed Matt and Clair in close conversation, serious expressions on their faces. Was he also being given friendly advice? She walked over to Duncan to thank him and was pulled into a friendly embrace.

'I'll be eternally grateful to you for helping Clair and boosting her esteem. Other technicians made her feel inadequate though she hid it well.'

'It wasn't much compared to your company and hospitality. I've loved every moment.'

'Then come again—plan for a holiday in the spring or in December. Despite the heat, we always have a festive season, including long evening walks followed by hot or cold drinks on the veranda.'

'It sounds inviting.'

'Then be here.' He smiled down at her. 'Pity you're based in Sydney. It's such a long way away.'

The farewells lasted another ten minutes and included more hugs for Lauren as if they feared they wouldn't see her for a long time. Finally they were on the road, and she let her head fall back and closed her eyes.

'Tired, darling?'

Every cell in her body sprang to high alert at his endearment, the second time he'd used it. Was it an automatic name for the women he made love to?

'A little. It's been a full weekend.'

'Any regrets, Lauren?' Low, and slightly hesitant. Not like him at all.

'None, Matt.' She paused and grinned. 'Well, maybe the purchase of a T-shirt depicting a joey in its mother's pouch, waving an Australian flag. I'll give it to a friend with quirky taste.'

Matt chuckled. His mood lifted. The idea he'd been contemplating was the best option for both of them. All he had to do was find the words to convince her. In his usual competent way, he rehearsed the phrasing, while negotiating the bends and merging onto the freeway. Lauren was lost in her own thoughts.

Satisfied he was ready, he glanced across and forgot it all in a rush of affection when he saw her lovely features relaxed in peaceful sleep. He faced the road again, tightening his grip on the wheel to conquer the urge to caress her cheek.

He had the rest of the day for gentle persuasion. If she agreed they'd spend all their free time together for the two weeks she had left. Fourteen days, and he'd count down every one.

Moving into the left lane, he slowed down. There was no urgency, Lauren was peaceful and the hectic uncertainty had eased from his life. He didn't know exactly what he faced legally but he'd been totally honest and had good representation. He had no idea how bad the backlash might be if, more like when, his father's duplicity became public but was assured of Duncan's full support.

He had faith in his own ability to reform the company and keep it viable. And—he shot an affectionate look at his sleeping passenger—he had Lauren. Sweet, adorable Lauren, who hijacked his thoughts at inopportune moments and flipped his heart with a wisp of a smile. She even had him questioning his steadfast beliefs.

A semi-trailer whooshed past in the next lane, too close, causing him to veer to the left. Lauren stirred and stretched her back, blinked and gave him an apologetic smile.

'I fell asleep.'

'I noticed. Sweet dreams?'

'I can't remember. Why?'

'You sighed a couple of times, low and contented. Cancel the hotel booking, Lauren. Stay with me.' Blunt and rushed—not as he'd practised. 'Sorry, I had a persuasive speech planned. Logical reasons to…'

He stopped midsentence as she silently bent, took her mobile from her bag and scrolled for the number. He shook his head to clear his muddled brain and closed his open mouth. Elation zapped along his veins. She'd be there to welcome him in the evenings. They'd have quiet hours to talk and long nights to hold each other.

'Done. I can do one-day trips to the southern area or the hills.' She dropped her phone into the drinks holder.

They were approaching the turn-off sign and he checked his rear-vision mirror in preparation for switching lanes. Pulling up at the lights, he covered her hand and revelled in the heat surge that simple act generated.

'And be home for dinner?'

'Oh, if you're expecting meals like Clair served us, you'll be disappointed. I'm very basic, usually cook for one or have cold meat and salad.'

'You've seen my fridge. It's been takeaway or dine out since I arrived home. We'll improvise as we go. I have dinner with my parents on Mondays and call in after work whenever I can.'

'They need your support so that mustn't change. And you can't neglect your sister's family either.'

'I won't. They and Alan are the ones who've kept me grounded and sustained me through it all.'

'You're lucky to have them.'

He flicked her a quick glance. It was a genuine remark with no undertone of acrimony.

'We never tried that pub near the unit. Wanna give it a go tonight?'

Wednesday's dinner was crumbed lamb chops and salad, followed by bakery fruit pie and carton custard. As basic as you could get. Lauren thanked the stars for the local butcher whose selection of ready-to-cook meals was superb and included helpful advice.

She'd revised her plans, exploring Adelaide suburbs and southern coastal areas on alternate days to limit the long drives. Today she'd been to the museum and art gallery in the city, tomorrow's choice was the Fleurieu Peninsula's historic towns.

Their evenings were casual yet special to her. They'd have a quick run of the taped news followed by lively discussions as they watched a favourite programme or two.

The nights held mutually shared passion and deep, peaceful sleep.

They lived in the moment. The future was never discussed but she wondered if he thought about it as much as she did.

Anticipation thrummed through her at the sound of his car. Soon she'd have to learn to live without the tingles over her skin, the breathlessness and the tom-tom racing of her pulse.

'Lauren.' She loved his homecoming routine: the same raspy greeting, the same admiration in his midnight-blue eyes, and the deep loving kiss, lasting until the need for air broke them apart. Plus for her the same intense pang to her heart.

'Mmm…' He nuzzled her neck, then sniffed appreciatively. 'Dinner smells almost as good as you. Let's talk 'til it's ready.'

What had happened? Bad news about his father's actions or the company? Serious talking was for as they ate, then forgotten in the pleasures of the evening. The way he grasped her fingers as they sat on the sofa was different, and disturbed her. *He was nervous.*

'What do you have planned for Friday?'

'A tram ride and walk on the beach.'

'Without me?' His eyebrow quirk and sudden grin confused her even more.

'Drive in with me, process the work I need done then go for your walk.'

'And?'

He seemed loath to continue, his eyes dark and intense, trying to predict her reaction to his announcement.

'I've got tickets for the Crows' game in the evening.'

Relief had her sagging into the cushions. That was all? He didn't want to upset her by leaving her alone for a few hours?

'That fine, Matt. It'll do you good to let off steam and I can amuse myself.'

Matt knew damn well she could, how self-reliant she was. While relishing the times she'd depended on him, he also loved her independent spirit. She'd admitted to rethinking her relationship with her family. Now he was hoping Friday's outing would help her move on.

'Two for Alan and his date and one for me.' He paused, eyes on her face. 'The fourth is for you.'

Her reaction was everything he'd hoped for. Wide eyes, gold specks sparkling. Red lips parted and inviting. Index finger pointing at his chest.

'I told you I don't attend matches, only watch bits when I'm visiting friends who have the television on. Take some-one else.'

She was magnificent, head high, chin jutted and eyes that flashed defiance. He stored the memory and prepared to counter.

He caught her finger in one hand, and cupped her chin with the other, stroking the silken underside of her stubborn jaw. Inhaled deeply as her eyes softened in response to his action. He so wanted to let her off the hook but it was more important to have her exorcise this demon.

'Lauren, you bound the whole concept of your perceived lack of parental attention with the sports your brothers played. Come and put it to the test. One game. Share a Crows win with me. Supper's on Alan.'

She looked down, bit her lip, and made a flimsy attempt to free her hand. It took little effort for him to hold on. She finally peered up at him and tilted her head.

'Do they still sell hot dogs?'

His heart swelled to bursting point. She was adorable.

'As many as you want, darling.' He pulled her into his arms and if the oven's timer hadn't rung, dinner would have been served a lot later.

* * *

Lauren liked Kaye at first sight when she arrived in the office with Alan and pizza. She was a trim, toned extrovert and an avid Crows fan, wearing all the club regalia and waving a beanie at a protesting Matt.

She also had a photo on her mobile screen showing a litter of squirming newborn puppies. A wriggling mixture of brown, white and black.

'You promised to wear it for the rest of the year if I found a suitable puppy for your nephews. These are a cross breed of black Labrador and German shepherd. They'll be gentle and protective, perfect for active children. You get first pick and they'll be ready to take home in five or six weeks.'

'They're adorable. Are you going to let the boys choose?' Lauren enthused, wishing she could have one too. Not practical with her profession or in an apartment.

'Under supervision, otherwise we'll end up with a car full,' Matt insisted, jamming on the hat. He'd cleared his desk for the meal and, when the others went to fetch chairs from Lauren's office, he muttered in her ear.

'She cheated, made the deal when our forward was lining up for a winning goal, sixty metres out and less than a minute on the clock.'

'If you agreed, it's binding.' She grinned at the usually stylishly dressed man—even in casual clothes on the weekend—now in well-worn jeans, football jumper and that distinctive beanie. And loved him even more.

'You siding with Kaye?' He gave her a hard, lip-smacking kiss. 'I can think of a few bets I'd willingly lose to you.'

She recalled hours of sitting rugged up on cold benches, being bumped and bruised by excited supporters. She thought of days wasted setting up stalls, being bored and trying to persuade people to buy merchandise or raffle tickets. Now she looked into hungry blue eyes and knew she'd go through all of that in a thunderstorm if he were beside her.

* * *

Matt kept a tight hold on her hand as they walked to the stadium, joining an ever-growing throng that bottlenecked at the bridge over the river. He kept telling himself this was for her but that excuse was wearing thin. It was he who wanted to share his enthusiasm for their national game, who wanted to see her lose her inhibitions and cheer with the mob. It was he who wanted her with him when they played in the finals.

It was a full house by the time they bounced the ball for the start and the noise was deafening. For the first time ever his concentration wasn't out there with the players. He watched Lauren, quite prepared to take her out if she became stressed. Instead he saw interest grow as her eyes darted from the field to the big screens and back.

His heart usually pounded at the fierce interaction between players, now it was because she leant forward as they ran, held her breath as they shot for goal and flopped back when they missed. By the fourth quarter, she was on her feet with Kaye every time the lead changed, face flushed and eyes shining. And he didn't care an iota that he missed most of the action on the field.

'A twenty-eight-point win. Our best this year.' Kaye danced up the steps, arms swaying with her scarf held high. 'You must be our lucky charm, Lauren.'

Matt hugged her close 'You are definitely mine.'

Lauren clung to him, treasuring his words. The excitement had been contagious. Her head spun, whether from the buzz of the crowd or the shock of discovering the thrill of the game overrode her inhibitions, she wasn't sure. As if tied to Kaye with invisible bonds, she'd found herself leaping to her feet and calling out phrases she'd never spoken, hadn't known she'd memorised.

Matt was grinning as if he'd been the star forward. Not a smug, I-told-you-so smile; he was genuinely happy for her.

Had she been wrong all her life or was she seeing everything through new eyes? And if she had changed because she loved him, why couldn't he love her for the person he was helping her to become?

Monday afternoon Matt decided to grab a chicken wrap on the way back from the bank. Funny how easily he'd adapted to healthier meals and salads. Not funny that in a week he'd be eating alone again.

Lauren. His pulse hiked up, and he quickened his pace as he saw her opening the door of a café across the street. He halted when she spoke to the dark-haired woman entering behind her. She hadn't mentioned meeting anyone.

By the time he'd crossed at the lights and walked along, they were seated at a table studying menus. An old friend she'd caught up with? He wouldn't disturb them; she'd tell him over dinner tonight.

She didn't. She was quiet and withdrawn, claiming fatigue and a headache. Concerned, he persuaded her to take a tablet and go to bed. In the morning he left her sleeping.

Tuesday was no different. She blamed it on the current autumn virus and he had to admit she looked unwell, though she didn't cough or sneeze. Was she depressed thinking of the shrinking time they had left? That he understood.

He'd never considered a cross-country romance. There'd never been a reason to. The idea of seeing Lauren only on weekends was gut-wrenching but better than not being with her at all. Would she be prepared to try?

Alan's text came through as he was driving to work Wednesday morning, and he read the short, concise message in the lift. Apprehensive, and with fingers tapping his desk, he accessed the online morning papers. The small article tucked away in one of the business sections sent his world crashing in flames.

Names weren't mentioned but anyone with determination and knowledge of the company or his father could identify them. Obscure hints were made of illness, legalities and the long-term viability of the business. His temper rose as he researched the reporter, found her profile and photo.

And his fragile faith was obliterated in a torrent of bitterness, far worse than all the other betrayals combined. This was the woman Lauren had been with on Monday, the reason for her reticence since.

She was one of the very few who had knowledge of his father's dementia *and* fraud. What reason could there be for meeting that woman? Why?

His chest heaved, and anger ruled as he reached for his keys. Threw them down, snatched up his mobile, and paced the floor until Lauren answered.

'Matt?'

Diffident and wary. Guilty?

'Who was the woman you were with on Monday?' Grated out without polite niceties.

Her quick gasp sharpened his pain. Her silence exacerbated his temper.

'She's a damn reporter. What did you tell her?'

'You… I'm…'

'Lost for words, Lauren. What am I? A magnet for cheats and liars? Dad, Christine, and now you? Do you have any idea what I…? No, you wouldn't. I can't bear to see you. Don't want to hear your voice.'

He hung up, tossed his phone on the coffee table and sank into a chair, burying his head into his hands. This was it. He'd never fully trust anyone again.

CHAPTER SIXTEEN

LAUREN CURLED UP on his settee, buried her head into his cushion and sobbed at his tirade. How could he believe she'd break her promise?

Idiot, stupid, stupid idiot. She hadn't realised the woman was a reporter until she'd begun to ask about Marcus. Fearing he might be annoyed that she'd been duped into the conversation, she hadn't told him. Things the woman had hinted she knew could only have come from one of the select few people he trusted implicitly.

He hadn't said what the reporter had claimed to know, only accused her of telling family secrets, and she had no way of proving her innocence. Maybe if she had been truthful with him he'd be looking for the real culprit. Instead he'd condemned her without even seeing her, proof his caring had been superficial.

She rubbed the tears from her cheeks, and went to wash her face with a cold flannel. The red-eyed wreck in the mirror gave her no choice.

She loved him so she'd make it easier for him. He didn't want to see her so she wouldn't be here when he came home. She booked a flight, packed her belongings and called a taxi.

Matt hadn't needed his cousin's harsh rebuke over the phone to know he'd been wrong to call her in anger. Personal confrontation when he could see her eyes and read her expression would have been better. Didn't change the reality. Or did it?

Alan had rung to say he'd done what Matt should have—checked and found out the reporter was ambitious, and not particularly scrupulous in her methods of obtaining information.

He couldn't postpone the morning's scheduled meeting though he came close to doing just that. It was crucial to the company's survival, especially after today's media article. With the prospect of legal proceedings giving him motivation, he blocked Lauren from his mind and went to the boardroom to fight for his and the company's future.

He deliberately stayed late at the office, arriving home to a dark and silent unit. Refusing to acknowledge the sour churning in his gut, he walked in.

I can't bear to see you. Don't want to hear your voice.

His words echoed in his head. He sagged against the door jamb leading to the kitchen area. The table was bare. The vase had gone. Lauren had gone.

Lauren had never felt more alone. She ached for Matt's smile, his spine-tingling touch, and his midnight-blue eyes that could make her pulse race from across a room. She even missed his cajoling her to reassess her relationship with her family.

Knowing he believed she'd betrayed him tore her apart. Knowing she had unconditional support from her friends held her together. Whatever they suspected, they'd never push, would give her all the time she needed until she was ready to confide in them.

On Wednesday night, she cried herself to sleep, reliving his caresses, his kisses. The passion they'd shared. On Thursday she wandered aimlessly for hours, stopping only for drinks and an occasional snack. On Friday morning she went to see her employer and resigned. When she got back to the units, Pete was home so she told him.

'You can't, Lauren. You're the best. You love digging out the solutions where others have failed. You...' Words failed him and his arms flailed in the air.

Lauren shrugged. She'd lost enthusiasm for her work, and her heart hurt every second of every day. Matt didn't want her, didn't love her and had never really trusted her. He hadn't bothered to ring but she'd have blocked the call if he had. His throaty voice was implanted in her brain. She heard it every night as she lay alone in her single bed. Didn't need to hear the reality and have her heart ripped apart even more.

'I'm going to teach.'

Pete made a scoffing sound, and dropped down beside her on the sofa. 'You'll be bored and climbing the walls in a week. And the salary's crap.'

'Private lessons to adults. One on one showing them just the functions they want to use on their own personal computers. I've done it for friends, and they all said they knew people who'd pay for the service.'

'You've thought it through? It's really what you want?'

'For now it's what I need, Pete. Who knows what's ahead?'

Nothing but memories and what-ifs for her. Her throat tightened—it seemed to do that a lot lately—her breath hitched, and she shivered.

In an instant she was wrapped in friendly arms, her head was cradled to his shoulder and his hand made soothing strokes over her back.

'I'd like to find the guy who hurt you and feed the most destructive viruses I can find into his computer system. *And him.*'

She choked up at the thought of polite, pacifist Pete going into battle for her. She felt warm and cared for, knowing he meant it and that the others would back him up. They might not have Matt's name or details of the breakup but he was now the enemy.

Easing away, she stood up and brushed off the few tears that had escaped.

'Save your knight-in-armour mode for Jenny. He wasn't

completely to blame. He'd been betrayed by someone he trusted and circumstances showed me in a suspicious light.'

'Loving means trusting.'

Which again proved Matt didn't love her.

'And the only way is forward. I'll take each day as it comes.'

And hide my torment in the dark nights.

All Matt wanted to do was to cower in a dark corner and lick his wounds. Nothing he'd suffered before had prepared him for the gut-wrenching pain whenever he thought of her, which was almost every minute of every day. He lay awake remembering the nights they'd spent together, reached out for her in his restless sleep on the couch.

The sun was rising as he drove into the city on Monday, an unneeded reminder of last weekend. Telling himself he was better off without her had no effect. His brain kept repeating one word over and over. Why?

Mid-morning he brewed another mug of strong coffee, couldn't bear to drink it in his office. Even with the connecting door shut, he kept glancing that way as if she'd suddenly appear. He walked to the boardroom because she'd never been in there but she came with him now, in his head and his heart. There was no escape.

On the way back, the lift doors opened as he went through Reception and Clair stepped out. Surprised by her tentative smile when she saw him, he walked over.

'I didn't expect to see you, Clair. You're always welcome, of course.'

'I had to come. Can we talk?'

Her apprehension triggered a kindred unease. That damn article? Duncan had already assured him the reporter's insinuations hadn't affected his opinion at all. There was nothing he wasn't aware of and their association wouldn't change. He was also convinced the people who mattered wouldn't equate Marcus's condition with Matt's aptitude to run the company.

'Of course, this way.' He guided her to his office, and over to the window seats.

'Coffee or tea?'

'Not now. Please, Matt, sit down. This is personal and it concerns you.'

His gut tightened as he obeyed. Lauren? He'd told Duncan she'd returned to Sydney. Not why.

She fiddled with the handle of her bag then dropped it onto the floor. He leant forward and took her hand, shocked to feel its trembling.

'What's wrong, Clair? If there's anything I can do, just ask.'

'It's the other way round, Matt. I came because I'm partly responsible for that reporter's knowledge, limited though it was.'

'You?' He shook his head, couldn't take it in. A chill seeped into his muscles and he dreaded hearing more.

'Your mother came to our group lunch two weeks ago, first time for ages. We were chatting in a quiet corner and she began to tell me about her problems with your father and his deterioration. I should have suggested we talk later somewhere more private but she was desperate to let it all out.'

The chill became icy. Every cell in his body seemed to shrink and close down. He had a vague awareness of letting go of her hand, of his shoulders slumping.

'She said your father kept telling her things she knew weren't true or dropping hints about special funding for his secret hideaway retirement. She didn't want to worry you or the family with his fantasies, just wanted someone to sympathise with her.'

His mother had confided in a friend because he'd built barriers between them. She'd been overheard and Lauren was innocent. The reporter had been trying to get confirmation or more details. It was as if he heard the facts but couldn't process them through the fog in his head.

'Duncan showed me the article, and this morning I found out the woman who wrote it had been at the venue. I noticed her hanging around, and assumed she was a guest. I'm so sorry, Matt.'

Oh, Lauren, what have I done?

Guilt and anguish raked him, his throat clogged, and his stomach heaved. Condemnation roared in his head. Sweat dripped down his back, and his fingers balled into fists.

'Matt. Matt, are you all right?'

His mind cleared. Clair was leaning forward, regarding him with deep concern. He shuddered back to reality.

He'd listened to her, heard what *she* said. He hadn't heard Lauren's explanation because he hadn't given her a chance to tell him.

'No. I think I've made the worst, stupidest mistake of my life and I'm not sure she'll ever forgive me.'

'Lauren?'

He nodded, too ashamed to speak.

Clair patted his knee. 'Go and tell her in those exact words. Lauren loves you, Matt, and we women in love can forgive our men almost anything if they love us too.'

Could they? Would Lauren, after his bitter accusations?

Lauren stared at the four family-sized pizza boxes and clutched her fingers in her lap. She'd always begged off the Monday pizza, footy and whatever-you-want-to-drink evenings in Pete and Jenny's unit. Why had she agreed to come tonight?

Because she wanted to prove she could watch an Aussie Rules game without breaking down. And she would as long as she didn't think of the crowded Adelaide oval and being crushed against a warm, muscular body in the crowd.

'So, did you keep that appointment with your boss, Lauren? Has he made an offer you can't refuse to get you to stay?' Jenny leant forward and opened the top box, the aroma evoking memories of the last time she'd been in Matt's office.

'We talked. He wants me to consider freelancing for him whenever he gets a job he thinks worthy of my talents. His expression. Soft soap and flattery. I think he's hoping I'll relent and come back full time after I've had a break.'

'Could happen.'

'I doubt it but the idea of a real challenge now and again is tempting.'

The last one had been and look how that ended. No chance of a repeat. She'd fallen in love and lost her heart to Matt Dalton, irretrievable and never to be reclaimed. The pain would subside and become a dull ache she'd learn to live with.

Matt needed someone to confess to, someone who'd listen, tell him what a drongo he'd been, and offer to help find her. The one person who'd shared all his dreams and aspirations, almost every failure and heartbreak. As soon as he'd finished essential work, he took a taxi to Alan's city apartment, picking up Chinese food on the way.

The food was hot and spicy, and the cold beer from the fridge slid smoothly down his throat giving him courage to begin. He lounged back, crossing his ankles.

'Lauren was my balcony girl.'

Alan stopped chewing and stared.

'You're kidding? I don't remember seeing her that night and she'd have been noticeable even then. *You* definitely never forgot her.'

'No, she was always there, even when I was contemplating marriage to someone else. I didn't realise who she was until I kissed her again.'

He almost lost it as the memory seared his brain. Closed his eyes, picturing hazel eyes full of passion, and a smile that always sent his pulse soaring.

'I'm an idiot, Alan. A blind, insensitive idiot who didn't have the nous to see the truth in front of me or the guts to claim the sweetest prize any man was ever offered.'

His cousin nodded. 'I agree. Now you tell me what happened and we'll work out how you find her, grovel like a lovesick fool—which you'll happily be—and win her back.'

Matt spilled his guts, taking all the blame. He'd cursed himself for not asking more about her life, her suburb, or the names of her friends. She wasn't in the phone directory and he hadn't been able to locate her on social media. Her employer had offered to forward any mail he sent, after justifiably refusing to divulge personal information. Apologetic words on paper could never convey his guilt and remorse. He needed to see her, hold her and beg for forgiveness.

'My last hope is to contact one of her brothers but they'd probably ask why and refuse if I tell the truth. All I know is she lives on the same floor as her friends, in a suburban block of units in Sydney. I didn't bother to ask her anything—'

He jerked upright, beer spraying onto his jeans and the floor.

'The form.' He sprang to his feet, dumping the can on the table. 'Come on—you drive.'

'What form? Where?

Matt was already halfway to the door.

'The personnel form I filed without bothering to read it. Her name and address, contact number in case of an emergency, et cetera.'

Ten minutes later Matt perched on *her* desk and read the form out loud.

'"Lauren Juliet Taylor", her address and mobile phone number. And—' the rush of joyful adrenaline almost tipped him off the desk '—"Peter Williams", her friend in the apartment opposite hers.' He punched the air in triumph. 'I've got where she lives. I've got her friend's number. And with his help, I've got a plan.'

Lauren fumbled in her shoulder bag for her keys as she took the last few steps to the third floor. Her first private lesson had been a success and her next three Tuesday afternoons were taken.

If even half her future clients were as good as feisty seventy-two-year-old Mary—or seventy-two years *young* as she'd claimed—her new occupation would be a pleasure. She'd listened intently, made copious notes in a neat legible hand, and was willing to give anything a go. She claimed making mistakes was part of living.

If that was the case, Lauren was certainly alive, so why did she feel numb inside? There was…

A large vase containing an incredible arrangement of orchids on the landing outside her door. Her foot caught on the last stair. She couldn't breathe, couldn't form a coherent thought.

Orchids: deep reds, yellow with leopard spots, and lilac ones of every shade imaginable. She stumbled forward and fell onto her knees, her trembling fingers reaching out to touch the soft petals, confirm they weren't her imagination.

Tears flooded her eyes. Her heart hammered into life, sending her blood racing to regenerate every pulse point. Orchids. Matt. Linked together in her mind for ever.

'Lauren?'

Broken, rasping voice. Trembling arms clasped her in a strong embrace. Warm lips pressed to her forehead. Disbelief scrambled her brain, and hope fluttered in her stomach.

'Don't cry, my love. Please, don't cry.'

My love. Matt's voice saying words she wouldn't dare to dream. Matt kneeling beside her, his body warm and solid, and his heart thudding under her hand. Matt's fingers lovingly stroking her cheek, and tilting her chin.

She barely had time to register dark shadows under his compassionate blue eyes before he kissed her. Not with the smooth arrogance of the youth, or the competent skill of the sophisticated man. Hesitant, unsure of her response.

She wanted the passionate lover who'd taken her to the moon and beyond, and refused to settle for less. Wrapping her arms around his neck, she tangled her fingers in his hair, binding him to her. She teased him with the tip of her tongue and nipped his lip with her teeth.

In an instant he crushed her against him, chased her tongue back inside with his, stroking and tangling, claiming his rights as her man. His hands caressed her, fuelling fires she'd believed extinguished. His breathing was as ragged as her own.

Voices echoed up the stairwell and he lifted his head, chest heaving, throat convulsing and eyes gleaming.

'Inside?' Rough and barely audible.

Unable to speak, she nodded, and looked round for the keys she'd dropped. Matt picked them up and helped her to her feet. Her fingers trembled too much to take them, and her heart flipped at his unsteady attempts to unlock the door.

He followed her in, stopped just inside gazing wide-eyed at her home.

Her home, where she'd spent six tortured nights berating the fool that she'd been to fall in love with him. Where she listlessly performed necessary chores, and agonised over a solitary future without him.

He stood there as if he were a returning hero carrying his gift like the spoils of war. And the anguish and heartache she'd suffered surged into a torrent of anger at his injustice.

'No.'

CHAPTER SEVENTEEN

HIS BODY JERKED, his brow furrowed, and his mouth fell open.

'You bring flowers and expect what you did to be wiped away and forgotten? You judged me guilty without proof, willingly believed I lied to you.' She retreated as she spoke, torn between aching for him and never wanting to suffer like this again.

'You never trusted me from the day we met. You were willing and eager to take me to bed but never prepared to give anything of yourself. Except your body for your own pleasure.'

'No. No, Lauren. I was…'

'Protecting yourself.'

His features contorted. He raised his hands, blinked as the orchids came into his view, and strode across the room to place them on her bookshelf. He turned to face her, his hands reaching out to her, and his dark beseeching eyes pleaded for understanding.

Her heart clamoured for her to run into his arms, surrender and forgive. But he'd disowned her over the phone, without giving her a chance to explain.

She straightened her shoulders and lifted her chin. When his hands fell then one rose to rake through his hair, her fingers itched to join it.

Flowers and kisses came easily to him. If he thought he could win her over by…

'How did you get into the building?'

He broke eye contact, and stared at her cream velour sofa with its colourful cushions. Typical Matt, plotting his reply instead of saying what he felt.

'Can we sit and talk? Please, Lauren. I know I've been a drongo and selfish as hell. And the dumbest prize idiot for not admitting even to myself that I love you.'

Her world slammed to a shuddering halt. The air rushed from her lungs, her legs trembled, threatening to buckle, and she leant on the breakfast bar for support.

'No, you don't.' Breathless. Distrustful.

The adoration in his eyes stirred the cold embers in her core, and she scrunched her fingers, wouldn't fold. He'd coerced her so many times. She'd need more than words to risk her heart again.

She moved to the sofa, determined to conceal the effect of the hot tendrils of desire weaving their way to every extremity as he joined her. Leaving space between them, he spread his arm along the back and hooked one ankle over the other knee—a simple, familiar habit that chipped at her resistance.

'Pete let me in.'

This wasn't going the way Matt had planned. He'd been wrong in so many ways, including persuading her to face her demons while fooling himself about his own.

He'd banked on her being thrilled with the flowers, and melting into his arms. Seeing her on her knees with tears streaming down her face had shattered him.

Her response to his kiss had been all he could have wished for. She cared. They'd talk and she'd forgive him. They'd make love and work out how they could be together.

Lauren had stunned him with her hostile stance and accusation, her flashing hazel eyes demanding he fight for her, and prove he was worthy of her love. Living without her had been hell. Together they could build their own heaven.

'You named Pete as your contact on the company's personnel form I'd filed without reading. I had completely forgotten about it until yesterday. He was tough to convince, but finally agreed to meet me with no guarantees of help. He also threatened to take me apart if I ever hurt you again.'

Her lips curved and he found himself grinning at the

image too. He had height and weight advantages but he had no doubt Pete's threat was sincere.

'I have…had trust issues. I never saw my parents kiss or be affectionate, and rarely heard them argue. Came home one evening and it was full on. He'd been having affairs for most of their married life. She put up with it because she wanted the lifestyle he provided. I was gutted at their hypocrisy.'

'That's why you left Australia.' She leant towards him. The tightness in his gut eased, and he ground out the rest.

'He used his business premises for rendezvous.'

'The bedroom?'

'I've never been in there. It's a tangible reminder of his adultery, and I swore I'd never be like him. That's what always stopped me from kissing you in the office.'

She shuffled a bit closer, and covered his outstretched hand with hers. As always with her touch, his heart beat faster, and his temperature rose. He needed to get the truth out, have no more secrets. Then he could hold her again.

'Apart from the woman in London, I knew others, male and female, who believed fidelity was outmoded. Faithful couples seemed to be a minority, or maybe my pride saw it that way as proof my father wasn't so contemptible. If I didn't believe in love their relationship wasn't abnormal.'

He took a chance and moved towards her. She stopped him with a hand on his chest, eyes wary and sceptical.

'You didn't want any of the photos.'

He caught her hand, raised it to his lips and kissed her palm. Rejoiced in her quivering reaction, and his own. Regaining her trust was paramount so he fought the craving to enfold her in arms and kiss her the way he had in the hall.

'*They* were for you. I ordered another set, which should have told me how special the evening with you was, and how much you already meant to me. It came the day after you left.'

His thumb began an automatic caress of her knuckles.

When she didn't pull free, he closed his eyes and took a long breath.

'I refused to believe in love even though I knew couples who proved me wrong. My experiences, including suspicion of my father's computer deception, gave me little reason to trust in any sphere of life.

'Then you walked into my office and all my resolutions collapsed. I fell in love, probably had ten years ago and hadn't been mature enough to recognise it. I stubbornly ignored the reality when we met again.'

Her smile grew as he spoke, her beautiful hazel eyes glowed, and his resolve crashed. He gathered her into his arms where she belonged, setting his world right. A different aroma, as alluring as the other, filled his nostrils. He brushed his lips across her forehead, and if his heart beat any faster, he'd short circuit.

'Matt?' She raised her head, a tiny furrow creasing her brow. 'That reporter…'

'She overheard my mother talking at a luncheon and started digging. I should have come home and talked to you. Instead I let my past rule my head. I couldn't admit, even to myself, that only you had the power to break my heart. My stupid pride almost destroyed us both.'

'She said she knew Clair, implied things about your father. I swear I told her I didn't know what she was talking about.'

'I believe you. I'll never doubt you again, my darling. I love you. With all my heart and all that I am.'

He kissed her deeply, lovingly with no reservations. Cradled her as close as humanly possible, only breaking away to breathe. Found the air clogged his throat at the love shining in her eyes.

'I love you too, Matt.'

He slipped from the sofa onto his knees in front of her and held her hands in his.

'Lauren Taylor, you are sweet and courageous, and I'll love you 'til my last breath and beyond. I'm yours, only yours, for ever. Marry me?'

Lauren couldn't speak. Her head spun as if she'd drunk too much champagne; the electrical zing from his fingers through hers was zapping along her veins at airship speed. Her already pounding heart threatened to burst from her ribcage.

The love in Matt's eyes wrapped her in an aura of soft warmth, a haven where there were only gentle caresses and love. A special place of devotion and commitment. For two.

'Yes. Oh, yes, please. I love you, Matt. I'm yours, now and for ever.'

He let out a roar of triumph, scooped her up and swung her round. She clung to him as her joyous laughter mingled with his. When he stopped, his kiss was gentle, reverent. He laid his forehead to hers.

'I ache to make love to you, darling, but I promised Pete and Jenny we'd go and tell them the good news.'

'Confident, huh?' She tried to sound stern; it came out husky and adoring.

'Optimistically hoping I hadn't misread the signs when we were together, the passion when we made love. No way was I going to walk away unless you looked me in the eyes and swore you never wanted to see me again.'

He kissed her again then set her on her feet and nuzzled her neck.

'We'll still have all night.'

Matt missed the earliest flight home in the morning, caught the next and went straight to the office. He stood in the doorway, taking in the expensive décor, the stunning views and his father's top-of-the-range desk. He didn't need all this to define himself, never had.

Knowing Lauren loved him gave him a goal to be better than he was. It was time to lay the first ghost to rest. He strode purposefully across the deluxe tiles, through the first door and into the bedroom.

It was neat, tidy and impersonal. Overwhelming sorrow shook him as he thought of how much his father had risked for the brief encounters in this cold place. He thought of his mother knowing the truth and living a lie.

Closing his eyes, he conjured up Lauren's lovely face as he'd kissed her goodbye, hair tousled, eyes shining. Together they'd face the uncertainties ahead. Together—a couple united by a vow to share life's fears and sorrows, its triumphs and joys.

Leaving youth's judgement and bitterness behind, he scrolled for his mother's number. From today he'd make up for the years of estrangement.

That evening, Matt held his mother close without censure and, for the first time in nine years, embraced his father. The hug he received in return filled his heart with love and relief.

Marcus was almost his old self and pleased with the gift of his favourite wine. As Matt opened it he regretted missed opportunities like this, reflected on his culpability then let it go. The past couldn't be changed but it could be left behind if they were all willing to face the future.

'I'm in love with a very special lady and she's agreed to marry me.' He couldn't keep it in any longer, and was elated at how good the words sounded out loud. Even more so when his mother hugged and kissed him and his father shook his hand.

'She's flying in from Sydney on Friday and I'd like Lena, Mark and the boys to join us here for lunch on Saturday to meet her.'

Before he left he had a private talk with his mother, pledging his and Lauren's support in caring for his father.

They'd sworn together to keep their knowledge of his father's infidelity a secret from her, saving her any more pain.

Finally acknowledging that loving someone meant accepting their faults and weaknesses, he put his arm around her. Holding her close, he regretted the years they'd lost.

'I was young, arrogant and so very wrong to keep distance between us for so long. If I hadn't you'd have been able to confide in *me* and that reporter would never have had a story to write.'

'You have your father's pride, Matthew. Promise me you won't let it come between you and Lauren.'

'I promise. She's more than I deserve, and is willing to help us keep Dad at home with you as long as possible.'

She wrapped her arms around him and he clung tight, grateful that he had the chance to make amends and heal the rift between them.

Mid-winter, the twenty-third of June. Lauren woke before the alarm, stretched and smiled at the blue skies behind the treetops outside. Sunshine as predicted for her winter wedding day, though not even a cyclone could mar the occasion. Tonight she'd be Mrs Matthew Dalton.

She threw back the covers, and ran to the shower, leaving the door open in case he rang early. He did, but by then she was perched on the side of the bed, wearing her dressing gown, and combing her towel-dry hair.

'Happy wedding day, my love. I missed you.' The sound of his voice, gravel rough from sleep, was her favourite way of starting each day.

'Me too, Matt. I'm lost in this bed without you.' She lay back into the pillows, wishing he were here beside her in the Fords' guest suite.

'Wasn't my idea to spend the night apart. Clair and our mothers ganged up on me. Never going to happen again if I can prevent it.' The low growl in his voice skittled up and down her spine. He'd only begrudgingly agreed after she'd said it would please the older women.

'I'll make it up to you.' She dropped her tone, trying for seductive, laughed when he growled again.

'You will, my love. I kept myself awake compiling a list.'

She quivered with delight, imagined ticking off each item. 'I love you, Matt. Four o'clock is a long time away.'

'Longer until we're alone. Then we have two weeks, just you and me where no one can find us.'

Someone tapped on her door.

'I have to go. I've got company.'

'Look in the bottom drawer on my side of the bed, darling. I'll see you at four. I love you, Lauren.'

Her mother peeped in as she ended the call. Along with thrilling Matt and Lauren with the offer of their home and grounds for the wedding, Duncan and Clair had invited her parents to stay with them for the event.

Accepting there would always be differences between herself and her family had allowed her to form a real bond with them. Matt had ensured no one on her guest list was absent, and hotels and guest houses in neighbouring towns were filled with relatives and friends from interstate.

'You're awake. Happy wedding day, darling.' Her mother hugged and kissed her, and sat on the edge of the bed.

Do you want to come for a walk with me, Clair and the dogs after a quick breakfast? It's going to be chaotic once the trucks start arriving with the marquee, and everything.'

'Give me ten minutes and I'll see you on the veranda.'

As soon as her mother left Lauren dived over the bed, pulled the drawer open, and took out a small black box. She gasped with joy at the delicate yellow pendant and earrings. A real full orchid and two orchid centres preserved in resin with their true colours.

Matt's message, handwritten on the small white card,

was memorised, never to be forgotten. Every word of the text she sent him came from her heart.

It didn't turn out to be so long after all when the hours were filled with the walk, meals and watching the lawn areas being transformed into a perfect venue for her dream wedding. She agreed to a hair stylist but did her own make-up, her hand as steady as her heartbeat. And every two hours she slipped away to be alone when Matt called, their secret pact to keep in touch throughout their special day.

Marcus and Rosalind arrived and she shared a quiet time with the two sets of parents. Her future father-in-law had no idea he'd been spared prosecution because of his deteriorating condition and the fact that no withdrawals had been made from the secret accounts. Everything had been transferred into the company files and all due taxes paid with interest for late submission.

Dalton Corporation had a new direction, the contracts for the new project had been signed last month, and Matt was the official CEO. He and his colleague in London were negotiating the sale of his flat and his shares in the consultancy firm.

The way everything fell into place, and ran smoothly to favourable solutions, sometimes scared her. Then she'd look into Matt's eyes, and know that, whatever troubles they encountered, he'd be there to love and support her, and smooth their way forward.

It was ten minutes to four. There was a chill in the air, and all areas were dotted with outdoor heaters. Somewhere in the garden Matt was waiting for her, as impatient as she was to make the vows that would join them for life.

She saw the rows of seated people waiting as her father escorted her across the veranda, looked beyond them to the decorated arch where the celebrant stood with…

Everything bar the man who'd turned towards her became lost in a haze that surrounded her. Matt, who'd taught her to let her true self shine, and showed her she was worthy of being loved. There was only Matt and his irresistible smile, his electric touch and those oh-so-persuasive lips drawing her closer. Only his midnight-blue eyes growing misty as she reached him. Only him, his gentle kiss and whispered words as he embraced her.

Matt would never find the words to express the emotions that rippled through his body when he turned to see Lauren at the top of the veranda steps. A vision in white was inadequate. She was gorgeous, stunning, and wearing his wedding gift.

This beautiful woman who'd captured his heart and soul as she helped him save his father's company and reputation. His own special angel who filled his days and nights with love and laughter.

Their eyes locked and the world disappeared as he willed her to his side. He acknowledged her father's traditional greeting automatically, his focus on Lauren's dazzling smile. Drawing her into his arms, he kissed her soft lips and whispered how much she meant to him.

They stood face to face, hands joined. Ten years ago he'd asked for a prize and claimed a kiss. He might not deserve her, but today he was claiming the best, the sweetest, the most loving woman as his for ever.

* * * * *

*If you enjoy office romances,
look out for the next 9 TO 5 title,
MISS PRIM AND THE MAVERICK MILLIONAIRE
by Nina Singh—on sale next month!*

WILLA'S FAMOUS S'MORES

A long time ago back in LA, I made this with my— well, let's just say with some people I shared my life with. They're gone now, but I've always held tight to the special memories of making this recipe with them. I'm in Thunder Ridge now, a town full of caring people... and a sheriff who keeps challenging my heart. I'm not sure I'm ready to love again, but I am ready to share these homemade treats with you.
PS: I'm letting you in on my closely guarded secret!

Ingredients:
4 graham crackers
2 marshmallows
2 chocolate squares
2 metal skewers
metal grill basket

1. Lightly warm the graham crackers and chocolate by placing them in a metal grill basket high over the flame. The secret is making the crackers soft. Like love, it's all about not getting broken!

2. Skewer the marshmallow and hold it far enough away that the flame is just teasing it. Be careful not to burn it.

3. Stack a graham cracker, chocolate square and marshmallow, and top with another cracker.

This recipe makes two, so share them with someone you love. Tell them Willa sent you.

—Willa

* * *

The Men of Thunder Ridge:
Once you meet the men of this Oregon town,
you may never want to leave!

KISS ME, SHERIFF!

BY
WENDY WARREN

MILLS & BOON

First Published in Great Britain 2017
By Mills & Boon, an imprint of HarperCollins*Publishers*
1 London Bridge Street, London, SE1 9GF

© 2017 Wendy Warren

ISBN: 978-0-263-92282-0

23-0317

Our policy is to use papers that are natural, renewable and recyclable products and made from wood grown in sustainable forests. The logging and manufacturing processes conform to the legal environmental regulations of the country of origin.

Printed and bound in Spain
by CPI, Barcelona

Wendy Warren loves to write about ordinary people who find extraordinary love. Laughter, family and close-knit communities figure prominently, too. Her books have won two Romance Writers of America RITA® Awards and have been nominated for numerous others. She lives in the Pacific Northwest with human and non-human critters who don't read nearly as much as she'd like, but they sure do make her laugh and feel loved.

This book is dedicated to LaCorius Jenkins,
who is smart and kind, courageous and true, and a
bunch of other wonderful things. You inspire me.

"In a gentle way, you can shake the world."
—Mahatma Gandhi

Chapter One

For the folks who cared to rise early enough, 6:30 a.m. was as fine a time as any on Warm Springs Road in Thunder Ridge, Oregon. The twinkle lights that glowed steadily through the night were still on. The Valentine's Day Decorating Committee met companionably at The Pickle Jar Deli for an early breakfast and a lively debate about whether to hang cupids or giant red hearts from the corner street lamps. And, next door to the deli, Willa Holmes opened the doors to Something Sweet, the bakery she'd been managing for the past two months. Her morning regulars typically arrived shortly after she flipped the "Done for the Day" sign to the side that announced, "Yep, Open."

Now, at precisely 6:32 a.m., Willa was at work behind the counter.

"Can I tempt you with a fresh Danish this morning, Mrs. Wittenberg?" She smiled at the tiny woman whose white curls bobbed just above the top of the glass pastry case. "They're still warm from the oven."

Baking since 3:00 a.m., Willa appreciated the early start time of her new job. The wee hours of the morning used to be for sleep or, back when she was first married, for lovemaking, but now she found late night and early morning to be the most difficult parts of her day. There was too much quiet time to think. And to remember.

Having breads to proof, cookies to shape and food costs to calculate provided relief from the thoughts that kept her awake at night. Her only coworker in the morning was Norman Bluehorse, who was either fortyish or sixtyish—it was seriously hard to tell—and who worked with earbuds in place and spoke only when he needed to ask or to answer a direct question. A few years ago that might not have suited Willa, but these days she appreciated Norman's unspoken you-mind-your-business-and-I'll-mind-mine policy.

Short on sleep due to the early morning and a restless night, she tried not to yawn. Mrs. Wittenberg peered closely at her.

"Sweetheart," the older woman said, "I hope you don't mind my asking, but is your red hair natural? I'm thinking about having a makeover. I used to have beautiful long hair, too. It fell out during The Change. Did you bake anything new this morning?"

Actually I think of my hair as light auburn...yes, it's natural... Your hair is lovely as it is...the pomegranate-orange bread is new. Willa only had time to think her responses before Mrs. W moved on to a new question or comment. This was their ritual six mornings a week. Mrs. W chattered brightly, examined every potential selection in the pastry case, then chose the very same thing she'd chosen the day before and the day before that—two lemon cloud Danishes and one large molasses snap to go.

"I added a touch of ginger to the lemon clouds today," Willa told the older woman, whose pursed lips were carefully lined and filled with a creamy rose shade even at this hour of the morning. "I think you'll like them."

Mrs. Wittenberg wagged her prettily coiffed head. "I don't know, dear. I think possibly I should choose something different this morning. It's a very special day."

"Oh?" Before Willa could ask why, the door opened to admit her second customer of the morning. A zing of pure adrenaline shot through her veins with such force, she actually felt weak. While Mrs. W tapped her upper lip, trying to make a selection, Willa's attention turned to the six-foot-two-inch sheriff of Thunder Ridge.

She hadn't interacted in any meaningful way with Derek Neel for the past couple of months, except to greet him and fill his order in the morning. She'd seen him around town, too, of course—he was fairly hard to miss, patrolling Thunder Ridge's wood-planked sidewalks on foot, or making the rounds of the broad streets in his squad car. He didn't just work in town, he lived here. Two weeks ago, she'd bumped into him in the cereal aisle of Hank's Thunderbird Market on a Monday night at 9:00 p.m. Impossible to ignore each other when you were shoulder to shoulder, contemplating breakfast. He'd smiled easily, asked if she thought "instant triple berry oatmeal" sounded good and then tossed the box into his cart after she'd replied that, sure, it was worth a try (which had been a total lie, because instant oatmeal was an abomination of the real thing and never a good idea). While he'd strolled off, she had remained rooted to her spot in the aisle like the proverbial deer in headlights, her thoughts rushed and confused, her emotions in turmoil.

Fact: she and the handsome sheriff had almost... *almost*...gotten to know each other in the biblical sense on one crazy, ill-advised night two-and-a-half months ago. It had been one of those evenings when sitting with her own thoughts had seemed painful, practically impossible. She'd been filling in for a sick waitress at The Pickle Jar, next door, and when a couple of the other servers mentioned they were heading to the White Lightning Tavern for a beer and a burger, she'd invited herself along.

Derek had been there, dining with Izzy Lambert Thayer, who co-owned both The Pickle Jar, where Willa had worked as a server when she'd first arrived in town, and the bakery Something Sweet. Izzy's new husband, Nate, had arrived at one point, and when he and Izzy got up to dance to The Louisiana Lovers, a visiting country western band, Derek had approached Willa's table and asked her if she would mind dancing with someone likely to two-step all over her toes. His eyes had sparkled, his lips had curved in good-humored self-deprecation, his open palm had hovered, steady as a rock, in front of her. He had made it so easy for her to say yes. So easy to laugh as they'd danced (and he hadn't stepped on her toes once). Easy to walk out the door with him later that evening, and easy— shockingly easy—to forget everything but the feeling of strong arms wrapped around her back as he'd kissed her.

Now, as Derek stepped into line behind Mrs. Wittenberg, he filled the small bakery with his bigger-than-life presence, neat and handsome in a crisply ironed beige uniform, his thick black hair still damp from a shower. Charcoal eyes met hers.

Just to prove she didn't have a cool or sophisticated bone in her entire body, heat instantly filled Willa's face.

Ducking her head, she refocused on the woman in front of her. "So what's the special occasion, Mrs. Wittenberg?"

Blue eyes, pink cheeks, and the tiniest, straightest teeth Willa had ever seen, beamed with pleasure. "Mr. Wittenberg and I are celebrating our fiftieth anniversary today."

"Oh. Oh…" *Wow.* A stab of pure, unadulterated envy caught Willa off-guard. "That's—"

Amazing. A gift. A reminder that life does not deal equally with everyone.

"Wonderful. That's really, really wonderful. Are you celebrating with a party?"

"No, dear. Our children wanted to, but Mr. Wittenberg and I have decided on a quiet time at home. Just the two of us. We're going to take an early walk along the river. We got engaged there. This morning, we're going to visit the very same spot. There's a little rock shaped like a chair. I sat on it while Mr. Wittenberg got down on one knee and proposed."

It was impossible not to be swept along on the tide of Mrs. W's pleasure and anticipation.

"Are you going to reenact the proposal?" Willa grinned as Mrs. W nodded vigorously.

"That's the plan." She giggled like a little girl. "Afterward, we'll walk back home, have a leisurely breakfast… And then I'm going to take that man into the bedroom and seduce him."

Willa's smile froze on her face. Her gaze shot to the sheriff. He was watching her. One eyebrow, as midnight black as his hair, arched in devilish humor.

"Do you have something sexy I could serve?" Mrs. Wittenberg continued. "The Food Network says breakfast can be a potent aphrodisiac."

The mischief in the sheriff's expression flared to a broad grin. A very sexy broad grin.

Alrighty. Willa looked at the pastries she'd baked with fresh appreciation. Up until now, the most interesting question she'd fielded was, *Do you make gluten-free strudel?*

"A sexy breakfast, hmm?" she said. "I have a chocolate chip babka Mr. Wittenberg might enjoy." She pointed to a tall, dome-shaped breakfast bread filled to bursting with chopped chocolate and cinnamon sugar.

Mrs. Wittenberg eyed the coffee cake. "It looks good." Her penciled brows knit together. "I don't know if it's sexy enough, though." Turning, she enlisted the aid of Thunder Ridge's finest. "Sheriff Neel, do you think a chocolate chip babka is sexy?"

Appearing to give the elderly woman's question his serious consideration, he drawled, "I don't watch too many cooking shows, Mrs. W, but I like to think I'm a fair judge of desirable. If the Food Network thinks you need an aphrodisiac, they're underestimating your charms." Because he towered above her by more than a foot, he had to bend down quite a bit to whisper loudly in her ear, "You're already irresistible. Just think of the coffee cake as an appetizer."

Turning back to Willa with a smile that seemed bigger than her face, Mrs. Wittenberg crowed, "I'll take the babka! Can you put a bow on the box?"

"Of course." Willa's glance lighted on Sheriff Neel. He winked. Once again, heat filled her face. *Like I'm a teenager*, she thought disgustedly, giving herself a mental shake as she went about the business of wrapping the coffee cake.

Apparently Sheriff Neel was perfectly relaxed and comfortable continuing to have casual encounters with her after their episode of very heavy petting. It was, after all, the twenty-first century. Plus, there was no shortage of women in town who spoke frankly about their interest in bringing Thunder Ridge's sheriff home for a night—or forever. What happened between him and Willa at the end of summer had probably happened to him a bunch of times.

Well, all except the part where Willa had pushed him away, exclaiming, "I can't do this!" and then ran away as

if the devil were on her heels. *That* had probably been a
new experience for him.

"Here you are." Handing Mrs. Wittenberg a white box
with red lettering and a glittery gold bow, she said, "I
added a couple of molasses snaps. For later."

"Oh, thank you so much, dear. I'll let you know how it
goes!" Showing her deep dimples, Mrs. Wittenberg hugged
the box to her as she exited the store.

Which left Willa alone with her next customer.

It was too quiet, too still in the bakery. Willa made a
mental note to ask her boss if she could play some music
during the day. Even the large fan that pulled heat out of
the kitchen sounded like nothing more than a faint hum.

Derek didn't seem bothered by the stillness. He was
pretty still himself, watching her, waiting patiently. He
had sought her out the day after their near miss, looking
concerned rather than angry. He'd asked her why she'd
run away, of course, and hadn't been satisfied with her
insistence that she'd simply been having a bad night, had
thought a little socializing might do her some good, but
hadn't meant to let things go that far.

He'd frowned, staring at her, waiting for a fuller explanation, and she'd felt so guilty, because he was a good
guy. When she'd waitressed at The Pickle Jar, she'd seen
him nearly every day. Her employer, Izzy Thayer, was
his best friend, and he'd come in regularly to have a cup
of coffee, do some minor repairs or keep a very wary eye
on the progress of Izzy's relationship with Nate Thayer
before Nate and Izzy married. Derek just seemed like a
natural protector, and that was nice. *Very* nice. But Willa
had learned there were some things from which no human
power could protect you.

So she'd stuck to her guns, claiming that what had happened between them was a mistake and wouldn't happen

again. "I'm very, very sorry for the…" She'd stumbled, not knowing what to say. "For leading you to believe I was…" *Ugh.* "I mean, if I led you on in any way." She was *so* not cut out for dating.

With the sexy, easy smile that was his trademark, he'd stood on the front porch of her rented cottage and shrugged away her apology. "No harm done. I just wanted to make sure you're okay."

"Me? I am." She'd nodded vigorously, as if being emphatic would turn her lie into the truth. She hadn't been "okay" in two years. But that had nothing to do with him.

Now, this morning, he transferred his gaze from her to the pastry case. "Got anything to tempt *me*?"

The words didn't sound utterly innocent, but his tone did, so she took them at face value. Reaching into the case, she withdrew a large flaky golden rectangle.

"Our signature cheese Danish," she said.

He squinted at the glazed pastry. "Where's the cheese?"

"Inside. It's filled with a blend of ricotta, cream cheese and honey. And a touch of orange zest and cinnamon."

"A Danish with hidden charms." He nodded. "Okay, I'll try it. And a large black coffee." Withdrawing his wallet, he pulled out a few bills. "I'm going to need the caffeine to stay extra alert now that I know Mrs. W's plans." He looked at Willa with a straight face, but roguish eyes so darkly brown they appeared black. "Mr. Wittenberg is ten years older than his wife, you know. If that babka really is an aphrodisiac, he may not survive the morning. I hope I don't have to bring you in for aiding and abetting an aggravated manslaughter."

The comment made Willa smile, and she remembered that he'd made her smile quite a lot, actually, that night in the tavern. "It isn't my recipe," she countered, "so I don't think I should be held responsible." She shrugged. "On the other hand, forewarned is forearmed, so thanks. I'll go home at lunch and pack a duffle bag in case I have to run from the law." She turned, the curve of his lips an enjoyable image to hold on to as she got him a large coffee to go and slid the Danish into a bag.

Derek paid her, the expression in his eyes that mesmerizing combo of sincere and humorous. "I hope you won't run from the law. I'm here to help." He gave her a quick nod. "Morning."

She watched him go, sharing a few words with an older gentleman who walked in as he walked out.

"Good morning, Mr. Stroud," Willa greeted the new arrival as he approached the counter. "Toasted bialy and cream cheese?" She named the savory round roll he had every morning. Soon, Jerry Ellison, who owned First Strike Realty up the block, arrived and sat with Charlie Stroud at one of the six small tables in the bakery. Business picked up the closer they got to 7:00 a.m., and Willa stayed busy throughout the morning.

"I'm here to help."

A couple of hours after Derek left, his parting words continued to play through her mind. She'd heard those words, or a variation of them, before.

"Don't try to do this on your own."

"You've been through so much. Let us help."

Didn't people know that their help was sometimes the cruelest of gifts? What they really wanted was to help her "move on," to "let go," to be happy again the way she used to be. To forget. And she couldn't let that happen.

"I don't want help. I don't need help," she muttered to herself as she slid a fresh tray of oatmeal chocolate-chip cookies into the oven. Kim Appel, a mother of young children who worked from nine to three or seven at the bakery, depending on whether her husband was available to pick the kids up from school, was now behind the counter while Willa toiled in the kitchen. That gave Willa plenty of time alone to obsess.

Her mind raced, her heart pumped too hard, her stomach churned. What was the matter with her?

"You're tired and you need some sleep, that's what." Wiping her perspiring palms on her apron, she gathered up bowls and utensils to stack them in the dishwasher. Maybe she should go home for a couple of hours. Kim could handle it; she was a capable worker. Willa could come back after a nap and close up shop.

Yeah, except whom was she kidding? She wasn't going to sleep. She was going to hear Derek's words over and over, see his sincere face, imagine his strong arms.

"I'm here to help."

For nearly a year now she'd caught him watching her and had sensed all along that he was interested. Interested in a way that, in a vulnerable moment, could make her skin tingle and her veins flood with heat.

He'd been unfailingly polite, courteous, gentle—never pushy—almost as if he sensed he would have to move softly if he hoped to get anywhere with her at all. And that agonizing yearning to lose herself in his arms, to forget for a night, for an hour…that yearning would sometimes overtake her like it had in the tavern. Her heart would race, and she would imagine surrendering to his arms and to his smile, to the unbridled laughter of lovers.

She would sometimes dream of *really* moving on.

Willa set the timer on the oven so she wouldn't burn the cookies while she cleaned the marble countertop. She hadn't moved to Thunder Ridge, eight hundred miles from family, friends and a brilliant career as a chef and culinary arts instructor so that she could forget everything. No. She'd moved so that she could live the way she wanted to—quietly, privately. She'd moved so she could hang on to the one thing that still held her broken heart together: her memories.

So far, she saw no reason to change.

When Derek walked through the door to the sheriff's office at seven-twenty, the sun was still trying to make its first appearance of the morning. The lights inside the large boxy room, however, were burning and emitted a warm, welcoming glow completely at odds with the rubber band that whizzed past his head with such force it could surely be classified a lethal weapon. Rearing back, Derek tightened his hold on the coffee cup, popping open the plastic lid and sloshing hot coffee over his hand and onto the linoleum floor.

"Russell," he growled.

"Sorry!"

Derek's deputy, Russell Annen, whipped his feet off the wide desk in front of him and stood. "I was aiming for Bat Masterson." He jerked his thumb at a poster of Old West sheriffs on the wall opposite him as he ran to fetch paper towels and sop up the spill.

"I hope you aim a gun better than you shoot rubber bands." Derek had almost had his eye put out on several occasions by Russell's wayward shots. "Slow night?"

"Yup." Russell bent to clean the mess. "Slow morning, too."

"You might as well take off then."

"I have another forty-five minutes."

"That's okay. You can get an early start." Heading for his desk, Derek noted the remains of Russell's breakfast littering the blotter: a liter bottle of soda and an open, half-eaten box of chocolate-covered donut holes. "Get a blood panel, would ya, Russell?" he suggested. "Check your sugar and cholesterol levels."

His deputy grinned. "Hey, I have to get my fix somewhere. LeeAnn watched some video about diet and heart disease, and now all she makes when I come over is vegetables and beans."

"Smart woman. You should marry her."

"I hate beans. Before that video, we used to look for the best burger-and-brew pubs. Now when we go to Portland, she wants to find vegan restaurants. Do I look like I'm meant to be vegan?"

Derek eyed his six-foot-tall, two-hundred-pound deputy. "You do not."

Russell began to wander toward their work area instead of toward the door, and Derek felt his shoulders tense. Seating himself behind the big oak desk, he pretended to become engrossed in his computer screen. Every morning after seeing Willa at the bakery, he required a few minutes alone to debrief himself. Willa took up residence in his thoughts more than anyone or, lately, anything else. It took some effort to refocus, and he liked to do that in private. His love life—or current lack of one—was his business, no one else's.

On that note, he said pointedly before Russell could sit down, "Enjoy your time off."

"I was planning to." Russell sighed heavily. "Before."

Do not, I repeat, do not take the bait. But Russell looked like a giant puppy whose favorite chew toy was stolen. *Give me patience.* "Okay." Derek crossed his forearms on the desk. "Before what?"

Closing the distance between himself and the desk, Russell dropped into the chair opposite Derek's. "See, it's this way. I made reservations for dinner up at Summit Lodge. Tonight. Their special is prime rib." He practically moaned the end of the sentence. "Eleven o'clock last night, LeeAnn tells me her cousin is in town today through the end of the week."

"So?"

"So, LeeAnn is refusing to go anywhere unless Penelope has something to do, too. And, someone to do it with."

"Can't she find something to do on her own?"

Russell slapped his palm on the desktop. "Dude, right? That's what I said. But Penelope and LeeAnn are females, see? They don't think like us."

Derek waited for more. "Okay. And?"

"So the only way I can go out with LeeAnn this week is if we double date."

It took a couple of seconds—only a couple—to understand. "No." Laughing humorlessly, Derek shook his head. "No way."

"It would just be for a couple of dates."

Picking up what was left of the coffee he'd brought over from the bakery, Derek leaned back so that his chair tilted on two legs. "No."

"Three dates, tops."

The front chair legs landed on the floor again with a thud. "Maybe you don't know this about me, Russell. I don't go on blind dates. Ever." He took a sip of coffee. "Good luck. I'm sure you'll find someone."

"LeeAnn thinks you and Penelope—"

"Someone *else*."

Blowing his breath out in frustration, Russell stood. "Fine." He turned and took several steps toward the door. Derek began to relax, but obviously everything was not fine, because Russell turned back. "It's not that you turn down blind dates. You don't date *at all*."

Narrowing his eyes, Derek warned, "Russell—"

"Not since that night at The White Lightning when you left with the woman who works at the bakery—"

"—you should go *now*."

"I saw how you looked when you left with her. Everyone saw it. LeeAnn gave me holy hell for a week after that, wanting to know why I didn't look at *her* that way."

Derek was on his feet before he realized it. He didn't even remember putting down his coffee. *Laugh it off*, he advised himself, but he didn't feel very humorous. Covering his eyes, he took a deep breath and dragged his hand over his face. "What is your point?"

"I expected you to tell me you went to Vegas that night and got married by Elvis. But ever since then, you act like a monk. You wouldn't talk about what happened with her, but it obviously didn't work out, so why not go out with someone else? Why not Penelope? LeeAnn says she's fun, and she's not even vegan. I asked."

Derek looked down at the desk. His feelings for Willa baffled even him; the last thing he wanted to do this morning was attempt to explain them to somebody else. "I'm going to make a pot of coffee now, while you get going." He glanced up again. "If you don't, *I* may decide to take a few days off and put you on extra shifts."

The phone rang before either of them could say anything more, and Derek snatched it up. He listened for a bit, said, "Don't do anything. I'll be there in ten minutes," and hung up. "Jerry Ellison's potbellied pig knocked down Ron Raybold's fence again," he told Russell, "and Ron is threatening to shoot it and have a luau. I'm heading out."

Resignedly following his boss to the door, Russell asked, "Jerry is single, isn't he?"

"Yeah."

"When you talk to him, ask if he wants to go out with Penelope."

While Russell headed to his car, Derek put the "On a call... Back later" sign on the front door and went to forestall a neighborhood feud. Being the sheriff of Thunder Ridge was nine parts relationship mediation and one part active police duties. Truth was, most of the time he wouldn't have it any other way. He might not have been born here, but he'd found a home for the first time in this place where, rogue pot-bellied pigs aside, people cared about each other's business mostly because they cared about each other.

His life was good, and he hadn't thought much was missing until Willa Holmes had moved to town.

While Derek drove to Ron's place, he thought about the woman who had made him break one of his cardinal rules: no high-speed chases where women were concerned. If a woman didn't want to be caught, MOVE ON.

Like any lesson that made a lasting impression, he'd learned that one the hard way. Maybe it was the curse of having raised himself until he was nineteen, but for a while he'd pursued unavailable women. An attempt, he supposed, to prove to himself that he could make someone stay. He'd sworn off that kind of bull a long time ago.

Until Willa.

When he was near her, his heart revved like a car with the accelerator pressed to the floor. She'd turned away after what had to be some of the best kissing he'd ever experienced. No, *the* best. And he knew she'd felt it, too, because when he let himself think about it, he could still feel her fingers clinging tightly to his shoulders...then moving like smoke up the back of his neck...threading through his hair... The longer they'd kissed, the more her body had melted into his, and the more his had felt as if it were about to burst into flame.

Just when he'd been certain he was experiencing the

best moment of his life, Willa had cut and run. No real explanation given. Ever since then, he'd been on a high-speed chase all right, one with no end in sight.

But something in those mesmerizing eyes of hers, eyes with all the storminess and all the sunshine of a spring day in Oregon, told him to keep chasing. That she needed him to catch up even if she didn't know it yet.

Was he nuts? Behaving exactly as he'd sworn he wouldn't? Yeah. And he figured there were only two logical outcomes. Either he was someday going to become the luckiest man on earth, or he would realize he'd been the jackass of the century. He only hoped he could handle the fallout if the latter turned out to be the truth.

Chapter Two

"You sure you want to stay and close by yourself?" Kim looked at her manager with worried brown eyes yet not a line or a pucker on her silken brow, which reminded Willa how young her assistant was.

"I'm sure," she said. "Go home to your kiddos. The sun's actually out. If you hurry, you might have an hour left to get them outside before the stir-crazies set in."

"You're right." Kim laughed. "Three and six are probably the worst ages when you have to stay inside because of the weather and dark nights. They fight like crazy."

"Go on then." Willa shooed her employee toward the door. "Put on their mittens and let 'em duke it out at the park. Play structures are a mother's best friend."

As Kim left, Willa returned to work. She hadn't gone home after all, though she had taken a long lunch and had driven to Long River to go for a walk with other lunch-timers taking advantage of the unseasonably sunny winter day. Now, at 4:00 p.m., she was tired, but the more exhausted she was, the better her chances of sleeping tonight.

She began the process of wrapping up the leftover goodies in the pastry case so she could take them next door to the deli. Izzy would sell what she could tonight at half price, and tomorrow Willa would take the rest to Thunder Ridge Long-term Care for the staff and residents to enjoy.

The after-school crowd had already come in and cleaned her out of the most popular cookie selections, but there were still apricot rugelach, buttery shortbread and chocolate chip mandelbrot. The folks who would come in before closing would be interested mostly in bread, rolls and cakes for the evening meal, so she started packaging the cookies first. As Willa worked she flicked on the radio, opting for an oldies station, and didn't see her next customer come in until he was standing directly in front of the counter.

"Oh!" Using her upper arm to brush a stray hair from her eyes, she smiled. "Hello. You're here at a good time. All the cookies, bagels and rolls are two for the price of one."

The boy—ten or eleven, she guessed—pressed his lips together in a sort of smile and nodded. He wore a dark blue coat, pilling on the body and sleeves, and a knit hat that had also seen better days. His skin was a beautiful caramel color, his eyes as dark as onyx. He looked shy, and she couldn't recall seeing him before, either in the bakery or the deli.

"Do you like chocolate?" she asked.

He nodded, and she handed him a brownie. "Try that. On the house. Then you can look around and see if you want another one of those or something else."

He stared at her without moving. She nodded encouragingly. "Go ahead, take it. It's good. I like to think of it as a cross between a truffle and a brownie. Maybe I should call it a bruffle. Or trownie." He didn't smile.

"Free?" His only word to her was soft, a little suspicious.

"Yep. Bakeries give out samples all the time." Gingerly, he accepted the treat. "I'll be over there—" Willa pointed to the counter behind her "—working. If you decide to get something else, just holler. We have hot cocoa and cider, too, on the house in the evening." Beverages weren't really on the house, but what the heck? She'd drop a dollar fifty into the till. Sensing that her observation was making the boy nervous, she turned her back, slipping more cookies into the plastic bags she would deliver next door.

Something Sweet's grand opening had been in September, and Izzy had already orchestrated Dough for Dollars and other promotions with the local schools, plus there had been a back-to-school special the first two weeks the bakery had been operational. Now, every afternoon they had several kids from the local K-8 and high school stopping by for snacks, but she'd never seen this kiddo before. She'd have remembered him. His shy, almost distrusting demeanor stood in stark contrast to a face that was exotically beautiful.

Everyone, children included, had a story. What was his? As her curiosity grew, Willa shook her head. His story wasn't her business; she was just here to provide sticky sweets that temporarily soothed the soul and gave people a reason to brush their teeth. That's what she'd wanted when she had first come to Thunder Ridge—a simple job with work she could leave at the "office."

Several minutes had gone by when Willa realized she hadn't heard a sound from her young customer. Glancing over her shoulder, she saw him hovering near a large plastic canister she kept on the low counter near the cash reg-

ister. There was a slit cut into the top of the lid and a big
picture glued to the front and covered with tape to protect
the photo. *"Help Gia."* Gia was fifteen and had lived at the
Thunder Ridge Long-Term Care facility for the past ten
months, after an auto accident that had taken her mother's
life and left her father with ever-mounting medical bills
and lost workdays. Thankfully, the canister was stuffed
with bills and coins. Every Friday, Willa deposited the
contents into a bank account set up for Gia and her family.

The boy had eaten his brownie and was frowning at
the jar. He looked anxious, conflicted. Was he thinking
about donating his money instead of buying something?

A sweet, sharp pang squeezed Willa's chest. Wow. People his age rarely gave the jar more than a passing glance.
She understood that. It was so much easier to pretend bad
things didn't happen to average kids. But maybe this boy
was one of the unusually empathetic ones. She was going
to give this cool kid a box of cookies and a hot chocolate
if he dropped even a penny in that canister.

When he looked up and caught her watching him, she
smiled. He appeared startled. Completely self-conscious.
You know what? She was going to give him a box of cookies and a hot cocoa just for *thinking* about—

"Hey!"

Like a lightning strike, his hands were around the canister, pulling it beneath his coat. He turned and ran for the
door with such speed, Willa was still standing in shock
when the door harp pinged behind him.

For a second, she merely stared. Then outrage, pure and
robust, rose inside her like a geyser. Gia's family needed
that money. They needed the support it represented. They
needed to know they were not forgotten, that *Gia* was not
forgotten as she lay in a hospital bed in a long-term care
facility.

Veins filling with adrenaline, Willa abandoned her post at the bakery, running full throttle after the boy. Twilight had turned to dusk, and the sunny day had given way to clouds that inhibited her visibility, but she caught sight of him up ahead.

To avoid running into a family, the kid dodged right, which forced him to skirt around a bench and slowed him down.

"Stop! You stop right now!" Willa hollered. Pedestrians turned to stare. Briefly, the boy looked back at her, too, his eyes wide. Then he jumped over a dog tied up to a street lamp and kept running.

Sophie Turner, who owned A Step in Time New and Vintage Shoes, was outside sweeping her front entrance when Willa raced by. "Willa?" the young woman exclaimed. "What's wrong?"

"He took my canister," she panted. "I've got to get him."

"He took…what? Do you need help?" Sophie called after her.

"No!" She cupped her hands around her mouth. "I'm warning you, you little twerp!" Really, she had been so wrong about this kid. "Stop. Right. Now!"

"Who are we chasing?"

Willa glanced to her right to see Derek Neel, out of uniform, jogging beside her. For a second, she was discombobulated. She'd seen him in street clothes before, of course, but tonight off duty Sheriff Neel seemed taller, more rugged and somehow relaxed even as he ran with her.

"He stole my donation jar," she said, panting.

"Who?"

"That kid!" Pointing, she accused, "That tricky little— Wait a minute, where'd he go?" Her eyes searched the darkening streets, but all she could see were a few scattered citizens of Thunder Ridge watching their sheriff and Willa run down the block together. "Darn it!" She stumbled to a stop, her breath heavy, her skin at once hot from exertion and cold from the thirty-five-degree evening. Suddenly, not even adrenaline could make her forget how tired she was, and how frustrated. "You made me lose him," she said, putting her hands on her thighs and bending over to catch her breath. "He's got all the money we've been collecting for a week. Do you know what that represented?"

"I'm not even sure what you're talking about." Derek's characteristic unruffled demeanor was intended to defuse the situation, but it had the opposite effect on Willa when he asked, "Who do you think took your jar?"

"I don't *think* he took it. I *know* he did." Her sudden fury at the kid was out of proportion, but she didn't care. "I was standing right there."

"Okay. And you say he looked like a kid."

"He didn't *look* like a kid. He *is* a kid." She started walking again, searching up and down the side streets, exasperated. "A kid with someone else's donation money."

"Okay, look, why don't you come on back to my office. You can give me a description, tell me what happened and how much money you think he's got."

"No." The word emerged too sharp, so she added, "Thank you. I'm going to find him."

Derek reached for her arm. "It's getting dark. He could have ducked into his house by now."

"Then I'll go door to door." Turning on Ponderosa Avenue toward the residential area, she strode up the block, searching. When she felt tears at the corners of her eyes, she swiped them away and kept walking. Derek stayed by her side, keeping pace until they had gone two blocks. Then he reached for her arm again, refusing to let go when she tried to pull away.

Because she was over-the-top, clearly, and probably irrational and maybe even a little scary, he looked at her in concern. "What is this really about?" His eyes searched hers as if he was trying to read what she wouldn't tell him.

She felt grief and fury rise inside her like dirty flood water. *I thought I was past this. I thought I'd cut this part of me out.* A couple of years ago, blinding anger had sprouted inside her as if it were a new organ. She'd worked hard to excise it, but tonight she felt as if she could scream— loudly and long enough to punch a hole in the night sky.

It had nothing to do with Derek. He was simply the hapless boulder standing in the path of her raging river. Willa's mind was on Gia—unable to speak clearly since the accident, barely able to walk and only fifteen. And her father, her poor father, probably felt responsible and utterly helpless.

Traumatic brain injuries were cruel. She'd wanted so much to show him his family was remembered every day.

"Never mind." She turned toward Warm Springs Road. She would get a new jar tomorrow, refill it herself and take it to the care facility. That, of course, was the reasonable solution. The boy was not her business. She shouldn't have interacted with him so much to begin with.

It took a moment to realize Derek was still holding her arm.

"I have to go. I left the store unattended." Which was a pretty stupid thing to do and an even dumber thing to admit to the owner's best friend. Great. Crazy Woman Loses Job would probably be the headline on the next *Thunder Ridge Gazette*.

"Okay, let's go."

"What? No. You were probably headed somewhere, and I'm fine. Really. I was over-the-top. Sorry." How many times could you apologize to someone for erratic behavior? "It was a long day. I'm fine now." She forced a smile. "Not crazy."

He didn't bother to answer. Didn't let go of her arm, either. With his jaw set in *capable sheriff mode*, he accompanied her back toward Warm Springs Road, Thunder Ridge's main street.

For future reference, Willa thought, *never tell someone you're not crazy. It makes you sound crazy.*

When they passed A Step In Time on their way back to the bakery, Sophie, who was young and pretty and single, ran to the door and smiled when she saw Derek. "Hi! Did you help Willa find her thief?"

"No, no need." Willa tried to sound philosophical. "He was just a kid. I lost perspective there for a few minutes. It's over and done now."

Beneath the street lamps that had switched on and the glow from the exterior light at Sophie's store, it was easy to see her brows pucker beneath a mop of caramel-brown curls. "I don't have kids, but if I did, I'd want to make sure they were held responsible for stealing. That boy's parents should hear about it." She divided her glance between Derek and Willa. "I hope you guys follow through."

"We will." Derek responded firmly. "Good night."

On they walked until they reached Something Sweet. Standing before the glass door, with the shop aglow inside, Willa hoped she would find the cash register exactly as she'd left it and figured she probably would. Crime was a relatively rare occurrence in Thunder Ridge. Before she opened the door, she said, "Everything looks fine." What were the odds she could persuade him not to come in? She needed some time alone to collect herself. "Thanks for walking back with me. I appreciate your help. I have some work to do and then I have to close, and I've taken enough of your time, so—"

"You're going to need to give a statement and a description of the suspect."

"No. I overreacted. Frankly, I'm embarrassed. Can we just forget it?"

Derek frowned. Disapprovingly. "This is about the boy now. I need to talk to his parents."

"Sure. Of course. It's pretty clear you aren't on duty right now, though." Her gaze traveled over his off duty attire—well-fitting black jeans and a zipped-up gray hoodie—and she wondered if he was meeting someone. A man that handsome, after all... Changing her train of thought, she offered, "So maybe I can swing by the station later tonight and talk to whoever's on call."

Derek reached around her for the door. He held it open and waited.

Quickly assessing the outcome of making an even bigger deal about this than she already had, Willa brushed past him. She didn't bother to walk behind the counter or into the kitchen. He wasn't going to leave, so she turned to face him in the middle of the bakery. Beneath the hoodie, she spied the top of a black turtleneck sweater that was exactly the shade of the thick waves that fell across his forehead. Yep, he definitely looked like a man with better things to do than solve the puzzle of her lunatic behavior.

"It seems I keep owing you apologies."

Raising one shoulder in a brief shrug, he said, "Nah. I'm not big on apologies. An explanation about what happened out there would be nice, though."

God knew she owed him one, but it would entail too many personal revelations, so she shrugged, too, hoping irony would diffuse the situation. "I'm not big on explanations."

"That's a problem then," he said. Hooking his thumbs

in his back pockets, he narrowed his gaze. "How do you feel about baos?"

"About what?"

"Baos. They're Chinese dumplings filled with meat. Sometimes beans."

"I know what they are." She'd once taught a class on Asian fusion cuisine.

"Good. How about eating some with me?" he invited. "Have you ever been to The Twin Dragon in Zig Zag? Best baos this side of Shanghai."

"Have you been to Shanghai?"

"Only in my dreams."

"Well, maybe someday you'll really go," she murmured. She *had* been to China. It had been a wonderful trip.

"I've been waiting for the right time," Derek said.

Her head rose at that. "You shouldn't. If you want to travel, you should just do it. Don't wait."

He gazed at her curiously, and she realized she'd sounded emphatic. "I'll take that under advisement," he said. He gestured toward the street beyond the window. "It's a big world out there. I'd like to see it with someone. That enhances the view, don't you think?"

"Yes." Uncomfortably aware that she hadn't responded to his dinner invitation, she clasped her hands in front of her. "I'd really rather not pursue finding that boy," she said, glancing everywhere but at Derek. "I think he was just… impulsive. I don't think he's a criminal."

"He'll be impulsive again."

"Still—"

"I'm not going to send him to juvenile hall. I want to talk to him and to his family. See if they're aware of what he's up to. Assuming he's never done something like this before, I'd like to make sure he doesn't do it again."

Reasonable. Derek was being very reasonable. She

couldn't argue without explaining her reluctance. "All right. After I close up here, I'll go over to your office to file a report and then head home."

The arch of his brow, the flare of awareness in his eyes and the near-imperceptible quirk at the corners of his masculine lips told her he got the message. No baos; just business. And no explanations, either.

"My deputy, Russell, is on duty all night. I'll text and let him know he should expect you."

She wanted to assure him that her rejection of his dinner invitation was not personal, but he was already on his way to the door. His broad, relaxed shoulders gave no indication that his feelings were wounded. Pausing with his hand on the door handle, he turned to consider her. "Maybe I should have been a detective. I like puzzles. Here's one I'm working on— beautiful woman—young, intelligent, capable of running her own business—moves to a small town in Oregon where she didn't know anybody and doesn't seem to want to. She takes a job working as a waitress in a deli. What would her motivation be?"

"For taking a job as a waitress? That's a rather elitist attitude."

"You have to consider the question in context," he said pleasantly enough. "The woman is clearly overqualified."

"Maybe she thought waitressing would turn out to be an upwardly mobile position."

"Could be." He nodded. "I doubt she would have assumed that at the start, though. There was no evidence that it would be."

"Well, it's hardly a mystery. Plenty of people move to Oregon because they want less stress and a pretty place to live. As for not socializing constantly, some people are naturally introverts."

"Maybe." Derek considered her for a long time. "Then again, maybe she's afraid."

"Of what?" Willa shook her head. "Never mind." She wagged her finger, trying to keep the moment light. "This is annoying, Sheriff. You're talking about me in the third person."

"I apologize. I had to repeat Language Arts in high school. Let me try it again. When I look at you, Willa, I see someone who wants to reach out, but won't. Or can't. I see something behind your eyes. Something you want to say or do, but wouldn't dare. And I can't help but wonder what it is. And why it's so hard." He opened the door, admitting a blast of cold air, and gave her one last look. "I'm not the enemy."

With that, Derek headed out onto the streets that were his to serve and protect.

Willa remained alone in the shop, shivering even after the door closed. The image of his searching dark eyes lasted long after he had disappeared.

Chapter Three

"You need to leave my employee alone, let her concentrate on her work, and go find a woman who actually wants you, because right now you are barking up the wrong tree." Izzy took a bite out of her pastrami and coleslaw on rye then spoke with her mouth full. "Gosh, I hope that didn't sound harsh."

"Gosh, it did." Derek unwrapped the deli sandwich Izzy had brought him. Once a week when the weather was decent, and often when it wasn't, he and Izzy met in Doc Howard Memorial Park. She supplied lunch from the deli, he supplied the appetite, and they sat by the river, talked and ate. Today he wasn't in the mood for food. "Is there mustard on this?"

"Of course."

"What about mayo?"

"Derek, please—" she sounded offended "—you've been eating the same sandwich for—what?—ten years? I know

how you like it, and I respect your condiment selections."
She poked at her own mammoth concoction, adding, "Even
though I think they're misguided."

Brisket on challah had been his go-to sandwich since
he'd had his first meal at The Pickle Jar. He liked it with
mayo, spicy mustard, and—Izzy's main objection—ketchup.

"Since I can see that you are not ready to stop obsessing about the manager of my bakery, let's return to our
regularly scheduled programming." Extending her legs and
crossing her ankles, Izzy flexed her feet inside fuzzy faux
fur–lined boots. "Recap. Willa turned you down for baos,
which is too bad, but at least you asked, which is progress
over last year when you were so afraid to be rejected you
barely spoke to her."

"I was not afraid to be rejected. What the—" Sitting
up straight, he glared at his best friend. "I didn't want to
pressure her or put us both in an uncomfortable situation."

"Ooh. Good thinking, Dr. Phil."

"I didn't want to come off like a stalker. Okay?"

"Mmm. And now?"

"Now it's different. At the tavern, I saw that she *is* interested."

Lowering her sandwich, Izzy gazed at him, her sparkling eyes turning serious and more sensitive. "Derek, was
she interested in *you*? Or was she interested in, you know,
a man in general?" Obviously trying not to hurt him or to
see him hurt himself, she rushed on. "Willa has been alone
here for over a year. She doesn't really socialize with anyone at work. Maybe she's lonely and it was just…time."
Placing a hand on his arm, she said, "I wouldn't hurt you
for all the world, you know that. I know how much you
have to give, and I want to see you happy. You said you
weren't going to date unavailable women, anymore. Re-

member? You said you were going to be sane about your relationships. Unlike me." She grinned.

She can afford to grin about it, Derek thought, gratitude for his friend's happiness softening his mood somewhat. On Izzy's left ring finger were an engagement ring, the wedding band Nate Thayer knew he should have given her fourteen years earlier and an eternity band to signify Nate's commitment never to leave her again.

To say Derek had disliked Izzy's now-husband when he'd first met the man…well, that was an understatement. Nate Thayer had hurt Izzy once, before Izzy and Derek had met. After hearing the story and being Izzy's best friend for all these years, Derek had given Nate as hard a time as he could when the other man had shown up again, suddenly, last year. But Nate had turned out to be a good guy—hard to intimidate, too—and Izzy was nuts about him. Eventually, despite the trust issues born from his own past, Derek had given the pair his blessing, and they seemed to be doing fine. Great, in fact.

So, yeah, Izzy could afford to smile about it all now.

"That night in the tavern," he said slowly, looking at the river, "I sensed from Willa what I've been feeling all along. *Some* of what I've been feeling," he amended, figuring honestly that Willa wasn't as invested as he. "It was more than physical."

Izzy shook her head. "Even after a year of working together, I hardly know anything about her, beyond the fact that she has a strong work ethic and is completely reliable." She reached for a dill pickle. "You know, if I got a dollar every time someone asked me to set you up with them—or with their daughter or their cousin or their cousin's daughter's cousin—over the years, I could retire. So why this woman, this time? I mean, yes, she's lovely and I know you've had the hots for her, but, really, why Willa?"

The stretch of Long River where they sat flowed quietly, with little fanfare, but it was beautiful, mysterious and multifaceted as any white water Derek had ever seen. It reminded him of Willa. Her silvery eyes were soft, keenly observant, kind, sad—it all depended on the hour and the day. He could study her endlessly and still not see everything he knew there was to see.

"When we were in the tavern, I told her a joke. A really silly one."

"One of Henry's?"

"Yeah." Izzy's former boss, Henry Bernstein, used to offer his customers "A joke and a pickle for only a nickel." Derek had heard plenty of them (and had eaten a lot of pickles) over the years. "Willa liked it. She laughed. Really laughed. For the first time, her smile was in her eyes, too, and I could see…" He held up a hand as Izzy gaped at him. "Don't say anything. No wisecracks." He waited until Izzy nodded before he continued. "I could see what the future might be with her. And, yeah, there was something kind of desperate about the way she was behaving, but for a moment there, I think she was wondering what a future might be like, too." Izzy was looking at him seriously, as seriously as she ever had. He took a deep breath. "My gut's been telling me for a long time that this is different. This is special. So even when I took her home, I knew we weren't going to do anything more than kiss."

Izzy's brows rose to new heights. Stretching his own legs out toward the water, Derek shrugged. "I *might* have taken some upper body privileges. But that's it. When we—" He stopped. Too much information. But as he stared at the river, he let his mind float and thought, *I want Willa for more than a night*.

"You don't know much about her. Nobody does. There

isn't a lot of information to be found apparently. A lot of people have Googled her," Izzy confided.

"What?"

"Yeah. Come on, you haven't?"

"No." Not that he hadn't been tempted, but… "No. Someday she'll tell me what I need to know."

"Okay, well we mere mortals are curious right now. And you know what we found out?"

"No. And don't—"

"Almost nothing. There isn't much information to be found. Isn't that weird in this day and age? No Facebook, no Instagram—"

"I don't have that stuff, either—"

"—and while I support her desire to stay off social media, you have to admit that it's weird not to be able to find her somewhere online. These days, you can get a history of addresses for people who've lived under rocks—"

"That's an invasion of privacy. That kind of information should only be available for legal purposes."

"—and there are, apparently, over nine hundred Willa Holmeses, but none of them jump out as our Willa Holmes."

Derek told himself there was nothing unusual about someone living under the radar of the internet.

"Some folks are saying she's running away from a bad relationship," Izzy continued. "Marcy Anneting thinks Willa is in the Witness Protection Program, but Marcy belongs to a mystery book club. And Jett Schulman says you can tell by her manner that she was born into a life of luxury and is just here temporarily to see how the other half lives."

"When did you become the town crier, Izzy?"

He saw the sting of his words as her eyes flickered, but she didn't back down. "Since my best friend started to fall for a woman I don't think will ever love him back."

Unmindful of the sandwich she was squeezing tightly in her hand, Izzy exhaled noisily. "I don't think she *can* love you back. I don't know what the truth is. Maybe she was a mafia wife or her high school sweetheart died tragically and she can't get over it, or she's just a very normal, exceptionally private woman who is emotionally closed off. Whatever it is, she's not the woman I want for you. Derek, everyone thinks of you as having it all together, and you do. *Now*. But I've known you since you since you were the original rebel without a cause. We come from the same place, you and I."

"That was a long time ago. When I left my uncle's house, I didn't even know what I was running from."

"I think you were trying to run *to* something. Just like me. You've been searching for a loving family that was all yours ever since I met you. I don't want you to be hurt again."

"And you think one small, shy woman can do that?" He smiled, hoping to tease Izzy out of her concern, but she refused to be distracted.

"I think she could, yes. I want to protect you, because I love you. Like you tried to protect me when Nate came back."

"Yeah, and I was wrong," he pointed out. "Everything turned out all right. Better than all right."

She stared at him a long time then slowly wrapped the remainder of her now squished sandwich and put it in the insulated lunchbox she'd brought with her. "Okay."

"Izz, I love you. But I've got to go with my gut on this."

She wouldn't look at him. "Yeah. Well, I hired her, you know? I brought her into our lives, so I guess I feel responsible."

He chucked her on the chin. "Okay, you can be the best man at our wedding." When she swiped at a tear, he realized how serious she was and felt a pinch of surprise. But he'd already considered all the possibilities. He knew where he was headed, and he wasn't changing direction. "Izz, I know this may turn out to be nothing. I do. I accept that. I'll deal with it."

She sniffled. "You want to get married. You want a family."

"Yeah," he admitted. "I've borrowed yours long enough."

She pulled back. "Derek! Don't even say that."

He smiled. "Hey, you and Eli are stuck with me." For the past ten years, he'd spent nearly every holiday, every birthday and plenty of days off with Izzy and her son, who was now fifteen and getting to know his father for the first time. Eli didn't need "Uncle Derek" constantly in the way. "I'm ready to branch out, that's all. Widen the circle a bit."

"Okay, I get it, but you *are* family, and my being with Nate doesn't change that." Izzy spoke emphatically, even though she'd said it all before.

She still couldn't accept that the past Thanksgiving and Christmas had been different. On this first holiday as a family, Nate would have preferred to keep his wife and his son all to himself. It had been obvious, no matter how Nate had attempted to mask the feeling. Derek would have felt the same.

He rose. "I should get back to the station. Russell thinks he has the flu, so I'm on duty the rest of the day and night. I'll take the sandwich with me."

"Yeah, I need to get going, too. We ordered Pickle Jar hoodies for Thunder Ridge Community Church's Souper Bowl. I have to pick them up. I got you a hoodie, by the way. You're still going to serve soup with us, right?"

"Right. But if the hoodie has a giant dancing kosher dill on the front, I'm not wearing it." Izzy busied herself with reassembling the lunchbox. Her silence confirmed that the design was the same as on the T-shirts they'd worn for the Hood-to-Coast Relay last summer. He shook his head. "What is it with you and pickle promos? First it was the giant foam costume and now shirts with vegetables."

"The name of the deli is The Pickle Jar. Obviously, we need to promote. Besides, in case you haven't heard, pickles are hip. Don't be surprised if they turn out to be the staple snack food of the twenty-first century." When Derek started to laugh, she socked him in the arm. "I'm serious. And the shirts are terrific. The pickles aren't dancing this time. They have a cartoon face with a pickle mustache and the caption Got Pickles? Isn't that great?"

He looked at her in disbelief. "I'm not wearing that."

"Yes, you are." Izzy reached for her backpack then looked beyond Derek and frowned. "What are those kids doing?"

Derek turned. Beneath a madrone tree about a hundred yards away, two boys, one a teen and the other a bit younger, appeared to be engaged in some sort of transaction with money changing hands. It was a school day; neither of them should have been in the park to begin with.

Keeping his gaze on the duo, Derek uttered, "See you later, Izz," and started walking. About halfway over, he saw the smaller boy glance at him. Their eyes met. In one hand, the boy held a wad of bills he was about to pass to the teenager. As soon as he registered that the man walking toward him was an officer, his expression filled with trepidation. Before Derek could call out a word, both kids were off and running.

Adrenaline flooded Derek's system. Making a split-second decision, he took off after the younger boy, his feet pounding the grass, sure this was going to be anything but another ordinary afternoon in Thunder Ridge.

Can U come back to bakery? Sorry to ask, but it's important. Thx. Izzy.

Ordinarily her boss's text would not have frustrated her, but Willa hadn't slept at all the night before. She'd come home after her confrontation with Derek Neel and had done the worst thing she could do before trying to sleep, the very thing she had promised herself she would *stop* doing, in fact. She had watched a series of DVDs, each one labeled simply with her last name and the year the video had been shot. She kept them stored separately from the remainder of her modest DVD collection, and she never shared them with anybody else. They were hers and hers alone.

She'd finally fallen asleep around midnight, after plowing through half a box of tissues and taking two aspirin for the headache that followed her crying jag. The alarm had gone off at 2:30 a.m. and, after pressing the snooze button as many times as the clock allowed, she'd dragged herself into the shower and over to the bakery to begin work at three-thirty. It had taken an entire pot of coffee to push her along until noon today, which was when she'd cried uncle and headed home again.

Before Izzy's text, Willa had done one load of laundry, eaten two sticks of string cheese and a banana and, at 2:30—p.m. this time—she was wondering if she'd completely throw herself off by taking a nap. And then her phone had pinged. She often went back to work without any prompting from her boss, but this afternoon she thought she might fall over just thinking about returning to the bakery.

Sure. Be there in a few, she texted back. At least she'd be closer to her regular bedtime when she came home again. Maybe tonight would be merciful, and she would fall asleep easily and stay asleep until morning.

She'd already changed out of her flour-dusted jeans and into a pair of soft plaid lounging pants, a gray thermal top and her thickest socks. Piled into a half ponytail/half bun, her hair was no longer work-ready, but she really, really, *really* did not have the energy to get herself dressed and coiffed again. So for the first time since she'd gotten her job in Thunder Ridge, she stuffed her feet into boots, grabbed her coat and headed to work looking, she figured, like a soccer mom with a hangover.

Willa shoved her hands into the pockets of her coat and ducked her head against the chilly wind that had kicked up. As she neared Warm Springs Road, the main street through Thunder Ridge, she raised her head to nod at the locals who greeted her. It was easier to remain private, she had discovered, if she smiled and seemed happy.

She arrived at Something Sweet hoping to be done in record time with whatever business Izzy wanted to discuss. Noting quickly that the store seemed to be doing a brisk late business, Willa opened the glass door and scanned the room for her boss.

"Willa!" Izzy called. She was seated at the table nearest the kitchen. All four chairs were taken.

Rats. Instantly, Willa felt dizzy with fatigue. Multiple-person meetings often meant sitting through a sales pitch about some brilliant new mixer or a better brand of bread flour. Willa honestly didn't know if she could remain upright for that today. And then she focused long enough to recognize someone else at the table.

Derek. Sitting with his back ramrod straight, hands resting on his thighs, he was looking, not at her for once, but at the people seated opposite him. One was a dark-haired man in his twenties and one was a boy.

"Thanks for coming." Izzy got up and motioned Willa to the seat she'd just left.

Derek took a moment to nod at her, but kept his attention mostly on the young man and the boy seated with them at the table. The young man was scowling and turned his glare on Willa as she sat. The boy refused to glance her way at all.

"Sheriff Neel asked me to call you," Izzy explained, standing beside the table, "since you were the one who saw the donation jar being stolen."

"Thanks for coming in." Derek nodded at her. "Gilberto—" he gestured to the boy "—admits to taking the donation jar. Unfortunately, the money has already changed hands. Gilberto was using it to purchase a bike. When I ran after him, the teen selling the bike took off in another direction. So far, Gilberto doesn't want to give me the name of the other boy."

"You better give it." The younger man leaned across the table, his dark eyes flashing dangerously. "You want to go down for some jerk who left you to face a cop on your own? You're bringing disrespect to your family, Gilberto. You better pick who you're going to be loyal to, and pick fast."

Willa saw Derek's chest rise on a deep inhalation.

The boy cringed. *You're bringing disrespect to your family.* So the boy and the man were related. It seemed obvious now. They both had latte-colored skin, black hair, dark eyes and similar features. The resemblance stopped there, however. Gilberto had a shy, nervous demeanor; by contrast, his relative wore resentment and belligerence like a second skin.

"I'm telling you, Gilberto, if you bring any more trouble

home, I'm going to—" Cutting himself off, he thumped his balled fist against the table.

Derek's entire body tensed.

Like a puppy trying to evade his master's anger, Gilberto kept his eyes averted. He blinked several times rapidly. Willa recognized that expression: a child trying desperately not to cry in public. A child in pain.

"Excuse me," she said to the man, "I didn't catch your name."

"Roddy."

"Roddy. And are you Gilberto's...father?"

"Hell, no! That would make me, like, fifteen when he was born. I been more careful than that." He pointed between Gilberto and himself. "We're blood, so anything anybody's got to say goes through me. If he stole from you, *I* deal with it."

"If he stole, the *law* will deal with it, Mr. Lopez," Derek interjected, his voice calm, but every muscle in his body rigid. "What is your relationship *exactly*?"

"He's my cousin. I can take care of him."

Derek nodded slowly. "I appreciate your taking responsibility and asking Gilberto to do the same, but the law is involved now. We'll be keeping our eye on the situation. The *whole* situation."

"What's that mean?"

"Just what I said. Our interest in Gilberto will continue."

Derek was giving the man a clear message that abuse would not be tolerated. But Mr. Lopez was a bully, and Willa knew Derek wouldn't be able to intervene in their daily lives. More sadness washed through her. *Not your business. Stick to your own business.* She looked at Gilberto. "He didn't steal from me. He looks a lot like the boy who was in here yesterday, but...it's not him."

Gilberto's surprise was palpable. Derek looked at her. "He nodded when I asked if he took the donation jar."

"He's not the one."

Derek turned back to the boy. "Why did you nod?" he asked.

Evading everyone's gaze, Gilberto shrugged.

It was clear the men were about to cross-examine him. "Maybe he was afraid," she offered, "and thought things would be easier if he told you what you wanted to hear."

"Is that what happened?" Derek questioned.

Gilberto shrugged again.

Roddy smacked his hands on his thighs and slid low in his seat, tossing back his head. "Aw! Are you crazy? You lied to get *into* trouble. Cops love stupid suspects like you." He looked at Derek. "No offense, man."

Derek stared long enough to make Roddy sit up in his seat. "None taken." Then he turned his attention back to Gilberto. The next obvious question was *Where did you get the money you were exchanging for the bike?* but Derek didn't ask it. After a moment, he rose. "Make sure you're in school when you're supposed to be. I'll be checking with your teacher and the principal. Don't make me come look for you."

Gilberto nodded. He looked miserable still, but relieved and more than a little surprised. Was it over?

Willa supposed she was excused from the meeting and pushed back her chair.

"Walk me to the door, Ms. Holmes." In an official tone, Derek commanded rather than asked for her compliance.

Izzy appeared bemused by the entire exchange and simply shook her head. "I'm heading back to the deli. I'm sorry for the confusion, Mr. Lopez. Please feel free to order something on the house." Walking around them all, Izzy was the first out the door, followed swiftly by Roddy, who pushed Gilberto along in front of him, saying they'd take a rain check on the free snacks.

Now that her burst of adrenaline was spent, Willa felt exhausted all over again and proceeded heavily to the exit. Every movement felt like a Herculean effort. Raising his arm over her, Derek held the door while she passed through. Willa burrowed into her jacket, as she stepped onto a rain-sprinkled sidewalk. By tacit agreement, they walked several paces past the bakery then stopped.

"Thanks for going to the station last night to give the description of the boy who stole the money." Not bothered by the cold or the rain, Derek towered above her, six foot plus of straight-backed sheriff. "And for coming back to the bakery this afternoon. I thought it might be easier for everyone if we handled it away from my office. You know, still official, but less intimidating. I anticipated that would make it easier to figure out where we would go from here to help Gilberto."

Willa felt Derek studying her, but she kept her tired gaze on the street, watching the occasional car roll past.

"What I didn't figure on," he continued, "was walking away with mud on my face. I didn't figure on *you*."

She glanced up to see the first hint of anger she'd ever noticed him directing toward her.

Resting both hands on his gun belt, he shook his head. "I'm a good judge of people. In my line of work, you have to be. But this time, I blew it. I never, ever judged you to be a liar."

Chapter Four

"A liar?"

Fire-engine red filled Willa's body, flared in her face. She wouldn't be surprised if the color poured in jets of steam from her ears. *He was calling her a liar?*

Okay, she *had* lied. But the reason ought to be obvious.

Her fists were stuffed into the pockets of her thin coat. Pulling one hand out, she jabbed a finger toward the end of the street and stormed off, rounding the corner, not stopping until she reached the alley. "How dare you?" Her voice shook. "I told you I didn't want to get involved in this, but you had to keep pushing. If you could take no for an answer, there wouldn't be a problem."

The implication of her words hit them both at the same time. He hadn't accepted her "no" regarding Gilberto, and he hadn't accepted her "no" regarding the two of them.

Derek's face grew stormier. "The problem was already here. If you think anything else, you're being naïve."

Was he talking about Gilberto now or her? Willa pointed toward the bakery. "That man—Roddy," she said. "He was going to make that poor kid's life a nightmare."

"That 'poor kid' is going to make his own life a nightmare if he meets his needs by stealing. Roddy talks big, but he has a record, too. Petty crime is a family affair."

"I'm sure there are ways to help Gilberto that don't involve the law, exactly. His school—"

"'The law' is a set of boundaries designed to establish and maintain order. That's exactly what Gilberto needs and exactly what he's not going to get if bleeding hearts make excuses for him."

"Bleeding hearts! I can't believe you said that." Willa shook her head as if to dislodge his words from her brain. "Life does not respect rules and regulations. Life just happens, and it doesn't ask your permission before it gets messy, although that might be hard for you to accept, Sheriff. I've seen the way you run around town, trying to convince people we're all characters in a nineteen fifties TV sitcom."

"What are you talking about?" The words emerged muffled as Derek's jaw and lips barely moved.

"I'm talking about your town meetings and visits to the chamber of commerce and all the other places you go to tell people that as long as they do the right thing, they'll stay safe and happy and the world will be a better place, now let's all go have donuts. The end."

"I'm sorry you dislike the message that playing by the rules does make the world safer and better. I've found it to be true."

"Lucky you."

Derek's entire manner was different from anything she had seen before. His body looked stiff enough to break, and Willa sensed she should stop talking, just let it go, but he was so *sure* of himself, so smug about the world and how it worked, and she couldn't stay quiet. Especially since he'd called her a bleeding heart. "If you think Gilberto is going to have a better life because I rat him out to his bully of a cousin, then *you're* the one who's naïve, not me."

There were no lights in the alley, save for porch lights above the back doors of the businesses along Warm Springs Road, but Willa could see Derek's expression—closed and distant—and knew he could see hers.

In the chilly night, her breath came in small, visible puffs. She didn't feel cold, though. Her face and hands felt hot enough to fry eggs.

It wasn't like her to confront and criticize. She wished he'd say something back. Something stubborn and intractable, so she could walk away thinking, *See, I knew it. He's just another lucky-so-far chump who thinks he's in charge of his fate. Boy, is he in for a shock someday.*

Derek's granite features changed not one whit as he tipped his head. "Thank you for coming tonight, Ms. Holmes. It's dark out. Do you need a ride to your house, or are you alright?"

Willa's emotions slammed to a roadrunner-like halt. He was the sheriff again, *just* the sheriff. A lump filled her throat, making it hard to swallow. "I'm fine."

"Good night." With another professionally polite nod, he turned. Willa watched him walk to the end of the alley and round the corner without a backward glance.

Usually, Willa awoke a good half hour before her alarm. Taking a shower before bed, all she had to do prior to heading to work was brush her teeth, comb her hair, pull on jeans, a Something Sweet T-shirt and her work clogs and head out the door. Once again, she'd barely slept at all, however, after the scene with Derek, and on this dark winter morning, she drank black tea and watched the digital clock until it read 2:45 a.m.

Instantly speed-dialing Daisy Dunnigan, Willa waited for the grumpy, caffeine-deprived "I can't believe it's morning already" that was her best friend's characteristic greeting. A renowned New York chef, Daisy owned and operated two unpretentious but fabulous restaurants—Goodness in Soho and More Goodness in Jackson Heights—and was one of the judges on a top-rated cable cooking show. Basically, she was a star, but Willa had known her since they'd attended culinary arts school together, and they were, above all, each other's support system.

This morning, Daisy answered on the fourth ring. "Damn, what time is it?" She sounded sleepier than usual.

"Five forty-five in your neck of the woods," Willa informed. "Didn't your alarm go off?"

"It must have been about to." There was a rustling of sheets. "What's up, tootsie? How's life in Mayberry R.F.D.?"

A smile rose to Willa's face, and she was grateful already that she'd phoned. Padding to her kitchen, she pulled several carrot-raisin muffins out of a plastic container, drizzled them with water and popped them into the microwave so they would steam.

"I pissed off the sheriff," she said baldly, placing a challah bread she'd brought home from the bakery into a picnic basket.

"Sheriff McYummy?" Visiting Thunder Ridge for a weekend the previous spring, Daisy had noticed Derek immediately. "Is he still stalking you?"

"He doesn't stalk me."

"With his eyes, he does. I would *love* to be stalked by eyes the color of a Mississippi mud pie. So how'd you piss him off?"

Ignoring the comment about Derek's eyes (which, yes, were almost impossibly dark and chocolaty and, well, deep) Willa said as casually as she could, "We had a disagreement about how to handle a petty theft at the bakery. A child took a few bucks. Sheriff Neel wanted to do something about it, and I didn't. Should have been the end of the story, but we got into a… I don't know, I said some things I shouldn't have, I suppose. Now I feel guilty. I mean, the whole thing—it's no big deal, right? You can't please everyone." She shoved a can of cat food and a small plastic bowl into the basket. "You're so good at saying what you think and damn the torpedoes. That's how I want to be." She forced a laugh. "That's how I am *going* to be! I'm so glad you picked up the phone. I always feel better after we talk."

The silence on the other end was deafening. There weren't even sounds of coffee preparation. Finally, Daisy commented with uncommon gentleness. "You're starting to feel again."

Right in the solar plexus. That's where Daisy's comment struck. Waves of nausea and pain and anger washed through Willa. "I don't know what you mean," she half whispered, half gasped. "I've done nothing but feel for two years."

"No." Daisy's voice remained calm and low. "Honey, you felt pain and grief more than anyone should have to for longer than anyone should have to. Then you moved to that tiny Main Street, USA and buried yourself right along with—"

"Stop! Don't say it. Don't—" Tears choked her throat, blocking words. *No. She didn't want to feel this. Didn't have to.* She shoved the pain away. "I actually have to go to work."

"Wills," Daisy said, anxiety creeping into her voice, "I didn't mean—"

"No. It's fine."

"It's not fine!" Daisy grew adamant. "You should do more than argue with that sheriff. You need to live again. Really live."

Willa bit her bottom lip so hard, it hurt. She couldn't even remember what lust felt like.

"This was a piss-poor way to start your day, huh?"

Willa heard the self-deprecation in her friend's awkward chuckle and felt guilty. "No, it's fine." Extracting the muffins from the microwave, she tried hard to infuse her tone with positivity. "Everything is fine. I do have to go, though. I'm sorry I had to call and run."

"Right." Daisy clipped the word. "Just do me one favor, okay?"

"What?"

"Stop saying everything is fine."

A mouthful of hot black coffee kept Derek awake. He wasn't on patrol tonight, but had rolled out of bed in the wee hours, showered, dressed in street clothes then grabbed a heavy jacket and a thermos of coffee to ward off the 3:00 a.m. chill. Now, as he sat in his truck, waiting, he felt the lack of sleep catching up to him.

He wasn't up this early to watch over the streets of his town; he was up this early to watch over...

Someone.

She was late. Usually, she hit the corner of Pine and Fourth before his watch read three-oh-five. It was already ten minutes past.

"You're an idiot." Sinking down into his coat, watching the windows on the cab of his truck fog up from the cold and his breath, he thought about the previous night. Frustration welled inside him all over again.

She thought he was a joke. Out of touch. Annoying.

Insensitive toward young children. A nineteen fifties TV sitcom.

The cynicism in her voice and face last night had surprised him.

"But then, you don't really know her." That was the problem, wasn't it? He'd turned Willa into a fantasy, not a real woman. He only *thought* he knew everything he needed to. Izzy was right.

His current fatigue and irritability aside, his body reacted like a sheriff's the moment she came into view, one lone figure bundled into a puffy jacket that just barely covered her perfect jeans-clad bottom, a wool hat covering the red-gold hair that had made her blend into fall like a fairy. She typically wore her clogs on these morning strolls through town, and he was always afraid she was going to slip on black ice in those damn shoes.

Staying in the truck for the first leg of her journey, he watched as she climbed the porch steps to Belleruth Hudson's house. Belleruth was in her sixties, had famously suffered from insomnia since the death of her husband some ten years earlier and clicked her lights on around 2:00 a.m. She was one of the first customers at The Pickle Jar every morning. Willa had gotten to know her there. Shortly after Something Sweet had opened, Willa had begun carrying her picnic basket to the Hudson home in the wee hours. Sometimes she went in for a brief visit, but most of the time, like this morning, she dropped off some food and continued on her walk, in the opposite direction of Derek's truck.

He'd worn sneakers this morning, for their footstep-muffling effect. When Willa was far enough along the street that he could see her without risking her hearing him, he exited his vehicle.

There were no sidewalks in this part of town, so he

stayed close to the lawns belonging to the cottages and wood-sided, two-story homes that looped like pearls on a necklace through Thunder Ridge's downtown residential neighborhood. At the corner, Willa turned left and headed to Doc Howard Park. Derek paused, mostly hidden from view behind Rand Moser's fifth wheel. He knew it would take a few moments for Willa to complete this part of her nightly ritual, so he blew into his cold hands and waited.

Before too long, the visitor she was waiting for arrived, pausing some distance from the bench. Reaching into the basket, she withdrew the container of cat food, emptied it into a bowl and it on the ground. The cat that had slithered out of its hiding places lunged for the food and ate voraciously. When the meal was over, Willa held out her hand, presumably holding another morsel, until it dared to approach. It was the same every morning. Still as a statue, she waited for the cat to sniff her hand. Eventually it ate the tendered treat then sat and stared at her as she slipped off the bench, crouched on the frosty grass and spoke patiently until the animal allowed her to stroke it. Sometimes she tucked the skinny feline into her jacket to warm it up, but tonight a dog barked in the distance, and the cat ran off. Willa looked after it for a while then rose to collect the empty bowl.

And this was the cynical woman who had accused him of trying to recreate Mayberry.

As she continued on her walk to the bakery, Derek started after her, but slipped on a patch of black ice. Grabbing for the bike rack on the back of Rand's fifth wheel, he hung on while his feet flailed. The fifth wheel rocked, and a shouted cry of "Earthquake!" came from inside just moments before the trailer's side door banged open to more shouting. "It's The Big One!"

"Shh! For Pete's sake, be quiet, Rand!

"Who's there? Who's that?"

"It's me, Derek." Regaining his footing, Derek faced the man who had emerged wearing nothing but a pair of thermal underwear.

"Derek? Did you feel the earthquake?" Rand's question was practically a shout.

"Shhh. There was no earthquake."

Lights clicked on next door at the Newman's and across the street at Jim and Ellen Lathrop's place. *Aw, criminy.* "Rand, go back inside."

"Can't. Patty says she can hear my snoring clear into the living room."

"Well, go back in the trailer then."

"Sheriff?" Denise Newman, wrapped in a thick robe, called from her front door, "What's wrong?"

"Nothing. Please, go back in—"

"Did you feel the shaking, Denise?" Rand called to his neighbor. "This could be The Big One. I say we all gather in the center of the street."

"No! No one gather in the center of the street." Derek held up his hands. Glancing quickly toward the park, he noted it was empty. *Damn.* Willa had moved on and would now be walking by herself in the wee hours of the morning with no one to watch over her. Later this morning, he was going to talk to Izzy about changing Willa's hours, so she didn't have to go to work in the dark.

Joining the modest throng around the fifth wheel, the Lathrops arrived, huddling in their pj's. "We're all wide awake now," Jim observed in his eminently reasonable, retired radio announcer's voice. "Perhaps this would be a good time to discuss the value of forming a disaster preparedness committee in Thunder Ridge."

As murmurs of assent rose around him, Derek clapped a palm to his forehead. Patty Moser opened her front door, first asking what all the commotion was about and then offering to start a pot of coffee and make cinnamon rolls from a can. "You'll join us, won't you, Willa?"

Willa? Glancing all around until he saw a small figure standing quietly by the trailer's bumper, Derek felt his heart lurch. She was staring at him.

"I'm on my way to work, actually."

"Oh, that makes sense." Denise Newman nodded. "I didn't think you lived around here."

"Nope," Willa agreed. "I live a few blocks south." She continued to gaze at Derek. "How about you, sheriff? Do *you* live around here?" She tilted her head, brows arched. "You don't look like you're on duty."

All attention focused on him. Derek's blood pressure spiked. "I'm not on duty, no."

"What were you doing around my fifth wheel?" asked Rand. "Were you staking out someone suspicious?" He glanced around.

"No, Rand. Everything's fine. I was…doing a foot patrol."

"Off duty?" Jim asked.

Denise clasped her hands beneath her chin. "This is just why I moved from Portland. The caring, the concern. Sheriff, I sleep better knowing you're near."

"We *all* do," Patty enthused.

In the glare of the sensor light above the Mosers' garage, it was easy to see the amused quirk of Willa's lips.

"Thank you," Derek replied, "it's nice to be appreciated."

"Come inside for a cinnamon roll," Patty urged. "It'll only take a minute in the toaster oven."

"You all go ahead and go inside now, folks," Derek nodded toward the house. "I'll walk Ms. Holmes to the bakery. It's too dark to be out alone." He took Willa's arm as the party moved indoors.

Derek escorted her up the block. Once they'd cleared a couple of houses, she asked curiously, "Have you been spying on me, Sheriff?"

"Spying?"

"Yeah. It's the word we non–law enforcement folks use for sneaking around, watching people without their knowledge." Stopping, she turned toward him in the dark, barely reaching his chin. "Why have you been doing it?"

Chapter Five

"I haven't been spying on you, Willa. Spying implies looking for information. That's not what I was doing."

Without touching her again, Derek crossed the street toward the park, listening for the sound of her rubber-soled clogs following him. He stopped when he reached the bench where she sat so patiently every morning.

Patience was not the feeling that exuded from her now. Below the rim of her knitted hat, her auburn brows—so silky and perfect they looked like a child's—drew together in a troubled pucker.

Desire punched him in the gut. And upside the head. His whole life he'd waited for the feeling he got when he looked at Willa, was near Willa, thought about Willa. It was a feeling of hope so broad and deep that it set his imagination on fire. He saw them together, bodies tangled, hearts beating in time. He pictured living in a home instead of a house, lifting a laughing child who looked like her over his head. He could imagine for the first time quenching his soul-deep thirst.

And now he understood, finally, that it was just a mirage.

"You feed stray cats," he said, his voice hoarse.

She looked at him, perplexed. "So?"

"You deliver food to lonely insomniacs."

Willa blinked owlishly. "How long have you been following me?"

"Since the week the bakery opened. I was on patrol the first time I saw you walking through town. I know you work early, but two-thirty, three in the morning? No one should be out wandering the streets. I don't care how safe or quaint or backward you think this town is."

"I lived in Los Angeles, Sheriff. I've taken self-defense classes, and I carry pepper spray. I can take care of myself."

He nodded. "Glad to hear it. But Thunder Ridge is mine to protect." May as well get that out of the way. She could liken him to a TV character if she wanted, but that wasn't going to change who he was. "Mine to watch over."

"So you followed me that morning. And you've been following me ever since?"

He nodded.

"Even when you're not on duty?"

Hands in his pockets, he stared over her head. How much should he say? Did it matter? He wasn't trying to "win" her anymore. "I like a puzzle." Lowering his gaze to her face, he added, "Here's one I've been trying to solve. A beautiful woman, generous and kind, wants to be left alone, but reaches out to widows and spends hours coaxing scrawny feral cats to come to her so she can feed them. She doesn't ask anything from anyone. In fact, when you reach out to her, she takes flight like a wild bird."

Under the dim street lamp, he caught her wince. "You're trying to analyze me."

Nodding, Derek just barely refrained from touching the soft auburn waves that flowed from beneath the wool cap to caress her shoulders. "True. And, really, I should be analyzing myself. Why can't I stop thinking about you?"

The space between them buzzed and crackled like water on a hot skillet. She could have walked away then, but didn't. Derek knew that after tonight he would discipline his mind to think of anything but the woman in front of him. He would force himself to accept that she would never be his, but in these final moments of longing, he wanted one—just one—taste of the heaven he'd hoped for.

Suddenly, there was less space between them. One hand left his jacket pocket and touched the back of her head, the knitted hat rough and nubby, the auburn hair soft as a dove.

Remember it all, he told himself, knowing he wouldn't fall this hard again for a long, long time.

Willa's lips parted, and her breath escaped in a wintery puff. He could see her white, even teeth and wished not for the first time that he'd been able to make her smile or laugh more often.

"Who have you loved?"

He realized he spoke the question out loud when her eyes, misty gray and achingly beautiful, filled with tears.

"Don't," he whispered, not wanting to be the cause of her pain, remembered or otherwise. Raising his free hand, he thumbed away the first tear that fell, and a force as powerful as gravity gripped him. It was the pull of the moon, heaven reaching down to earth.

Just this once…

Her mouth was warm and sweet beneath his. He meant to stop at just the barest touch of lips, but desire fired his veins when she leaned into him. One hand cupped her jaw, the other the back of her head. He let his kiss communicate what he hadn't been able to say up to now.

He kissed the corner of her mouth, inhaled her scent, nuzzled her jaw. She let him. Her skin was like silk.

"Sorry, I didn't shave," he murmured. Sometimes before he arose to watch over her solitary walk through town, he would shave to be ready for the day ahead. He'd tossed and turned so much last night, however, that this morning he hadn't had time. "Too rough?"

In lieu of answering, she sought his lips again, and his body felt as if it were expanding to fill all of Thunder Ridge. Light as a butterfly, her hands settled atop his chest as she kissed him. He could tell when she began to surrender to the heat and the need, but then he realized something: while he was finding himself in their kiss, Willa, he sensed, was trying to lose herself, to lose for a moment the pain she refused to discuss.

Disappointment began to dull some of his lust. With one gentle, final kiss, he drew back. She seemed dazed. They stood still, foggy breath mingling in the cold, as he waited for her to steady herself.

"Almost time for you to get to work," he said roughly, as if that were an explanation for ending one of the best sensations he'd ever had. Willa was obviously perplexed.

Toward the latter part of his turbulent teens, Derek had learned the art of disciplining himself to think first, react later, but when Willa's brow knit more deeply, it was all he could do not to kiss the confusion away.

Knowing better than to keep touching her, he shoved his hands back into his jacket pockets. "Come on," he said, shooting for a lightness he sure didn't feel, "I'll stalk you to the bakery. One last shadow for old time's sake."

The irony didn't relax her. Nodding mechanically, she fell into step by his side. Neither spoke as they walked through the quiet streets of Thunder Ridge. Frustration rocked Derek's body, and his mind spun. He wondered if Willa felt the same.

Barreling through the door that was stenciled *This Way to The Pickle Jar,* Willa's boss began talking before she was fully across the threshold. "Okay, the cinnamon–hot chocolate cake was a total hit. We sold every piece at lunch, and people are asking if they can buy whole cakes. That toasted Swiss meringue frosting?" Izzy grinned. "Genius."

Willa nodded from where she was putting stickers on bags of the *zimmel* rolls that Izzy stacked by the cash register in the deli every evening. "Oh, good. Good." Distracted, she didn't even notice Izzy coming round to the clerk side of the counter until a hand shot out, grabbing one of the still-warm rolls.

"I am ravenous lately," Izzy said. "It's always that way in winter." Tearing off a hunk of the soft bread, the energetic blonde dunked it in the coffee she'd brought with her and popped it into her mouth. "So. How would you feel about baking cakes regularly? We would hire more help, of course, to free up your time. Someone else could come in early and bake the breads and rolls—although, oh my lord, you have a way with dough—and we could hire more counter help, too. Because if you agree, I'm thinking we could actually expand the bakery to provide more special occasion cakes."

"Oh, yeah?"

Izzy nodded, making her curls bounce. "You can get a basic wedding cake out here, but if you want something truly fabulous, you need to order it from Portland and transport it yourself."

"Wedding cakes?"

"It's only a thought for now." Clearly hearing Willa's

hesitation, Izzy dialed down her enthusiasm a notch. "It just seems that you know your way around flavors and decorations. And if that part of the business should take off, you could become a kind of artistic director. Anyway, mull it over." She dunked more of the roll into her coffee. "Plus, it would mean you wouldn't have to come to work so early. You could start, you know…after sunrise."

Something about her boss's tone made Willa suspicious. "After sunrise," she repeated. "I don't think so. I'd probably start the same time as usual."

"Oh. Really?" Izzy continued to dunk the roll hypnotically, unmindful of the fact that it was becoming so saturated with liquid that a sizable piece of it was about to fall off into the coffee cup. "Hmm. I don't know. There might not be enough room back there—" she gestured to the kitchen "—for you *and* someone baking the bread. And bread and coffee cakes and Danishes would be a priority, time-wise. Actually, now that I think of it, maybe we should switch up your schedule anyway. Move Norman into the opening shift. He *loves* to get up early…although, wow, you *really* do make great dough." She caught the soaked roll on her tongue just before it fell.

"Izzy," Willa ventured, "is my coming in later *your* idea?"

Izzy's faux-innocent expression was comical. "Yeah. I just thought, you know, there's a new yoga class starting at six a.m. at the community center. You wanna go? Very relaxing, I'm sure. It's just, you know…yeah."

All day, Willa had tried to understand how Derek could have begun kissing her the way he had and then stop abruptly. She'd tried to figure out whether she was glad he'd agreed not to "stalk" her in the morning anymore. And, she'd tried to tolerate the restlessness she'd felt when he'd failed to appear for his usual bagel and coffee for the first time since the bakery's grand opening.

"Did Sheriff Neel suggest I come in later?"

"What?" Izzy exclaimed, embarking on the conversational equivalent of a dog paddle. "Derek suggest that you come in later? Nooooo! Why would he? He never talks about you. At all. I mean except to say something nice. And impersonal." Izzy's fake laugh made it clear that participating in the Thunder Ridge Community Theatre would be ill-advised. "I just thought, you know, we women need our beauty rest, and it's not good to mess with our circadian rhythms." Her shoulders flagged. "Okay, yeah, it was Derek. But only because he's a very conscientious sheriff. Not for any other reason." Setting her coffee on the counter, she covered her face with her hands. "I am so bad at this. He told me not to let you know he talked to me, so please don't say anything?"

A strange, sweet relief curled through Willa's stomach. Last night the thought of his following her, watching her, getting too close raised all her alarm bells, but after that kiss... "I won't say anything," she assured.

"Thank you." Izzy's expression relaxed. "I was serious about the wedding cakes, though. Your baking is out of this world. And when you think about all the people who rent the Summit Lodge for weddings and anniversaries and birthday bashes...ooh, I would love to get a piece of that business! We wouldn't necessarily have to stay local, either."

As Izzy began to rhapsodize about a new branch of the bakery, Willa's attention drifted to dark chocolate eyes, broad shoulders, warm skin and a kiss that made her forget everything but the lips moving on hers. She couldn't figure out why he'd *stopped* kissing her, unless the experience had disappointed him? She hadn't kissed anyone in a long time; she was certainly out of practice. And he had caught her off guard. Although, let's face it, in vulnerable deep-of-the-night moments she had relived their first kiss a time or two and wondered if it would be that good again. And it had been, as far as she was concerned. Keeping her eye on the clock all morning, she'd wanted Derek to come in to order his bagel and give her a clue about where they went from here. When he'd failed to show, her mind had refused to stop thinking about him.

"I'm getting ahead of myself, aren't I?" Suddenly contrite, Izzy interrupted her own soliloquy about the business. "Never mind. I'll do some market research, and we can talk about it another time. If it doesn't suit you—"

"No, no." *For heaven's sake, focus. You're at work.* "It's a good idea. Great."

"You really think so?"

"Absolutely," Willa confirmed. "Special occasion cakes are a big industry."

"Exactly! Look at *Cake Boss*."

"That's right. And imagine the advertising possibilities. We could wear T-shirts that say Got cake? above a three-tier, tap-dancing mocha sponge covered in vanilla buttercream." Izzy's T-shirt designs were infamous. Willa joked so infrequently these days, it felt good to tease.

Izzy, who was in fact wearing a gray hoodie sporting a dancing pickle, nodded knowingly. "Fine. You're making fun of me." Grabbing a sugar packet, she slapped it against her palm before opening it and pouring it into her coffee. "Just like Derek. He disses my Pickle Jar hoodies every chance he gets, but I sold a bunch of them over Christmas."

The mention of Derek's name made heat rush to Willa's face, and Izzy noticed. "Derek had breakfast at the deli this morning," she mentioned, picking up her coffee and another roll and taking them with her to the door adjoining

the deli and bakery. Before she opened it, she looked back
soberly. "I've known him since he was nineteen. He's as
good as they come. I'm not sure what's happening between
the two of you, but if there's no chance for a relationship,
please make that clear to him. Really clear. His life hasn't
always been easy, and sometimes I think he—" She gri-
maced. "Okay, never mind. I am such a buttinsky!" She
knocked herself in the head with the *zimmel* roll. "Like
I'm such a relationship expert." With a wry expression, she
shook her head. "Sorry. Really. Forget I spoke."

Willa gazed at her boss, letting the words sink in. *Don't
hurt my friend* was what she was saying. Ashamedly, for
the first time, Willa realized Derek might not be the im-
perturbable Rock of Gibraltar she imagined. She'd been
hurting for so long that, selfishly, she forgot how easy it
was to wound someone else.

"You seem to have done quite well in the relationship
department," she commented admiringly, sincerely, and
a pretty pink filled Izzy's cheeks.

"It took a while, but yeah."

Reunited with the father of her son, Izzy was now part
of an adoring trio. But that wasn't all that Willa meant.
Prior to Nate Thayer's return to Thunder Ridge, Izzy had
already turned her friends and coworkers into a family.

Chewing the inside of her cheek, Willa wondered what
the people in this tightknit town thought of her unwilling-
ness to become personally involved? Perhaps she should
have remained in a big, anonymous city, after all.

"Hey, isn't that the kid Derek thought stole the donation
jar? Did you hire him to clean the windows?"

Willa looked at Izzy to see her peering at the large window in the front of the shop. With a spray bottle containing a blue solution in one hand and a wad of newspaper

in the other, Gilberto was staring at the gold letters that spelled *Something Sweet*.

"Yes, that's him. But I didn't hire him." Willa walked around the counter. "What's he doing?"

"Looks like he's going to wash the windows. I wonder if he's trying to earn money? Why don't you ask him, and if that's what he's trying to do, pay him out of petty cash. He can come next door, too."

Willa nodded, waiting for Izzy to close the door to the diner before she headed outside. Gilberto startled a bit when he saw her, even though he knew she worked there. Guilt crawled across his features. He and Willa knew what Izzy did not, of course: that he *had* stolen the money.

"Hello."

"Hi," he mumbled.

"What are you doing?"

"I'm gonna clean your windows."

"Well, thank you, but I actually cleaned them this morning. Are you trying to earn money?" If he was, she would send him next door right away.

He shook his head. "I can't earn money for this. I'm supposed to do it for free."

"Supposed to?"

"When you didn't tell on me, the sheriff said you saved my butt, and I better figure out how to show you I'm worth it."

"So you decided to wash the bakery windows?"

"No. The sheriff, he said I look like a good window washer. And after I wash the windows, I'm gonna sweep inside the bakery."

What? "That sounds like a very long afternoon. What grade are you in?"

"Sixth."

Sixth. That made him eleven or twelve. Remembrance

pierced Willa like an arrow. "I'm sure you have home-work—"

"Sheriff's going to help me. Afterward. I come here every afternoon when school's out, and then he helps me with math and stuff. Then he's going to drive me home. He's driving me *in the squad car.*"

"Every day? Is that what the sheriff told you to do?"

"He says a boy runs away, but a man pays his debts. So I'm here, paying them."

The tug on Willa's heart was not the least bit com-fortable. "I appreciate what you're doing, and the sheriff was right about making restitution for what you took, but, um…" A thought, stuck her. "Does your cousin agree to this?"

Gilberto's gaze shifted downward. "He doesn't know," he mumbled.

"Gilberto," she began carefully.

The boy's eyes widened. "The sheriff's here to check on me. I gotta get to work." Spraying the windows with vigor, Gilberto used the wadded newspaper to scrub the glass.

Willa turned around, to where Gilberto had been look-ing, and there, indeed, was Derek, striding down the street with his customary confidence. His features were neutral, unreadable. When he made eye contact with her, Willa couldn't see his expression change one bit, even though her body reacted instantly and without her permission, simply to the sight of him.

She was pretty sure that for the rest of her life, when she thought about Derek Neel, she would picture him first in his uniform. Its desert-sand color was a perfect comple-ment to his deeply tan complexion and black hair. Crisp, always perfectly ironed, the uniform emphasized his lean, muscular frame, which in turn spotlighted his height. He looked like he could whip the bad guys with a flick of his wrist.

Exactly how a lawman should look.

Why had she called him a TV sitcom sheriff? That was so hurtful. So unlike her. And, really, if he did remind her of a TV sheriff, it was in all the good ways. He was honest and ethical, and he made people feel better. Safer.

"Afternoon, Ms. Holmes." He tipped his head to her, and she noticed he'd had his hair cut. The thick waves were shorter on the sides.

"Sheriff."

"Gilberto," he said. "Right on time."

"I was early."

Derek's eyes glinted with approval. "Good man."

Gilberto nodded, hair the same shade as Derek's flopping into his eyes. Standing taller, prouder, he used both hands to wipe down the window.

Willa was struck by the similarity between the two of them. They both had café au lait skin, hair as dense as a string mop, and eyes so dark it was hard to distinguish the iris from the pupil.

"Sheriff," she said, "may I speak with you, please? In the bakery?"

He glanced at his watch. "I have a couple of minutes." *Only* a couple, his tone stated.

"Fine." She led the way inside and rubbed her arms as warm, bread-scented air welcomed them in from the cold. "Would you like a cup of coffee?"

"No, thank you."

All right. Down to business. "Sheriff, I think what you're doing with Gilberto is admirable. No one could argue that you're influencing him in a positive way. But I would rather that you leave me…leave the bakery…out of it."

"Yes, you made that clear."

"Well, then you can see that his being here every day when I am trying to stay out of it might be awkward."

Derek appeared to ponder what she was saying. "Actually, no. How is it awkward? He's just a kid doing some chores."

Emotionally speaking, there was no such thing as "just a kid doing some chores." Not in Willa's world. And especially not when the kid was preteen and obviously aching for a parent.

"He could go to the deli. Izzy was saying she could use someone to do the windows over there. I have plenty of time in the mornings, so I always clean the bakery windows myself."

"Gilberto stole from the bakery. He's going to make amends to the bakery."

"Actually, he stole from the donation jar—"

"Same difference."

Derek's body and even his tone remained calm, but he was as immovable as the mountain that stood sentry over their town.

Willa swallowed, her initial fear turning into embarrassment that she was, once again, making a big deal of something in front of Derek. "Sure, sure. I don't mind taking a break from window washing for a few days."

"There was almost a hundred dollars in the jar. It'll be more than a few days. And I'd like to suggest you empty the jar more frequently."

He sounded impersonal, as if he was giving safety tips to the senior center. She said nothing.

"Was there anything else you needed to discuss?" he asked.

Yes, why did you stop kissing me last night?

"No. That was it."

"Alright." Derek glanced to the window, where Gilberto was working particularly hard on a spot. "I'll be supervising him. If anything comes up, call me."

She nodded. *Don't let him go. Find out why he didn't come to the bakery this morning. Tell him...tell him you missed seeing him.* Because it was true. There had been a gaping hole in her morning routine.

"Sheriff!" she called as he headed toward the door. Derek looked back. "I didn't thank you last night. For watching me on my way to work. I've become used to taking care of myself, so... Well, I'd just like to say thank you. I should have said it last night."

The muscles in his face relaxed. His eye color seemed to change from cold onyx to hot fudge. After gazing at her for a time without speaking, Derek gave a small shake of his head, more to himself than for her. "That's a relief," he said finally. "Now I won't have to figure out new ways to stay out of sight."

"You mean you're going to keep following me?"

"It's not safe to walk around town at three a.m." His rapid return to law enforcement mode made him look very, very cute. "If you insist on going for walks before work, I'll have to keep watch. Unless you're planning a change in schedule?"

Willa feigned an innocent expression. "You mean like if my job description were to change? If I started decorating cakes or something, for example?"

Derek rubbed his brow. "Izzy obviously handled that well."

Willa smiled. "Don't blame her. I'd probably still come to work early. I'm already awake in the morning, so—" She stopped, but not before raising his curiosity.

"Awake before three?" She expected him to question her about *why* she was awake so early, but instead he commented, "It's supposed to be a creative time, the very early morning. In days gone by, more people were awake in the wee hours. They worked or visited with neighbors. Or made love." He nodded. "Very powerful time."

There wasn't an iota of suggestiveness in his tone, but heat rose inside Willa like mercury in a thermometer. She felt herself blush from the tip of her toes to the top of her head.

"You can Google it," he added.

"I'll do that." Her voice was hoarse.

"Good afternoon, Ms. Holmes."

"Good afternoon, Sheriff."

Chapter Six

Crossing her arms on the desk, Holliday Bailey, local librarian and continual burr under Derek's saddle, beamed up at him. "I told you, in order to fulfill your request for a library card, I will need two pieces of mail with the potential cardholder's name and address."

"And I told you, I don't have two pieces of mail with Gilberto's name and address. So, can you make an exception?"

Holliday gasped. "What? Are you, Sheriff Follows-The-Rules, asking me to make an exception in library protocol for you? To, in fact, *break the rules*?" She placed a heavily jeweled hand over her chest. "I'm shocked. I'm appalled. I'm… I'm feeling faint." She glanced around. "Medic?"

"Hilarious," Derek affirmed since she seemed to need that. "You're hilarious. Now can you give me the library card, please?"

She started to respond, then looked beyond him. "Hi,

Willa! What can I do for you?" Glancing back at Derek, she widened her eyes. *Look who's here!*

Derek gritted his teeth. Holliday was one of Izzy's best friends. As such, Holliday and Derek had spent more time together than they otherwise would have. Over the past year plus, she'd figured out he had a crush on Willa.

"Hi," Willa responded, approaching the reference desk. "Hello, Sheriff."

"Ms. Holmes."

Holliday laughed. "You're so formal, you two. Let me introduce you. Derek, meet Willa. Willa, this is Derek."

As if God wove strands of hair out of autumn leaves, Willa's soft waves cascaded around her shoulders as she smiled his way. "Sheriff," she acknowledged, steadily meeting his eyes.

"Ms. Holmes," he responded once again, and the moment became private, all theirs, as together they affirmed that they would not be pushed around.

"Hopeless." Holliday wagged her head. "I have that book you put on hold, Willa. *Decorating with Gum Paste.* Looks fascinating."

"It is. But if you're helping Sheriff Neel, I can wait."

"I'm trying to get a library card for Gilberto," Derek shared. "He's never had one."

"Never?" Instantly, Willa's brow furrowed with concern. "I would think he'd need one for school, if nothing else."

Gilberto had been working at the bakery for almost a week. Derek picked him up in the squad car or in his truck—both of which Gilberto loved—after work, and drove him out of town to the house he shared with his cousin's family. Invariably, Gilberto would mention that Willa had provided a snack. He also said that she corrected his grammar, and when he stayed late asking for more chores, she told him he should be doing his home-work or playing a sport. Gilberto seemed to like that she talked to him that way.

"He does need a library card." Derek studied Willa, wondering if she would always remain a puzzle to him. She had seemed almost frantically opposed to Gilberto work-ing at the bakery at first, yet she cared about his welfare. She'd protested when she'd found out Derek was following her, yet kissed him back. Kissed him hungrily.

"Here's the application." Holliday slid a rectangular printed card toward Derek. "Fill it out to the best of your ability. Let me get your hold, Willa." Pushing away from the desk, she rose and walked away on teetering high heels.

There were few similarities between Willa and the li-brarian. Holliday's bold, in-your-face sex appeal was a lightning storm; Willa's soft sensuality reminded him of a gentle rain. Not that she was simple, though. Nope. Any-thing but.

"So." Off duty, Derek slipped a hand in the pocket of his jeans. "Anything new?"

"Yes, actually. I'm thinking about decorating wedding cakes." She grinned. After unzipping the puffy white jacket that made her look like she was about to push off a ski slope, Willa unwound the raspberry-colored scarf around her neck. "Gilberto told me you're helping him with homework. Sounds as if he's behind in most of his classes?"

"All of them. A couple of years behind in math. I spoke with his teacher. He has no learning disabilities, just a poor attendance record since first grade."

"What happened in first grade?"

Derek glanced around the area in which they stood. Gilberto lived outside of town, but he attended school in

Thunder Ridge. He had a right to some privacy. "Are you really interested in this?" he asked.

Willa looked offended at first then seemed to understand why he would ask. "Yes," she said solemnly. "I'm interested."

"I'm off duty. If you have a couple of minutes, I can fill you in once we're done here."

Willa nodded. Derek filled out the application for the library card with as much information as he knew. When Holliday returned with Willa's book, he handed her the application. In return, she gave him a plastic library card on which she instructed him to write Gilberto's name.

"I can take that to the front desk." Holliday pointed to the cake-decorating book in Willa's hand.

"Don't bother. We'll use your self-checkout," he said.

"Want me to walk you through?" Holliday asked him with feigned concern, her implication obviously that he was going to have trouble.

"Between the two of us, I think we'll manage."

"Yes, two is always better than one." She smiled benignly, but Derek knew she'd be on the phone to Izzy before he and Willa were out the door.

"Holliday was behaving a bit oddly," Willa commented as they emerged from the library.

"Holliday *is* a bit odd," Derek groused, but in truth the flaming redhead was more outrageous than odd. With her leopard-print sweaters and platform shoes, she was no one's idea of a small-town librarian. "She likes to poke at me."

"Hmm."

It was another cold winter day. Willa was already zipping her coat again.

"Let's find someplace warm and private, and I'll tell you what I know about Gilberto," he said.

"Someplace private doesn't exist in Thunder Ridge." Willa smiled as she wrapped herself in the scarf.

Derek's fingers itched with the urge to free her hair from beneath the knitted tube. "Do you have anywhere you need to be?"

"No. It's my day off."

"I know. I slept in."

Willa's pretty lips pursed as her smile widened. "You're doing a good job."

"At what?"

"Hiding when you follow me. I haven't seen you once all week."

Which meant she'd looked. "I've had practice."

Lately, it was all he could do at three in the morning not to join her on the park bench when she was feeding the damn cats and make out with her under the stars. But what had changed? He didn't want a relationship that was a mosaic of secrets.

"Come on." Escorting her to his restored fifty-seven pickup, he couldn't squelch the flash of pride and pleasure when she ran her fingers over the highly polished red hood.

"This is beautiful. How long have you had it?"

"Since I was nineteen. It'll be warm if I turn on the heat, and it's private if you don't mind sitting in a truck in the parking lot."

"I don't mind at all."

Opening the door, Derek had a feeling of déjà vu as she climbed in. How many times had he imagined Willa snuggling against him in the cab?

"Is it authentically restored?" she asked, touching the dashboard as he slid in on the driver's side.

"When I was nineteen, my friend Walt offered me a chance to restore the truck with him. I thought we were restoring it for him, and that was okay with me. It was the most fun I'd ever had. We worked on it for two years whenever he had spare time. In the second year, he let me work on it alone."

"He must have been a very good friend."

"The best."

Derek put the key in the ignition and let the engine idle so the heater could work. "Should get warm in here in a minute." Relaxing against the embossed vinyl seat back, he rested his wrist on a steering wheel that was approximately the diameter of an extra-large pizza. "Walt was a great man."

"How did you meet him?"

"Walt Martin was the sheriff of Thunder Ridge for nearly three decades. We met shortly after I arrived in Oregon. I'd been living with an uncle and aunt I didn't get along with very well, and I headed out on my own at seventeen. Back then my favorite sport was fighting anyone who was willing." Willa's slack-jawed surprise was almost comical.

"I'd been bumming around Portland," he continued. "I made my way out here, because I wanted someplace new to steal from." This time, he almost laughed out loud at Willa's expression. "I like to think I've changed for the better."

"So what kind of shenanigans brought you and Walt together?"

"I was a really clumsy burglar. Tripped alarms, alerted dogs. I never actually made it all the way into anyone's house, but I scared quite a few people. As the sheriff, Walt decided that rather than arresting me, he would take me under his wing. He held me accountable, though. I had to apologize to everyone I'd attempted to burgle. Walt saved my life."

Willa's once-again kind, always gorgeous, silver-blue

eyes glittered with understanding. "You're paying it forward with Gilberto."

He didn't need her admiration to know he was doing the right thing, but it sure felt good.

"Did Walt give you the truck when you were done working on it?" Willa asked.

"In a way. He offered to let me buy it, but for much less than he could have gotten from anyone else. He knew it would mean more to me if I could sit in it and say, 'I earned this.' Of course, at the time I had no idea he was deep, deep discounting it for me. All I knew was that it was the first thing I'd ever owned, and it made me feel like a king. In later years, I tried to pay him more, but he always refused to take my money. He said I could pay for the truck by being the man he knew I could be."

"So you became a sheriff like him."

"I'll be lucky to be half the man Walt Martin was. But, yes, I wanted to be a sheriff, because I saw how much he gave to the community. How much he belonged to it and how the community belonged to him."

The glance she gave him was heart-meltingly sincere, and suddenly the cold winter day felt like summer in the cab of his truck. Without a few dozen more sets of fingers and toes, it would be difficult to count the number of times he'd imagined being with Willa as they drove the River Loop on a day off from work, or parked behind the hay bales for the summer drive-up movies at Gold Meadow Farm. Sitting in a parking lot together was nowhere near the same as the scenarios he'd played out in his mind, but if this was as close as he was ever going to get, well, he'd take it.

He'd make a mental snapshot of her, this haunting, elusive woman whom he'd sometimes thought about day and night, and he'd store the memory away, taking it out when he needed a buffer against the solitary times ahead.

Willa couldn't believe she had dissed this very good man. "I truly am sorry I made that comment about TV sheriffs," she began.

He stopped her with a laugh. "I'm a big Andy Griffith fan. I like Westerns, too." His expression—amused, self-deprecating, and irresistibly boyish—made her toes curl in her boots.

"You know, I think Gilberto is a lot like me. He needs to belong somewhere. I never felt like part of something until Walt showed me I could be part of Thunder Ridge. It made all the difference to my motives. Changed me in a way I might otherwise have missed." He fiddled with the heat knob. "You warm enough?"

Willa nodded. It was impossible to feel cold sitting so close to him.

"Gilberto's parents are out of the picture," Derek went on, turning the subject toward the boy who was the reason they'd climbed into the truck to begin with.

A stab of frustration surprised her. She wanted to hear more about Derek. Marshaling her focus, she nodded for him to continue.

"According to his school records, he was being raised by an aunt who was a single parent with a few kids of her own. When the burden on her became overwhelming, Gilberto moved in with one cousin or another until he wound up with Roddy. Gilberto's teachers say he's smart and is always eager to learn when the school year begins, but as the lessons pick up steam, he falls behind and his absences begin to increase. It's a vicious cycle. Since first grade, he's been truant nearly fifty percent of the time."

Willa gasped.

"At this point," Derek said, "it's a pattern everyone's come to accept. But we're going to break the pattern."

So determined. So confident.

"Can the school give him extra support?" she asked.

"He doesn't qualify. Truancy isn't a learning disorder." Derek's fingers drummed the steering wheel. "Academics weren't my strength, but I'm going to help him any way I can."

Eyes narrowed, jaw set, he looked like a cross between heroic warrior and plain old determined dad when he spoke like that.

Gazing thoughtfully out the windshield, Willa made eye contact with Jeanne Frank and Myra Newsome as the duo crossed the parking lot on their way to the library. Both women exhibited obvious surprise at seeing her in the truck with Derek. Jeanne waved wildly, and Willa raised her hand limply in response. Myra was an inveterate gossip. Tempted to sink low in her seat, Willa looked at Derek for his response. If he noticed the women at all, he didn't seem to care that he and Willa were about to become headline news. He was still watching her.

"I thought you should know more about Gilberto," he was saying. "I want you to understand the impact that doing chores at the bakery is going to have on his life. I know, or I think I know, that it's been hard for you to have him there."

"Not hard," she said carefully. "He's fun to be around. He hums and dances now when he works."

Surprise and then gratification deepened Derek's smile.

"You'd be a good father," Willa blurted before she had time to think. She reached toward the dash, trailing her fingertips along the smooth, shiny red metal. It was cold, of course, a hundred and eighty degrees different from his skin, which had been warm the other night and downright hot to the touch the evening they'd made out after leaving the White Lightning Tavern together.

"I make whole grain bagels now," she said overly loudly to fill the conversational vacuum left by her awkwardness. "They're good, not too heavy." Her eyes were still trained on the dashboard rather than on the man who kept it polished. "We have a new cream cheese, too. Sweet Marionberry. In case you were thinking about coming in for breakfast again. Sometime."

Dear lord. Bagels and cream cheese? Seriously? Why couldn't she simply say what was on her mind? "We make our own jam now." *Oh, please.* "You haven't been in for a while, is the thing, and…you're missed. By everyone. All the regulars, everyone who's there in the morning, you know, misses seeing you." *Coward.*

Derek's expression did not say, "*This chick is crazy,*" but she figured that's what he was thinking. She needed to get honest. Just spit out what she wanted. And what she wanted was…?

His touch. His warmth to melt the chill in her soul. She wanted the feeling his arms and his lips had given her—the feeling of summer in the midst of an achingly long personal winter.

Her throat threatened to close with nerves, but she forced herself to speak. "I've missed seeing you, too."

One second passed. Then two. As she counted to five, she began to worry, stopped fiddling with the dashboard and chanced a look at his face.

Derek's brows were still pulled together. Rather than softening, his features were once again set in stern granite. "I need to head to the office. I have some paperwork to do."

Whoa. For the first time since she was engaged to be married, she'd told a man she liked him and that was his response? *"I need to head to the office"?* Attempt to flirt with the sheriff: total fail.

"Do you need a ride somewhere?" he asked, clearly being polite. "I can drop you at—"

"No. No, no," she said cheerily, her hand already going to the door. "Such a beautiful day. I'm going to walk. That's what I was doing before I stopped at the library, actually. I was walking. I do that now later in the day. In fact—" extricating herself from this embarrassing situation now seemed tantamount to anything else "—I'm not going to walk in the morning at all anymore. Nope. I'll just drive myself to work. Sleep in a bit. Walk when other people are out walking. So, you won't have to follow me around." She emitted a trill of laughter that sounded faintly maniacal. "You'll be able to sleep in, too. Unless you're working, of course, following suspicious people. But you won't have to follow *me*." Now he was scowling and looking at her as if he might call for backup. She opened the door and slid out. "Bye."

She gave a quick wave, shut the door and was off, walking as quickly as she could toward home.

That could have gone worse, she thought, nodding to herself. If there had been, say, a sudden tornado-like gust of wind that picked up the truck with them in it, whirled it through the air and dropped them on top of the General Store, sending terrified shoppers running for their lives into the street, that would have been worse.

Willa watched her square-toed boots eat the pavement. He'd kissed her, she'd kissed him back, he'd changed his mind. End of story. Not flattering, not encouraging, but certainly not the end of the world. And maybe she was being protected. Maybe she only *thought* she was ready for a man's arms, for his company, for the physical plunge that offered oblivion even as it reminded a person she was, in fact, very much alive.

"I need a hobby," she muttered.

As time marched on, Willa decided, she would try very hard to be proud of herself for acknowledging that she wanted the sheriff to kiss her again. For the first time in nearly two years, she had been willing to admit she needed something more than a life frozen in time and memory. For just a moment, she'd glimpsed the spring thaw, and she'd been glad.

Chapter Seven

She handled the DVD delicately, reverently, the way one might handle a Fabergé egg, removing it from its case, blowing specs of dust off its glassy surface, touching it only by the edges as she set it in the DVD player and closed the little door. The motor whirred, the TV screen assured her that her video was loading and gave her enough time to seat herself on the edge of her couch, her posture and her breathing both strained.

This was something Willa hadn't watched in the past two years, unlike the other home videos she had watched and rewatched so many times that she'd finally burned them onto additional discs to avoid losing them.

When the menu screen came up, she chose Play All. A young woman dressed in bridal lace and satin appeared on the screen, grinning at the camera as a small group of bridesmaids surrounded her. They were helping her don a garter, and the bride, with cascading auburn hair held back on one side by a jeweled clip, looked up at the camera and mugged, waggling her brows and pursing her lips in mock flirtation.

The next scene showed Willa again, this time walking toward her groom, who grinned like a fool. Lighthearted, winsome joy defined the ceremony and reception, befitting two kids who were barely out of their teens, but sure they had found their forever.

As the wedding portion of the video wrapped up, the screen went dark then lit again with a beatifically smiling Willa, only a year older, and a sleeping baby wrapped in the palest pink. The tiny girl had cupid's bow lips, skin like strawberries and cream, and auburn lashes that fanned her round cheeks as she snoozed. Willa cuddled her daughter close and looked at the camera, mouthing so as not to wake the baby, *I love us.*

The video stopped then started again. This time Willa was behind the camera, and her husband, Jason, held their still-sleeping Sydney. Jason's face, trustworthy and triangle-jawed, open and approachable (perfect for the doctor he planned to become, everyone always said) beamed contentment. Unlike Willa, he had no fear of waking Syd, because he complained that she was never awake enough when he was home.

Now he looked straight into the camera lens and proclaimed, "I'm the luckiest man in the world." The pride and gratitude in his eyes left no doubt that he was sincere.

Picking up the remote, Willa hit Stop. She remembered that day so well, zooming into Jason's face so that in the decades to come their daughter would see her father's eyes and know: *you are loved fully and completely.*

Tossing the remote onto the coffee table as if it were burning her fingers, she rose and wrapped her arms around herself. She had loved that life. Had felt grateful for every single day, even the messy ones, the boring ones, the worrisome ones. Never in a million years had she thought it would end so soon.

Still hugging herself tightly, Willa crossed to the window and looked out. After the sunny morning, the afternoon sky had turned gray. Now Thunder Ridge was being sprinkled with a dusting of snow. School was out for the day, and the kids across the street were standing on their lawn, jacketed arms outstretched, heads back and mouths open as they caught snowflakes on their tongues.

Their joy was vivid and fresh and real. Hers was a faded photograph, something she could no longer feel, only take out and look at. She felt as if she were fading, too.

"This is no good." Moving quickly, she grabbed her jacket off a hall tree, jammed her arms in, slipped on her boots and went outside. At first she didn't know where she was headed, but as she marched along, snatches of her conversation with Derek played in her mind, and she followed their path.

According to the sheriff, Gilberto needed focused help to catch up to his academic benchmarks. If he didn't catch up, his future would be dim, for sure, yet the school couldn't provide the extra help the boy needed. Derek didn't think he was capable, and tutors were expensive. Willa, on the other hand, was familiar with fifth-grade curriculum.

An idea began to take shape in her mind.

Checking her watch, she saw that it wasn't yet four o'clock. Gilberto's teacher might still be at school. Her footsteps struck the sidewalk with more resolve.

The snow was delicate, melting as it touched the ground, and merely being out in it made her feel more alive. By the time she reached Vista Road, leading to the elementary school, Willa knew exactly what she wanted to do.

* * *

"I'm telling you, dude, it's her birthday, and she's not doing nothing."

"Anything."

Gilberto growled. "That's what she always does. Tells me how to talk. Anything…nothin'…whatever. That's not the point."

"It's absolutely the point." Derek turned from the window, where he'd been contemplating his thoughts more than the view outside his office. "Your education is the reason Willa started tutoring you. She wants you to have a future."

"Yeah, which is why I want her to have a present for her birthday. You get it, dude? She cares about my *future*, I want her to have a *present*. Oh, man, I'm good."

"Uh huh. You are good." Since the evening Gilberto sped off with the donation jar, he'd changed from a furtive kid who seemed moody and awkward around adults, to an outgoing, far more confident young man. And the change in the two weeks since Willa had begun to tutor him in all his subjects was even more profound. Derek wasn't sure what had sparked the change in Willa, but her willingness to help Gilberto had unlocked a door.

Gilberto might still voice a casual attitude toward his schoolwork, but now that he was beginning to grasp a few things, his posture was straighter. He looked happier, chatted more and was currently chatting with Derek about Willa's birthday, which was, apparently, tomorrow.

"Izzy, she come into the bakery—"

"Came into the bakery."

"I *know*. Dude!" The boy took a noisy deep breath. "Okay…*came* into the bakery, 'cause she needed Willa to fill something out, and she said—I totally heard her—'Hey, girl, your birthday is tomorrow.'"

"I've never heard Izzy say 'Hey, girl.'"

Gilberto shrugged. "I mighta got that wrong, but then Willa said, 'Yeah, I've got plans after work,' but, Dude, she don't. Wait—I know, *doesn't*."

"How do you know she doesn't?"

"Because I asked her if she could help me with my homework tomorrow, and she said, 'Sure.'"

"Her plans are probably for evening, Gilberto." Derek told himself not to wonder what those plans were, or with whom she was sharing them.

Two weeks ago, Willa told him she wanted him to come back to the bakery, and he'd had to force himself not to think about her, not to convince himself it was okay just to drop in to get a bagel and coffee or to see how Gilberto was doing. True, that day in his truck she had seemed to be telling him she was interested, after all. But he knew too much now. He knew Willa was not ready for all the things he wanted. And, he knew he wasn't ready to settle for less.

"She doesn't have *any* plans. That's what I'm trying to *tell* you." Impatience colored the boy's voice. "I told her I got a test on Friday, so could she help me a little longer tomorrow, and she said, 'Yeah, I've got plenty of time.' See? She forgot what she told Izzy."

"Or maybe she's making you her first priority." To give himself something to do, Derek reached for a stack of papers on his desk. "Want to hand me that stapler?" he asked the boy who was sitting in his desk chair, swiveling left and right in agitation.

Gilberto grabbed the heavy black stapler and handed it over the desk. "I'm telling you, she's not doing noth— *anything* for her birthday. And that's not cool, 'cause she's, you know, she's nice. She's good to people."

Derek nodded. Shortly after their conversation in his truck, Willa had told Gilberto that she was going to help him with school, and she was, apparently, quite proficient at it. "Like a real teacher, except that I understand her," Gilberto had become fond of saying.

Gilberto was a good person, too. He came to the office after finishing his jobs and his homework at the bakery. Derek had spent time with Gilberto the past two weekends, too. They had gone ice-skating at the temporary rink Jax Stewart set up in Trillium Park. Then they went to the movies, where Gilberto ate popcorn and chocolate-covered caramels until Derek was sure he was going to be sick. Derek's days off were more full and more fun than they had been since Nate Thayer had come to town, claiming Derek's best friend as his bride.

And now his new little buddy wanted to do something for Willa's birthday. Self-preservation warned Derek to change the subject. Pronto. But the image of Willa celebrating her birthday alone overruled. He squinted at Gilberto. "What do you have in mind?"

Willa did her marketing on Friday evenings. The large grocery store outside of town stayed fairly quiet at night, and she was able to wander the aisles, looking at ingredients and wondering what she could experiment with for the bakery. She saw no reason to alter her pattern on this particular Friday.

She'd already had phone calls from her parents, her aunt Esther and cousin Nancy. Daisy had phoned, too, singing "Happy I-Can't-Believe-We're-This-Old-Day to You" on Willa's voice mail then asking, "What are you doing tonight? It had better be good, and it had better involve a man."

Thirty-four is not old, Willa had texted back. Big plans for the evening. Many men involved. XOXO.

At the market, she had a nice conversation with the

butcher, who, yes, was a man. Then she chatted with the cashier, also male, and declined help out from the bagger, another XY chromosome carrier. So she hadn't lied, exactly.

Putting her groceries in the trunk of her car, she got in, turned the key in the ignition and hoped the heater would work quickly. After spending the afternoon helping Gilberto study for a math test he had the following week, she was surprisingly hungry. She planned to make a toasted pancetta and brie cheese sandwich with a smear of the homemade fig jam they sold at the bakery. Then she would eat in front of the television, watching an episode of *Downton Abbey* on Netflix. There was nothing wrong with spending her birthday like that, even if her family and Daisy disagreed.

Pointing her car toward home, she traveled less than a quarter mile before she saw a trio of lights flashing in her rearview mirror. Though no siren wail accompanied the lights, Willa knew she was looking at the lights of a police car. She pulled over, wondering what she had done wrong.

Rolling down her window, she smiled, hoping she could talk her way out of a huge fine on her birthday, "Hello, what did I do— Oh. Hi."

Derek nodded, looking official in his uniform and even a hat, which she rarely saw him wear. "Evening. Are you aware your undercarriage is sparking?"

"My…what is what?"

"I saw sparks coming from the undercarriage of your car. That's very dangerous. I've alerted the local fire department, who I'm sure will arrive shortly. For now, I'm going to have to ask you to step out of the vehicle for safety's sake." He spoke quickly, which emphasized the danger of the situation. "If you'd like to bring your purse and any other belongings you need to take with you, I'll have Dan Bowman tow the car in and look at it." He attempted to open her door, which was locked. "Dan will contact you. Will you unlock your door, please?"

Confused as heck and growing more alarmed, Willa clicked the lock. Immediately, Derek opened the door and reached for her arm to help her out. "Let's move quickly," he said.

"We're not even in Thunder Ridge," Willa grumbled. "What are you doing out here?"

"I'm a county employee. You're in my county. Now, do you need anything besides your purse?"

"I just went to the grocery store."

"Okay, get in the squad car, please. I'll grab the groceries."

She did as he asked, realizing as she slid onto the front seat of the police car that she was asking him to risk his safety for her pancetta. She watched him, big and strong and sure, and was going to call out to him to forget the groceries when he returned, three bags in his hands. He stowed everything in the backseat then slid into the driver's spot. The car filled with his presence. She felt sure she could smell his pheromones.

With supreme effort, she returned her attention to the car. "Where are the sparks?" she asked.

"They were visible while you were driving. It's a good sign that it stopped when you cut the engine. So." He glanced her way. "Got any plans for the weekend?"

"Is it okay to leave the car there if it could catch on fire?" She craned her neck to look back.

"Like I said, it stopped sparking. And I'm sure a fire truck will be there soon. Weekend plans?" he asked again.

The night was starting to feel truly surreal. Derek hadn't spoken to her this much in weeks. These days, she saw him mostly in passing or through the window of the bakery if he dropped by to pick up Gilberto. He didn't come in. She'd come to accept that whatever attraction he'd felt for her had ended, and she tried not to think about why.

"I'm working on Sunday," she said. "I thought I'd do some cooking tomorrow. Freeze a few dinners." *Wow. That ought to make his head spin with excitement.* "Maybe I'll take a drive into Portland." The urban area was a good ninety minutes away by car. And, actually, it seemed even further removed with regard to lifestyle. The uber-popular, quirky city couldn't be more different from the charming western vibe of Thunder Ridge.

"What are you going to do in Portland?"

Uh, nothing. Because I just made it up. "I might go to Powell's." She mentioned the multistory independent bookstore that was on every visitor's must-see list. "And I love Northwest 23rd." That much, at least, was true. Northwest 23rd boasted some of the city's best shops and eateries. Maybe she really ought to drive over. Get out of her rut.

"Have you ever eaten at El Gaucho?"

Willa shook her head.

"It's downtown in the Benson Hotel. Best steaks this side of Texas."

"You've been to Texas?"

"I'm from Texas," he confirmed.

"I assumed you grew up in the Pacific Northwest."

"I did." In the lights from the dashboard, she saw him smile wryly. "I 'grew up' here. Became a man instead of a would-be felon. But I was born in Lubbock, Texas, and lived there until I was almost seventeen. That's when the uncle I was living with told me to straighten up or get out. I chose to get out. Started hitchhiking and ended up here, thank God."

He kept surprising her. "You really did have a hard childhood."

Derek shrugged. "I had challenges." They drove in silence for a good quarter mile before he spoke again. "Gilberto is confused, because the only people he feels he belongs with are the ones he can't relate to. They're people he doesn't want to become, and they're not what I'd call attentive. *Not* belonging to them, though, makes him feel panicked. Like a boat bobbing alone in the middle of the ocean. He wants mooring, and he'll take it where he can get it. Even if that means looking for it in all the wrong places."

Everything he said made sense, but somehow his words left her with a burning discomfort in the pit of her stomach. "You're offering him the chance to belong somewhere," she observed. "You're doing everything you can to help."

He cut a glance at her. "*You're* giving him the opportunity to belong, too. Every time you work with him."

"But my help is temporary." Suddenly, she felt sick with worry. "Maybe the last thing he needs is someone transient in his life. What if that makes things worse?"

"What you're giving him isn't temporary, Willa. The time you spend with Gilberto is something he'll take with him wherever he goes, from now on." He paused. "And how do you know when your relationship with him is going to end? It doesn't have an expiration date."

They were nearing Thunder Ridge. The twinkle lights that had decorated every building since the weekend after Thanksgiving were becoming visible, a sweet beacon to guide them down an otherwise dark road. Derek had stopped talking, the silence in the car unexpectedly welcome as Willa tried to make sense of her feelings.

All her life, she'd had a place and people to whom she'd belonged. Why did talking about belonging, even thinking about it, make her feel so nettled? Being hesitant to put down roots in Thunder Ridge did not mean she didn't belong…somewhere. And if it turned out that all she was doing here was helping a young preteen set down roots that would allow him to grow tall, that ought to be enough.

As they reached the downtown area, Derek turned up Warm Springs Road. After 6:00 p.m., even on a Friday night, most of the businesses were dark, though a couple of diehards, notably the General Store and the pet shop that had opened last year, remained well lit and open for business. As Derek approached Fourth Street, Willa alerted, "You can turn here for me." His cell phone rang, and he answered it, passing the street. "Or not," she murmured.

"Hey, Izz," he said, using his Bluetooth. "Oh, yeah? Well, I'm close to the deli… Sure, I can check it for you… Right-o. Bye." He looked at Willa. "Octavio thinks he forgot to turn off the burners this afternoon. Izzy's at some function with Nate and asked me to stop by and take a look. Do you mind coming along?"

"No, I don't mind. That's really weird. Octavio crosses every *T*. If anything, he's a tad obsessive."

"We all have an off day occasionally."

"I guess so."

Derek drove around the corner and into the alley behind The Pickle Jar. "Come with me," he said to Willa. "You can show me how to turn off the burners."

As they stood at the back door, she asked, "How long have you had keys to Izzy's restaurant?"

"Pretty much forever. Henry and Sam gave them to me years ago." Henry and Sam Bernstein had owned and operated the deli for decades before giving 60 percent of the business to Izzy, who'd started out as a waitress and manager before becoming their partner. The two men had happily semiretired and were currently at a cousin's home on Kaua'i, where, according to Izzy, Sam had fallen in love with shave ice and was trying to convince Henry to open a stand in Thunder Ridge upon their return.

Unlocking the door that opened to a storage area, Derek said, "Here we are," his voice sounding overly loud in the empty restaurant. He stepped back, allowing Willa to enter first. Knowing exactly where to find the light, she clicked it on, then led the way into the kitchen. The aromas of deli fare—potato and fried-onion knishes, corned beef, all the yummy comfort food—teased her nose as if the deli was open and ready for business, and she realized how hungry she was. "Octavio must have been cooking ahead for next week," she surmised. Why else would a restaurant that had been closed for a couple of hours smell like it was in the middle of a dinner rush? "I wonder if they're catering something?" Usually when the Pickle Jar catered, Izzy tapped Willa for cakes and cookies, but no one had mentioned an upcoming event.

"I don't know," Derek said, "but it's making me hungry. I haven't had dinner."

"Me, either." She glanced over. A smile (truly adorable, let's be honest), played at the corners of his mouth. She began to imagine a private picnic in the closed restaurant. Raiding the walk-in refrigerator and the adjacent bakery, lighting a candle and setting it on one of the tables or at the counter. Maybe she would say something like, "You've never had a cheese blintze with marmalade? You have to taste it" and use her fingers to pop a bite into his mouth.

Why not? Do it. Don't think. Just—

"You know," she ventured, interrupting her own thoughts before they talked her out of it, "if we're both hungry, we're in the right place." Her heart pounded with every word. "I bet we could find something to—"

"Surprise!"

Willa squealed as dozens of familiar people popped out from behind booths and tables in The Pickle Jar's dining room.

A hand reached out to steady her. A big, warm, supportive hand. Derek leaned close. "Happy birthday, Willa."

His calm murmur tickled the hair by her ear and sent shivers all the way through her. It took several seconds to find her voice. "This is for me?"

His smile gentled. "All for you."

Willa turned toward the crowd of people who were calling out, "Happy birthday!" and asking Derek, "Is she surprised?"

As her gaze roved around the crowd, she noted Izzy, along with Nate and their son, Eli; Holliday Bailey, the librarian; Kim, her coworker from the bakery, who was holding hands with her husband; and a good thirty other people. Standing in front of them all, holding a hand-lettered poster that shouted Happy Birthday, Willa/Teacher! was Gilberto. His grin held none of the shyness it had when they'd first met, the afternoon he'd decided to take the donation jar. Instead, he looked excited, full of importance in a really good way.

Derek placed a hand on the small of her back, gently urging her forward.

As she moved from the kitchen to the dining counter, around which most of the guests were crowded, Willa became aware that the chattering and greetings were becoming more subdued until they quieted altogether. Dozens of faces looked at her expectantly, making her acutely conscious that of all the folks here to celebrate her birthday, to celebrate *her*, she didn't know any of them very well, and they knew her…hardly at all. Not a one of them would be able to name the most important events of her life; that's how she had wanted it. Now her reluctance to let these people into her world made her feel awkward and kind of small as they waited for her to say something.

"Thank you," she started off breathlessly. "This is such

a surprise." *Duh*. "I mean, I truly, truly had no idea. I can't believe you went to all this trouble." She shook her head, shocked when tears began to prick her eyes. "I'm speechless," she concluded lamely.

Her relief was great when Derek took over. "Somebody said there'd be food at this shindig," he called out. "The birthday girl hasn't had dinner. Let's eat!" Enthusiastic applause traveled around the restaurant.

Izzy and Octavio—it looked as if the entire staff had given up their night off for her—sprang into action. Out came the platters of food whose aromas had enticed her as soon as she'd opened the door. A line formed at the counter, and plates were filled. Several people greeted Willa personally and urged her to eat. She promised to join everyone in a moment, but she wanted to talk to Gilberto first.

"You made that sign?" She pointed to the large electric-yellow poster board he held.

Nodding, he boasted, "I spelled everything right, too. Do you like it?"

"I love it. Thank you. And thank you for spending your Friday with me. I know you usually watch a movie with your cousins on Fridays."

His gaze shifted. "We don't do that so much anymore."

She frowned. He'd only told her about his busy Friday nights two weeks ago. *"Me and my cousins do a lot of fun stuff,"* he'd said.

"Well, people have busy seasons sometimes," she reasoned. "Schedules can change temporarily."

Gilberto shrugged, but some of his joy seemed to evaporate.

"If you're free tomorrow," she said spontaneously, "there's a theater in Portland that plays reruns. They're showing *Hotel Transylvania*, one and two. I love those movies. And there's an ice cream store nearby that's serving Vampire Blood ice cream and another flavor called Creepy Cake Batter, which has actual bug brittle in it. That's a crunchy candy with pieces of real bugs. I dare you to taste it."

Gilberto screwed up his face. "Gross! I'll taste it if you will."

Willa laughed. "I'll decide after the movie."

"Did I hear someone mention ice cream?" Derek appeared beside them, making Willa's skin tingle from the nearness.

"Bug ice cream," Gilberto crowed, socking Derek on the arm. "Willa dared me to eat some."

As he chattered on about the kinds of bugs he imagined would be in the ice cream, Willa realized she envied Gilberto's easy way with Derek.

"*Mi abuela* grew up eating a dish called *sompopos* in Guatemala," Derek said when Gilberto dared *him* to eat an insect. "*Sompopos* are ants. She cooked them in butter."

"No way!" Gilberto found this fascinating.

Actually, so did Willa. "You're Guatemalan?"

"My grandmother was mestiza, half Indian and half Spanish. Her daughter, my mother, married an Irish lad."

"Guatemalan," Willa mused. "Is that the reason for your year-round tan?" She touched his wrist—a purely unconscious gesture that, paradoxically, made her hyperconscious of, oh boy, everything about him. Conscious of the hair on his arm and the smoothness of the skin beneath. Conscious of the scent beneath his clean-soap smell and the subtle aftershave he wore. The scent she most often associated with Derek was just him. Warm, comforting, enticing, stirring… Derek.

He glanced to her fingers, resting light as butterflies on his wrist. His gaze seemed to electrify their touch, but when his brow lowered, she pulled away self-consciously.

Derek's big hand clamped onto Gilberto's shoulder. "Grab some food and a booth. We'll be right behind you."

Gilberto didn't require a second invitation to eat. Presenting the Happy Birthday sign to Willa, he jumped into the buffet line, where several people pushed him on ahead of them, making sure his plate was piled.

"He really is becoming part of the community," Willa observed softly, looking up at Derek to find him watching her steadily. He relieved her of the large cardboard sign, tucking it behind a stool at the counter, then returned to her. Derek stood a good ten inches taller than she, and she felt at a slight disadvantage. "I'm guessing my car is actually okay?"

"It's fine. I'll take you back to get it in the morning. Or tonight, if you need it."

More time alone with him sounded good to her, or it would if she didn't sense the distance between them.

"It was incredibly good of you to go to all the trouble you did to get me here." She surveyed the scene around them. Someone had added music to complete the party atmosphere, and for the first time she noticed the balloons. "I still can't believe Izzy organized this, as busy as she is."

"She's capable of it, but it wasn't Izzy," Derek said. "It was Gilberto's idea. Izzy was all for it." He stopped, shaking his head. "Actually, she was a little concerned you might feel uncomfortable with the attention, but Gilberto insisted."

"Gilberto did?"

"He heard Izzy mention your birthday and came to me so fired up to throw you a party, I couldn't have talked him out of it if I'd tried."

"He came to you." She frowned. "That means *you* planned this?"

"Gilberto planned. I facilitated." Derek crossed his arms

in the classic sheriff stance she was starting to find more endearing than intimidating. "I'm not big on parties, but he's right. You deserve one."

The word "deserve" deepened her frown. "I haven't done anything to deserve all this—"

He silenced her by pressing his index finger to her lips, and if touching his wrist was electrifying, that was nothing compared to the pad of his finger on her lips.

"You're important." His voice was husky, heavy. "To this town. To Gilberto." His eyes, deep and dark and burning like the core of a volcano, told her what he didn't say out loud. *To me. You're important to me.*

"I thought you didn't like me anymore." Though she attempted to say it ironically, Willa heard the faint pleading tone that turned her statement into a question. She cringed inwardly, wanting to take the words back, but Derek's lips curved in the most mesmerizing quarter smile.

"That would be way, way too easy." He wagged his head. "And so far nothing with you has been easy."

"I know. I'm sorry."

"Don't be." After a moment of what appeared to be an internal battle, he announced, "I'm driving you home tonight after the party. Could your car use an oil change?"

She nodded.

"Dan Bowman will take care of it and bring your car over in the morning."

Done. His tone said not to argue. A thrill shivered up her arms.

"Okay, you two, time to hit the buffet." Izzy slapped Derek on the shoulder—rather hard, Willa thought. "You're monopolizing the birthday girl. Let her eat and mingle."

Derek glowered at Izzy. Willa smiled at the knowledge that he really did want to spend more time with her. Even as she slipped into the buffet line ahead of Derek, she imagined inviting him into her home later that night. Anticipation rose, and she felt like one of the sparkling cider bottles Jax Stewart was opening at the beverage table. Any more internal pressure, and she'd bubble up all over the place.

No. That was way too tame a comparison. She didn't feel like a bottle of apple cider; she felt like a woman who knew exactly what she wanted. And what she wanted was Sheriff Derek Neel—out of uniform, thank you very much.

A millisecond after that thought, his hand settled on her waist, and lust erupted inside her, like a long-lost friend she hadn't expected to see again. *Turn around. Let him know what you're feeling. That's how this is done.*

She looked behind her, and the moment they made eye contact the inferno spread, heating the space between them. Suddenly Willa was ravenous, but not for dinner. The feeling was frightening and exhilarating and wonderful.

"Knish?" A Pickle Jar employee stood behind the counter, a smile on her pretty, young face, and a fat square pocket of golden dough balanced on the spatula she held out. "Happy Birthday, Willa," she said brightly. "I'm so glad I could come tonight. Do you want meat or potato?" She nodded to the knish.

Derek's hand fell away, leaving a void that acted like a rush of cold wind to cool Willa down. She answered the question then struggled to make small talk. When she glanced at Derek again, he was listening to Ray, the barber, complain about the new construction in town wrecking the "legitimate authenticity of original structures."

Derek looked over at Willa, his expression impassive. He gave her one slow wink. It was all she needed to begin counting the minutes until her birthday party was over and the main event of the evening began.

Chapter Eight

The full moon peered down from behind a misty cloud cover as Derek helped Willa out of his squad car. Foggy breath mingled and hovered between them under the old-fashioned iron street lamp as the evening's first fat flakes of snow began to float to the ground.

When Willa tilted her face up, Derek caught the child-like wonder in her smile. "I never get tired of the snow," she said. "We haven't had enough."

"That's unusual around here." Ordinarily he thought an inch or two of snow was plenty, but seeing her expression and the flakes of snow that clung to her hair could make him revise his opinion. "Some years, we'd be up to our ankles in it by now."

Together, they stood on her sidewalk, watching the snow begin to dance and swirl around them in the circle of lamp-light. The happy, relaxed sound of Willa's sigh burrowed into Derek's heart.

"Really, I don't mind going out and getting my car," she offered. "We should probably do it, before the streets get super slick."

And end this moment? "Nope. It's late, and you don't have snow tires. Besides Dan Bowman really wants to throw in a lube job. He'll have your car here first thing in the morning. It's his birthday present."

"You've gotta love a small town." A poignant smile made her face shine. "I can't thank you enough for throwing me such a wonderful birthday party."

"You're welcome. I'm glad you had a good time. Gilberto was so happy that we actually managed to surprise you, he told me he's going to throw parties for a living." They'd dropped the boy off at his cousin's house before heading to Willa's, and he'd jabbered the entire way.

Willa giggled, the first time he'd heard that particular sound from her. "I know." She nodded. "He was so excited and so full of sugar, I wonder if he'll sleep a wink tonight."

Derek touched a snowflake that landed on the tip of her nose. It was all he could do to keep from threading his fingers through her gorgeous red waves. "How about you?" His murmur produced another puff of cloudy breath. "Are you tired?"

Her eyes were wide, her smile knowing and somewhat shy when she assured him, "No. Not a bit."

He took her elbow, and they headed up her porch steps.

Willa's home was one of the post-WWII cottages that were typical in this area, with a steeply pitched roof and a wide porch that spanned the front and two sides of her house. Matching wooden keg planters with large winter cabbages and a few hardy pansies in purple flanked her front door. The taupe-color siding appeared to have been recently painted, as did the black shutters framing the windows. Off to one side a two-seater swing hung from the porch's ceiling, and beside it, at first glance Derek thought he spied a bronze floor lamp. Closer inspection revealed that it was the kind of outdoor propane heater used to warm restaurant patios.

He gestured in its direction. "You use this thing much?"

"All the time."

"This time of year?"

"Especially this time of year."

"You're kidding." He took several steps to better look it over.

"No. I love to see the stars on a clear night. Makes me feel closer to…" she shrugged and looked wistfully into the misty heavens. "Nature, I guess."

Derek watched her face angle toward the cloud-filtered moonlight. What did she see that drew such pensive thoughts?

Giving her head a shake, Willa stepped over to plug in a strand of star-shaped twinkle lights that rimmed the porch ceiling. "This is how I combat a cloudy day," she explained, switching on the propane heater. Suddenly, an orange light cast a pool of warmth, transforming her porch into a cozy room. "Hang on a minute," she said, a mischievous note in her voice as she unlocked her front door.

Since he wasn't invited inside, Derek used his time unobserved to glance around the porch. Noting homey touches that spoke of the hours she spent here, he walked over to examine a forgotten book that sat on a small table next to the swing. He picked up the slim hardcover, running his thumb across the title. *Coming Back from Grief.* A bookmark stuck out one third of the way into the pages.

It didn't take a private investigator to understand that Willa was trying to heal. But from what? Replacing her reading material, he ambled to the opposite end of the porch and looked out across the street, his mood taking a

sharp downturn. Would she ever feel safe enough to confide in him? He suspected some of the answers to the Willa
puzzle were inside the house. Is that why she hadn't invited
him in? Briefly, he thought about following her inside, but
before he could act, Willa reappeared carrying two beach
towels and a large Pendleton blanket.

The unspoken invitation to stay softened his sudden
grumpiness. "Beach towels?" he asked. "In the middle
of winter?"

"Feel," she invited, holding the pile out to him.

"They're warm."

"I keep them hanging on a quilt stand in front of the
radiator."

After she'd arranged the towels on the plump outdoor
swing cushions, she sat and gestured for him to join her
under the toasty wool blanket.

The swing creaked as they settled on it.

Tucking the warm blanket all around their shoulders,
Derek deliberately pressed his thigh against hers. She
didn't move away. In fact, she leaned against his arm as
she arranged the blanket over their laps.

Derek arched a brow at her. "So this is what it means
to be snug as a bug in a rug."

"Yup. Magical, isn't it?"

"Pretty much, yeah." Illuminated by the heat lamp and
twinkle lights, Willa's skin glowed, as smooth and creamy
as peach ice cream, and her eyes sparkled with enjoyment,
for once undisturbed by shadows from the past. "You're
magical."

To his own ears, Derek's voice sounded as thick and
warm as the wool that wrapped them both in one cocoon.

Beneath the cover, he reached for her hand, threading
his fingers through hers. Her smile deepened. All along
his left side, their bodies touched. The snow was swirling

out of the sky with increasing gusto, coating her lawn and the grove of trees across the street. The weatherman's report that Derek had seen earlier said they'd get five or six inches tonight. He was glad she wouldn't be out driving in it. The first day of real snowfall each year equaled fender benders and worse. Before morning, he would no doubt get a call or two requiring him to lend a hand directing traffic around someone in a ditch.

For the time being, he didn't want to think about that. Didn't want to think about going anywhere. This was perfect.

Around them, the world fell silent except for the dulcet hum of the heater, and off in the distance a train whistle sounded its haunting song. The train's rumble gently vibrated the floorboards.

Slowly, Derek reached out from under the blanket to pull a snow-dampened strand of hair away from her cheek and lower lip. He'd been dreaming about her every damned night for a year. He inhaled as his desire for her surged.

Easy now. Take it slow.

The muscles in his jaw worked with the effort it took to relax.

A sigh, so light that only her misty breath told him he hadn't imagined it, made him lean closer. His resolve crumbled like the walls of Jericho. She was completely intoxicating. Giving into the heady rush of adrenaline that rocketed through his gut, he released the fingers he held beneath the blanket, cupped her jaw in his hands and pulled her mouth firmly beneath his.

He'd promised himself that tonight would be his very last attempt to woo her. Yeah, he'd said it before, but this time… If she rebuffed him now, he would force himself to move on in spite of the fact that he was pretty convinced this woman was his destiny.

Immediately Derek sensed this kiss was different—hotter and more urgent than the others had been. Relief flooded every cell as she kissed him back with the same passion he felt, and soon, like a door opening on a flaming backdraft, they were consumed. Cold noses, warm lips and tongues, their lungs laboring—it felt to him as if they had stopped being two distinct individuals and instead were one heart pounding with want. With need.

One kiss became two, then three. Derek took Willa into his embrace, her lower back resting against his lap, her shoulders cradled in his arms. Their kisses gave way to guttural whispers shared in the hushed snowfall.

"I haven't made things easy on you, have I?" She stared up at him.

"Hell, no."

Willa traced his lips with gentle fingers, which nearly drove him mad. "I'm sorry."

He kissed the tip of her nose, her jaw and an apparently sensitive spot beneath her ear. "You're forgiven."

She looped her arms around his neck. "Thank you for hanging in there with me. You know, for being so patient and persistent."

"You're worth the wait."

"You, too."

Derek allowed himself to bask in this victory. Pulling her more firmly against his chest, he murmured against her hair. "I could sit here like this forever."

Willa leaned back, pressing her lips together. "I'm not so sure about forever."

"Too cold, huh?"

"It's just that I'm more about being in the moment."

Uh oh. Derek took a deep breath and held it. Was she erecting barriers again?

As if he were trying to capture a bird poised to fly, he

locked his fingers behind her back. "Are you making small talk or trying to tell me something?"

Her sigh was heavy, underscored by a barely audible moan. She plucked at a bright red thread of wool hanging loose on their blanket. "The whole 'forever' thing... I just don't believe in that."

"Do you trust me enough to tell me why?"

"It's me I don't trust, not you." She was still cradled in his lap. Warm and soft and utterly right in his arms, a position definitely to her advantage when she ran her fingers across the stubble on his cheek and asked, "Do you really want to stop what we're doing to have a philosophical conversation? Does 'why' matter tonight?"

It mattered. But he knew the conversation wouldn't change anything in this moment.

Beyond them, the world was now covered in a downy comforter of sparkling white. A clean slate. Derek knew the presence of the grief books and someone in her not-too-distant past held the answers she was reluctant to give. Did she have a new beginning left in her heart, in spite of her words to the contrary? Her kisses promised so much more than she would admit.

"Anyway," she said, "This...what we have here...we should let it be what it is."

"What do you think it is?"

"It's wonderful. And temporary."

"An affair."

She wrinkled her nose. "That sounds tawdry."

Actually, his blood heated at the image, but as he kissed her again, he couldn't quite bring himself to believe she meant it.

As if she could read his mind, she admonished breathlessly, "I'm serious. This won't ever lead anywhere permanent."

"Okay." He nodded solemnly. "Of course, it's your loss. You said yourself I'd make a great dad someday."

"You will. You do." She spoke carefully. "But not with me as the mom."

She was watching him, waiting for him to show that he understood. Which he sure as hell did not, because everything—every little thing—he knew about her said *love, family, forever.* But for now he decided to give her what she was looking for, because there was so much more to discover. "All right, Willa. We'll play by your rules. For the time being," he murmured, hauling her closer for several more kisses, meant to distract. When she was breathless, he asked, "So this affair. Care to elaborate?"

Looking beautifully mussed and a bit dazed, she shook her head. "No. Just the standard, exciting, clandestine, secret, middle-of-the-night rendezvous will do."

"Secret, huh? Will I have to climb out of your window, or will you allow me to use the front door? Or, are you planning to keep this affair of ours confined to the front porch?"

Her mood lifted once more, and her giggle rocked the swing. "Definitely not the front porch. Remember, my neighbor Belleruth is an insomniac. If she saw us, the entire block would hear about it before breakfast."

"Small town. Big talk." He massaged her back. "Can't have that." Though he couldn't have cared less.

"No," she whispered against his mouth. "We can't have that. Myra at Hair Today would start some under-the-hair-dryer gossip that would spread to the *Tribune* by the end of the week."

"Okay then. A tawdry affair it is." He kissed her until he was pretty sure she'd have trouble stringing together the words to make a sentence.

Then, just as she was completely limp in his arms,

Derek marshaled every ounce of strength in his nearly two-hundred-pound body and lifted them both to their feet. "Good night, Willa."

The slack-jawed expression she wore on her face was priceless. Clearly, she expected their affair to begin that night. But Derek wasn't in this thing for short-term success. He was in it to win it.

"Since every tawdry affair should begin with a real date," he told her, "I'll pick you up tomorrow night at six. Hooligans. Dinner, dancing. Dress accordingly."

And with that he strode, whistling into the dark, to his car.

He left? Stunned, Willa stood, staring at the tracks Derek's tires left in the pristine snow. A minute ago, she'd thought they were really headed somewhere. Specifically, her bedroom. And then?

He'd up and left. Just like that, leaving her heart hotly pounding blood through her veins with no avenue of release. Mind whirling, she gathered the blanket and towels and stepped inside her house, closing the front door behind her.

Surely, she'd made herself clear. She didn't need to be wined and dined. They could dispense with the whole getting-to-know-the-real-you process.

She did not want strings. Ties. Knots in her stomach.

Ties could bring love, and love eventually brought sorrow. And Willa had sorrowed enough for one lifetime. Slowly, she folded her blanket and towels over the quilt stand and crossed to the mantel of her fireplace.

"Hey," she whispered to a framed photograph, tracing the face she found there with her fingertip. "What would you have me do?"

As Willa pondered the lively, sparkling eyes that looked at her with such adoration, she began to sense the answer.

"But am I ready?" she whispered. "I know it's been two years, but I'm just so—" her sigh clouded the glass "—so very tired."

She scrubbed the fog with the tip of her finger so that the eternally smiling eyes came back into focus, ever encouraging.

"I don't think I can," she admitted. "Missing you has used me up."

The expression in the photograph would never change. As long as she peered at the picture, she could slip, if only for a twinkling, into that glorious time when love had been mostly pain-free. Her memories lent her the encouragement to live again. But to love?

Picking up the frame, she cradled it in her arms and headed to bed.

As Derek rounded the corner to city hall, he spotted a lone figure shuffling along the sidewalk. The snow had started to come down something fierce, and though his wipers were set to high speed, he was having trouble seeing. This person was either a very small adult, or a child. Deciding to err on the side of caution, he slowly pulled up next to the pedestrian and rolled his window down.

"Everything all right?" he called.

The small person stopped and squinted into his headlights.

"Gilberto? Is that you? What the devil are you doing out here?" Derek glanced at his dashboard. "It's nearly eleven o'clock at night."

Shoulders hunched against the weather, Gilberto came around to the driver's side and poked his head inside the window. "I was looking for you."

"Well, you found me." Hitting the unlock button, Derek nodded toward the rear passenger door. "Hop in." Rather than climbing in the back, Gilberto wasted no time diving into shotgun position and pulling the door closed. "You eighty pounds?" Derek asked skeptically.

"You kidding me? I'm almost eighty-five!"

"My bad. Belt," Derek reminded him as he pulled back onto Ponderosa Avenue. Lucky thing he'd decided to make a quick sweep of the town before turning in for the night. "Wanna tell me what you think you're doing out for a stroll at this time of night in the middle of a snowstorm?"

"I didn't want to call 911."

"Why would you need to do that?"

"I didn't. That's why I was walking."

"Dude, help me out. Why *didn't* you need to dial 911?"

"Oh! Roddy and his friends were getting really drunk. Music was so loud, I couldn't sleep. So I go out to the living room to tell Roddy I can't sleep, and *Roddy* is sleeping. I couldn't wake him up, and his friends were all laughing and doing stuff to him."

"What kind of stuff?"

Gilberto made a valiant effort not to laugh, but failed. "One of 'em was putting lipstick on him and another guy was taking pictures. But when they wanted to do some of that crap to me? I was outta there, man."

Derek cut a glance over at the kid and nodded. "Did the right thing, buddy boy. But next time you might want to call me and have me come get you, instead of freezing half to death."

"I don't have your number."

As Derek reached for his radio he said, "We'll have to fix that, huh." Then, thumb to the talk button, he called, "Russell, you out there?"

Static crackled as Russell responded, "I'm here, dog. What can I do ya for?"

"I need you to run over to check on Gilberto's cousin." He gave the address. "I got a report that Roddy is passed out on the couch, but just in case it's more serious than that…"

"Ten-four. I'm leaving now."

"Great. While you're there, make sure Roddy knows Gilberto is with me, and see if the music needs to be turned down."

"I'm on it."

"Thanks. I'm out." He snapped his radio into its holder and glanced at Gilberto. "Wanna make some rounds with me?"

"You mean like a deputy?" The boy's obsidian eyes shone in the dark.

"Just like a deputy."

"Hell, yeah!"

Given that he wanted to laugh, Derek directed toward his young passenger the sternest glance he could manage. "You mean heck yeah."

"Right!"

"Good. When we're done, we'll head to my place. You can spend the night at my ranch."

"That would be awesome! So, you live on a ranch? Do you have cows?"

"No. But I have several horses. You can help me feed them in the morning."

Gilberto pumped his fists, not the least bit tired. "Yes!"

"You hungry?"

"Totally."

"Figures." He'd eaten plenty at dinner, but Derek remembered his own predilection for consuming as much as possible at that age. "Okay. Since it's the weekend—and only because it's the weekend—you can stay up late. I'll make you an early breakfast when we get home."

"Oh, man, this is turning out to be the best night ever."

Smiling, Derek wagged his head. The kid was easy to please. He thought about what he'd started on Willa's porch, about the fact that he was going to see her the next day, and about how much he enjoyed the company of the eleven-year-old beside him. He wasn't thrilled about Roddy's behavior, not one little bit. Nonetheless, he was inclined to agree: this was a pretty good night indeed.

Chapter Nine

"Is that Gilberto in the backseat of your truck?" Willa asked Derek as the grinning child hung out the window and waved at her. From where she and Derek stood on her front porch, she lifted a hand to wave back then shot a quizzical glance at the man beside her. Didn't they have a dancing date right about now?

"Yeah. That's him," he confirmed. "There's been a slight change of plans. A little more than slight."

Willa's face crumpled with disappointment and she instantly felt foolish. "Oh." She strove to find a blithe recovery. "That's okay. Really. Another time, then?"

He looked confused. "What? No, no, I want to spend the evening with you. I mean, if *you* still want to. But it's going to be a group date…type…thing." He dragged a hand through his hair. "The kid's bunking with me for a couple of days."

Along with surprise, Willa felt a frisson of alarm. "Is he in some kind of trouble?"

"No." He took a moment to explain how he'd found Gilberto on the road. "You remember his cousin Roddy?"

"Who could forget?" Roddy's belligerence at their meeting left a strong impression.

"He ended up in the hospital with a pretty serious case of alcohol poisoning. Some of the other party animals were booked with MIPs."

"What's that?"

"Minor in possession. Roddy was playing bartender and some of his patrons were underage. Needless to say, Roddy had a little visit by DHS this morning. The caseworker informed him that she decided to remove Gilberto from his custody temporarily until they can investigate Roddy's ability to provide safe care. So, I've got the kid until further notice."

Willa was instantly sympathetic. "He's so lucky he has you. You stepped right up to the plate."

Derek obviously wanted to shrug away her praise. "Yeah, well, we didn't really have much choice. The closest DHS office is closed today, and I have a foster care certification. We're going to play the next few days by ear."

"Why are you certified to do foster care?"

"I have been since I started the job. Walt was certified and suggested I do it, too. Said you never know when you're going to make a difference in someone's life. I maintain the license every year, but I've never needed it before. Anyway, when I told Gilberto that I was supposed to have dinner with you, he came up with a pretty cool idea. Unfortunately, as much as I hate to say it, you might want to change out of that knock-out dress and into something more suited to the great outdoors."

Willa swallowed her disappointment. On her lunch hour that day, she'd bought a sexy new dress just for the occasion. And the appreciative look currently in Derek's eyes made it worth every penny of the exorbitant price she'd paid. Counting the seconds until he'd arrived, she'd even braved her front porch with her coat over her arm instead of snugly around her. "Why don't you and Gilberto come in while I change?"

She caught the surprise that crossed his face before he turned and gestured to Gilberto.

"You might want to think ski gear," he suggested as she opened her door.

"We're going skiing?" No wonder he looked like an ad for the local Summit Lodge mountain resort, in a chocolate cable-knit sweater that gorgeously accented his tanned skin.

"Not skiing, exactly. But I think you'll enjoy yourself. Gilberto and I put our heads together and…well, you'll see. I would have called to tell you about the change in plans—I should have called you—but I didn't want you to change your mind."

"I wouldn't have."

The small, pleased quirk of Derek's lips gave her goosebumps.

"You got a swing!" Gilberto's voice rang from outside Willa's front door. His face popped into view. "Can I swing on it?"

"Sure," she laughed. Being around Gilberto had reintroduced her to the irrepressible energy of childhood. It had been a long time since she'd experienced it up close and personal. "Close the front door if you're staying outside, though, okay?"

"Yep."

He did as requested, and a moment later the creak of the thick chains holding the swing was audible as he sat. Willa shook her head. "I forgot that the simplest things are often the most entertaining when you're young."

When she looked at Derek, he was studying the fire-place mantel. Instantly, her heart began to hammer. She had removed the photo last night, hadn't she? Scanning the heavy oak shelf, she saw a picture of herself and Daisy Dunnigan on a trip to New York, and a photo of her parents together in Paris for their thirtieth anniversary. Other than that, the mantel held only her small collection of candlesticks.

Relief flooded her. Time with Derek was meant to be an escape. She wasn't ready for questions that would jerk her back into the past.

"I'm going to change. It'll just be a minute." Heading to the bedroom, she rummaged through her dresser for a heavy sweater and her Lycra ski pants. She shimmied out of her dress and pantyhose and into a pair of pink long johns and heavy socks. Not quite the seductive effect she'd been shooting toward, but it would have to do. He was a rare man in this day and age, this sheriff of hers, putting the needs of a child who wasn't even his above his own desires. He knew how to look at life in the long run.

In just a couple of minutes, she'd shed her earrings, pulled on her ski clothes and tamed the static electricity in her hair.

"So, will you take a rain check on the dancing?" Derek called from her living room.

Willa grinned at her reflection in the mirror and nearly didn't recognize herself. The woman smiling back looked both excited and happy. "Of course."

"And…" He drew out the word, an interesting note in his voice. "Will you wear that dress for me again?"

Laughter rose into her throat. She glanced at the clingy jade-colored wraparound she'd tossed onto her bed. "You like that dress, hmm?"

"*Ohhhh*, yeah."

When, she wondered, was the last time she felt this good? "I'm almost done. Just tying my boots. Would you mind grabbing my ski jacket from the hall closet? Next to the front door." When she came out of her bedroom, Derek helped her into her jacket. A pair of gloves, a hat and a scarf from a drawer in the entry credenza were the last touches. "Ready," she finally announced.

"Not just yet." Reaching for the ends of her scarf, Derek drew her close for a kiss that instantly had her blood boiling and wanting to shed her down jacket. "I can't do that in front of the kid," he murmured. "And I didn't want to wait."

"I like the way you think, Sheriff Neel." Her voice emerged husky and flirtatious. Her heart began to thrum so hard, she could actually hear it and wondered if he could, too. Oh, how she wished they could stay here tonight.

As things were getting interesting, Gilberto pounded on the front door. "We should go now!"

"Gilberto is a little excited," she observed wryly.

"Not as excited as I am," Derek groaned, dropping one more kiss on her waiting lips. Gilberto tried the knob then rang the bell. "I'm glad that door was locked."

Once they were all on the road, Gilberto regaled her with the tales of last evening. "I was a real deputy. I got to wear a badge. Right here." He thrust his skinny chest between their seats and pointed to the spot just above his heart.

"Belt on," Derek commanded.

"Okay, right! And then," he continued as he dropped back into his seat, "we went home and ate breakfast in the middle of the night. And this morning I fed Derek's horses. When you hold out a carrot, they eat it out of your hand. But they don't bite you or nothing."

"Anything," Willa and Derek chimed.

"Okay. They just go like this." He demonstrated. "Their lips are soft and fat and have sharp hairs."

While Gilberto waxed on in the backseat, Derek reached over and took Willa's hand. "They just go like this." He brought her hand to his mouth and oh-so-gently nibbled the palm.

Pleasure filled her. *Oh, good golly.* "That's how they do it, hmm?"

"Hey!" Gilberto called. "What are you guys doing?"

"Just showing Willa how the horse eats," Derek said.

"Oh." And Gilberto talked nonstop the rest of the way to the ranch.

Derek's place was only about fifteen minutes south of Thunder Ridge, but the snow made the going a little slower. When they turned down his long driveway, Willa spotted a charming log home nestled in a grove of giant fir trees. To the left of the house stood a stable and paddock. Immediately behind Derek's home was a snow-covered hill adorned with two rows of flaming tiki torches. The entire scene was a Thomas Kinkade painting come to life. Willa felt her pulse accelerate in a way it hadn't since she was a child.

Unable to control her giddy grin, she glanced quickly between Gilberto and Derek. "What on earth is this?"

"It's cosmic sledding," Gilberto informed, looking mighty pleased.

"Or our version of cosmic sledding, anyway," Derek said, returning her grin. "We don't have the big slides and colored lights, but we did our best."

As they pulled nearer the hill, Willa could see myriad trails had already been blazed between the torches and the snow between them was packed hard. Unbridled glee rose in her throat, making her voice squeaky. "We're going sledding?"

"Yes." Gilberto flung his seatbelt off. "We're gonna let the horse pull us to the top of the hill, and then we're gonna ride our sleds down. We already tried it out, and it's pretty cool."

Making eye contact with Willa, Derek arched a brow suggestively. "I can think of one or two things that might be better, but it *is* a total blast."

Willa couldn't stem the grin that felt as if it swallowed her entire face.

"We thought we'd sled for a bit and work up an appetite, before we head inside for some grub."

"We made barbecued chickens," Gilberto announced, opening the car door as Derek came to a stop in front of his house.

"I'm no chef like you," Derek told her, "but I figured you probably like to have someone else do the cooking once in a while."

"Is that what smells so wonderful?" Willa's mouth began to water as they got out of the car. The scent of mesquite and barbecue sauce was unmistakable. "Are you cooking outdoors?"

"Yep. Treated myself to a Traeger grill last Christmas."

She inhaled deeply. "Mmm. I smell sage. And rosemary."

He chuckled. "You're good. The chicken should be ready in about an hour. Till then, go with Gilberto to choose a sled, and I'll harness Autumn."

Once she and Gilberto had trudged to the bottom of the hill, Willa turned to take in the view of Derek's spectacular property in the waning twilight. His log cabin had huge mountain-facing windows that extended from the first floor all the way up to the peak of the second floor.

Indoor lamps cast pools of golden light through the glass and onto the snowpack below, and the entire forested countryside was awash in moonlight. Icicles clung to the eves spanning his rustic front porch, and smoke snaked from the river rock chimney. Willa could easily imagine enjoying this view with a cup of coffee first thing in the morning in one of the several rockers that flanked the living room windows.

Gilberto was already in the sled, making *shooshing* sounds as he pretended to be on a thrilling slide down the slopes. In response to the fun he was already having, Willa felt a rush of pure joy moments before guilt whomped her in the solar plexus with the force of a wrecking ball—not because she was at Derek's or planning to go sledding, but because for a moment she'd felt *only* happiness and anticipation. She'd just taken a giant step into a future that was hers. Hers alone.

Steadying herself, she took one breath and then another, letting go of self-reproach, willing herself to stay in the moment.

"Everything okay?"

Lost in thought, she didn't notice Derek had come up behind her. Guiding the horse he called Autumn, he looked as if he'd stepped off a poster for a movie Western. His gaze was watchful, concerned. Autumn blew a noisy puff of air through her wide nostrils and shook her head till her bit jangled. Derek stroked the horse's forelock, his big, gentle hands obviously welcomed by the mare.

I'm with you, sister. She didn't want to crawl back to the cave in which she'd been living the past couple of years. It was a nicely adorned cave, with windows to the outside world, but now that she truly had moved beyond its walls, she knew she couldn't retreat. Not yet, anyway, not while this man was standing right in front of her.

"Everything is fine." Smiling brightly, she joined Derek in petting the horse's broad forehead. "So this is Autumn," she said. "Glad to make your acquaintance." Derek had hitched a long toboggan to the horse's traces. "You going to tow us up that hill, girl?"

"She's ready if you're ready."

Willa was glad to see that his expression already had begun to relax. Rubbing her mitten-clad hands together, she nodded. "As I'll ever be, I guess. It looks a little scary."

"That's what makes it exciting." He stared at her, long and deep and mesmerizing. "I'm not going to let anything happen. To you or Gilberto. The thing about sledding is that to get a really good ride, you have to let go. Completely. Can you do that?"

She couldn't look away. "I can try."

"Good enough."

After some brief instruction by Derek on safety, she and Gilberto clambered aboard the long wooden toboggan behind him. Holding onto their sleds by ropes, they rode up the substantial incline to the crest. Impossibly, the view was even more stunning at the top. The twin rows of tiki torches glinted, beckoning them with the promise of adventure.

"C'mon, Willa, let's go," Gilberto urged, thrashing off toward the starting gate, his Flexible Flyer sled bobbing along behind.

Willa glanced at Derek. "It's a lot steeper than it looks from down there." Shadows flickered across the snow.

"It's not bad. Hang on tight, and you'll be fine. You steer this thing with your feet." He demonstrated on her sled as Gilberto took off down the hill on his, whooping with wild abandon. At her dubious expression, Derek laughed. "Come on, then. I'll go with you the first time." Tethering Autumn to a small tree, he positioned the sled, pulled Willa onto his lap and wrapped his arms around her waist. "You okay?"

"Yes. Now." And she was. Something about Derek's strong embrace made her fear evaporate. No wonder everyone seemed to trust the sheriff of Thunder Ridge, she mused as she looped her hands around his arms.

The air fled from her lungs as they took off after Gilberto. Giddy squeals filled her ears, and it took a moment before she realized they were coming from her mouth. *They were flying!* Rapidly they soared, up and over the occasional bump that tickled her stomach and stole her breath. The flames from the torches blended into an orange blur and all too soon they were at the bottom of the hill, plowing into a snow berm and panting with laughter.

Willa's face was nearly frozen, her nose dripping snow, and her wool hat sagging over her eyes. She felt *alive*, a feeling that was familiar and foreign and fantastic all at once. Pulling her to her feet, Derek straightened her hat, kissed the tip of her nose, then set off to get Autumn for a ride back to the top.

For over an hour Willa heard herself rivaling Gilberto's shrieks all the way down the hill, and then chatting over each other as the horse towed them back up. And, like the young boy, she was disappointed when Derek finally announced it was time to head inside and eat—although she had to admit, the aroma from his back deck had her stomach growling. Besides, it was snowing again and visibility was growing sketchy.

Caked with snow, her boots crunched along after Derek as he led Autumn to the stable. "You were right—that was so exciting! Much better than dancing."

Derek mock glared at her. "I'm going to take that as a challenge." Slipping an arm around her waist, he kissed her temple. "I'm glad you had a good time. I was looking forward to Hooligans, but I appreciate your going with the flow."

"Anytime you want to do this again, count me in."

"It was my idea," Gilberto announced, trudging up behind them. "Can I comb Autumn's hair with that one thing? You know?"

"Yup. Curry comb's in the tack room. Run ahead and open the stable door, sport."

They watched the preteen hike through the snow toward the sliding wooden door.

"He really seems to love it here. With you," Willa observed. She couldn't blame him. The ranch was a great place for a boy like Gilberto. And Derek... Derek was fun and funny and encouraging. A perfect role model. "Do you think he'll ever go back to live with Roddy?"

Derek's reply was swift and decisive. "I sure as hell hope not."

"Does he have other relatives he can live with?"

"I don't know. Doesn't sound like it. Sometimes DHS can dig up a distant relative who's willing to help."

"When they can't," Willa ventured, "what happens then?"

From the grim expression on Derek's face, Willa sensed that Derek had already begun to care pretty deeply for the child. "When no relatives are available, or capable, the state assumes guardianship."

"Foster care."

With one hand on the reins leading Autumn, Derek used the other hand to whip off his sodden wool cap and stuff it in his pocket. "We've got a long way to go before any permanent decisions are made." He shook his head at her. "This evening has been perfect so far. I don't want to worry about tomorrow's problems. And that's saying something for me."

Willa reached for his free hand and continued walking, a silent agreement to keep the night light.

Even so, as their boots and the horse's hooves stamped the snow and the tiki torches flickered on, she worried about the conscientious sheriff at her side. Because where Gilberto was concerned, Derek wasn't simply a sheriff taking care of a community matter. The boy's future had become personal to him. She saw the telltale signs of true affection, maybe even love. Without actually meaning to, she squeezed Derek's hand. Smiling crookedly, he squeezed back.

Please don't let him get hurt, she prayed. But even as she sent the prayer up, she knew it would be futile if he crossed the line from affection into love.

A blast of warm air greeted them as Derek held the kitchen door open for Willa and Gilberto. Immediately, Willa was in love. His kitchen was gorgeous. Knotty pine walls and cabinetry were the perfect backdrop for the chocolaty granite countertops and island. The appliances were state-of-the-art stainless steel; he even had an eight-burner stove that made her fingers twitch with the desire to grab a saucepan and start cooking. Beneath their feet, the hardwood floors were softened by colorful throw rugs.

"This is a beautiful remodel," she stated, knowing it couldn't be original to the house. "It should be on the cover of *Better Homes and Gardens.* Must have been a big project."

"The house deserved it. I had some money saved. Remodeling seemed like a good investment in the future."

A quiet *woof* punctuated his explanation, and Willa turned toward its source.

In one corner of the kitchen, an ancient dog, a shepherd

mix, lay on a bed in the corner, slapping the floor with his tail in greeting.

"Hey, Captain," Derek murmured as they walked over. He bent to scratch the grizzled head. Captain honored Derek with several kisses before he curiously eyed the new visitor. "Willa," Derek said, "this is Captain. He's about ninety in people years. He doesn't see too well anymore, so you always want to let him smell you before you touch him."

A dog lover her whole life, Willa extended her hand, grinning at the large twitchy nose that examined her thoroughly. At last, the old fellow decided she was kiss-worthy and licked her with the slowest, gentlest canine kiss she'd ever felt.

"What a lover," she cooed to him.

"Captain was named after Captain Hook in *Peter Pan*," Gilberto explained. "Tell her, Derek. Captain was a brave dude when he was younger."

"Later, sport. Why don't you two wash up at the sink and then, Gilberto, show Willa to the table while I rustle up the food."

"Can I help you?" Willa asked.

"Nope. Everything's under control. You relax."

"I want to light the candles." Already becoming familiar with Derek's house, Gilberto zoomed to the correct drawer to locate matches.

"Okay. Willa, make sure he doesn't set the house on fire."

Gilberto snorted. "Please, I'm eleven. I can light a match. Been doing it all my life."

"I hope not." Willa caught Derek's eye and returned his grin.

"Hey, I'm in the fifth grade."

"In that case, maybe Derek will let you drive me home tonight."

"Fifth graders aren't allowed to drive, but I could do it," Gilberto mused as he led Willa to the dining room. Tongue protruding slightly as he worked, he managed to light the match on the ninth or tenth strike. Soon, the candles on the table were flickering happily, lending a festive mood to the evening.

"You sure I can't help you?" Willa offered again as Derek moved back and forth from the deck and kitchen with mounds of food.

"Positive. You're our guest. Gilberto, help me with the dishes so Willa can relax."

While Gilberto willingly trotted behind Derek, Willa took the opportunity to make an exploratory stroll around the open-concept living and dining area. Much like the man who owned the house, the surroundings were ruggedly masculine, yet a woman would feel right at home here, too. Safe. Isolated from the outside world and its cares. Maybe that's what he meant when he'd said he'd remodeled with an eye toward the future—not merely that he was thinking about his investment, but that he wanted the ranch to be less a bachelor's retreat and more a family dwelling.

The living room was outfitted with large leather chairs and couches, covered with ivory and beige throws so soft they begged you to cuddle up. Hand-woven Indian blankets and artifacts adorned the walls, lending color and character. Soft music came from speakers in the polished wood ceiling, and built-in bookshelves bore evidence of a well-read owner. A fire crackled merrily in a river rock hearth.

Setting the last dish onto the farmhouse table that divided the kitchen from the living area, Derek called, "Dinner is served." Ravenous, Willa found her seat opposite him.

"I'm starving!" Gilberto announced as he watched Derek dish up a steaming plate of barbecued chicken, baked potatoes and savory roasted vegetables for Willa. "But I don't want any of that veggie stuff. I hate green junk."

"Fine. But, if you expect to get any of the dessert you ordered, green junk is on the menu." Derek's tone, though placid, brooked no argument, and Willa hid her smile behind her water glass. He really was a natural father figure. Someday, some lucky kid would no doubt reap the benefits.

Just…not with her.

Because the very idea threatened the cozy mood the evening had invoked, Willa pushed away all thoughts of tomorrow and simply allowed herself to revel in the delicious food and easy conversation. There were no lulls in said conversation, either. Gilberto treated them to an insane number of knock-knock jokes as they ate, and she and Derek laughed or groaned on cue. When they'd done justice to the meal, Gilberto moved into the kitchen to feed Captain a few remnants of barbecue that he'd saved from his plate.

"How did you end up living on a ranch?" Willa asked over a cup of after-dinner coffee.

Setting his napkin next to his plate, Derek leaned back in his chair. "Walt and his wife, Julie, weren't able to have kids. We became like family. When Walt was diagnosed with lung cancer, I was in the police academy, but came back to help. Julie had had heart surgery and wasn't doing well. When she passed, it took the wind out of Walt's sails. He went downhill pretty quickly."

"I'm—" Willa swallowed "—so sorry. I know how hard it is to lose someone you love." Eyes downcast, she twisted her napkin between her fingers, and blinked back the sudden, unwelcome urge to cry.

"Right before he passed, Walt claimed he was going to leave the acreage to his horses." Derek smiled wryly. "And the old codger actually did. But, there was an addendum that left the horses and everything they owned to me. And that's how I came to own a little piece of paradise."

"That's amazing," Willa murmured. "Walt sounds like he was a real character."

"He was. One in a million. Everybody in Thunder Ridge loved him. I figure…" Derek glanced over his shoulder at Gilberto, who lay on the dog bed with his arms around the snoring Captain. "I figure that Walt is the reason I give a damn about what happens to that kid."

Chapter Ten

"Dang." Gilberto sagged as yet another marshmallow fell off his stick in a flaming ball of goo. "Willa's come out way better than mine."

"She does seem to have the Midas touch, doesn't she?" Derek scowled at the black char on the end of his own skewer, adding another failure to their ever-growing discard pile.

Relaxed, happy and sated with food, Willa laughed at her two dinner companions. "*Now* are you willing to let me teach you how to make the perfect s'more?"

Together, they had cleared the dining table and settled onto a pile of pillows in front of the fireplace for dessert. Gilberto had lobbied to put s'mores on the night's menu, eager to try them for the very first time. Derek had loaded a tray with graham crackers, chocolate bars and a mountain of jumbo marshmallows, but so far the results were sketchy.

"I can't believe I need a lesson for this," Derek grumbled as he attempted, mostly in vain, to clean his metal skewer.

"Humility is the first ingredient in any successful recipe."

"You made that up."

"Not at all." Taking a sip of incredibly good coffee, Willa smiled. "In my former life, I taught at a culinary institute. The best chefs were invariably the ones who were the most teachable."

Derek's attention peaked. "Where was this culinary institute?"

"South Pasadena. I taught at Le Cordon Bleu," she shared. "It's not there anymore, unfortunately. I was also a pastry chef at a restaurant on Lake Boulevard."

"Lake Boulevard?"

"It's the South Pasadena equivalent of Rodeo Drive in Beverly Hills, or—" she paused to think "—Northwest Twenty-Third Avenue in Portland."

"Overly trendy and expensive?"

She laughed. "An epicurean's delight," she countered. "A hub for the most creative food in the city."

Pleasure filled Derek's face, and he nodded. "I like your confidence."

It was true: when it came to career, she'd rarely faltered.

"Confidence is very…" *S-e-x-y.* He mouthed the word, even though Gilberto was too involved in biting burnt marshmallow off his skewer to listen.

"Oh, I agree." Connection sizzled between them.

"So you had a great career," he observed. "Why did you leave?"

Crud. She'd walked right into that, and the answer was guaranteed to open the floodgates of her past. It would happen eventually, she knew, but she wanted to control when, where and how much she revealed. Tonight had been light and fun with moments of unexpected bliss. It had been, so far, much more than she'd expected. Discussing her past would change all that.

She shook her head. "I didn't leave. I'm still doing what I love, but now I'm doing it in Thunder Ridge. And I don't have to tell you why living in Thunder Ridge is so attractive."

She considered that an excellent save, but Derek's eyes narrowed. He knew she was hedging.

Curved around his skewer, his hands looked tense. Taking a chance, she covered his knuckles with her palm. "I like where I'm at right now, working in Thunder Ridge. Being here, with you and Gilberto. I loved today. And tonight has been perfect."

Let it stay that way, she implored silently, breathing a sigh of relief when his hand relaxed beneath hers.

"Rrrrrrrgh." Gilberto's frustrated growl claimed their attention. He thrust his skewer at them. "I can't get it right. Willa, can you do mine?" he requested.

"Of course. I'll show you a few special tricks for the perfect s'more." She sent Derek a benevolent smile. "And may I say that the willingness to be taught shows true strength of character."

As she leaned forward to take Gilberto's stick, Derek whispered, "I'm going to remember you said that when it's time for me to show *you* a few special tricks."

His words filled her with a flush of anticipation. Quickly, she glanced at Gilberto, but he was busily engaged in choosing the perfect marshmallow for her to roast.

Ordering herself to focus on dessert, Willa cleared her throat. "Alrighty. Lesson one. Lightly—very lightly— warm your graham crackers and the chocolate to prepare them for the marshmallow."

"Prepare them. Check," Derek murmured.

Willa placed the crackers and chocolate in the metal grill basket Derek had bought especially for tonight and held it high over the flames. "We're not trying to toast these or melt the chocolate yet, remember. We're just getting them ready."

She jumped slightly as Derek's hand slid up her back. Softly, he kneaded the muscles at the base of her neck.

"What are you doing?" She sneaked the question out the side of her mouth.

"Getting ready." Smooth as silk, his voice matched the ministrations of his hand—soothing, confident, sexy. Willa's vision blurred a little.

"Now can we do the marshmallow?"

Gilberto's pleading question jerked her back to attention. "Right! So. You hold the marshmallow far enough away that the flame is just teasing it."

"That makes sense," Derek agreed in a tone that could only be called a purr. His fingers wandered to a spot—ooh, it was a very sensitive spot—below her right ear. "Only enough heat to tease…"

She closed her eyes for a second—honest to Pete, no more than a millisecond—until Gilberto shouted, "Look out!"

"Oops!" Willa yipped, laughing sheepishly as her marshmallow burst into flame.

"A little too hot for you there?" Derek goaded. To Gilberto he said, "She's demonstrating how *not* to do it, I guess."

"That's exactly right." Reaching for her own skewer, she jammed a fresh marshmallow onto the tip. "I allowed myself to get distracted. That's very bad."

Serenely, utterly serenely, she held the marshmallow over the flame, proud of how steady her hand was. "There.

See how it's light brown all over? That's what we're look-ing for. It's per-FECT!" Nearly shouting the second syl-lable, she sat bolt upright. Was that Derek's hand dipping below the waistband of her jeans?

While she sat there stupidly, doing absolutely nothing with the marshmallow, he let her go, took the skewer from her useless fingers and started to make the s'more for Gil-berto exactly the way she had shown him. He presented it to the boy, who announced, "This is the best s'more ever."

"Isn't this your *first* s'more ever?"

"Yeah. It's the best."

Derek laughed.

He was acting as if nothing at all had happened. Sev-eral s'mores later, a few of which Gilberto proudly made on his own and served to them, Willa began to relax again.

"That's it for me. I pronounce you top chef," she told Gilberto, leaning back and holding her belly. "I'm retiring my skewer. I'm stuffed."

"Lightweight," Derek said good-naturedly as he, too, settled back.

"Hardly. I probably gained five pounds tonight."

"I don't see it. You'll have to show me where."

He was doing it again. Sounding innocent, but giving her a look that sent her blood pressure through the roof. She narrowed her eyes. This was definitely a game meant for two.

While Gilberto constructed yet another s'more, she took advantage of the unwitnessed moment. Scooting closer to Derek, she nudged his arm with her shoulder and reached for his hand. Instead of linking fingers, however, she drew her forefinger along his palm…his wrist… Then she curled her fingers under the sleeve of his sweater and explored his arm, loving the strength of it. When she felt his muscles tense and goose bumps cover his arm, she let a satisfied smile crease her face.

Now we're talkin'. She could feel the energy filling Derek's body and recognized the victorious sensation of her own sexual power. It had been ages.

"I don't want this s'more," Gilberto announced from his position in front of the fireplace. He plopped back on his heels. "I don't even know why I made it. I already ate, like, six."

"Uh oh." Willa sat up, pulling her hand away from Derek, but he refused to let go, sitting up with her. "I wasn't paying attention."

"Me, either." Derek thoughtfully studied the boy. "On the other hand, I don't think we have much to worry about. At least two of them are still on your face."

Gilberto probed the area around his mouth with his tongue.

"Why don't you head on upstairs and jump into the shower, since it's already past your bedtime. I'll be up to say good-night when you're done, okay?"

"Okay. What should I do with this?" Gilberto offered his latest creation to Derek. "Do you want it?"

"Nope. I can't eat another bite. It'll be too hard to eat by morning. You can toss it in the fire," he advised.

Gilberto looked affronted. "No, I don't want to burn it up. It's one of my best ones. This marshmallow is perfect. Look, Willa." He held it up for her to admire one last time. "Can I give it to Captain instead?"

Derek shook his head. "Sorry. Chocolate is bad for Captain."

"It is?" Gilberto's brow creased with worry. "Why?"

Willa nodded. "Unfortunately, chocolate is poison to dogs."

Alarmed, Gilberto gasped. "Chocolate is *poison*?"

Derek chuckled. "Not to humans, bud." Having heard

his name, Captain limped in from the kitchen to nose his master's outstretched hand. "Hey, Captain. Did you hear us talking about you?" With happy grunts, the old dog curled up by Derek's side.

Gilberto watched his s'more go up in flames then leaned over to embrace the dog before he hugged Derek and Willa. "'Night, Captain. 'Night, Willa."

"Good night, buddy."

"Don't forget to brush your teeth," Derek ordered, "so they don't fall out after all that sugar."

"If they fall out, you've got to put money under my pillow, dude, so I'll believe in the tooth fairy. You don't want to, like, destroy my innocence or nothing."

Willa and Derek started laughing so hard, neither of them bothered to correct his grammar.

Clearly pleased to have received this reaction, Gilberto got to his feet, beaming. "You're both weird," he said contentedly, heading to a staircase constructed from split logs that had been polished to a soft golden sheen. Trailing his hand along the bannister, he called, "'Night, weirdos," from the landing and disappeared toward the room Derek had given him.

Turning to the man who still held her hand, Willa observed, "Considering he hasn't been here that long, Gilberto seems to have made himself right at home. You're good at this."

The muscles worked in Derek's jaw. "I suppose anything's better than bunking with Roddy and his idiot posse."

"Maybe, but don't sell yourself short. I barely recognize that boy from the one who was lurking in the bakery, trying to figure out how to steal. I wonder if Roddy wants him back?"

Derek's hand tightened on hers—unconsciously, Willa

guessed. "I don't know," he responded. "Gilberto doesn't talk about him much, but he's shared a couple of incidences that make me suspect longstanding neglect." His expression clouded. "Unfortunately family can become territorial. They may fight for their right to raise one of their own even when they're not committed to doing a good job of it."

Willa watched Derek's free hand gently stroke Captain's face and head. "If you had the option, would you be interested in becoming his foster parent?" she asked.

Derek thought for a long moment as on the other side of the wall of windows, the snow continued to fall. Occasional flurries swirled before being swept away by the whistling wind. Anticipating Derek's answer made Willa's stomach feel like those flurries. He was a born family man; anyone watching him with Gilberto would be able to see that. Of course, being good at something and being willing to do it every day, possibly for the rest of your life, were two different things. Did Derek have any idea what raising a child involved, far beyond the daily needs?

He inhaled long and deep, slowly exhaling before he answered her. "I try not to get too emotionally involved."

Unbidden, Willa's snort of laughter made Captain's tail thump on the floor. "I hate to break it to you, but you're already emotionally involved."

Derek appeared to be about to deny that, but his shoulders sagged. "Is it that obvious?"

Empathy welled as she smiled. "It's who you are. Caring. Sweet. Optimistic."

He tugged her close. "I'm no boy scout."

"In some ways you are. You're such a boy scout, you're a…a…*man* scout. People trust you. They're attracted to you."

"Right now, I'm only interested in whether one person is attracted to me."

She could feel the warmth from his skin. "Isn't it obvious?" she breathed. "I wouldn't be here if I wasn't attracted. Very."

They shared a kiss, each of them struggling with the self-control to make it last…and last. Willa expected to be interrupted by Gilberto, calling down that he was ready for bed, but, instead, Captain became the culprit. Hefting himself to his feet, he walked around until he was between her and Derek, forcing them to break apart. The old shepherd nosed Willa's hand until she reached out, weaving her fingers into the surprisingly soft fur.

Derek groaned in frustration. "I should have found you a different home when I had the chance."

"How could you say such a thing? Don't listen," Willa crooned in the old boy's ear. "He's just jealous."

"Damn straight."

As Willa scratched the dog's back, Captain lay down, swishing his tail across the floor.

"You like Willa, too, hmm?" Derek asked, and the dog crooned in delight, making her laugh. "He rarely trusts anyone this quickly."

"Really?" From upstairs, they could hear the sounds of Gilberto getting ready for bed. "What happened to Captain's paw?" she asked, referring to the strange-looking boot the dog wore below his right knee.

"He lost it in a trap."

"No!" She leaned in for a closer inspection of the Velcro and ripstop fabric sheath that secured a springy metal J-hook to his leg. "How horrible. Was it recently?"

"No, no. It happened about the same time Walt passed, so I guess it's getting close to a decade ago now. I was out one day, exercising one of the horses on an old forest-access logging trail up behind where we went sledding, and Stark, who has always been a pretty mellow horse, started acting real skittish. At first I thought maybe he'd picked up the scent of a bobcat or a bear, because we have plenty of those around here."

Willa watched his handsome face process the past in the firelight.

"After I got him settled down, I took a look around with my binoculars. Didn't see anything, but after a while, I heard a sort of high-pitched whine. Sounded like an animal was in pain."

"Captain." Willa murmured.

"Yeah."

You have a sad story, too, Willa thought as she gently stroked the intelligent face.

"Since I wasn't able to convince Stark to head toward the sound, I had to tether him and head into the woods on foot. Took me a while to locate him. I think he stopped moaning now and then as he heard me coming closer. Probably pretty afraid of me, too, right old man?" Derek's expression softened. He scratched a sweet spot just above the dog's tail.

"Anyway, I found him cowering on the ground, his paw caught in an illegal small-game trap. He was half starved to death and in obvious pain. He was real sweet as I released the trap, and let me tell you, trying to get that thing off him without doing more damage was tough. He whined more than once, but never tried to bite me."

Willa winced at the image of big-hearted Captain in a sawtooth trap.

"I took him into the local vet, but he couldn't save the paw. Together, though, we came up with a pretty cool prosthetic for him. We've refined it a few times over the years, but even in the beginning it wasn't too long before he was fat and sassy and off running around again, just like a pup."

"Wow. You are a lucky dog," Willa said to Captain.

Again, Willa was struck by how deeply Derek cared. Not only about Captain. About any underdog. "It's going to be so hard when he goes," she said, then realized how tactless that sounded. "I'm sorry. I didn't mean to say that out loud."

"No, it's okay. It's nothing I haven't already thought of. Or had to deal with before. I had another dog, back when I was in the police academy. When I adopted her, she followed me everywhere. People would laugh at me because I'd talk baby talk to her."

"Baby talk? Like?"

"You know. Things to build up her self-esteem."

"Ah. And she understood you?"

"Of course." Derek grinned.

"Adorable," Willa murmured. Like the man telling the story. "What were her favorite affirmations?"

"Nothing out of the ordinary. All the stuff a woman likes to hear." Both she and Derek were lying on their sides now, gazing at each other over Captain, who had lapsed into a soft snore. Derek ran the back of his finger ever-so-gently down Willa's cheek. "I'd tell her she was beautiful. And that failing puppy class did not make her a loser. She worried about that."

He has the softest, sweetest eyes I've ever seen. "Did she?"

"In weak moments. So I'd remind her that her struggles didn't define her." He spoke softly. "They made her stronger. More beautiful."

"I bet you say that to all the girls," she whispered back.

"No. Only to the strong, beautiful ones."

Willa felt as if she'd been in the desert for years, and Derek was a tall, cold glass of water. Every cell in her body drank him in. Thirsty for his touch, his kiss, she inched forward…

"I'm ready!"

Gilberto jumped down the stairs, swinging himself with both hands on the bannisters then crash landing three steps below where he'd started. "You can come up now."

As self-conscious as if she'd been caught buck naked, Willa sprang back.

Derek put a calming hand on her arm. "I'll be right up." To her, he said, "Can you hang tight? I won't be long."

She nodded. At least, she thought she nodded. Her heart was pounding so hard, she felt faint. And it wasn't pounding because they'd been caught off guard, either. Oh, no. It was pounding, because she realized she was starting to need this man's touch and his gazes and his words the way she needed food and water and sleep. They breathed life into her.

She watched him jog up the stairs to join Gilberto, ruffling the boy's hair as they walked companionably side by side the rest of the way.

Rousing from his brief nap, Captain lifted his head, looked for his master, and, when he saw that Derek was leaving without him, let out a whimper of protest.

"Yeah, me, too." Willa rubbed his tummy, settling him down so he wouldn't have to tax his elderly joints by getting up to follow. With a sigh, the dog flopped back to the floor, allowing Willa's touch to mollify him.

If only she could be appeased that easily. For her, however, one thing was clear. No man's touch, no man's presence but Derek's was going to suffice. For the first time in forever she knew exactly what she wanted: more. More kisses, more whispers in the night. More of the feeling she had when he looked at her, his eyes heavy with desire.

Lifting Captain's ear, she murmured, "Can you keep a secret? Tonight's the night. I'm going to seduce the sheriff. And defeat is not an option. Okay with you?"

Captain swished his feathery tail. His tongue lolled out of a doggy grin as he panted.

She patted his belly. "Good doggy. I'll take that as a yes."

Chapter Eleven

It took Derek longer to put Gilberto to bed than he'd intended. The kid had never had a bedtime routine before, and he loved to review his day—in detail. They were also reading the first *Diary of a Wimpy Kid* together, a very big deal since Gilberto previously thought he hated to read. Being read to for the first time in his life had proved to be the game changer for him, and Derek didn't want to break the spell. Try as he had to shorten their routine tonight, it had still consumed thirty minutes.

He'd come back downstairs concerned that Willa might have gotten bored or annoyed because yet another moment rightfully belonging to her had been handed over to Gilberto. He was being the kind of date most single women he knew would lambaste, unless they were parents. Or wanted to be.

As he reached the living room, he saw Willa curled up on the floor pillows with Captain. She'd tucked an afghan around the old dog, and her hand rested on his side. Silhouetted against the firelight, the curve of her waist and hip made his fingers tingle with the desire to trace them. Her hair glowed with red and gold flames.

He paused on the last step, unsure of his next move, which had happened more since he'd met Willa than at any other time in his life. Knowing what he wanted did not translate easily, however, into knowing how to get it. He'd spent a day and an evening so close to the life he wanted, he could taste it.

When she turned her head and smiled dreamily, he knew he couldn't trust himself to walk over and kiss her; the night would end up very quickly in his bed. And as much as he wanted that, he refused to settle for it. He wouldn't accept anything less than everything she had to give.

So instead of joining her, he walked to the kitchen, grimly holding himself in check and returning a few moments later with a mug of hot cider, which he handed to her.

Resettling herself on the sofa, she accepted the mug, inhaled the aroma of apple and spices, and peeked up at him. "This smells incredible."

"I buy it from Springer Sisters. Have you been out there?" Willa shook her head. "It's an orchard on Highway 35. Four sisters run it. They have a store and a restaurant, too." He gave his stomach a pat. "I ate a lot of their pies before you showed up."

"You wouldn't know it," she complimented, and he felt his ab muscles flex involuntarily.

There was something different in her manner tonight. Her tone bordered on flirtatious. Her gaze was bolder. When she patted the sofa cushion next to her, his self-control became a bad joke.

Taking the mug from her hands, he set it on the table

and cupped the back of her neck, pulling her in for a kiss. Warm and pillow-soft, her lips tasted of apples and cinnamon. When he nudged them apart, she complied eagerly, turning the teasing nibbles into something deeper and more urgent. *Oh, man, the woman knows how to kiss.*

Clinging to Derek's shoulders, Willa pulled back and glanced toward the top of the stairs. "Is Gilberto all settled in?" she asked breathlessly.

"Asleep before I left the room."

Her forehead against Derek's, she nodded slightly. "It's getting late."

His gut clenched as he tried to stem the tide of desire rolling through him. "I didn't expect the night to go so long. I can't leave Gilberto. How am I going to drive you home?"

"Hmm." Brow furrowed in a mock frown, she murmured, "That is a problem. Let me think. I suppose, if necessary, I could stay the night. Just to help you out." Her eyes were large and bright.

"I appreciate that more than I can say." Derek's breath felt labored, and he was sitting still. As far as his libido was concerned, all systems were go. There was a guest bedroom on the first floor, far away from the child sleeping upstairs. Perfect.

As his body prepped for a touchdown dance, however, his brain slapped him upside the head. He'd learned a long time ago that dreams required time and patience, two things in short supply when he wanted Willa with every fiber of his being.

Reaching for her hand, he got to his feet and pulled her with him toward the stairs. He was about to take a calculated risk.

When they reached the second-floor landing, he said, "I always have an extra toothbrush on hand."

"For all your women friends?" she teased.

"I have only one." He planted a swift, hard kiss on her upturned lips.

The flush of pleasure that filled her cheeks made it nearly impossible to do what he knew he had to.

At the end of the hall, two broad double doors led to his master suite. Inviting her into the most intimate space in his home, he watched her reaction. Would she view it the way he had the day the ranch had become his? More than any other room in the house, this one beckoned him to picture a future here with a partner to share it.

Slowly, Willa turned to take in his California king-sized bed and the puffy comforter in an earth-toned Aztec print. The walls were made up of the flat side of split logs, sanded and polished with white chinking in between, giving the room a lodge-resort feel. But his favorite part was the wall of windows facing the now-dark Thunder Ridge range.

"Amazing," Willa murmured.

"I like it a lot. I like it even more with you here."

He wanted her in that king-sized bed, opening her gorgeous stormy eyes to the sight of the mountain. He wanted a love as strong, as permanent as Thunder Ridge itself.

If he and Willa made love tonight, it would be incredible. But dangerous, too, affirming that they were having an affair and suggesting he could be satisfied by the bits and pieces of her life that she was willing to share.

The parameters she'd set for their relationship were built on a foundation of some trauma she refused to confide. Someday, it would be different. He would wait. He would wait as long it took.

"I have a T-shirt you can wear," he told her.

"Will I *need* something to sleep in?"

Time stopped. Their gazes caught and held. Taking a big breath, he tucked her hair behind her ears. "Couple years ago, I came home after a really hard day and made a pan of brownies. I couldn't wait for them to be ready, so I took them out of the oven early. After the first bite, I knew I'd blown it. They were like pudding in the middle. I figured I could put them back in the oven and try again, but they were never right after that, and I realized it was possible to ruin something that should have been great, by trying to hurry it. Know what I mean?"

Willa frowned heavily. "I know you need baking lessons. And this is a really weird time to be talking about brownies."

His laughter was self-deprecating. "Right on both counts. I suck at parables." Holding her face between his hands, he looked into her eyes. "I don't want brownies. I want us. I want us to come out right, Willa. I think that's going to take more time."

Her lips parted. Two spots of color appeared on her cheeks. "But we've known each other over a year."

He could see her confusion. She was trying to process his sudden change in direction. *Damn.* He wanted to kick his own butt for not handling this better. Tamping down his guilt, he crossed to his dresser, withdrew the T-shirt and handed it to her.

"Clean towels are in the master bath and toothbrush is in the medicine cabinet. TV, radio, phone are at your disposal. Use anything you want." Her gaze lowered to the cotton T she held tightly in her hands. "I'll be in the guest room, second door on the left as you enter the hallway, if you need anything. Will you be all right?"

She nodded without looking up.

"Sweet dreams," he said quietly.

He left the room, acutely aware that she hadn't answered.

Two mornings later, the bells on Something Sweet's door jangled, alerting Willa that another customer had arrived. The early birds had already come and gone, and the eight o'clock, post-school drop-off crowd wouldn't swoop in for several more minutes.

Willa nearly dropped an entire tray of onion bialys as Derek filled her doorway. Instantly, her pulse accelerated in anticipation, flagrantly disobeying her brain, which said, *He has a lot of explaining to do.*

Last night, she had slept in her own bed again, though "slept" was a misnomer. Mostly, she had tossed and turned and wrestled with covers that had felt too hot and too heavy even though it was still snowing outside.

She hadn't stopped thinking about Derek for more than a couple of minutes at a time in the past thirty-two hours, having tossed and turned all night at his place, too. For the second time, Derek had primed the pump like a man dying of thirst and then walked away from the well. *What was up with that?* His stories about immediate gratification and undercooked brownies did not cut it as an explanation.

Smiling, he ambled up, resting his arms on the high glass display case. He looked clear-eyed, energetic, fresh as a daisy. *I hate him.* Lack of sleep had drawn dark circles beneath her eyes, and, having spent her mental energy on fretting, she hadn't had the motivation to do anything more this morning than swipe on some lip gloss and sweep her hair into a bun.

"Good morning." His voice reminded her of the coffee she was brewing, smooth and rich.

With Gilberto present the morning after she'd slept at Derek's, Willa hadn't had the opportunity to address her confusion over the way the night had ended. Truthfully, she hadn't even known how to go about it. Now, with him standing right in front of her, she felt heat rise up her neck and into her cheeks. She still had no idea how to ask, *Why don't you want to make love to me?*

Her eyes pricked with tears just from thinking it. Lowering her head, she gave herself a stern talking to while she transferred bialys to the display case. *Keep your cool. Do not hint that you feel rejected. I forbid you to sound pathetic. He's acting like nothing happened, so that is exactly what you'll do.*

"Hi there," she said breezily. "Nice to see you this morning. Would you like some coffee? There's a fresh pot brewing." With rapid movements, she placed the last of the bialys in the case. "Not that you look like you need the caffeine. Uh-uh. You seem very well rested. I'm going to put this tray away and be right back." Baking sheet in hand, she stomped to the kitchen, let the tray clatter into the sink and, ignoring Norman Bluehorse's uncharacteristically inquisitive look, returned to the front.

Back behind the counter, she refused to look Derek in the eye. For the first time, she saw that he'd placed a sheet of neon-yellow paper on the glass top. "What's that?" She pointed.

Glancing down as if he hadn't noticed it, either, he looked so gorgeously masculine and thickheaded, she almost forgave him on the spot.

"It's a flyer. About Rudy Gunnersun's barn dance." He sounded as uncomfortable as she felt. "This Friday."

"I heard about it. Do you want me to put the flyer up in my window?"

His expression said that was the furthest thing from his mind. "No. I came to ask if you'd go with me."

"Oh. I see." She heard her foot tapping the stained-concrete floor. "Actually, no, I don't see." Had he somehow missed the signals she was giving him? "Look, I appreciate the dates, this whole courtship thing, but in case I haven't made myself perfectly clear—I'm easy."

Her heart thumped against her ribs. Well. That was

more forward than she'd been in years. Actually, more forward than she'd ever been.

Derek put his hands on his hips, studying her. "No." He shook his head. "You sure as hell are not."

"Okay, I walked right into that one. I realize I'm not the easiest *person*. We've already covered that territory. But as far as a sexual relationship goes, I invited you back to my house with no time limit on how long you could stay, which I think was a pretty big hint, and the other night, I told you I wanted to spend the night with you at your place."

"You think that makes you a sure bet?"

She gaped at him. "Uh…yeah. Derek, I flat out told you I'm ready for an affair. And you walked away. Twice. What more does a woman need to do to convince you she wants to sleep with you? Put a rose between her teeth and dance naked on the coffee table?"

"Sounds promising," he said drolly. "You said some pretty important things just now. I want to address them. But not here."

"I shouldn't have even brought it up. There are too many ears, and I have too much to do."

"Okay. Tonight then? No, wait—" He frowned. "I have Gilberto now, and I haven't asked anyone yet if they'd be willing to babysit an eleven-year-old boy."

"With an excess of energy," she added.

"Exactly. And I'm not comfortable leaving him on his own yet."

"I'd offer to watch him, of course, but…"

"That would defeat the purpose."

"Right."

"And I want to talk soon. Which brings us back to Friday."

"The barn dance?" she said doubtfully, setting the plates on a serving tray. "Not exactly private."

"Could be. I responded to a suspected prowler call once at Rudy's place. I know all the hideaways. And Gilberto will have other kids to hang with. My guess is we won't have any trouble finding time to talk about…your concerns."

Her biggest concern was that she'd somehow misread him. But he was right: she didn't want to spend any more time obsessing about it, so they needed to talk about it soon.

As the bell on the door jangled again, she said, "The morning rush is about to start. I'd better get to work."

"Okay." Derek cocked his finger at her. "Friday. 'Berto and I will pick you up at six." Leaning close, he murmured, "I'd like to kiss you."

He would? She pulled her lower lip between her teeth to keep from smiling like a ninny. "Oh?"

"Yeah, but that would be like taking out a front-page ad in the *Thunder Ridge Gazette.*"

She nodded. "That's probably pushing it."

He reached for her hand and raised it to his lips. Goose bumps shivered along her arm.

Releasing her with a smile, he headed for the door, holding it as moms in sweatpants and heavy boots tumbled in. "Good morning, ladies," he nodded, tossing one final look back at Willa, who stared after him as he walked down the street.

Okay, snap out of it now. Immediately, she started a second pot of coffee, knowing she'd be pouring steadily for the next hour. It was back to business as usual. *Thank heavens.*

Rudy Gunnersun's giant barn was so well lit, Willa could see the glow spilling over the landscape and into the hills.

As she, Derek and Gilberto walked from Derek's truck to the wide-open doors, she spied half the town inside, warmed by a wealth of heat lamps and the music of Hanging by a Thread, an all-female, all-strings band. Entertained by vigorous fiddling, Rudy's guests gathered around food tables set against the far wall under the haymow or lined up in front of kegs that flowed with cider and beer.

Everyone knew the festivities were part of Rudy's bid to oust Thunder Ridge's incumbent mayor, and it wasn't as if Rudy tried to hide that fact. Giant posters with his smiling face decorated every wall.

"Vote FUN, Vote GunnerSUN?" Derek read one of the captions. "It looks like Rudy's running for the mayor of Never-Never Land."

"Shh," Willa chided, trying to stifle a grin. "Do you think Mayor Ellison is concerned about an upset? There are an awful lot of people here."

"Ellison has an indoor softball tournament scheduled for next week. The same people will be there."

The hand Derek placed on the small of her back and the grin he sent her made her feel as if they'd been a couple for years and that this was simply another of those small-town social engagements they were required to keep. It didn't feel bad at all.

"I see my friends," Gilberto told them, waiting for the okay from Derek before running off to hang with them.

Out of uniform tonight, Derek was hands down the best-looking man in the barn. Or in town.

Or possibly in the state, Willa thought as she studied her date. A V-neck knit sweater in a deep wine color topped black jeans that left no doubt about the sheriff's level of fitness. His arms looked as strong as a lumberjack's, and his belly was flat. Over the sweater, he wore a leather jacket as black as his hair.

She had decided to wear heels tonight, hoping to make it easier to dance with a man ten inches taller. Even in her stack-heeled boots, however, he dwarfed her by the sheer breadth of his shoulders and chest. Still, his gaze, his touch, left her feeling strong as well as cherished.

"What are you thinking? Right now," he demanded.

Willa responded immediately with the truth. "That you're not at all my type."

Rearing his head back, Derek released the most robust laugh she'd heard from him yet. She loved that he was so settled in his own skin, so comfortable he didn't offend easily.

"What's your type?" he asked.

She considered. "Refined. Intellectual. More yuppie, less classic macho hero."

The hand on her back began massaging in slow circles. His eyes lowered in heavy-lidded seduction mode. "You had me at 'classic macho hero.'"

It was Willa's turn to laugh, pleasure filling her right down to her toes. She was happy when she was with Derek. Just…happy. "Would you like to dance, Sheriff?"

With the hand that was on her back, he pressed her close. "I sure would. As I recall, dancing together is something you and I do very well. Let's go."

Taking her hand, he led her to the dance floor, where they started out two-stepping to "All About Tonight" and slow danced while Hanging by a Thread played "Bless the Broken Road." The band announced a break, and the couples on the floor began to disperse, all except Willa and Derek, who continued to sway while looking into each other's eyes.

"You wanted an explanation for why we haven't made love yet."

The mere thrum of his voice sent internal shivers racing through her veins. Everywhere they touched, her body felt awake and on fire.

"Now would be a really unfortunate time to mention that you're gay." She spoke hoarsely, relieved when the corners of his eyes crinkled.

"I'm not."

"Whew." She glanced around them at the nearly empty dance floor. "So, it's not exactly private out here. Given the nature of our conversation, I mean."

"Hide in plain sight. Best tactic ever invented."

"If you say so." A devil dancing in his eyes mesmerized her. He could tell her almost anything right now, and she'd believe it.

"I'm not a one-night man," Derek said, his expression and voice turning instantly more serious. "And you are not a one-night woman."

She blinked, genuinely confused. "Who said anything about one night?"

"One night, one week…if you put a time limit on it, it's sex, not a relationship."

"Okay, you kinda sounded like a girl just then."

The cockeyed grin she loved came out in full force. "I may be macho, but I'm also deeply sensitive."

"That time, you managed to sound sexy. Bravo." Facetiously, she asked, "Sooo, you're afraid I'll take you for granted?"

Until that moment, they had continued to sway, even though the music had stopped. Now Derek stilled. "I don't want to take *you* for granted."

This time, emotion caused the shivers that ran through her body, and that was far more dangerous than sexual shivers. "You would never take me for granted," she whispered, knowing it was the absolute truth. "Ever."

Tightening his hold on her waist, he lowered his head.

They stood on the dance floor, forehead to forehead, the sliver of space between them electrified by anticipation. Just a tiny move toward each other, and they'd be kissing. They both knew how good that was.

A bright flash temporarily blinded Willa.

"What do you think you're doing?" Derek's irritated snap surprised Willa almost as much as the flash of light.

"Smile! You two look so cute together. Can I interest you in a souvenir photo? All proceeds go toward the Gunnersun mayoral campaign."

"I don't believe it." Derek rolled his eyes. "Who gave you a camera?"

Holliday Bailey shot Derek her trademark wide, sexy smile. "Rudy. He saw some of my photos in the library. I'm taking a photography class online. It turns out I have a natural gift. Just one among many." She batted her long lashes.

When Willa had first worked at the deli, she'd spent a fair amount of time wondering if the ever-bickering Holliday and Derek were interested in each other. Now she knew the opposite was true: they annoyed the heck out of each other. Sometimes on purpose.

"If this dance had a king and queen, you'd get my vote," Holliday purred then opened her eyes wide. "Hey, what a great idea! We'll start an impromptu ballot. I'm sure I can scrounge up a tiara."

"Don't even think about it." Derek glowered in warning.

The redhead laughed. "Speaking of killjoys, you'd better check on the little man you've been palling around with. He was last seen polishing off the dessert table."

"So that's where he's been." Willa looked at Derek. "He's going to make himself sick. We'd better go."

"How about we let Derek do the dirty work?" Looping her arm through Willa's, Holliday tugged her away. "He's not allowed to keep you all to himself now that you're finally out of the bakery. We girls can grab something to eat with Izzy and a few members of the Thursday night book club. I know they'd love for you to recommend your favorite cookbooks."

Holliday kept chatting while Willa tried not to look back at Derek for rescue, or to think about the almost-kiss Holliday had interrupted. She spent the next quarter hour or so chatting with Izzy and with Holliday's book group, which included Carly Levine, Gilberto's fifth-grade teacher.

"It's amazing, the progress Gilberto has made since he moved in with Sheriff Neel." Carly, who, Willa guessed, was in her thirties, beamed. "And the tutoring you've been giving him has been seriously helpful, Willa. He talks about it. His self-esteem has skyrocketed, and his attendance has jumped from forty to one hundred percent. Everyone at school is thrilled. Thank you."

"Don't thank me," Willa demurred. "Derek's the one holding the reins. I think Gilberto is his special project."

"That's great, but don't sell yourself short," Carly said. "If he's ever had a woman in his life before, this is the first time it's shown." She looked around the room. "I'd better go find my husband. I've left him alone far too long to talk local politics with city council members. Makes him cranky."

After Carly left, Izzy said, "She's right. You're both doing a great job with that boy."

"Well, Derek is doing the lion's share. I'm only helping out." Her gaze swept the room, lighting on Derek and Gilberto next to one of the dessert tables, deep in conversation with Izzy's husband, Nate, and their son, Eli. As she and Izzy watched the foursome, Derek said something that made Eli laugh and sock him on the shoulder. Gilberto guffawed so hard, he doubled over. "He really is a natural with kids," Willa murmured.

Izzy grinned fondly. "Always has been."

When she'd first worked at the deli, Willa had been struck by the extent of Derek's involvement in Eli's life. A single mother until recently, Izzy's situation apparently had been complicated by a lack of education and a family to whom she could turn for help. On top of that, Eli had been severely hearing impaired since age two. As Izzy's best friend, Derek had learned American Sign Language to communicate with Eli and had been the central male figure in the young man's life until Nate returned and began to build a relationship with his son.

"I don't know if you remember," Izzy said, watching her men, "but Derek tangled with Nate when they first met."

"I do remember."

"Derek was the main man in Eli's life for so long. He had to slide over to make room for Nate. It was difficult."

Oh, my gosh. How dumb am I? Willa thought abruptly. Taking care of Gilberto represented a whole lot more than an act of extreme volunteerism. In a very real sense, Derek had lost his "family" when Nate arrived on the scene. Taking care of Gilberto filled a big, big hole.

"He's wanted a family of his own for a long time," Izzy confirmed. "Is that what you want?"

She said it kindly enough, but her concern was evident.

"Derek knows where I stand," Willa said carefully. "I've been clear." But then Derek's words leaped to mind. *If you put a time limit on it, it's sex, not a relationship.* "And, of course, we're still talking about it," she stumbled as worry niggled at the back of her mind. But he *did* know where she stood, didn't he?

Izzy stared at her a moment longer, then nodded. "Have you tried the pear and gorgonzola crostini?" She reached for one of the hors d'oeuvres on the table beside them and took a bite. "Delicious. You think a pear-gorgonzola knish would fly at the deli?"

With the subject changed, they spent the next few minutes discussing new recipes Izzy wanted to introduce at The Pickle Jar. Willa's attention, however, never strayed from the man they both cared about so deeply.

Chapter Twelve

Once the applause died down and the lights in the Thunder Ridge Elementary School gymnasium buzzed back on, Willa allowed herself to exhale. The fifth-grade history pageant was now history itself, and Gilberto had rocked the part of Daniel Boone. She and Derek had been clutching each other's hands since Gilberto's first appearance onstage.

"I think I'd have been calmer during a high-speed chase," Derek said, looking quite adorably serious about that.

Willa laughed. "It might have been less nerve-racking if we'd had more notice he was going to be Daniel Boone. Under the circumstances, I think a little anxiety is justified."

Originally cast in a less pivotal role, Gilberto stepped up to fill Daniel Boone's moccasins when the boy previously set to play the part announced that his family had sold their home and was moving. Willa was sure Carly

Levine had transferred the role to Gilberto to boost his self-esteem now that she knew there were adults who could be counted on to help. Although the teacher had assured Derek that Gilberto could carry the script if he needed to, the eleven-year-old had refused even to consider that option. Offered his first chance to shine in school, he'd been determined to give it all he had.

Derek squeezed Willa's hand. "If it wasn't for you, the kid would have had to wear a cardboard sign that said 'I am Daniel Boone' as a costume. Thank you for not complaining that every would-be date seems to turn into a family affair. The next date is ours alone. You have my word." He rubbed the back of her neck and the spot right below her ear. "Have I told you how grateful I am that you've been by my side through this?"

"One hundred and forty-two times in the past ten days alone. This makes a hundred and forty-three."

Shaking his head regretfully, he murmured in that resonant baritone, "I should have done it more."

How did he make the most innocuous statement sound like verbal foreplay? "I enjoyed it," she murmured back, and she really had. Gilberto's enthusiasm was always infectious, and Derek's fumbling attempts to sew had been flat-out endearing. Willa had wound up making Gilberto a Daniel Boone costume with a fringed jacket and faux coonskin cap. And, when she wasn't sewing or helping him draft his speech, she and Gilberto had hiked one of her favorite sections of Long River to gather props and get into character.

If she and Derek hadn't found the time to resume the discussion about whether they were going to have an "affair" or a "relationship," well, that was a bonus as far as she was concerned. Everything was so good right now, so easy and natural. Couldn't they just enjoy it awhile?

"I don't think he took his eyes off you during his entire speech," Derek commented.

"Because he was afraid of forgetting his lines." Willa laughed. "Daniel Boone was supposed to have said, 'I have never been lost, but I will admit to being confused for several weeks.' Not the other way around."

"I wondered about that." Derek chuckled. "Come on. Let's find Mr. Boone before he's mobbed by fans."

His proud smile tugged at her heart.

"Sounds good."

As they blended into the line of parents and other family members snaking into the hallway, he brushed a light kiss at her temple.

She inhaled sharply. Sometimes she got swept up in the idea that she wanted this to last. As the throng milled around them, pressing them toward the PTA's snack tables, Willa tried to focus on the smell of hot coffee, the freshly popped corn—anything but the temptation to stay where she was, right here with Derek and Gilberto, finding her place in life again by loving a man and a child.

They inched forward, and her gaze roved the art projects that covered the hall walls. Did one of these drawings belong to Gilberto? Did anyone care? She did, she realized, as children pushed through the crowd to reach their parents. She cared very much.

"How'd I do?"

It took a moment for Willa to realize Gilberto had squeezed between her and Derek and was peering eagerly into their faces.

"My man, Daniel Boone! Is it really you?" Derek leaned far forward, pretending to scrutinize Gilberto's face and the faux fur hat. "You were amazing up there, Dan. Can I have your autograph?"

"Cut it out," Gilberto complained, looking around to

see if anyone was listening, but his grin conveyed more pride than embarrassment. "What did you think, Willa?"

He looked so earnest, so desiring of her approval. Memory pinched her heart. *Ignore it. This is a different time, different place. Different people. It's nowhere near the same.* "You were great." Bending close to Gilberto's ear, she said, "The audience loved you. Your research paid off, buddy. Everyone totally believed you were Daniel Boone."

"You really think so?"

"I sure do." It was so easy to fill Gilberto's tank. Her compliments had him beaming.

"There's the man of the hour!" Izzy approached from inside the auditorium to give Gilberto a hug and add her praise to Willa and Derek's.

"You came to see me in the play?" Gilberto asked Izzy in wonder.

"Wouldn't have missed it." She handed him a paper bag tied with a ribbon. "I brought the cream soda you like from the deli. Opening night gift."

"Wow! Thanks. I'm opening it now." Catching himself, he looked up at Derek. "I mean, *may* I drink it now?"

Derek nodded. "Sure. Knock yourself out."

"Can I go find Tyler and share the soda with him?"

"You bet." Derek turned to Izzy as Gilberto trotted off. "Where's Nate?"

"Stacking chairs in the auditorium. Wanna help?"

Tucked into his back pocket, Derek's phone vibrated. He pulled it out and checked the screen. "Sorry, Izz, gotta take this." Kissing Willa on the cheek, he said, "Back in a minute."

"Pretty cute," Izzy commented, taking a few steps forward alongside Willa in the coffee line.

Willa nodded. "He looked adorable in that 'coonskin cap,' didn't he?"

"I meant the three of you."

Oh. Heat suffused Willa's cheeks. Their conversation at the barn dance loomed crystal clear in her mind even though neither woman had referred to it since. Over the past two weeks, Willa had watched Derek in full fatherhood mode and could honestly say he was one of the best men she'd ever known, devoted to his work when he was at work, but equally committed to Gilberto—and to her—when they were together.

Gilberto wasn't the only one blooming in Derek's care.

Emotion welled rapidly, closing off her throat. Feeling foolish, she blinked away the burning sensation in her eyes.

"Hey." Concerned, Izzy tugged Willa out of line. "Everything all right?"

Intending to deny there was a problem, Willa instead heard herself exclaim, "I don't want to hurt him." And then she was crying. *Oh, for pity's sake.* Had she held on to her precious control for all this time only to let go now?

Izzy spoke quietly. "I'm assuming that by 'him,' you're referring to Derek." She dug into her purse for a tissue and handed it to Willa, who accepted gratefully.

"Yes. Derek."

"Then come clean with him."

Willa froze mid nose blow. She'd never discussed her past with Izzy. "What…what do you mean?"

"Whatever is bothering you—*whatever it is*—Derek can handle it. Truly. He has very broad shoulders." For the first time in their acquaintance, Izzy put her arms around Willa, giving her a reassuring hug. "I know how hard it is to trust yourself with his heart. But it really will be okay."

"I—I know," Willa whispered, but she didn't. Not really. Izzy had hit the nail on the head. Could she count on herself to take care of Derek's heart? If they were ever going to move forward, she had no choice. A voice inside her head said loudly, *He deserves the truth.*

As they arrived at the head of the concession line, Derek reappeared, looking shell-shocked.

Willa handed him a coffee. "You look like you could use something stronger," she said. "What's wrong?"

Accepting the cup, he nodded toward the quiet hallway where he'd taken the call. "Let's talk over there. Is 'Berto still off with his friend?"

"Yes." Willa traded a concerned glance with Izzy.

"The call was from Jeanne," Derek said when they reached a relatively private spot, "Gilberto's social worker. She phoned to tell me Roddy's gone."

"Gone?" Willa shook her head. "Where?"

"No one knows. According to his roommates, he packed up all his things along with plenty of theirs and split. No forwarding address. They want to press charges for theft." Derek's eyes flashed lightning. "He's completely abandoned Gilberto."

Unmindful of Izzy or anyone else who might be watching, Willa wrapped Derek in a hug. She felt his strong body relax into her embrace as he allowed her to comfort him. "What happens now?" she asked.

Derek pulled back enough to be heard by both women, but kept an arm firmly around Willa. "According to Jeanne, this wasn't the first time Roddy was caught giving alcohol to minors. He's permanently off the list of potential providers for Gilberto, and there are no other family connections suitable or interested in providing care at this point."

"That stinks," Izzy exclaimed, her own background no doubt adding fuel to the fire in her tone. "Gilberto is at the mercy of people who can't get their acts together?"

"Not necessarily." Derek looked into Willa's eyes.

"Jeanne asked if I'd be on board for long-term foster care." He paused. "Or permanent guardianship."

"Are you?" Izzy asked.

Willa knew the answer before he gave it.

"Yes." He was still looking directly at her, searching for her reaction.

The truth was she'd have been disappointed if he'd made a different decision, because this one was pure Derek. He was a man who stepped up to the plate every time.

She smiled and nodded to offer her support. Even as she did so, however, worry gnawed at her. This complicated things. He needed people who would stick with him and stick around, no matter what challenges came his way.

Now, she realized, they had even more to talk about on Friday—the night they planned, at last, to have a real date, only the two of them. Derek had found an adult eager to hang out with Gilberto for the evening, so they were all set. Willa knew she'd have to do a lot of thinking between now and Friday night. One thing was certain, however. It was time to tell Derek everything.

The week flew by. Even the weather had changed significantly enough to turn the previous days into a distant memory. It had stopped snowing, and though the cold front continued, the streets were clear. By Friday, Willa still hadn't decided exactly how she was going to broach the topic of her past with Derek. The past that, no matter how she tried to deny it, still affected every nook and cranny of her present. Burning off nervous energy, she tidied her house from top to bottom in preparation for his arrival.

The bungalow looked good. Flickering candles emitted a subtle spicy fragrance, and light jazz played in the background. The lamps were on dimmers, and the fireplace was ready for the strike of a match. She had an elegant Hudson

Vineyard Syrah and her grandmother's wine goblets poised on the table. She still needed to put the flowers into vases.

In the kitchen, a sage-and-thyme-crusted prime rib filled the house with its succulent aroma, and her Yorkshire pudding waited patiently to be put in the oven, where it would puff to golden perfection. Lord-of-the-manor food. I-care-about-you-and-want-you-to-feel-special food. Her signature bourbon-spiked creamed spinach still needed to be prepped, but that wouldn't take long, and first she wanted to double-check her bedroom.

From the doorway, she scanned the area, trying to see it through Derek's eyes. What about candles in here? Should she light them now or wait until he arrived? Moving to her bed, she smoothed her hands over the comforter. Fresh sheets? Check. Pillows plumped? Check.

Sexy lingerie? Check.

She fingered the lace peignoir and satin robe she'd laid out. She'd bought the sexy duo only yesterday. The nightie with its plunging neckline and see-through skirt had looked so glamorous, so confidence-inducing in the shop window. Suddenly, though, it seemed dangerously scanty. Playing the seductress had never been her MO, yet tonight she wanted to try it, and she wanted to do it *before* she told Derek about her past life.

Because it's easier to bare your body than your soul.

Sharing her history with him signaled not only the beginning of a new phase in their relationship, it signaled the end of something, too. Up to now, her grief had been private, fierce yet somehow delicate, like a butterfly she had to shield to keep alive. Because keeping the grief alive kept the people for whom she grieved alive. That's how it felt, anyway. If she wanted Derek, she was going to have to slacken her hold on the past. Allow others to disturb her status quo.

A quick glance at the clock told her Derek would be there in just over an hour. Her stomach felt like a crazy soup of foreboding and anticipation and yearning. She didn't even bother to convince herself she was ready for this moment; she knew only that she wanted it. *Seduce first, talk second. Everything will be okay.*

And then the doorbell rang.

What?

Derek had said he'd arrive at eight. It was only seven.

Willa's pulse leaped wildly. Dinner wasn't ready, and she still hadn't decided for sure about the negligee.

"Just a minute!" she called then glanced at the mirror, flustered. *Crumbs*, she hadn't even had time to do her hair and makeup. Derek was always punctual, sometimes early—and he had called twice today, saying he couldn't wait for this evening—but an *hour* early? For a date? No fair.

As suddenly as it arrived, though, her panic subsided. She'd wanted to be naked at some point on this date. Might as well start with a naked face. Apparently, she wasn't meant to hide behind anything tonight.

Taking a deep breath, she headed for the front door.

Although she hadn't yet turned on the porch light, through the leaded glass panes, Willa could see the shadow of a man. As she unlocked the deadbolt, she teased, "You must be as excited about tonight as I—"

Her voice faltered.

Time and her pulse both seemed to stop as she realized that the person on her porch was not Derek.

"Jase?" she whispered. Or thought she'd whispered. Had a sound actually emerged?

It's an illusion. Your mind is playing tricks.

But he smiled, and it was the smile she remembered,

the one that had once made her feel all was right with the world.

She raised a trembling hand to her lips. The blue eyes she knew so well filled with too many emotions to count… apprehension, guilt, gratitude…

"Hello, Willa," he said raggedly. "I'm back."

Chapter Thirteen

The man Willa had married when she was still just a girl reached out and hugged her tightly, almost uncomfortably so, but she understood the impulse. It was nearly impossible to believe he was here, that he was alive at all after so much time without a single bit of contact. The emotion she'd staved off for two years broke loose, bit by bit, like stones tumbling from a cliff in the moments before an avalanche, and she felt her arms wrap around him, holding him. Her crying left wet patches on the front of his shirt, and she could feel his own tears dampen her neck as he pressed his face into the crook of her shoulder.

She curled her right hand into a fist and thumped it against his chest. "Dammit, Jase. I thought you were dead." His shirt muffled the last, sobbed, word.

"I'm sorry. I'm so sorry."

They stood for a long moment, he just outside her front door and she on the threshold. They clung to each other, attempting to pull themselves together. Finally, Willa leaned back to peer at him through the blur of her tears.

He was leaner now. Almost hollow. His clothes were far more casual than the designer shirts and suits he'd once favored, their starched-and-pressed perfection gone entirely. The Jase she remembered could have stepped out of a menswear catalogue. The man in front of her looked disheveled.

"Any chance you'll let me in?" he asked, uncharacteristic hesitation shadowing his words.

A tiny hiccup escaped her. "Of course." She stood back and held the door wide. "Please."

Jase stepped past her into the cozy cottage she'd so carefully set for seduction and glanced around with abject curiosity. "You…uh—" he cleared his throat, running a hand over his stubbled jaw "—expecting someone?"

"Yes." The blood surged hotly to her cheeks as she nudged the door shut with her hip. "But not for an hour. Sit down." She gestured to the sofa.

Awkwardly, he nodded, sitting on the edge of a cushion as if he couldn't quite commit.

"This is a nice place," he said.

She shrugged. The house they'd shared in California, a remodeled Mediterranean that he, especially, had loved, had been four times the size of this one. "It's small. But I like it. It's home now," she acknowledged simply.

He nodded. Long fingers, perfect for a surgeon, curled over his knees. "I rehearsed what I was going to say. You know? And now here I am, and…" He shrugged, getting to his feet, his body a bundle of nervous energy that refused to let him settle. Willa watched him cross to the fireplace as if he knew exactly what he'd find there.

Slowly raising a hand, he touched the framed photo she'd kept in her bedroom the past several weeks. Tonight she had brought it into the living room again, because she wanted Derek to see it.

"This is the only photo I took with me when I left," Jase commented. "It's my favorite."

Willa felt the muscles in her stomach clench. She forced herself to inhale. "Mine, too."

The picture showed their daughter, Sydney, at age ten, in a photo snapped right before her fifth-grade spring dance.

"Everything made sense before she died. Nothing made sense after," Jase said roughly. "I honest-to-God don't know how you went through it stone-cold sober, Will. You were the strong one."

Willa's body gave a little jerk while her mind tried to process that. Did simply surviving mean she was strong? Hiding in a new town, in a tiny bungalow meant for her alone, sidestepping human entanglements? She hadn't felt strong at all. After their beautiful Sydney died, the world turned upside down and stayed there, until just recently.

She looked at her candles, smelled the prime rib still cooking, remembered the nightie. Unbidden, anger joined the myriad other emotions rocking around her body. For so long, she'd dreamed of the moment he would show up unexpectedly, and she would realize he was still alive. But that moment hadn't come. Now, without a call, without the merest hint of warning, he was here.

"Where the hell have you been, Jason? It's been two years of pure torture. I thought you were dead. We all did. You sent me divorce papers and a note that told me basically nothing except that you couldn't handle our marriage anymore. You haven't even contacted your *parents* in all this time. After losing a child yourself, how could you—" She slapped her hands over her mouth. She'd relegated rage to the back of the line behind worry and grief. Now it was front and center, poised to launch an arrow straight into Jase's heart for leaving her to handle so much on her own and for making them all grieve twice.

"Go on," he said when she stopped. "Whatever you have to say, I deserve it. And I've probably already said it to myself." He returned Sydney's picture carefully to the mantel and faced his ex-wife. "I was a fraud, Willa. I loved medicine, but I worshipped the idea that I could fix whatever was broken, and when I couldn't help our own daughter—" He blew a frustrated sigh at the ceiling. "The guilt drove me to my knees. I damn near—" Raw emotion twisted his features. "I didn't think I was going to make it. Leaving everyone seemed like the right thing. I'm not saying it was, only that my mind made it seem that way. I'll never be able to tell you how sorry I am for putting you through everything I did. I don't expect you to give me your forgiveness. I just need you to know that I'm asking."

Outside, a dog barked. A siren rose then faded into the distance and a car whooshed down the street, too fast. Life in Thunder Ridge carried on, oblivious to their struggle.

There were so many questions, but Willa knew the most important ones couldn't be answered. Not in this lifetime. They would never understand why they had been so lucky, so blessed with the magic that had been their family. Or why it had all had to end.

Jase managed a wobbly smile. "Thanks for keeping my lawyer in the loop about where you're living."

Wordlessly, she nodded.

He glanced around again. "You're building a life for yourself here."

"Trying to."

"I'm proud of you, Will. You're a survivor."

Silent tears slipped down her cheeks. He had come to give her the gift of closure on a marriage that had taken her from girl to wife to mother. He'd given her Syd, and the truth was that as long as she lived she would be Syd's mother, her favorite role of all. In return, Willa could give Jase the one thing he couldn't give himself.

"You're forgiven," she whispered. "Believe it, Jase. You're forgiven." She wasn't sure who made the first move, but suddenly they were in each other's embrace for one final hug.

The familiar arms tightened briefly before he leaned back to look at her. "How long did it take you to believe you really could move forward?"

"I think...it took until just now."

They shared a long moment of understanding neither would ever have with anyone else. The doorbell jarred them both.

Through the picture window to the right of her front door, Willa saw Derek, standing close to the glass. Close enough for her to see that he wasn't merely standing on the porch; he was staring into the house at her and Jase.

It didn't take long for her to react. She left Jase's arms immediately and ran to the door, flinging it open. "Derek! Come in."

A burst of cold air entered with him. Willa felt so overheated, she welcomed it.

"I'm glad you're here," she said, the words rushing out. This was so *not* how she wanted him to find out about her life as a wife and mother. Her mind raced as she tried to figure out what he was thinking.

"I'm early." Voice and expression grim, he stared at Jase as he asked Willa, "Bad timing?"

"No," she lied and gestured to Jase. "We were..." *Oh, boy. What?*

Derek looked at her. His shoulders squared, his brow lowered, he had an *I-could–kick-this-guy's-ass-easily* look on his face. Yet, underneath, she saw an uncertainty that made her want to kiss him until he looked like Derek again.

"I get the feeling I'm interrupting," Derek deadpanned.

"No. I am." Stepping forward, Jase extended a hand. "Hi. I'm Jason Holmes. And you are?"

"Derek Neel. Sheriff of Thunder Ridge." Warily, he reached for the outstretched hand, his expression puzzling out the connection. "Holmes? You're related to Willa?"

"In a manner of speaking. I married her about fourteen years ago, just out of high school."

Derek went pale. A long, awkward moment of silence followed before he found his voice. "In that case, I suppose you two have a lot of catching up to do. I'll leave you to it." Turning, he strode through the still-open door.

"Derek," Willa called, gripping the doorknob, "don't go."

He crossed the porch and headed down the steps toward his truck.

"Derek, you don't understand." Willa ran after him. His driver's side door slammed. "Please wait!" But he couldn't hear her over the roar of the engine or the angry squeal of tires as he drove away.

It took every ounce of strength, emotional and physical, for Derek to walk calmly into his house, excuse the sitter on the pretext that his stomach was acting up, and spend the rest of the evening watching dumb movies with Gilberto. Every time the phone rang, Derek ignored it, grumbling about telemarketers until he eventually just yanked his landline from the jack and put his cell on "vibrate only" to stave off Gilberto's innocent questions.

Willa had called at least six times, but he was in no mood to talk to anyone, especially not to her, not yet.

Gilberto seemed to sense that he was struggling and

actually went into the kitchen on his own to make Derek a cup of tea laced generously with honey. Then he made sure the throws were tucked in around Derek's legs. The boy's clumsy, well-meaning ministering was the only thing that kept Derek from tearing his house apart, stud by stud.

Once Gilberto found the antacid bottle in the medicine cabinet and offered "something for your sick tummy," he burrowed in next to Derek, peering up every so often with such tender adoration that Derek could barely swallow around the lump in his throat. The kid was so sweet, looking at him as if he hung the moon, when in reality, Derek felt his world crumbling around him.

She was *married*. Married to her high school sweetheart, yet hadn't considered that important enough to tell him. What a fool he'd been. After all the opportunities he'd given her to tell him the truth about her mysterious past, she had a damned husband. One to whom she was obviously still pretty close.

And here he was, the complete dumbass, showing up at her front door, thinking forever was in the cards.

Blood surged through his body like molten lava. Muscles tensed, fists clenched, he muttered an expletive under his breath. Gilberto squirmed around under his blanket and peered at Derek curiously.

"Do you need to throw up? Cuz, if you do, I can go get you a bowl." He looked worried.

Derek inhaled deeply and made a concerted effort to reassure the child at his side. "No, little buddy, I think I just had some heartburn. It's going to be fine, and you know why?"

Gilberto shrugged. "No."

Derek looped an arm around the child's shoulders and pulled him close. "Because you are the best doctor in the whole world. That tea you made me? Has me feeling almost a hundred percent. I'm telling you the truth. I don't know what I'd do without you here to help me through this rough patch."

Gilberto puffed like a peacock. He nodded manfully. "'Kay. I think you probably should go to bed now. I can tuck you in." He looked at the clock and calculated. "It's already past ten, so I'll turn off the TV and let Captain out. You go upstairs, put on your pajamas and brush your teeth, and I'll be up there to say a prayer and stuff, okay?"

Derek pulled the kid up against his chest and ruffled his hair. If Willa had sent fissures splintering through his heart, Gilberto was the sealant that kept it from breaking altogether. "You're the best, buddy. I'll meet you upstairs after you take care of things down here."

Thrilled at the opportunity to play master of the house, Gilberto completed his chores and met Derek, who had watched everything from the top of the stairs.

"You know, because of your help tonight, I feel good enough to tuck you in, dude," Derek said. "I think you totally cured me."

"Yeah, well, I've been thinking 'bout being a doctor."

"No kidding? I always hoped I'd have a doctor in my family." He'd already told 'Berto about Roddy leaving, letting the confusion and grief and anger sit for a day or two before mentioning that Jeanne was trying to find someone who could keep Gilberto safe and take care of him until he was an adult. Then Derek had shared that he'd told Jeanne *he* wanted to be that someone.

Now, as Gilberto heard Derek say the word "family" in relation to them, his mouth dropped open before he snapped it shut and acted too cool for his shoes. He turned away, but not before Derek caught the beginnings of an enormous grin. Another crack in Derek's heart filled as he followed the boy to his room. They were almost through their good-night routine when Captain began to bark incessantly.

Gilberto sat up in bed. "Captain hears something."

Derek had heard a car a couple minutes earlier when Gilberto was starting to nod off during their book time. "Probably some pest getting into the garbage out there. You go to sleep, and I'll take a peek outside, okay?" he said, though he was pretty sure it was Willa.

'Berto nodded and yawned, scooting back down in the bed and rolling onto his side. "If it's a burglar, call me and I'll come and kick him in the yayas for you, okay?"

"Will do." Derek had never had a deputy offer to kick anyone in the yayas for him. He gave the boy a fist bump and left the room telling himself that he and the kid would be fine, just fine on their own. If Willa was outside? She could stay there. He was in no mood to hear an explanation now.

A soft but insistent knocking had Captain doing his ancient best to guard the fortress from attack. Unfortunately, the rusty barking and doused porch light failed to sway Willa, who continued to knock in a restrained way Derek knew was intended not to disturb Gilberto. Hovering at the top of the stairs, he watched her move to the plate glass window. She cupped her hands on the glass, trying to catch a glimpse of life.

He stood silently, willing her to go.

"Derek, I know you're there. Please open up." There was a slight pause. "It's freezing out here." She knocked again. Harder.

He wavered. Just a little.

"Derek?" Gilberto's voice, sleepy yet filled with worry, called out from the bedroom. "I think Willa is here."

Derek sighed in heavy frustration. "I'm on my way down to talk to her. You go to sleep, okay?"

"Okay." Gilberto sounded hesitant. "Good night."

"'Night, partner."

Captain was working himself into an early grave, clawing at the door and whining now that he realized who was there. Using the need to save his dog as an excuse, Derek pushed himself off the top step and walked heavily down the stairs. Flipping on the porch light, he opened the door. Willa huddled inside her coat and rubbed her ungloved hands together. Instantly, he wanted to haul her into his arms and warm her.

Sucker.

Steeling himself, he said, "Willa, go home. I don't feel like talking."

"Derek, hear me out. That's all I'm asking. I was going to tell you everything tonight, but Jase… He showed up and beat me to it."

Her auburn hair was loose, the way he liked it most, cascading in angel-soft waves around her face and her shoulders. Her features looked strained and tense, and her splotchy cheeks told him she'd been crying. His jaws clenched tighter than a vise.

"It's freezing out here," she reiterated. "Let me come in for a few minutes to explain. Please."

He hesitated, and her face filled with uncertainty.

I don't care.

But he did and damned himself for it.

They hovered on the threshold until finally he took a step back. She walked past him.

Shutting the door, he fumbled with a lamp that sent a yellow glow throughout the room.

"Sit." He gestured to a chair in the living room and moved to stoke the fire that he and Gilberto had let die. Shyly, she moved to the chair nearest the hearth and sat, shivering.

"You should have worn mittens."

"I ran out of the house too quickly." Her teeth chattered. "I left right after Jase did."

Jase. "I'm going to get a cup of tea. Want anything?"

"No. I'm good. Thank you."

"Okay. Tea it is." Abruptly, he turned and strode to the kitchen.

No matter what she said, no matter her reason for refusing to share with him a fraction of what she had obviously shared with *Jase*, he wasn't going to give in to his heart, which was once again telling him to let it go, to listen, to love her. His heart was such a dumbass. Well, he was all through letting himself get whomped in the gut. If the question was, "When are you going to learn your lesson?" the answer was, "Right now."

Willa knew Derek could tell she was freezing. Even though she'd caused him great pain, he was still worried about her.

She leaned forward on the sofa, her chilly palms pressed together and tucked between her knees. As he clattered around in the kitchen, she tried to remember everything she needed to tell him tonight, so she could get it all out before he tossed her on her ear. She wouldn't blame him if he did. What he'd walked in on tonight would have thrown anyone for a loop.

After five of the longest minutes in Willa's life, Derek returned with two steaming mugs of tea, their bags bobbing in the water. He pressed one mug into her hands then sat in the recliner across from her. *Fair enough.* An involuntary shiver racked her entire body, and she sloshed her tea. Derek stood, dropped a throw in her lap then returned to his own chair.

"Okay." His sigh was filled with a mix of impatience and resistance. "What do you need to tell me?"

"Everything. From the beginning. Which is what I'd planned to do tonight, before Jase showed up. His arrival was totally unexpected."

"Is that so?"

She didn't know what he disbelieved—that she'd been planning to tell him about her past or that Jase's appearance had come as complete surprise, but the answer to both was, "Yes."

With a steady, uncompromising stare, he said nothing more, merely waited for her to begin. So she did, however awkwardly.

"Jase… Jason Holmes…was my husband. *Was*, being the operative word. Our divorce was final about a year ago, although the marriage ended before that. Before tonight, I hadn't seen Jase in over two years, right before he served the divorce papers."

"He served you?"

"Yes. We'd gone through a rough time. He'd started drinking and taking prescription medication. I wasn't really myself at that point, either, and, well, since I didn't want to kick him while he was down, he went ahead and filed for the divorce himself. Then he disappeared. No one, not even his parents or sister heard from him. To be honest, until I saw his face this evening, I thought he might be dead."

Derek's brows shot up, and she could tell she had his attention. "Why would you think that?"

Willa kept her hands cupped around the hot mug. She took a sip of tea, willing its warmth to penetrate the places inside her that were filled with icy fear.

"Let me back up," she said, "so it'll be easier to understand. Jase was a very gifted surgeon. Pediatrics. We got pregnant when I was twenty. Sydney was a surprise. At first we sort of freaked out, but she was a golden child from the very beginning—happy, funny, healthy and a great sleeper. You can't complain about that, even if the timing isn't what you expected."

Derek set his mug down, his attention riveted, his brow lowered.

"We had help from very doting grandparents. Jase went to medical school and on to his residency, and eventually I went to culinary school. Life was hectic and intense and wonderful. I was happier than I'd ever been. We were all happy."

Derek's jaw worked over that bit of information, but the time for sparing feelings, his or her own, had come to an end. He needed to understand and that meant she had to tell the truth. "You know," she confessed softly, "as much as I loved my culinary career, being Sydney's mom was far and away the best part of me. Nobody could make me laugh like Syd. She practiced jokes before she went to sleep at night."

Willa watched Captain slowly clump around the coffee table, making his way toward her. Ever-so-gently, he laid his graying head in her lap. If she didn't know better, she'd say she saw compassion in his old eyes.

Upstairs, the floor creaked. Gilberto heading to the bathroom, she assumed.

"Oh, I brought a picture to show you." Reaching for her purse, she pulled out the framed 8x10 from her mantel and handed it to him.

Derek studied the photo. "She's the spitting image of you. Beautiful. Really. Beautiful."

Willa smiled. "She was way prettier. Her features were bolder. *She* was bolder. That was taken before her first formal school dance. We went shopping for a dress and spent hours getting her ready."

She watched him read the note and signature slashed across the bottom of the 8x10. *To Mom, From Syd. I love it when you do my hair.*

"She gave me the photo on Mother's Day," Willa said. "That weekend, we were all invited to go on a vacation out at Big Bear Lake with a couple of Syd's friends and their families. Jase was working at Los Angeles Children's Hospital, and I was an executive pastry chef in South Pasadena. He didn't have any surgeries scheduled, but there was no way I could go. Mother's Day weekend is one of the busiest in the food industry. I didn't want them to miss out since I had to work anyway, so I insisted they go without me. Syd gave me my present before they left."

"How old was she in this photo?" Derek asked.

"Almost eleven."

"Same age as Gilberto," he murmured.

"Yes."

"Tell me more about her."

The guarded look that had been on his face since he'd opened the door gave way to an expression of intense listening. Willa took a ragged inhalation. "Syd was a big heart with arms and legs. She never had a 'best' friend, because she loved everyone and assumed they loved her back. Her room was always a mess. She was crazy good at most sports. Swam like a fish. Nothing scared her. Not even the things that should have."

With shaky hands, she raised the mug of tea to her lips and took a long swallow before continuing. "On that Mother's Day weekend, Syd, Jase and a couple other families and their kids camped by the lake near a popular swimming and diving area. From what I was able to gather, Syd watched someone do a backflip off the rocks and decided she wanted to try it. Jase had seen some pretty serious injuries from that kind of thing, and he told her no. I guess when he and the other dads went to turn on the propane tanks in the motorhomes, Sydney climbed up the rocks. She told her friends she wanted to see how high it was. No one knows whether she'd decided to dive despite her father's warning or whether she lost her footing and fell."

Derek's own tea sat untouched on the coffee table now, and he was as still as stone.

"Syd didn't surface. The kids started screaming. One of the mothers searched for her while the other ran for Jase. By the time he reached Sydney, she was out of the water, but unconscious. And by the time Life Flight got her to the hospital and I arrived, she was on life support."

Willa tried to tell the story as a series of facts, but each word that fell from her lips felt like a self-inflicted blow, and she rounded her torso over her legs in a kind of upright fetal position, as if she could protect herself.

"While I stayed with Syd round the clock, Jase called in every favor from every expert he'd ever consulted with and then some, searching for a miracle. He wouldn't leave his office for days at a time. And I sat alone in Syd's room, searching for her in the hospital bed."

Once more, Willa saw the clinic-green walls with their outrageously cheerful decals and the tubes and wires and brilliant, heartbreaking machines that sustained her daughter's breathing.

She closed her eyes. "I thought if I believed hard enough, she would wake up. Be my Syd again." Opening her eyes, she sought Derek's face, willing him to understand. "The moment you stop fooling yourself is the worst moment of all."

"You weren't fooling yourself," Derek responded roughly. "You were hoping. Hope is never wasted."

"Thank you." She wondered if Derek realized he was massaging her back? She didn't want him to stop.

"Where was Jase in all this?" he asked.

"Still wrestling with his own demons. We'd begun to visit Sydney separately. We were arguing horribly, saying things to each other we wouldn't have been able to imagine before the accident."

"What did you argue about?"

"Jase refused what his education told him it was time to admit. That our daughter was gone. And I began to think we'd go crazy if we didn't admit it. I knew I would never, ever, ever understand, but it was time." Her throat closed around the words.

"You took her off life support?" he inquired gently.

"Not right away. Jase fought it. He fought until she began to have complications." She took a big jagged breath. "Afterward, his guilt and grief and rage consumed him. We wound up in limbo—unable to go back, but not able to move forward, either." She wiped away a tear, then looked at him. "I'm sorry I kept you in the dark. You've been nothing but wonderful, and I hate that you were blindsided tonight. My only excuse is that in my mind, the private grief kept Sydney alive in some way. Does that make any sense at all?"

"I can't pretend to understand it the way you do, but yeah. I guess it makes sense." He reached for her hands, holding them between his own. Willa could feel their wonderful heat warming her fingers. "I wish I could have comforted you. I wish I'd known your daughter."

Her eyes stung. "Me, too. On both counts."

"So it's really over between you and Jase?"

"It is." Now that she'd given him the facts and an apology, she wanted to tell him what she'd planned to say before Jase's arrival, but her nerves skyrocketed. With her heart flopping like a flounder in her chest, she looked into his eyes. "I'm ready to move forward now. With you."

Chapter Fourteen

Letting go of her hands, Derek leaned back, raising his face to the ceiling and exhaling a breath he seemed to have been holding for ages. Without looking at her, he put a hand on her thigh, squeezed and said, "Wait here." Then he rose and crossed to the coat tree in his entry.

Willa sat, baffled. Had she blown it? Stretched his patience to the snapping point? Waited too long to realize she wanted to realize her feelings ran deeper than those of a mere lover or friend?

On pins and needles, she watched him root through a pocket in his leather jacket. When he found what he wanted, he returned to her. Clearing his throat, he sat.

"I knew you'd lost someone. I saw the books on your front porch, the ones about grief. But I never dreamed you'd lost a child." He met her eyes. "You humble me. I don't mean that lightly, and I'm not patronizing you. There's not a doubt in my mind that you were an amazing mother to Sydney, because I've seen you with Gilberto. You're a natural."

Willa's heart beat in an erratic rhythm. Derek was unusually nervous.

"The thing is," he continued, "I knew from the beginning, from the time you first came to work for Izzy, that you were special. Loving and good in a way that didn't jive with the distance you were keeping. I told myself not to stalk you. I mean, if you weren't interested then how warped was it to keep pursuing you? But my gut said you were the one."

"Derek, I think... I... I should—"

"No, let me say this. It's what I meant to say when I got to your house tonight." His elbows were on his knees, his head turned toward her, his expression as open and vulnerable as she'd ever seen. "You're the love I've waited for. The past two weeks, while we were helping Gilberto with the play and couldn't even squeeze in a real date—they've been the most mundane, wonderful weeks of my life."

He looked down at his hands. Concentrating on his face, Willa had neglected to look at the item he held. Now she noticed it. *Oh. Oh, my. Oh, no.*

"I planned to do this earlier." Turning over his hand, he revealed a small, sapphire-blue velvet box.

Willa felt as if she were in a dream, the kind in which everything moved in slow motion, and you couldn't react quickly enough no matter how hard you tried.

"I love you, Willa. I don't want to waste another minute living without you. Whatever life brings, I want to be by your side." He opened the box. An absolutely stunning ruby-and-diamond ring glowed in its velvet bed. "The ruby reminds me of you. Unique, rare." The first genuine smile of the evening lit his face. "And, it goes real well with your hair."

Slipping from the sofa to the floor, with one knee bent, Derek asked humbly, "Will you marry me?"

"Oh, Derek." She reached for his hands, not the ring. Tears sprang to her eyes. "When I said I want to move forward, I... I meant it, but...in a relationship that's open-ended. I want to be there for you, too, but as a...a..." She struggled to find the right word. "A girlfriend." Derek's brows swooped abruptly. "A steady girlfriend," she assured, but she could tell by his expression that she was making it worse. The intensity of his stare unnerved her even more.

Silence as heavy as an anvil fell onto the conversation.

Slowly, Derek raised himself to the sofa. He snapped the ring box shut and dropped it on the table in front of them. Elbows on his knees, he put his head in his hands and spoke with great care. "I can see that after what you've been through, it would be hard to commit again. But I'm not Jase. I'll never walk away."

"That's not what this is about—"

"Of course it is," he insisted. "If you'd had someone to help you get through the pain—"

"It would have helped, yes, but it wouldn't change my mind about today. It was wonderful with Syd, but—" Anguish clogged her throat. "I don't want children of my own again, Derek. I just can't do it."

"You're still grieving. You don't know how you'll feel in time."

"I know how I *don't* want to feel again. It's been two years. You have to accept what I'm telling you."

"But you could be a girlfriend," he said, making her wince at the mocking tone. "So, if it was just me, you'd consider marriage?"

Willa had a hard time meeting his gaze. "I don't know how you did it," she said, "but you managed to break through every rational reason I ever had not to fall in love again." She shook her head rapidly. "I'm botching this so badly. I'm sorry. I know how much you want to be a father. The thing is, you *are* one. You and Gilberto are a package deal. I know how much having him here means to you. I do, and I'm happy for you. I just can't risk—" She blinked at the welling tears and fanned at the sudden heat in her cheeks with her fingertips. "I won't risk feeling that kind of pain again."

"And you think being a girlfriend will keep you safe?"

She felt like an idiot when he put it that way. "Maybe not completely, but…"

The tension in the air crackled to an uncomfortable level. "But as a girlfriend, you could walk away if you felt yourself getting in too deep. Right?" he demanded harshly then raised a hand before she could respond. "Never mind, I've heard enough." He stood and took a step back.

"I'm sorry."

"You said that."

Willa shook her head. She really was an idiot. It was over. Why hadn't she accepted the fact before she'd come here tonight? It had been selfish to assume she could chop her affections into carefully controlled bits, like a dieter trying to make a chocolate bar last as long as possible. Why would anyone be satisfied with that? Why should he?

Clasping her hands beneath her chin, she said, "I'm so sorry—okay, I know, you've heard that already. I don't know what to say except… I have to know my limits."

He swung around, his expression filled with disbelief. "That's the coward's way of saying you're still running away. Like Jase did."

"That's unfair! Jase had started drinking," Willa argued, feeling defensive now. "He was actually trying to protect me by leaving!"

"No, Willa. Jase was protecting *himself.* He ran away from the reality that life dishes out crap sometimes, and it's up to us to turn the crap into something decent. Something meaningful, even if we wouldn't choose it for ourselves in a million years. But you don't run away."

Standing now, Willa faced off with him. "You don't understand. You can't possibly understand."

Striding forward, Derek grasped her upper arms. "I know I love you. I know we should be together. Not only when it's easy and not just for a while. Forever. For better, for worse."

"Derek." Willa groaned with frustration. "You don't know what you're talking about. You don't! Don't tell me about forever."

"You're right. I've never lost a child. I don't know what that's like, not at all. But I know one thing—" he paused and took a deep breath "—I want a woman to love and a house full of kids to share that love with. I want pets and chaos and the whole messy works. I want it with you. And I believe, deep down, if you'd let yourself, you'd want that again, too."

No. Just...no. Though she wanted to explain, there were no more words. She couldn't do it again, and it was beyond her at the moment to make him understand.

No matter. He obviously read it in her face.

A log fell in the fireplace, sending a shower of sparks up the chimney as Derek scooped the ring box off the table and looked down at it. Captain's head swiveled toward them before he yawned noisily.

Derek bobbed his head once. "Okay."

Her chin wobbled miserably. "I'm—"

She stopped herself, but he knew what she was about to say and raised his eyes to hers. "No. If you were really sorry, you wouldn't be doing this."

She had no retort.

Derek shrugged. "Well, I guess this is it." He moved toward the foyer.

Wordlessly, Willa followed.

"Good night, Willa," he said, holding open the door.

She nodded, not trusting herself to push words through the new spate of grief that rose like a tidal wave.

Frigid air stung her lungs as she stepped onto his front porch. The click of the door behind her seemed as final as any sound she had ever heard.

Two nights later, Willa was wide awake and staring morosely at the shadowed ceiling above her bed when the phone rang. Yellow light pooled as she turned on her bedside lamp then searched the nightstand for her cell. DEREK, the screen read.

Pushing herself up against the headboard, she held her breath. They hadn't spoken or seen each other since he'd closed the door on the night he'd proposed. She'd moved like a zombie through the past two days, the grief she'd tried to avoid front and center no matter what she was doing. Now merely seeing his name on caller ID filled her with adrenaline. Had he changed his mind about insisting on marriage? Was he phoning to say he wanted to try being in an open-ended relationship after all?

Did it matter?

Since she'd left his house, Willa had become more convinced with each passing minute that it had been ludicrous to believe she could be Derek's "girlfriend" and still maintain a safe distance from Gilberto. Or, a safe distance from him, for that matter. Her mind and emotions were already in turmoil. Imagine if they'd been in a long standing relationship and *then* broke up. Or if they were together, in love, and he was killed on the job, God forbid. The very thought made her feel so sick, she thought she might throw up. What had she been thinking, getting involved with someone in his line of work?

While she fretted, the phone stopped ringing. Before she could decide whether she was relieved or disappointed, it started in again, and this time she checked the clock: 1:18 a.m. Emotionally and physically drained, she wondered whether she had enough energy to tackle another charged conversation.

Biting the inside of her lip, she gazed at the small screen. Curiosity was seductive.

She took the call.

"Hi," she murmured, hunkering back against her pillow and pulling the covers up around her shoulders.

"Willa?"

Instantly, her heart slammed into her throat. Once before, she'd answered a call in which she'd heard the same note of urgency when the caller spoke her name. Sitting straight up, she clutched the phone in a death grip. "What happened?"

"I'm sorry if I woke you up."

"Derek, what's wrong?"

"Gilberto is gone."

"What do you mean, gone?"

"I went into his room to check on him about an hour ago, and he wasn't in his bed."

She tried to swallow, but her throat felt like sandpaper. "Did he run away?"

"I don't know." It sounded as if Derek was pacing as he talked. "I don't know why he would. We've been doing great."

"You looked all over the house and grounds?"

"I searched every corner and called his name till I was

hoarse. Look, the reason I called is I thought maybe he'd hitched a ride to town and somehow made it to your place?"

"No and if he had, I'd have called, immediately."

She could tell he was grasping at straws. Head swimming, Willa jumped into a pair of jeans. "Where are you now?"

"I'm in my squad car. Over in Roddy's old neighborhood. I've got the entire force out looking for Gilberto, and we've put out an Amber Alert and an APB."

"Do you really think Roddy could have something to do with this?"

"I don't know. I have to explore every possibility."

"Of course. Does Roddy know where you live?"

"I don't know. Possibly. But Captain didn't bark, and he always lets me know when someone drives up."

"If Roddy did come back, do you think Gilberto went with him willingly?" The alternative made her blood freeze.

"I'm not sure. I didn't give enough consideration to the family bond." Remorse warred with the panic in his tone. "There've been so many changes for the poor kid. What the hell was I thinking, expecting everyone to move on from their pasts because I said so? I've been so damn blind—"

"No. Stop." Willa interrupted the self-condemning rant. "Derek, that boy loves you. He wants to live with *you*, not Roddy. He told me that several times when we were working on his costume for the school play. Whatever is going on, it has nothing to do with him feeling pressured to let go of his previous life. If he left with Roddy, it's because of divided loyalties, not because he wasn't happy where he was."

Derek fell silent, and she could tell he was pondering her words. Unfortunately, Gilberto was not with her.

"He's not here," she said.

"Damn it." Derek's worry and frustration were tangible. "Hang on."

In the background, Willa could hear him communicating on his radio. The muffled conversation made it clear that no one had seen Gilberto yet. When Derek came back on the line he said, "Look, I'm going to let you go so that I can focus here."

"Oh. Okay, right. Of course." She hated the idea of letting him go. "Just one more quick question. Did he take anything with him?"

"His backpack. And I'm pretty sure he had that Daniel Boone outfit you made him. I don't know what else." His radio squawked, and Russell began to relay some information. "I've gotta go."

"Let me know the second you hear anything," Willa said right before he hung up.

She sat on the edge of the bed. Her gut told her Roddy had not come back, but why would Gilberto run away? Something had to have happened. Something he couldn't cope with. But what? And, where would he have run if he was feeling some kind of emotional turmoil?

Her mind moved so fast she was breathless. And, why on earth would he have taken his costume? Unless…

She remembered the hike they'd taken in the days just prior to the history play. They'd driven out to a heavily forested area of a national park near the Long River called Winter Forks to get the feel of pioneer life. And to gather the sticks he needed to make his bow and arrow set.

"I could live out here," the boy had boasted. "I could use my bow and arrow to hunt rabbits. I'd build a fire to cook and keep warm. And I could build a lean-to right over there. It wouldn't be that hard."

She'd thought his bluster was endearing at the time, but now? Could he have been serious? And if he was, could he have gone back to the spot under the fallen tree he'd insisted would be the best place to set up camp? It was about two miles past Derek's place. He could have made it out there in under an hour, even in the dark.

Dear God. Don't let him get hit on the road.

A feeling deep in her gut urged her to head in that direction. Without further consideration, her feet were in motion. Quickly she found a backpack then put some leftover pizza in the microwave. While it was heating, she grabbed the blanket she kept hanging by the radiator and stuffed it into another bag. Once in the car, she tucked everything under the heating vent to keep it all warm.

Within minutes, she was backing out of the driveway, but stopped before she pulled out onto the street. Reaching for her cell phone, she texted Derek.

Heading to Winter Forks to search. Long shot. Will let you know ASAP if I find him.

During the seemingly interminable drive, turmoil over Gilberto's safety took on a life of its own. If anything happened to him, she knew Derek would never forgive himself.

Anxiety threatened to give way to panic and Willa had to fight to control her rapid breathing as she found the correct cutoff. Gravel crunched under her tires as she flipped her headlights on high beam and slowly worked her way down the crude forest access road. Trees cast long, eerie shadows and Winter Forks looked so very different than it had in broad daylight. Gaze roving from one side of the road to the other, Willa searched the woods for any sign of a young Daniel Boone making a campfire. Eventually, the spot she'd parked in the last time came in to view and she pulled over and cut the engine.

Please, God, don't let this be a wild goose chase. Or, if it is, let Derek find Gilberto right now. Right now!

Shoving her keys and cell phone into her backpack, she grabbed everything she'd brought with her, locked her doors, clicked on her flashlight and strode down the formidable forest trail, rage beginning to replace the fear that wanted to consume her.

This is not happening again. Nothing bad was going to happen to Gilberto. *I will not allow it.*

With a mother's intuition, she followed the path her heart told her to take.

Chapter Fifteen

It had to be close to freezing. Gilberto had complained that his Daniel Boone coat was too warm. Now Willa was grateful she'd ignored his protest. In the back of her mind, she could hear the echo of his young voice as they'd explored this trail the first time. *I could live out here, all by myself. I wouldn't be scared. Daniel Boone did it. I could, too.*

"All alone?" Willa had asked. "I think people need other people to live with."

"You don't," the boy had pointed out. "And you're not scared of anything."

How ironic that at this very moment her rage was underscored by the terror of losing Gilberto before she ever had a chance to tell him how much she loved him.

In the distance, she heard the sound of Long River rushing over a ravine filled with boulders. A coyote set up an alarm that was repeated across several hilltops, while, closer by, an owl hooted. The trail they'd taken several weeks ago was difficult to make out in the dim beam of her flashlight, but she forged on.

"Gilberto?" she shouted, swiveling the light from right to left. "Gilberto? Are you out here? If you are, please answer me!" She paused to listen. Nothing.

They'd hiked for quite a while that day, so she probably had another quarter mile to go? Maybe he couldn't hear her yet. "Gilberto?" she repeated every twenty paces.

Finally, she reached the spot where Gilberto had declared he'd easily forge the life of a pioneer, but there was no sign of him. "Gilberto!"

Battling back another wave of panic, Willa was about to admit her intuition had mislead her when she spied a backpack. Her heart lurched. It was his.

But where was he? "'Berto, answer me, please!" Heading more deeply into the woods, Willa continued to call his name. She was nearly at the riverbank when she heard a whimpering sound up ahead.

As she stumbled along the path, Willa's light illuminated the outline of a boy, shaking in his hiking boots.

"Gilberto? Oh, thank God!" She ran to his side. "Are you alright? Are you hurt, honey?"

When he didn't immediately answer, she followed the direction of his gaze with the beam of her flashlight.

Her relief proved short-lived. Up ahead about thirty feet, a black bear stood, head swaying as he stared into the light. *Dear Lord.* Spring was on the horizon, and hibernation must have given way to hunger. Frantically, Willa tried to remember everything she knew about bears.

Nothing.

What was it the old-timers in town said? What was that one rhyme? If it's black, attack. If it's brown, lie down? It was hard to tell what the hell color this guy was, but she knew black bears were more common in this area. Why had she left her pepper spray in the glove box?

"I… I think he wants my sandwich," Gilberto managed to croak.

Willa wasn't sure it was a sandwich the bear wanted, but she wasn't going to quibble.

"Sweetie." She pushed the fear-frozen boy behind her. "Yeah, he's probably hungry, huh? So, I have some pizza in my backpack, and we're going to slowly take it out and toss it at him, okay? And then we're gonna run like crazy." In her peripheral vision, she could see Gilberto nodding. "Good. Now, just unzip my—"

Their slight movements seemed to encourage the bear to rise up on its haunches and emit a noise that smacked of his impatience.

"Change of plans," Willa whispered, slipping the backpack off her shoulders. With strength worthy of a Scots log thrower, she hurled it at the huge animal. She grabbed Gilberto by the hand. *"Run!"* she screamed.

Behind them, the bear wasted no time tearing into the pack and locating the pizza. Unfortunately, the animal was now also in possession of Willa's cell phone and car keys, but she would worry about that later. Much later. After she and Gilberto thrashed their way through this blasted forest and out to the main road.

By the time they reached her car, Willa's breath was coming in knife-like jabs. Bent over, Gilberto sucked in heaving lungfuls of air. Willa didn't pause long, however, before she pulled the boy into her arms.

"What are you doing out here? You scared me half to death. Don't you ever run away like that again, do you hear me?" She pushed him far enough away to scan his head and body, checking to be sure every finger and toe was intact, the way one would with a newborn. Then she swept him against her heart and held on, whispering fiercely in his ear. "I love you. I couldn't stand it if anything happened to you."

Gilberto cried, clutching her as they stood outside her parked car and rocked together. When the flood of emotion subsided some, Willa thought of the blankets she'd carried in the second bag and realized she'd dropped it somewhere on their flight through the woods.

"I think the bear ate my car keys," Willa said, "and my phone." Attempting to add a little levity to the situation for Gilberto's sake. "We're sort of on our own at the moment. But that's okay. I told Derek where I thought you might be and knowing him, he's going to find us real soon. We just need to keep moving," she told the teeth-chattering boy, "to keep warm. And, to get back to the main road, okay?"

He nodded in assent and meekly followed her lead.

Willa kept the pace at a good clip, not only to create warmth, but also because the idea that there were other predators lurking in the shadows had her spooked. When she saw the highway up ahead, she knew they had two miles to Derek's house.

"How are you doing?" she asked her companion, who still looked shaken.

"Good."

"Good. So. Want to tell me what made you leave your warm, comfortable bed in the middle of the night and move in with the bears?"

Misery filled his voice. "I heard what you and Derek were talking about the other night."

She swallowed. "You did? I must have woken you up, huh?"

"Nah. I was already awake. But I knew something was wrong with you guys, so I listened in." He shrugged and shot a guilty glance up at her.

Hot shame filled her belly. What had the conversation sounded like to his young ears? She'd told Derek she didn't want to love a child again.

"You left because of what I said?"

"Uh, uh. I left because Derek was really sad, and I knew he wouldn't feel better until you married him, and you wouldn't marry him until I left."

"No!" She swept him into her arms. "No, that's not right. Oh, buddy, listen to me." Holding him at arm's length, she stared hard at his face in the moonlight. "If you were eavesdropping, you know I had a daughter. And that I lost her. I want to talk to you more about that when we're not freezing half to death, but for now, you need to understand that I didn't turn down Derek's proposal because of you. I turned it down because of me. Because I'm scared of being married again."

Gilberto's brows were pulled tightly together. "How come?"

She shook her head. "I'm scared of lots of things, I guess. And that's something I have to work on. But it's my problem, not yours. Not Derek's, either. He's…he's great, and he loves you. Do you know he'd go nuts if anything happened to you? So you can't ever run away like that again, right?"

A tear slipped silently down his smooth cheek. His lower lip trembled as he wiped the moisture from his eyes and nodded, and she hugged him again, squeezing so tightly, he eventually wriggled to be free.

Before they could say any more, the sound of an engine slowing and tires turning onto the access road was followed by the blinding glare of headlights on high beams. Red and blue lights swirled from the approaching car and bounced off the treetops.

Derek!

Awash in the lights, Willa and Gilberto stood in the middle of the road as the squad car sped up beside them and skidded to a stop. Derek leaped from the car, pulling Gilberto into his arms. There were tears in Derek's voice as he reached for Willa, too, and included her in the embrace. "Thank you. Thank you so much," he murmured against the top of her head.

Willa nodded. They hung on to each other as if each was afraid one of the others might disappear. She buried her face against Derek's chest.

The relief that should have washed away all else got dammed up inside Willa. Gilberto had run away, because of her. The beautiful boy huddled between them had believed he was nothing more than a stumbling block on the road to her romance with Derek, and it was her fault. As for the man who'd offered to love her through thick and thin…

A shudder ran through her. Her own aching heart had led her to break two more, and that wasn't okay. It wasn't okay at all.

It was almost 3:00 a.m. when they all trooped in through the front door, and four by the time Derek had Gilberto tucked into bed. When he finally came downstairs and into the kitchen, Willa could see the exhaustion in his eyes.

"Something smells good," he said.

The closeness they'd shared in the forest had yielded to lingering uncertainty. She gestured toward the frying pan on the stove. "Turkey sausage and scrambled eggs. I thought you'd be hungry."

"I am."

"Have a seat. It's ready."

He complied and, running a hand over his face, told her, "Gilberto overheard our conversation."

"I know." Serving up the sausage and eggs, she arranged triangles of buttered toast on the edge of the plate. "He was telling me that right before you arrived." Legs rubbery, Willa set the food down in front of Derek and sank heavily into the chair across from him. "I blew it."

Reaching across the table, he placed a comforting hand on her arm. "He's a kid. He couldn't understand the context."

"Neither did I, apparently. Everything was clear in my mind until you phoned to say he was gone. And then when I saw him in front of that bear—"

"None of that was your fault."

She shot him the kind of *puh-lease* look that Gilberto was mastering. "He wanted us to have a chance at a relationship. I'd say that was more mature than I was being."

The hint of a smile appeared on Derek's face. "As crazy and misguided and dangerous as it was for him to run away, the sacrifice he made was probably the nicest thing anyone has ever done for me."

"Children are like that. You think all they care about is themselves, and then they surprise you by how much they notice. How much they're willing to give to make you happy."

"Yeah." He looked down at his hands, folded now on the counter. "You were right. Gilberto is mine. I couldn't lose him now."

Willa nodded, mentally comparing the two great romantic loves of her life, Jase and Derek. They were both wonderful men, but fundamentally so different.

Jase turned in on himself during a crisis, withdrawing from her so totally it was as if they were in separate rooms even as they shared a bed. Derek's care was as reliable as the tide.

Suddenly, he looked up. "I didn't think this all the way through. You're locked out of your house, aren't you?"

Willa blinked. She hadn't thought of that, either. "Yes. I guess I am."

"Got a spare key hidden somewhere?"

"No."

"Good. It's not safe." He eyed her steadily. "Stay."

A simple invitation, yet one that sparked myriad possibilities.

"I want to," she whispered.

"Good. I'll make up the guest room for you."

"No. You've got to be exhausted. I can—"

"You can decide not to argue." He forked up a bite of scrambled eggs. "I'll draw you a bath, too."

"You certainly will not!"

Sternly, he arched a brow. "Arguing at four in the morning is exhausting."

That stopped her. Besides, a bath did sound heavenly. "Thank you."

"You're welcome." He tried the sausage then added, "Just because I'm being hospitable, it doesn't mean I'm not still angry you went off into the woods by yourself."

"I couldn't *not* go."

"Yes. You could have wai—"

"No." She shook her head when he tried to rebut. "Mothers don't wait." Leaning forward, she beseeched him with her eyes. "I think I've finally figured out some things."

The hand holding the fork slowly lowered. "I'm listening."

"When Gilberto and I were the woods, the only thing that mattered was getting back to you. I knew you were out there looking for us, that you wouldn't stop looking until you found us, and I realized you were right. Believing in the person you love, being one hundred percent certain you can count on him…it changes things. It makes you go the distance."

She reached for Derek's hands. He was so still, she knew he was listening to every word. "Before I met you, I didn't think it was right to let go of my grief. I thought if I let go all the way, it would be a betrayal."

"I'm not going to ask you to let go, Willa."

With her fingers curled around his, she could feel his reserve. He didn't pull away, but he wasn't holding onto her, either. Not the way he had in the past.

"You were right," he acknowledged. "There's no way I can understand what you went through. After tonight, though, I think I get it a little bit more. I was terrified I might lose the one thing that finally means more to me than my own life."

"Gilberto." Grateful on his behalf, tears filled her eyes, and she nodded. "That's exactly how a father feels."

"Yeah. I do feel like his father. But I don't mean only Gilberto." Fiercely, his gaze bore into hers. "First day I saw you in the deli, I started wanting something I'd told myself a long time ago didn't exist. I wasn't even eighteen when I figured believing in 'forever' was bull, and if people couldn't see that, then they were fools asking to be kicked in the teeth. All I knew about love was how to turn my back on it before it turned its back on me." Pulling one of his hands free of hers, he rubbed his forehead. "When I saw you with Jase, I was angry. I was stinking-ugly angrier than I had any right to be. I know you had what you wanted with him and Sydney. I know that was supposed to be your happily-ever-after. It should have been."

Her heart squeezed hard. For a second she almost wished for Derek's sake that he'd fallen for someone with a simpler past.

Releasing his other hand, she came around the counter to stand in front of him, eye-to-eye with him seated on the stool. "Listen to me, Sheriff. You are not my consolation prize. Do you understand? I have never—not for a second—thought, 'Well I already had the best in life, so now I'm willing to settle.' You're a gift."

Gently, she brushed the thick black hair that had fallen over his forehead. "The thing is, when reality blows happily-ever-after out of the water, you begin to think true joy is a gift with someone else's name on it. So when a man comes along—a very, very good man—and he reminds you that your heart may be broken, but it hasn't stopped beating…you don't necessarily know what to do with that. I can't believe you were so patient with me for so long, but I sure am grateful." She rubbed an index finger over his puckered brow, trying to erase the frown line. "If you're willing to give me another chance, I promise it'll be the last one I'll ever need."

Tension radiated from every muscle in his strong, hyperalert body. His expression was impossible to read, and Willa felt panic begin to stir.

"Tell me what you're thinking," she urged.

Slowly, he nodded. "Okay. I'm thinking that you'd better be planning to make an honest man out of me. Because if you're still talking about an affair—"

She threw her arms around his neck before he could finish the sentence. "I'm talking about locking you up and throwing away the key, Sheriff. As far as I'm concerned, this is for good."

Derek half growled, half grinned his response. "Oh, it's going to be a whole lot better than good." Pulling her onto his lap, he went for a soul-searing kiss.

When they came up for air, Willa felt dizzy. "Wow. You are a mighty fine kisser."

Pressing those magical lips into a tight line, he rued, "Darn it. I knew this was going to happen."

"What?"

"Now you only want me because of my amazing sexual prowess."

Even though he was kidding, she figured laughing *very* hard might hurt his feelings. It was nice, though, it was very nice, to feel as if her heart were light enough to float. She patted his chest. "Don't sell yourself short. You're a man of many layers, and I plan to explore all of them."

A smile of unbridled joy stretched across his face. "Better get started then." After another incendiary kiss, he pulled back to study her, using his thumb to trace her lips with a touch as gentle as summer rain. "We'll take this happily-ever-after thing one day at a time," he promised.

If Thunder Ridge could talk, it would have sounded just like Derek then. Powerful, reassuring, able to shelter the ones it loved from the harshest of life's elements. The perfect haven for a woman truly ready to start living again.

"Should we wake Gilberto?" she asked as she snuggled against Derek. "Tell him we kissed and made up?"

"Nah, let the kid sleep. I want him to be wide awake tomorrow when we propose to you."

This time, her heart leaped with excitement, not fear. Raising her head, she looked at him, adoring the crook of his dark brow. "It's going to take two of you to do the job, huh?"

"Absolutely. Like you said, we're a package deal." Reaching for her hand, he raised it, kissing her temporarily bare ring finger. "For better, for worse, from this day forward. I love you with all my heart, Willa Holmes."

"From this day forward," she agreed in a whisper, nodding. "I love you, too, Derek Neel."

If it were possible, Willa thought, she'd cling to this golden feeling and never let it go.

Slipping her arms all the way around Derek's waist,

she murmured, "You can kiss me again, Sheriff, whenever you're ready."

She didn't have long to wait.

Through the windows behind them, the sky began to glow pink as the sun rose on two people ready to face the beautiful, uncertain future together.

Epilogue

"What do you think?" Willa asked the marmalade tabby she used to feed in the park before work every morning. Growing courageous, he'd followed her to the bakery one day and had chosen not to leave. Together, they'd decided his name should be Harold and struck a bargain: he agreed to remain on the ground unless someone picked him up, and she promised to bring him whitefish and lox scraps from the deli as a reward. At night, he slept at her place.

"It's good, isn't it?" she said, scooping the cat up so he'd have a better view of the cake she'd been decorating for the past several hours. Instantly, he favored her with his bass, outboard-motor purr. "Really? You think I'm a genius? Nah, you're just saying that." He rubbed his nose against her chin. "All right, if you insist." In truth, she was one hundred percent satisfied with her efforts.

A knock on Something Sweet's front door startled her. The bakery was closed, chair seats resting on tabletops and only the work lights on. The wildflower-filled spring they'd all enjoyed this year was yielding already to verdant summer with longer days, but for now the sun still set before nine, and it was a full hour past that. She certainly wasn't expecting anyone.

Willa couldn't see the person standing outside the door until she was more than halfway there. When recognition hit, she gave a happy gasp. Setting Harold on the floor, she raced to the front, fishing the key for the dead bolt out of her pocket. "What are you doing here?" she asked as she opened the door, throwing her arms around Derek's neck. "I thought you and 'Berto were enjoying your last night as bachelors. Is he with you?" Leaning to the right, she tried to see around her husband-to-be.

Derek kissed her soundly on the lips before answering. "Izzy, Nate and Eli invited him to go bowling. The question is, what are you doing at work this late, bride-to-be? You're supposed to be home, getting your beauty sleep."

"I'm busy." Yesterday, he'd made her promise she wouldn't work all day before their wedding. Now she gave him a kiss that she intended to be thoroughly distracting, then said, "If you're all alone tonight, why aren't you home, dreaming about me?"

With a hand on her lower back, he pressed her closer. "I do that every day, with my eyes wide open."

"That deserves another kiss." Grinning, she delivered it. "Okay, now go," she ordered, making shooing motions.

"I just got here," he protested. "When you weren't at your place, I figured you were working on our cake, despite giving me your word you'd quit at six."

"I said seven."

"It's almost ten. Where's the cake? Let's see it."

"Before the wedding?" She crossed her arms. "Nope."

Tomorrow she was marrying Sheriff Derek Neel in a

wedding that had started out small and blossomed into a come-one, come-all bash. Derek was, after all, a beloved community member. So was Gilberto.

And so was she.

After more than two years of wandering, Willa had found her Promised Land right here in Thunder Ridge. That merited a rock-star cake.

"Time for you to scoot," she told him.

Derek adopted the stubborn expression she was coming to know quite well. "Izzy told me I couldn't see you in your wedding dress. She didn't say anything about the cake. Lead on."

After a moment's thought, Willa shrugged. It might be better for him to see it before their guests. She had, after all, planned a surprise that was exclusively for Derek.

Preceding him to the kitchen, she made a sweeping "ta-da" gesture.

"That's incredible," he said as he gazed in obvious appreciation at the six-tiered, white-chocolate, buttercream-covered pièce de résistance she had draped with the sugar flowers, leaves and branches she'd been making in her spare time for the past few weeks. "Wait a minute, is that..."

Willa watched closely as he peered intently at the top tier, the one intended to be their anniversary layer.

Derek began to laugh, a robust, pleasure-filled sound that invariably made her feel as if the sun was shining straight into her heart.

"Yes, indeed," she confirmed. "Our anniversary cake is a chocolate chip babka. It worked wonders for Mr. and Mrs. Wittenberg. She isn't here in the mornings anymore, you know. She and Mr. W 'sleep in' now." Willa winked broadly. "So, I figured a year from now on our first anniversary, when the flames of passion have died down..."

"I'll need a chocolate chip babka to bring them back?"

"Well, you're not getting any younger. Remember what Mrs. W said. According to the Food Network, breakfast treats can be a potent aphrodisiac."

"Is that so?" Sweeping her into a kiss so hot it could have set the bakery on fire, Derek took his sweet time making her eat her words. "Still worried?" he murmured finally, against her lips.

"Mmm, not so much." Willa felt decidedly, deliciously dazed as Derek released her.

"I brought you something," he said, brandishing a small square box she hadn't even noticed he was carrying. Opening it himself, he removed a few tissue-wrapped items and handed them to her. When she uncovered three ceramic figurines, she laughed with sheer pleasure. "Cake toppers!"

"Yep," he agreed as she held up a miniature Sheriff Neel, a baker Willa and a little Gilberto.

"They're wonderful. I love them." Moving to the cake, she arranged the little figures in the buttercream, one tier below the dome-shaped anniversary babka. "Now it's perfect."

"Not yet." Derek withdrew another item from the box.

This time when Willa unwrapped the gift, she gave a sharp intake of breath. No words could get past the sudden tightness in her throat.

"Is it okay?" Derek asked, his voice betraying his sudden nerves. "You've been so happy lately, and I don't want to make you sad—that's the last thing I want—but it's important, and… I hope it's okay," he concluded, his habitual strength softened by concern.

"More than okay," she whispered. "So much more than okay." Reverently touching the lovely ceramic creature, she looked up at him. "But how—?"

"I took a photo from one of your albums," Derek confessed, "so the artist could make it look like Sydney."

And it did. It looked like Syd at the spring formal dance, when she'd been so thrilled with her dress and her hair, so excited to feel grown up.

"Gilberto and I agreed the whole family needs to be on the cake," he said.

The whole family. Willa nodded.

Gilberto had started calling Derek "Dad"—often with a smile he couldn't hide—a couple of months ago. Then last week, during a break from a tournament of crazy eights, he'd shyly asked Willa if he ought to start calling her "Mom or something" after the wedding.

It had been too long since anyone had called her that, and she had realized a heart could break and heal in the same blessed moment.

Looking at the doll again, Willa shook her head in wonder. Derek had given her a son, and the two of them had decided she should never lose her daughter.

"I love you," she told her husband-to-be, knowing she'd never say anything truer.

Taking the Sydney figurine carefully from her, Derek placed it on the cake with the others, then stepped back and held Willa close as they admired their creation.

Safe in the sheriff's arms, Willa thought about the wedding and about their future and about all the good that had come before it, too, and for a second she could have sworn she saw the Sydney doll smile.

* * * * *

*When plain-Jane professor Gemma Gould agrees
to help her high school frenemy—football star
Ethan Ladd—care for his infant nephew,
sparks of every kind fly! But will the discovery of
Ethan's secret—and the truth about baby Henry—
ruin their chance at happiness?*

*Don't miss their story, the next installment
in Wendy Warren's new series,*
THE MEN OF THUNDER RIDGE.

Coming soon to Mills & Boon Cherish!

MILLS & BOON®

Cherish™

EXPERIENCE THE ULTIMATE RUSH OF FALLING IN LOVE

A sneak peek at next month's titles...

In stores from 9th March 2017:

- **Reunited by a Baby Bombshell** – Barbara Hannay
  and **From Fortune to Family Man** – Judy Duarte
- **The Spanish Tycoon's Takeover** – Michelle Douglas
  and **Meant to Be Mine** – Marie Ferrarella

In stores from 23rd March 2017:

- **Stranded with the Secret Billionaire** – Marion Lennox
  and **The Princess Problem** – Teri Wilson
- **Miss Prim and the Maverick Millionaire** – Nina Singh
  and **Finding Our Forever** – Brenda Novak

Just can't wait?
Buy our books online before they hit the shops!
www.millsandboon.co.uk

Also available as eBooks.

MILLS & BOON®

EXCLUSIVE EXTRACT

Griffin Fletcher never imagined he'd see his childhood sweetheart Eva Hennessey again, but now he's eager to discover her secret— one that will change their worlds forever!

Read on for a sneak preview of
REUNITED BY A BABY BOMBSHELL

A baby. A daughter, given up for adoption.

The stark pain in Eva's face when she'd seen their child. His own huge feelings of isolation and loss.

If only he'd known. If only Eva had told him. He'd deserved to know.

And what would you have done? his conscience whispered.

It was a fair enough question.

Realistically, what would he have done at the age of eighteen? He and Eva had both been so young, scarcely out of school, both ambitious, with all their lives ahead of them. He hadn't been remotely ready to think about settling down, or facing parenthood, let alone lasting love or matrimony.

And yet he'd been hopelessly crazy about Eva, so chances were…

Dragging in a deep breath of sea air, Griff shook his head. It was way too late to trawl through what might have been. There was no point in harbouring regrets.

But what about now?

How was he going to handle this new situation? Laine, a lovely daughter, living in his city, studying law. The thought that she'd been living there all this time, without his knowledge, did his head in.

And Eva, as lovely and hauntingly bewitching as ever, sent his head spinning too, sent his heart taking flight.

He'd never felt so side-swiped. So torn. One minute he wanted to turn on his heel and head straight back to Eva's motel room, to pull her into his arms and taste those enticing lips of hers. To trace the shape of her lithe, tempting body with his hands. To unleash the longing that was raging inside him, driving him crazy.

Next minute he came to his senses and knew that he should just keep on walking. Now. Walk out of the Bay. All the way back to Brisbane.

And then, heaven help him, he was wanting Eva again. Wanting her desperately.

Damn it. He was in for a very long night.

Don't miss
REUNITED BY A BABY BOMBSHELL
by Barbara Hannay

Available April 2017
www.millsandboon.co.uk

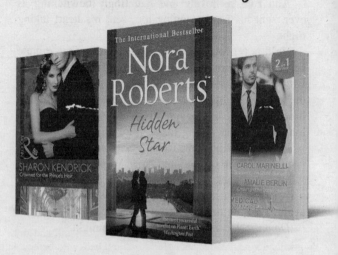

MILLS & BOON®

Congratulations
Carol Marinelli
on your 100th Mills & Boon book!

Read on for an exclusive extract

How did she walk away? Lydia wondered.

How did she go over and kiss that sulky mouth and say goodbye when really she wanted to climb back into bed?

But rather than reveal her thoughts she flicked that internal default switch which had been permanently set to 'polite'.

'Thank you so much for last night.'

'I haven't finished being your tour guide yet.'

He stretched out his arm and held out his hand but Lydia didn't go over. She did not want to let in hope, so she just stood there as Raul spoke.

'It would be remiss of me to let you go home without seeing Venice as it should be seen.'

'Venice?'

'I'm heading there today. Why don't you come with me? Fly home tomorrow instead.'

There was another night between now and then, and Lydia knew that even while he offered her an extension he made it clear there was a cut-off.

Time added on for good behaviour.

And Raul's version of 'good behaviour' was that there would

be no tears or drama as she walked away. Lydia knew that. If she were to accept his offer then she had to remember that.

'I'd like that.' The calm of her voice belied the trembling she felt inside. 'It sounds wonderful.'

'Only if you're sure?' Raul added.

'Of course.'

But how could she be sure of anything now she had set foot in Raul's world?

He made her dizzy.

Disorientated.

Not just her head, but every cell in her body seemed to be spinning as he hauled himself from the bed and unlike Lydia, with her sheet-covered dash to the bathroom, his body was hers to view.

And that blasted default switch was stuck, because Lydia did the right thing and averted her eyes.

Yet he didn't walk past. Instead Raul walked right over to her and stood in front of her.

She could feel the heat—not just from his naked body but her own—and it felt as if her dress might disintegrate.

He put his fingers on her chin, tilted her head so that she met his eyes, and it killed that he did not kiss her, nor drag her back to his bed. Instead he checked again. 'Are you sure?'

'Of course,' Lydia said, and tried to make light of it. 'I never say no to a free trip.'

It was a joke but it put her in an unflattering light. She was about to correct herself, to say that it hadn't come out as she had meant, but then she saw his slight smile and it spelt approval.

A gold-digger he could handle, Lydia realised.

Her emerging feelings for him—perhaps not.

At every turn her world changed, and she fought for a semblance of control. Fought to convince not just Raul but herself that she could handle this.

Don't miss
THE INNOCENT'S SECRET BABY
by Carol Marinelli
OUT NOW

BUY YOUR COPY TODAY
www.millsandboon.co.uk

Join Britain's BIGGEST Romance Book Club

50% OFF your first parcel

- **EXCLUSIVE** offers every month

- **FREE** delivery direct to your door

- **NEVER MISS** a title

- **EARN** Bonus Book points

Call Customer Services
0844 844 1358*

or visit
millsandboon.co.uk/subscriptions